He repeated what Giselle had said, eyes wide as saucers. "I go to this address tonight and you will help me. After that, I burn this paper to complete the spell."

Not that he would ever get that chance. "Good boy. Now go back to your room and wait until dusk, then come to me. Leave all your valuables behind."

With a final nod, he got up and disappeared into the crowd.

Her skin tingled with the sheer brilliance of what she'd just set in motion. Giselle thanked the goddess for sending the senator's son to her as she got to her feet and started packing up her things. She had to get to her sister Zara's. They had another ritual to prepare for.

Praise for HOUSE OF COMARRÉ

"Painter scores with this one. Passion and murder, vampires and courtesans—original and un-put-downable. Do yourself a favor and read this one."
—Patricia Briggs, *New York Times* bestselling author

"Gripping, gritty, and imaginative. If you love dangerous males, kick-ass females, and unexpected twists, this is the series for you! Kristen Painter's engaging voice, smart writing, and bold, explosive plot blew me away. Prepare to lose some sleep!"
—Larissa Ione, *New York Times* bestselling author

"Kristen Painter's *Blood Rights* is dark and rich with layer after delicious layer. This spellbinding series will have you begging for more!"
—Gena Showalter, *New York Times* bestselling author

"Prophecy, curses, and devilish machination combine for a spellbinding debut of dark romance and pulse-pounding adventure."
—*Library Journal* (Starred Review)

"Kristen Painter brings a sultry new voice to the vampire genre, one that beckons with quiet passion and intrigue."
—L. A. Banks, *New York Times* bestselling author

"A world full of rich potential. Excellent!"
—P. C. Cast, *New York Times* bestselling author

"Exciting and interesting!"   —*RT Book Reviews* on *Bad Blood*

"The romance is tense and fresh...I highly recommend this if you enjoy fantasy and want an original take on vampires."
—*USA Today*'s Happy Ever After on *Blood Rights*

GARDEN OF
DREAMS AND DESIRES

GARDEN OF DREAMS AND DESIRES

CRESCENT CITY:
BOOK 3

KRISTEN PAINTER

www.orbitbooks.net

Orbit
Hachette Book Group
1290 Avenue of the Americas, New York, NY 10104
www.orbitbooks.net

First Edition: April 2015

Orbit is an imprint of Hachette Book Group, Inc. The Orbit name and logo are trademarks of Little, Brown Book Group Limited.

The Hachette Speakers Bureau provides a wide range of authors for speaking events. To find out more, go to www.hachettespeakersbureau.com or call (866) 376-6591.

The publisher is not responsible for websites (or their content) that are not owned by the publisher.

The characters and events in this book are fictitious. Any similarity to real persons, living or dead, is coincidental and not intended by the author.

Library of Congress Cataloging-in-Publication Data

Painter, Kristen L.
   Garden of dreams and desires / Kristen Painter.—First edition.
      pages ; cm.—(Crescent City ; book 3)
   ISBN 978-0-316-27835-5 (softcover)—ISBN 978-0-316-27834-8 (ebook)
   I. Title.
   PS3616.A337845G37 2015
   813'.6—dc23

                                                           2014040062

10 9 8 7 6 5 4 3 2 1

RRD-C

Printed in the United States of America

*For Melanie Newton. Your help and support are priceless
and your friendship is a gift.*

Chapter One

New Orleans, Louisiana, 2068

O ne witch to rule them all.

Giselle almost laughed out loud at the cleverness of her thought. Instead, she kept her giddiness to a smile. A tourist passing through Jackson Square smiled back. Giselle let the woman think it was an invitation to duck under the pavilion Giselle had set up for reading fortunes, not her rising anticipation of what was to come.

The woman kept walking. Giselle's smile disappeared. One day after Mardi Gras and the city was still thick with tourists carrying on like the party had yet to end. She didn't mind. Much. It suited her purposes. Today might be a bust, however. It was afternoon and she'd yet to have anyone she could use sit across from her. Soon, when the spell she and Zara were working on was cast, she'd never have to sit here and pander to the masses again.

A young man approached her booth, a nearly empty plastic cup of beer clutched in one hand. "You're too pretty to be a fortune-teller."

She studied him. Expensive wristwatch. Manicured nails. Alligator loafers. This was not your average college boy. She smiled coyly. "Is that so? How should I look?"

He ducked under the ivory pavilion. "You know, wart on the nose, scarf on the head, that sort of thing."

He'd been drinking for a while, based on the cloud of alcohol surrounding him. She shrugged. "I'm sorry to disappoint you."

"I'm not disappointed." He drained the last of his beer and set the empty cup near the small ivory placard that displayed her prices in simple black font.

Beneath the pristine white velvet draping her table, she dug her nails into her palm to keep from hexing him. She pointed a few yards away. "There's a trash can over there."

He left the empty cup where it was and sat on the folding stool across from her. He stuck his palm out. He had the smooth hands of someone who'd never done manual labor. "Tell me my fortune."

She thought about telling him she was closed, but a sixth sense made her wait it out. She tapped the top of her sign. "One, you must pay me first, and two, I don't read palms. I read crystals."

He dug into the pocket of his shorts, pulled out a wad of plastic bills and dropped a few on the table. Quite a bit more than her rate. She didn't correct his mistake. He put the rest away and put his open hand back on the table. "How about now?"

"I still don't read palms." She tucked the plastic away, then placed a tall silver cup filled with crystals in front of him and went into her spiel. "I am Giselle, mistress of the crystals and keeper of the light. Cover the—"

"I'm Robbie."

She lifted her hand. "No names. I prefer to work without

influence. Now, cover the cup with your hand and think about one question you'd like to have answered, but don't tell me what it is. Keep the question in your mind."

Laughing like it was all a big game, he put his hand over the cup and squeezed his eyes tight. A moment later, he opened them. "Okay, I thought of a question."

Giselle took the cup from him. "Very good." Since Ian had tattooed her with a crystal, the source of her power, her ability to read the crystals was sharper than ever, which proved that his inherent gift was an extraordinary one. Even so, she whispered a few words over the crystals for clarity and guidance, then tipped the container and spilled the stones across the velvet. They twinkled with a rainbow of colors despite the shade of the pavilion. She stared at them intently, not saying anything for almost a minute.

Strong images of power, money and influence danced before her. Money she understood, but the boy across from her didn't look like anyone of importance.

"So?" He shifted impatiently.

"Silence." She moved her hands over the crystals but they never lied. One of the formations showed a strong family tie. That must be where the power and influence came in. "You live a blessed life."

He nodded like that was no revelation.

She continued, asking the crystals to show her specifically where this young man's power and influence came from. An image of a woman formed in her head. A woman she recognized.

He crossed his arms. "Is that all you've got?"

She looked up at him, seeing the resemblance to the woman in her head instantly. His mother. "You come from a powerful family."

That shut him up. She went on. "One that you both love and hate. You love the power, the influence, the money, but you hate the comparisons, the standards, the expectations, but most especially the consequences if you step out of line."

A plan unfurled in her head like the leaves of one of her sister's plants. Lush and verdant, the idea grew so large so quickly that the perceived reward overshadowed any possible risk. She smiled at him, offering him a safe place. A friend. "You struggle with so much. You deserve to be your own man."

"I do." He nodded.

"You are so much more than your mother's son." She pushed a relaxation spell into her words to make him completely receptive to what she was about to say.

His mouth opened and his pupils dilated slightly. "I am."

"But no one ever gives you the chance, do they?"

"No." He shook his head slowly. "They never do."

She whispered a few words to entrance him further, the alcohol in his system aiding her. "I can help you," she said quietly. "I can give you that chance. I can make your heart's desire come true."

Eyes glassed over, he leaned forward. "How?"

She smiled sweetly. "I'm a good witch. I know a secret garden where all your dreams and desires will come true and your troubles will disappear."

More nodding.

He belonged to her now. The plan branched into something greater. She pulled a scrap of paper and a pen from her bag and scribbled down an address while murmuring a disillusion spell over it so that he would see what she wanted him to see and not what she'd actually written. Then she held the paper up so he could read it. She spoke the address she wanted him to read three times, then folded the paper and placed it in his hand. "Come to this address tonight and I will help you. You must tell no one and when you return, you must burn this paper to finish the spell. Do you understand?"

He repeated what she'd said, eyes wide as saucers. "I go to this address tonight and you will help me. After that, I burn this paper to complete the spell."

Not that he would ever get that chance. "Good boy. Now go back to your room and wait until dusk, then come to me. Leave all your valuables behind."

With a final nod, he got up and disappeared into the crowd.

Her skin tingled with the sheer brilliance of what she'd just set in motion. She thanked the goddess for sending the senator's son to her as she got to her feet and started packing up her things. She had to get to her sister Zara's. They had another ritual to prepare for.

⚜

Augustine balled his hand into a fist, but kept it at his side. Smashing it through the bedroom door in front of him wouldn't do any good.

Although it might make up for the last three days of hell. He'd spent seventy-two hours knowing the woman he loved was suffering but had been unable to do anything about it. All because three days ago, he'd drugged Harlow in hopes of finding out if the rekindled spirit of her dead twin, Ava Mae, had truly possessed her.

He'd gotten his answer. Harlow was, indeed, possessed.

And now, three days later, Ava Mae had yet to come out of Harlow's room, claiming to be too sick to join him and Lally for meals. Or do anything else for that matter. Every time he asked, no matter what the reason, she refused.

He stood in the hall and stared at her closed door, his anger building. Had Ava Mae locked herself in there because she remembered that he'd drugged her and gotten her to admit she'd taken over Harlow's body? Did she know he was wise to her scheme? Was she afraid? He pondered that a moment. If she was, it was the first smart thing she'd done as Ava Mae. And if she was afraid of him, studying up on Harlow so she could appear more like her sister and not her sister's possessor was another smart move.

Whatever her reasons, he wanted her out where he could see her. Because while Ava Mae was essentially holding Harlow hostage so that Ava Mae could enjoy the pleasures of the corporeal world, that body still belonged to Harlow and he knew for a fact that Harlow was still in there.

He would set Harlow free. From that room. And from her sister. His hands ached from squeezing them so hard. He relaxed them, flexed all twelve of his fingers and took a deep, cleansing breath.

It didn't work.

What the hell was Ava Mae doing in that room? If he had to guess, she was learning everything she could about Harlow in order to pass as her more competently. At some point, boredom would set in and Ava Mae would have to come out. He lifted his hand, but used it to knock on the door instead of punching a hole in it. For Harlow's sake, he would continue playing this damned game and ask the same question he'd been asking every morning. He did his best to soften the frustrated edge in his voice. "Morning. How are you feeling today, Harley?"

Coughing answered him. "Morning." Some sniffling. "I'm just so-so. Would you have Lally leave my breakfast by the door again?"

As sick as she supposedly was, she hadn't lost her appetite. "Three days and you're still not well enough to get out of bed?" He exhaled, pushing his temper down, but anger put words in his mouth. Words that held a threat he should have made a day ago. "I'm getting the doctor over here immediately. You need medical attention before this gets worse. Maybe even a trip to the clinic."

He heard movement. Feet on the floor.

"That's not necessary," she answered. "I'm not that bad. Actually, I think I feel well enough to make it down for breakfast. Let me give it a shot. In fact, a nice hot shower would probably do the trick. I'll be down soon."

He grimaced at her lies. "Excellent." Except now he and Lally had to deal with Ava Mae face-to-face. He jogged downstairs to tell Lally the news.

The housekeeper stood at the stove, stirring a pot of grits. "Morning, Augie. Any word from the devil child or she staying holed up in that room forever?"

"Yes, I talked to her and stop calling her that. She's coming down for breakfast."

She stopped stirring, eyes wide. "She's joining us for a meal?"

"Yes. Did you make enough?"

She snorted softly. "Have you never seen me cook before?"

He grinned. "You're right. I already knew the answer to that one." He stared out the kitchen windows toward the pool, his smile fading. Steam lifted the aroma from the coffeepot and made his mouth water, but nothing could dislodge the pit in his stomach. He looked at Lally again. "Remember, it might be Ava Mae talking and running the show but Harlow's still in there. Somewhere." And he would find a way to get her out. Eventually.

Lally's brows lifted. "I hope you're right. Not that I doubt you, child, but this is one of those things we need to be sure about."

"I'm sure." He glanced toward the upper levels of the house. "While under the influence of bourbon and *nequam*, Ava Mae was subdued enough that Harlow could communicate with me. There is no doubt in my mind that the woman I carried into Harlow's room three nights ago and put to bed is physically Harlow, but mentally Ava Mae."

Lally returned to stirring the grits, going very quiet as she turned her face toward the window overlooking the backyard. He poured a cup of coffee, added sugar to it and was about to drink when she made a soft whimpering sound and covered her mouth with her hand. She looked at him. Tears streaked her face. "This is my fault. I never should have told that child about the tree."

Sometimes he wished neither of them knew. The lightning tree hidden in the center of the house thanks to centuries-old fae magic had caused all of this, but Lally telling Harlow about it didn't mean it was Lally's fault. "You can't blame yourself. Olivia handled it for years and there was never an issue." If only Olivia were still alive in this world and not trapped on the fae plane. Which reminded him he needed to visit her. Of course, if she were still alive, Harlow would never have come to New Orleans in the first place.

Lally dabbed at her eyes with the edge of her apron. "There was when I first told Olivia."

"You mean when Olivia attempted to use the tree to bring Ava Mae's ashes back to life." Which was how Ava Mae's spirit had first been freed. The tree had raised Ava Mae's spirit from infant to adult but Harlow's act of dumping the remaining ashes onto the lightning tree had finished the job, creating the monster they now knew as Ava Mae.

Lally nodded. "I shoulda known it would go the same with Harlow. She's her mother's child. Why should she act any different?" She sniffed and gave the grits another halfhearted stir before covering them and turning the heat off. "What are we gonna do?"

"I don't know. Yet. But Fenton's on it too. Maybe he'll have some news for me this morning. And I know you don't like him, but Nekai's also working on it." Neither he nor Lally was fond of the weaver fae, but the fact remained that Nekai had once saved Harlow's life and his skills were valuable. Augustine wasn't going to turn down help for this situation. "Fenton thought Nekai might know of another weaver fae who'd dealt with something like this before."

"Good. That's something." She checked on a pan of sausage links in the oven. "You leaving soon then?"

"Not until after breakfast."

"And until we figure something out, how we supposed to act around her? Like we know? Like we don't?"

"Like we don't." He sipped his coffee. "The less we set Ava Mae off, the better."

Lally nodded. "Okay, I can do that."

He smiled, more for her sake than as a reflection of how he felt. "I know you can. You're the strongest woman I've ever met, Lally Hughes."

"That's sweet of you. Speaking of strong women, you going to see Olivia anytime soon?"

"No immediate plan but I do need to visit her." He smiled. "You want to come?"

"You know I do. I'm gonna make some lemon bars to take." She hesitated. "So long as bringing me won't get you into trouble again."

Taking a human to the fae plane was a serious offense. One Augustine had already committed and one that had almost cost him everything. Now that he was Guardian, however, he was willing to bend that rule on occasion, as long as the visits were kept quiet. "It'll be fine. Do her good to see you."

"To see *both* of us."

"I'll make a plan."

The floorboards creaked and a moment later, Ava Mae meandered into the kitchen in her bathrobe, her beautiful cranberry-black hair in tousled waves around her shoulders. Harlow would have worn it knotted up in a messy loop. It gave Augustine some pleasure that he knew that much about the twin Ava Mae currently possessed.

She sighed and leaned against the door frame while nibbling on one fingernail. "What are you making a plan for? Something for me?"

Knowing that Harlow was Ava Mae's prisoner made him want to snap at her. Instead, he smiled and kept up the game. "It can be. I was talking about a visit to your mother on the fae plane. You must be dying to see her again now that you're feeling better. She'd certainly love to see you. I know you're still new at traveling by mirror, so I'd be happy to take you with me."

Her hand came away from her mouth to tangle in her hair. "I'm not sure I'm up for that just yet."

He hadn't imagined she would be. "Let me know if you change your mind. It's nice to see you after three days. I was really starting to get worried, but that shower must have done you a world of good. You don't look sick at all." She also didn't look like she'd showered, judging by her dry hair. "How'd you sleep?"

She shrugged, slanting her eyes at him coyly. "Could've been better. My head's a little foggy, though, and I still feel achy." She stretched and moaned for emphasis before peeling away from the door and making a beeline to the coffee.

Her lies were one on top of the other, but he had no problem going along with them. To a point. The overt flirting was so out of sync with the way Harlow would act. All it did was remind him that Ava Mae needed dealing with, which put him in a decidedly unromantic mood. "What are your plans today now that you're feeling better?"

She yawned as she poured a cup of coffee. "Shopping. I need to get out of the house and get some fresh air. Not to mention some new clothes. You wanna come with?" She leaned against him, looking up through her lashes. "We could make a day of it. You could watch me try on some new pretties. I have a lot of *underthings* to buy." She scooped up a heaping spoonful of sugar and stared at him as she stirred, her gaze holding the darkly wicked expression he'd come to recognize as purely Ava Mae. "Afterwards, we could grab some lunch. Or whatever."

He took his cup to the table, leaving her behind. "I can't, I have work to do. Being Guardian is a full-time job. And, like I mentioned, I need to visit Olivia."

She stuck her lip out. "What about the self-defense lessons we started?"

"If you're not up to visiting your mother, I doubt you're up to sparring with me. Besides, I thought you were going shopping today?" He'd enjoyed the few lessons he'd given Harlow, but that was before Ava Mae had taken over, and he had no desire to give her any more advantage than she already had.

"I *am* going shopping, but that's not exactly a high-stress activity. I guess there's always tomorrow." She huffed out a breath. "Unless you're going to be too busy chasing whatever baddie you're after now."

He drank his coffee, which was better than snapping back that *she* was the baddie he was after. It also helped to temper his response that he believed that Harlow, despite being Ava Mae's prisoner, was still capable of witnessing everything that was going on around her. He held his eye contact with Ava Mae, daring her to look away and praying that Harlow really could hear him. "I can't make plans for tomorrow until I see how today goes. It's my job to keep the city and *all* its citizens safe. And I'm not going to start shirking that duty just because Branzino is no longer a threat. There are still plenty of evils that need eradicating."

Whether it was the mention of her father or evils that needed eradicating, the tiniest hint of alarm flashed in Ava Mae's gaze. She spun toward Lally, who was watching with the sharp-eyed expression of someone who thought they might have to act on a moment's notice. "How long before breakfast?"

"Ten minutes or so." Lally turned and started cracking eggs with an unusual amount of force.

Ava Mae nodded. "Fine. I'll come back down then. I just remembered something I need to do." With a furtive look at Lally, she took her coffee and went upstairs.

⚜

Ava Mae set her coffee cup on Olivia's dressing table and pushed open the door to her mother's closet. The soft breeze wafting through the cracks of the door hidden behind the clothes greeted Ava Mae like an old friend. The tree sensed her just as she sensed it.

Deep within her, Harlow shifted uncomfortably. *What are you doing?*

What I should have done days ago. She walked in, closed the door and leaned against it. Whether or not Augustine had meant his words to scare her, they had. Did he know she'd taken over Harlow's body? She wasn't sure he even knew about the tree, but all his talk about eradicating evil made her think he was up to something. Something that involved her.

Leaving the house and being away from the tree for a short time wasn't an issue, but if he did something that prevented her from getting back here, she would be in real trouble. She'd weaken, and with the way Harlow had been fighting back, Ava Mae could lose her control. If she was away long enough, she might weaken to the point of no return.

That could not be allowed to happen. She needed some insurance. The kind only the tree could give her. She shoved the clothes aside to stare at the outline of the hidden door. Not so hidden now, not since she'd wooed Harlow into unlocking it and stepping through.

She pushed it open and walked out onto the small balcony that abutted the tree's trunk. She closed her eyes for a moment, inhaling the acrid, sooty scent that smelled like home because it was. The tree was the only home she'd known. She went to the edge of the narrow balcony and wrapped her arms around the trunk, pressing her face into the charred bark.

Harlow cringed, causing Ava Mae's stomach to sour, but the tree vibrated with welcoming power and after a moment of contact, she felt whole again and Harlow fell silent and still.

She released the tree and stepped back, staring up at the spiderweb of branches that mapped the space above her. Confidence filled her. No one would unseat her from this body. No one. She wasn't sure how she was going to make that happen, but she'd figure it out just like she'd figured everything else out.

The closest branch was above her head. She climbed onto the railing, using the trunk for balance, and took hold of one narrow offshoot. It snapped cleanly in her grasp. She hopped down off the railing and stuck the twig in the pocket of her robe. She'd carry it in her purse when she left the house today; that way, even if Augustine prevented her from returning, she'd have a piece of the tree with her to give her strength and keep Harlow from wresting control back. At least for a little while.

I hate you, Harlow whispered. She sounded very far away.

Don't worry, Sister dear. Ava Mae smiled as she left the closet. *You're only going to be with me a short while longer.*

❧

Neither Augustine nor Lally said a word until Ava Mae had gone back upstairs. Lally shook her head, her voice low but strong. "That woman makes me want to strangle her." She set the table. "Poor Harlow, trapped in there, unable to do anything."

"I know. It's hard not to do something physical, but I can't see how that would help Harlow. I will find a way to free her. I promise."

Lally nodded. "Well, if you're not going to be here today, I'm glad that woman isn't going to be, either."

"Lally, if she does anything to upset you—"

"Don't you worry about me." She patted his arm before returning to the stove. "She can't hurt me anyway. Not much."

For her sake, he smiled. "Good. But if you need a place to go, you can always go to the Guardian house. I'll make sure Beatrice and Dulcinea know, too. In fact, I'll ask them if they mind you having a key. Not that Beatrice goes out too much now that she's got morning sickness." His two lieutenants who lived there would be lucky to have Lally around. The woman was a treasure. "And I can have Nekai add you to the house's protection ward. It's a little hard to find otherwise."

"Thank you, Augie. I appreciate that, but you know I don't do well leaving this house." She dumped the eggs she'd scrambled into a pan slick with bacon fat. "You be home for supper?"

"I should be." Despite Lally's reassurances that she could take care of herself, he was loath to leave her alone with Ava Mae, no matter how briefly. "If not, I'll call, okay? And if I can get home early, we'll go see Olivia."

"Good enough."

Ava Mae's return for breakfast dampened his mood again

and after a tense meal spent dancing around Ava Mae's innuendos and deflecting Lally's pointed comments, Augustine busied himself with made-up chores until Ava Mae left. She took off in Olivia's Bentley convertible, ignoring the late-model hybrid Harlow had driven to New Orleans. He couldn't blame her. Harlow's vehicle had definitely seen better days and the deep red Bentley was a peach of a car. Didn't matter what Ava Mae drove, though; he'd still know where she was. He'd stuck a GPS tracker on both cars *and* dropped one in her handbag. He wasn't about to let her disappear with Harlow's body.

Fully kitted up in sword, knives and a new pair of fae leathers Fenton had ordered for him, Augustine gave Lally a nod. "All right, I'm off. You need me, you call." He kissed her cheek.

"I will. You be careful now." She smiled as she smoothed the collar of his long coat. "You look awful handsome in this getup. Wouldn't want any strange women getting ideas and following you home."

"Yeah, we have enough strange women in this house already."

She laughed as he left and in a few moments, he was in his car, the sleek Tesla Thrun he'd inherited with the job of Guardian. Driving such a fine piece of machinery usually righted his mood, but nothing could shake his worry for Harlow. He was so lost in thought he drove past the turn for Lafayette Cemetery Number One.

He swung around, parked on Coliseum and got out, going into his newly discovered smokesinger half form that allowed him to ghost through the high wall surrounding the hallowed site. He'd only used the form a few times now, but with each shift it got easier and his confidence in the ability grew, something he knew Fenton would appreciate.

Inside the cemetery, he strolled toward the Miller crypt with the collar of his long leather coat turned up against the chill of the February morning. Fallen leaves crunched underfoot, releasing the damp scent of earth. After a quick check that no one else was around, he took the few steps to the crypt's entrance and pulled on the rusted sconce beside it. Soundlessly, the door swung open.

He slipped in and used another sconce to close the door. Simultaneously, a section of the crypt's floor slid back, revealing a set of worn steps leading into the earth. Into the Pelcrum. The headquarters for all the secret and not-so-secret dealings of the fae. He strode down into the cavern, the soft glow of the gas lamps along the wide hall welcoming him as he made his way past a number of doors to open the double set at the end.

Fenton waited at the grand meeting table in the war room, as did a large mug of coffee at Augustine's place. "Morning. How are things?"

Augustine knew exactly what Fenton meant. He settled into his chair and took a drink of coffee before answering. "She finally left her room and came down to breakfast."

Fenton's brows lifted. "That's...good. I guess. Any change other than that?"

Augustine shook his head. "No. Ava Mae is still running the show. She said she's going out shopping today."

"Maybe you should have one of the lieutenants trail her."

"I planned to. I put a tracker on the car. Actually, let me call Cylo before we go any further." As an ethos fae, Cy could mimic anyone so long as he'd seen them. So even though Ava Mae knew what he looked like, he could choose a new identity and keep himself perfectly hidden. In fact, he could change his look throughout the day, never giving her the slightest hint she was being watched. Augustine grabbed his Life Management Device, unlocked the screen and tapped Cy's speed dial.

Fenton frowned. "Is your com cell not working?"

Augustine touched the tiny gray dot stuck behind his ear.

"It's fine. Just a little early for voices in my head." Using the LMD manually turned the com cell off automatically.

Cy answered. "Hey boss, what's up? How's our girl?"

"She's the same." Cy and Harlow had bonded over their shared geek love of online gaming and a sci-fi show called *Star Alliance*. "She's also why I'm calling you. Ava Mae plans to go out shopping today. I want you to tail her, make sure she doesn't do anything to harm Harlow."

"You got it. She'll never know I'm there."

"That's the plan. Check in with me when you can; otherwise, just call me when she returns home."

"You got it, boss. How do I find her?"

"She's in Olivia's red Bentley. The car has a tracker on it but so does her purse. As soon as we hang up, I'll send you the links for both. You shouldn't have any trouble locating her."

"Cool. I'm on it."

Augustine hung up, swiping his finger over the screen and sending the links as promised. Then he set his LMD down and picked up his coffee. "That's one less thing to worry about today. What else is new? Any ideas on how to get Harlow back? Nekai turn anything up?"

Fenton's slow nod was a sure sign there was something new. "I'll get to what's new in a moment. The best Nekai's been able to come up with so far is a spell that would put her in a type of stasis."

"You mean like a coma?" Augustine didn't like the sound of that at all.

Fenton made a face, tipping his hand back and forth. "Sort of. Because it would be magically induced and not medically, it wouldn't be as taxing on the body. More like a very restful sleep. But it's a stopgap measure, not a cure." He pushed his glasses back on the bridge of his nose. "At least we know it's possible if Ava Mae gets out of control."

"I guess. What's the other news?"

"In my research on Harlow's condition, it occurred to me that we fae may not be the most expert source of information on this type of possession." He slanted his eyes at Augustine. "I was thinking you might talk to your mother, see if she knows of anyone who might be knowledgeable about exorcisms. If we get to that point."

Augustine's jaw tensed. "The last time I tried to talk to my mother, she refused to even see me. I am done trying to reach her."

"But Harlow's life is potentially at stake. I just thought—"

"There is nothing I wouldn't do for Harlow." Augustine hesitated. "Do you really think this is a path worth pursuing?"

Fenton shrugged. "It might be grasping at straws but right now, straws are all we have."

Augustine grimaced. "Maybe there's someone else we can talk to then. My mother isn't going to help us. That bridge isn't just burned, it's gone. Besides, if there is any way around it, I will *not* put Harlow through an exorcism."

He stared at the enormous fleur-de-lis inlaid in the table's center, memories churning through his mind. His mother had done that to him as a child. He'd been terrified by the process, somewhat because of the mysticism surrounding it but more by the idea that he was possessed by something evil. All because he'd been born blatantly fae, unlike his half-human, half-smokesinger mother, who could easily pass for human. Not long after kicking him out of her home for being too fae, she'd gone to live at the Ursuline Convent. She still lived there, doing menial labor in exchange for her room and board.

Her faith had become her Guardian, but her son, who was Guardian of the entire city, she ignored. The irony was not lost on him.

"I'm sorry," Fenton said quietly. "I knew you'd...that is, I didn't mean to stir up your past."

The fact that Fenton knew what Augustine's mother had done to him those many years ago didn't surprise him. The cypher fae knew *everything*. "I know you didn't. Anything else?"

"Yes. I had a feeling you'd respond to my suggestion about contacting your mother the way you did, so I reached out to Detective Grantham—"

"What's he got to do with Harlow's situation?"

"Nothing directly, but he did tell us his grandmother was a mambo."

"I remember. She was the one who verified the powder we found in Dreich's home after his death was *bokura,* the zombie dust." The light clicked on in Augustine's mind. A mambo was a voodoo priestess and voodoo had many religious elements in it. "You're thinking a mambo could very well know how to handle a possession."

"I am."

Typically the fae avoided voodoo the same way they did witchcraft, but this was a special case. And perhaps, in some ways, a new age. What difference did it make where the help came from? "Is his grandmother well? I thought she'd been sick."

"She had been, but she's better now."

"Did you ask Grantham about her helping us?"

Fenton nodded. "I did. He talked to her and she agreed to meet with you, so long as Grantham is there, too. I'm sure she's as trepidatious about meeting you as you are about mixing voodoo into this situation."

"If it helps Harlow, I'm all for it."

"Good. You're to meet him at her house in a couple hours. She lives out in Treme."

"Near Father Ogun?"

"In that neighborhood, yes." Fenton tapped his LMD. "I'm sending you the directions now."

Augustine's LMD buzzed with the incoming info. "Thank you for setting that up."

"You're welcome, but it's not exactly free. Grantham needs our help with something, too, so you can expect to talk to him afterwards."

"Quid pro quo. What's he need?"

"Tourists have been disappearing."

"Sounds like a job for City Hall. Or the tourism board."

Fenton shook his head. "I don't mean tourism's down, I mean tourists have literally gone missing."

"Mardi Gras was two days ago. They're probably just sleeping it off somewhere."

Fenton shook his head. "Six tourists in three days. Valuables left in their hotel rooms, except for the things they might have been carrying on their person. This isn't just a case of someone passing out by the river, or in the wrong hotel room. And to make matters worse, it seems one of the tourists is Robbie Pellimento."

"The senator's son? You said seems. Does that mean you don't know if he's actually missing?"

"Correct. Robbie has a reputation as being quite the party animal. It could be he *is* actually sleeping it off somewhere. Or still partying. Or trying to avoid his mother, the senator. Whatever the case, Senator Pellimento was scheduled to arrive in two days to dedicate that new statue in Audubon Park." Fenton heaved out an unhappy breath. "However, since Robbie has been incommunicado, she's arriving today."

"And that's a concern because?"

"While it's pretty common knowledge that Irene Pellimento is on track to be the next president of the Southern Union, what's not well known is her hatred of othernaturals. If she had her way, we'd all be rounded up into camps. And we might be, if she ends up president."

Augustine frowned. "I'm not saying I doubt you, but this is the first time I've heard about this. Not that I follow human politics much."

"I do and I can tell you, Pellimento's sly about it, but digging into the legislation she's passed has brought to light a frightening number of anti-othernatural rulings."

"So basically, if her son is among these missing tourists and this turns out to be othernatural related, she's going to hate us more than usual?"

Fenton's eyes narrowed behind his glasses. "She has the power to take New Orleans away from us, Augustine. To destroy our Haven city designation."

"That's a fae thing. She has no say over that."

"She does if she makes it illegal for fae to own property or hold a job here." He pointed a finger at Augustine's smirk. "I'm not joking. If her son dies and she becomes the next president of the Southern Union, she will make our lives very difficult. Actually, it won't take her becoming the president to make our lives hell. As I'm sure you can imagine, Loudreux is very concerned this not happen."

"For once, the Prime and I agree on something." Hugo Loudreux was the leader of the fae Elektos but even his position as Prime didn't give him authority over the Guardian. In theory, they were supposed to work together, but Loudreux hadn't been in favor of Augustine becoming the Guardian and as such, made his life as difficult as he could whenever possible.

"I hope that means you'll give this some real attention."

Augustine sat back, his fingers on the handle of his coffee mug. It took a lot to rile Fenton. This was obviously serious. "I will. We'll find her son." Eventually. He still had Harlow's needs at heart. "Grantham have any leads?"

"Not on Robbie, no, but he does have an eyewitness who thinks she saw one of the missing tourists talking to Zara Vincent at the farmer's market."

"If you'd told me Giselle, I'd think it meant something, but Zara's the harmless one, isn't she?"

Seeming slightly calmer, Fenton shrugged. "She's never done anything to put a blip on the radar."

"Although now that her sister is the high priestess of the New Orleans Coven, maybe she's decided the time is ripe to make a move." His brain kept processing. "Or she could be working with Giselle."

Fenton lifted his hand. "To what end? Giselle makes her money telling fortunes in Jackson Square. I know she's got private clients that pay her a lot more, but those tourists are her bread and butter. I can't imagine her doing something that could possibly scare them away."

Augustine shook his head. "But as high priestess, she's now on the coven's payroll. I'm sure she'll keep her private clients but I can't see her wallowing with the unwashed masses in Jackson Square anymore."

Fenton lifted one finger. "Ah, but she has been. We've had eyes on her."

"Interesting." Augustine wrapped his hand around his mug but the coffee had gone cold. He let it go. "Almost as much as the fact that theirs is the one name that's been connected to this new issue." He sighed. "Talking to Giselle never does any good. I can't imagine talking to Zara would be any different."

"Agreed. Leave that to Grantham. Right now we have Harlow to think about."

"And finding Robbie." But finding that party boy was only peripherally on his radar. No matter how bunched up Prime Loudreux was. Harlow was his sole concern. Augustine pushed his chair back and stood. "If anything comes of the talk with

Grantham's grandmother, I'll let you know. Otherwise, I'll see you tomorrow morning. And I'll tell Grantham he's got our cooperation, but my involvement is going to be minimal until Harlow is herself again." The thought of another day passing and Harlow still held prisoner in her own body shot a sense of helplessness through him, a feeling he hated more than anything.

Fenton nodded. "I understand."

Augustine turned and strode out of the war room and down the hall toward the crypt's exit. Paying a visit to his mother, even under the guise of helping Harlow, would be worthless. Unless he commanded her to help.

As Guardian, he had the right to require any fae citizen of New Orleans to assist him. But as her son, he also knew that such a command would destroy her. She would be forced to face her fae heritage, the only thing she hated more than her own son.

He shut the crypt door behind him, blinking for a moment in the brightness of the clouded sky.

There was no question in his mind as to his decision if things got that desperate.

Harlow would always come first.

Chapter Two

Ava Mae couldn't stop smiling. The money she'd found in the duffel bag under Harlow's bed was stuffed into her purse. At least eight thousand dollars' worth of new, slippery plastic bills. They'd go a long way toward jazzing up her sister's boring wardrobe.

It's not boring, it's practical. And you have no right to that money.

Blah, blah, blah. All black is super-boring. Almost as boring as the whining you've been doing about this all morning. I'm doing you a favor by spending this money on something worthwhile. Now, let's try to have some fun, shall we? Ava Mae laughed. *Well, at least I will.* She ignored the rest of Harlow's comments, letting her simmer below the surface while Ava Mae poured herself into the task of shopping. It turned out to be one of her talents. In less than two hours, she'd spent nearly half the cash and loaded herself down with shopping bags, divesting the boutiques in the Quarter of their prettiest things.

You have the taste of a preteen girl in love with glitter and kittens. If you think Augustine's going to be attracted to someone who looks like a rainbow threw up on them, you're wrong.

Ava Mae shook her head. *I know you're jealous. I would be, too, if someone else was about to bed that gorgeous hunk of man and force me to watch.*

You are not taking him to bed. Harlow was practically shaking with rage, causing the edges of Ava Mae's vision to waver. *I forbid it.*

Pain shot through Ava Mae's head, another by-product of

Harlow's anger. She leaned against a building, letting it pass. *Calm down, Harlow. Do not make me do something you're going to regret.* But the realization that Harlow was growing stronger struck Ava Mae like a falling brick. She would have to do something more than just carrying around a twig from the lightning tree. She just didn't know what yet. Killing Lally, her first choice, could cause Harlow to fly into a greater rage. One Ava Mae might not be able to withstand.

The pain subsided and Ava Mae returned to ignoring her sister. She stopped at a café for hot chocolate with extra whipped cream and beignets. She'd earned it. As she settled into her table, she pulled out the new scarf she'd bought, snapped the tag off and draped it around her neck, distracting herself from the problem of Harlow. The distraction was brief.

Hideous.

Shut up. It's beautiful.

"Well, now, isn't that a pretty thing. Very nice."

She turned. The man at the table beside hers nodded at her scarf. She nodded back. "Thank you." *See, Harlow? I've already gotten a compliment on it.* He was a peacock of a man, dressed beautifully in a purple velvet suit, green patterned shirt and blue leather shoes, all topped off with a black fedora sporting a beaded band in the same colors. A few gold rings gleamed on his fingers and around his neck was a black silk cord from which dangled a little red pouch holding who knew what. "You're very colorful." She needed more jewelry. She smiled. "I like it." She stuck her gloved hand out. "I'm Harlow."

Liar.

He laughed and extended his hand. "Pleasure to meet you, Harlow. You can call me Rufus."

"Nice to meet you, too, Rufus."

An old woman walked by, giving them both a curious look. Ava Mae ignored her. Probably jealous of her new scarf.

He added three spoonfuls of sugar to his coffee, then a big glug of cream. "Are you visiting our fair city?"

"No, I just moved here. The city is still very new to me."

He pointed his spoon at her pile of shopping bags. "Seems to me you're finding your way around pretty well."

She smiled. "I needed some new things. My old wardrobe was boring and dull."

You're boring and dull. And not long for this world.

Ava Mae directed her thoughts inward with a hard shove. *Sister, dear, you really need to learn not to push me.*

After a small gasp, Harlow stayed quiet.

He sipped his coffee. "Boring and dull is no good." His face suddenly came alive. "You know whose style I always admired? Olivia Goodwin. You wouldn't know her being young and new to town, but now there was a woman who dressed with panache."

Ava Mae knew her mouth had come open and didn't care. "I know who she is."

"You do?" He looked shocked, but pleased. "Good for you. Most young people these days seem to have forgotten about the old Hollywood stars—"

"She was my mother."

He stared at her for a long moment. "I am so sorry for your loss. My apologies if I've upset you by bringing up her name, her having so recently left us." He crossed himself.

"No, it's fine. You just…surprised me." Ava Mae leaned forward. "Did you know my mother then?"

A slight smile brought up the corners of his mouth. "I did, but it was rare I got to see her. Those house companions of hers—"

"Lally and Augustine?"

He nodded. "They never cared much for me. Said I was a bad influence."

If they thought that, he is.

Ava Mae frowned. "You were a bad influence on my mother? How?"

He grinned. "I'll tell you, but if you tell Augustine you've met me, he isn't going to like it."

"I won't say a word." Anyone Lally and Augustine didn't like instantly intrigued her. "Tell me."

His smile broadened. "I'm what most would call a voodoo doctor. In truth, I am a follower and practitioner of the voodoo religion. Does that scare you?"

Harlow's panic turned the taste in Ava Mae's mouth bitter. *Get away from him.* Ava Mae blinked, her curiosity piqued by Harlow's instant aversion to the man. "No. I've never met a real live voodoo man before. You've just become twice as interesting as you were a minute ago. What did you say your name was?"

He laughed. "Most people call me Father Ogun. But like I said, you can call me Rufus."

"A real voodoo doctor?"

Rufus nodded. "I guarantee."

A jumble of thoughts swirled in Ava Mae's borrowed brain. A voodoo doctor might know how to silence Harlow for good. Ava Mae didn't want to lose her sister, but the incessant chatter and constant battles for control of the body wore her down. If there was a way for Ava Mae to be assured of always having the upper hand, she would gladly take it.

The bitter taste in her mouth remained. *Nothing good will come of this. Nothing.*

Ava Mae pointed. "What's that little pouch on your necklace?"

His hand went to the small red sack. "That's my *gris gris* bag. Brings me luck. Keeps me peaceful. Draws good things to me." He glanced at it, then at her. "Maybe you're one of those things, hah?"

She smiled, thinking the same thing. "Maybe I am. Could

you make one of those for me? Something that would protect me from those trying to harm me?"

Concern creased his face. "Of course, but my dear child, who on earth would want to harm you?"

She'd already been gone so long from the tree and even though she had a piece of it in her bag, she still felt uneasy at being away too much longer. She bit her lip. This wasn't an opportunity she could afford to lose. "I have to get home soon. Maybe we could meet again? I'd love to talk with you some more. Ask your advice on a few things."

He splayed his fingers against his chest. "I would be honored to help you out in whatever way I could. I'd be pleased to meet you again. Let's make plans, shall we?"

⚜

Augustine followed Detective J.J. Grantham into his grand-mother's house, a neat and tidy single story. Here and there were a few signs of her voodoo involvement, but it was nothing like Father Ogun's overwhelming collection. And instead of the powerful stench of incense, the warm embrace of freshly baked cookies greeted them. If this was the other side of voodoo, he could get real comfortable with it.

Grantham called out, "Mawmaw, it's J.J. and I've got that friend with me I told you about."

"In here, baby."

They followed her voice into the kitchen. J.J. kissed her on the cheek, then introduced Augustine. "Mawmaw, this is Augustine Robelais. Augustine, this is my grandmother, Queen Jewelia Grantham."

Augustine offered his hand. "Pleasure to meet you, Queen Jewelia." Grantham had prepped him on queen being the appropriate title for a woman of her position in the voodoo religion. "But you can't be Detective Grantham's grandmother. You barely look old enough to be his mother. More like his sister, I'd say." None of which was a lie. The woman before him had flawless mocha skin, hair as thick and black as any he'd seen, and she held herself with the perfect carriage of youth. All of it seemed proof of her skills as a mambo.

She smiled and before shaking his hand, wiped hers on the apron covering her long blue dress. "If you're trying to sweeten me up, J.J. has already told me to cooperate. But feel free to continue." She laughed. "Lally Hughes taking good care of you?"

"Better than you can imagine."

Queen Jewelia nodded knowingly. "You boys want some coffee? I just fixed a pot to go with the cookies." She pointed at her stove, where trays of chocolate chip cookies sat cooling.

"I'm in." Grantham took a chair at the kitchen table. "Especially because I know you made those cookies for me." He looked at Augustine. "I'm her favorite grandchild."

She waggled a finger at Grantham. "Now, don't go starting things or I'll move you down the list."

Augustine sat also. "Thank you very much. I never turn down a good cup of coffee or a homemade cookie."

She stopped pouring coffee to smile at him. "You fae like sweets, don't you?"

"Yes, ma'am, we do."

She went back to filling cups. "I don't know many of your kind. None, really. We don't tend to mix, do we?"

"No." He hoped that wasn't a point of contention for her.

She brought the coffee over on a tray with cream and sugar, three folded white cloth napkins and a big plate of cookies. "Help yourself."

Grantham reached for a cookie and she smacked his hand. "Guests first, Jeremiah."

"Yes, ma'am." Grantham made a face at Augustine as if to say, "You see what I grew up with?"

Augustine nodded, smiling more than was probably wise, and took his coffee. Grantham was a former lightweight championship boxer. Seeing him cow to his grandmother gave Augustine hope for the world.

She sat between them and helped herself to coffee.

The cookies were warm, but Augustine had too much to say to eat the one waiting on his napkin just yet. "I really do appreciate you seeing me on such short notice. Especially since this is a fae matter and not something you'd normally be concerned about."

"I wouldn't say that." She stirred sugar into her cup. "J.J. tells me there's a young woman's life in the balance here. If she wasn't one of yours, would it matter to you who her people were?"

"No, ma'am, but the fact that she is someone close to me makes it more pressing."

"I can understand that." She set her spoon down and looked at him. "Tell me what I can help you with."

"Olivia Goodwin's daughter, Harlow, has been...possessed by the spirit of her twin sister, Ava Mae. I don't know if it's an important detail, but her twin was murdered by their father not long after she was born."

Jewelia nodded but didn't act like anything he'd just told her was that unusual. "Could be. Some murdered spirits have a lot of anger in them. A lot of desire to do the things they were robbed of doing."

"That sounds like Ava Mae, but she was killed when she was an infant. Would she remember any of that?"

She paused a moment. "That wouldn't seem likely, but then the spirit world doesn't always follow the paths of what makes sense and what doesn't. You sure your friend is still in there?"

He broke the cookie in half. "I *know* Harlow is still there, but Ava Mae has completely taken over and is somehow keeping Harlow suppressed. If you have any ideas how to get Ava Mae out without hurting Harlow, I would be in your debt."

She took a long, slow sip of coffee as if considering the usefulness of having a fae she could call upon for a favor. "I might be able to help."

"Thank you." Relief flooded Augustine. He popped a quarter of the cookie in his mouth. As delicious as expected.

"I have a few more questions."

He nodded. Grantham was reaching for his third cookie.

She shot Grantham a look. He took the cookie anyway. Frowning, she looked at Augustine. "How long has Ava Mae possessed Harlow?"

"About four days."

"That's good. Not too long then. Too long and spirits latch on. Grow roots." She nodded like she was thinking. "Who raised the spirit?"

"Harlow."

"How?"

Augustine hesitated. "I'm not sure what you're asking."

"How did she bring the spirit into the mortal world? What kind of magic did she use? Fae magic? Witchcraft? Voodoo?"

"I...don't know." He couldn't tell her about the lightning tree. That was a sworn secret. But he also wasn't sure what kind of magic that was. "Natural magic?" He shook his head. "This is out of my area of expertise, I'm sorry."

Her gaze lingered on him a long while before she turned to Grantham again. "J.J., be a dear and give us a minute alone."

He stood without argument, almost like he'd expected it. "I'll be in my car. I have a few calls to make anyway." He grabbed one more cookie, then looked at Augustine. "We still need to talk when you're done."

"I promise it'll happen before I leave."

With a nod, he walked out.

She waited until the front door closed. "Lally Hughes made you promise not to tell, didn't she?"

"Why would you think Lally had—"

"It was the tree, wasn't it?"

He sat there, finding no immediate way to answer her. He didn't want to betray Lally, but Harlow was his first priority. "What tree?"

She smiled and patted his hand. "It's all right. I'm not going to tell anyone. That's why I sent J.J. out. I'm talking about the lightning tree. The one Olivia's mansion was built around. By your people. But then you know that already, don't you?"

"Yes." There was no point in denying what she already knew. Not if she could help Harlow. "How do you know about it?" Of course, if she'd been fishing, he'd just given her quite a catch.

"Lally and I go way back." The gleam in her eyes said there was more to that than she was telling him, but he let it go. "I take it you didn't tell her you were coming to see me today?"

"I didn't know I was until a few hours ago, so, no, she didn't know. I'm guessing you've known Lally a lot longer than I have. Like a lot longer than most people have."

She coughed out a laugh, her mouth bending into a sad, funny smile. "You've shared with me, so I'm gonna share with you. I'm actually J.J.'s *great-great*-grandmother." She lifted her cup to her lips and drank slowly, like she was giving him time to understand what she'd said.

Well, that was interesting. He leaned back a little. "I appreciate you balancing the scales with the exchange of information." He hesitated. "I'm curious, though...if you and Lally are so alike...it's just that Grantham said you were sick recently and Lally never gets sick."

The light in her eyes turned guarded. "I wasn't sick. Not in the way regular folk are. There are times when I need deep rest.

That was one of them. Lally never gets that way for a different reason."

He got the sense she'd shared more with him than she had with most. "The tree?"

She nodded.

"Thank you for identifying the powder we found as *bokura,* by the way. I appreciate you helping us with that."

The relief on her face said she was glad to be on to a new subject. "Didn't help much, did it?"

"It did, but since we couldn't link it to anyone..." He shrugged, not wishing to downplay what she'd done but the truth was the truth.

"Damn that Rufus Ogun. It *was* his, but you'll never hear me say that outside this house."

She'd just confirmed what he'd suspected all along, but without her testimony it was worthless. "Why? You aren't afraid of him, are you? Seems to me you're more powerful than he is."

"Hmph." She shook her head. "Power is one thing. How you use it is another. If there are shades of white and black in voodoo, then Ogun and I are at opposite ends of the spectrum. Everything I do is for good purposes. Ogun doesn't let such a concern bother him." She leaned forward. "You know why people think he's the head of all things voodoo in this city? Because everyone else is too scared to go against him." She tapped her finger on the table. "That man's done a serious disservice to our community and all we do is cower."

"I appreciate that info. I am doing my best to take him down."

"Do fae have black magic? Because that's the only way you're going to rid the world of that man."

"Thanks for the tip." Augustine filed that away for later. Time to return to his real purpose here. "Knowing what you do now about how Ava Mae's spirit was raised by the tree, do you think you can help Harlow? Is there a way to get Ava Mae out without hurting Harlow?"

Jewelia studied him for a few long seconds. "You love her. I see it in your eyes. That's why I'm going to say this in the gentlest way I know how." She laid her hand over his. It was warm from the cup she'd been holding. "That tree is bad business. Not evil exactly, but bent toward darkness and if dark magic put that spirit into your friend, dark magic is the only way you're going to get that spirit out. And I am truly sorry, but that is not something I can be a part of. You might find someone willing to practice that kind of craft but I would be very careful. A spirit like that cannot just be loosed. It must be contained somewhere new or it will wreak havoc on whoever cast it from its home. It might still."

"What if I destroyed the tree?"

Her mouth quirked up in a sad, strange way. "If that was possible, it would have been done years ago."

"So there's no other way?"

"No."

Her answer sent a deep ache through him, the kind of pain he'd felt when Olivia had lain dying in his arms. "I can't believe there's nothing that can be done. I won't accept it. I won't give up hope."

"Good." She wrapped her fingers around his. "There is always hope." She let his hand go. "Now listen to me. If Olivia's daughter is still in there, she may be able to fight her way back out. Surround her with the things she loves. Keep those memories alive. And if you truly love her—"

"I do."

"Then tell her. Love is a powerful magic in its own right. Give her a reason to want to fight. Something to fight for."

"If I tell Harlow I love her, the only one who's going to hear it now is Ava Mae and she's the last one who needs that encouragement."

Jewelia's eyes narrowed and her gaze swept him. "She's been after you, eh?"

"Relentlessly."

She nodded. "Girl knows sleeping with you would widen the chasm between her and her sister. Ava Mae must know Harlow loves you. If she could cause Harlow enough hurt, Harlow would most likely retreat and lose whatever hold she has left." She shook her head. "You must not let Ava Mae know how you feel."

"I have no plans to, I promise."

"But Harlow needs to know you love her. It will give her strength, I'm sure of it."

"I'm all for that, but how?"

Jewelia fell silent. "If you're willing, I have an idea."

"I'm willing. Whatever it is."

She folded her hands before her. "You must use *bokura*."

Augustine jerked back. "The same stuff that killed Dreich? No."

"The powder is only the tool. The one wielding the tool did the killing. A little *bokura* will put the dominant spirit to rest, letting Harlow come forward. You can tell her your feelings and reassure her that you are doing everything you can to set her free."

"I don't know."

"I am *not* Ogun. You can trust me."

The idea scared him, but the reward was worth the risk. "I . . . am willing to try." At least that way if Harlow didn't make it, a thought that tore a hole in him, she'd know how he felt.

Jewelia patted his hand again. "Let me get you some and then I'll tell you exactly how to use it."

Chapter Three

Giselle sat with her sister, Zara, in the sunroom at the rear of her sister's house. Her home had become their informal headquarters, a logical choice considering the plans they were implementing. Ian, one of the coven's Circle of Thirteen, the council who helped the coven leader rule, lounged nearby.

Since the death of Evander, their father, Ian had become quite a bit closer to Giselle and her sister than the average coven member. She smiled. That had more to do with his willingness to share his prodigious talents than his position in the coven.

A drop of condensation ran down the side of Giselle's sweet tea. She caught it with her finger and flicked it into the air. "How are things proceeding? I assume that's what you wanted to discuss when you asked me to come over." At some point, Giselle imagined their meetings would be held at her new home, previously her father's house, but that would be a while yet based on the way the remodeling was dragging on. And of course, that garden didn't hold the same promise as Zara's.

"It is." Zara shook her head, the lines around her eyes more pronounced. "Things are proceeding too fast. I want to unseat the fae as much as you do but we have to slow down." She ran her hand along the arm of the tufted chaise, her fingers worrying the slightly worn velveteen. Zara's sentimental nature had kept her from replacing anything when she'd moved into their late mother's Garden District mansion nearly twenty years ago. She had, however, added even more plants, to the point the house looked and smelled like a botanical garden, but then that wasn't so surprising. Zara was a green witch just as their mother had been. Plants were her source of power.

"I disagree." Giselle shook her head. Was Zara worried about something? About the danger of the spell? Green witches weren't typically known for their fearlessness, but Zara was no shrinking violet. She took after their mother, who'd proven herself a warrior in the never-ending battle against the fae. "Unless you tell me the pace is going to harm the magic, I see no reason to pull back. We've accomplished a lot. We're so close to being exactly where we need to be."

"Six souls in three days are too many. It raises suspicion." Stress cast little lines around Zara's mouth. Perhaps it was just tiredness. She *was* bearing the burden of the spellwork. "The spell will never be cast if we're in jail. Or worse. The fae will destroy us if we're caught."

"Which is exactly why we need to continue." Giselle refrained from rolling her eyes. Patience was difficult when you wanted something so badly. "You'd prefer what, that we cut that number in half? Take only three this week?"

"Three in a week?" Zara looked aghast, her fingers twisting together. "Even that's too many. One every few weeks. One every month. This pace you've set us on is a race toward disaster." She pushed a flaming red strand of hair away from her eyes. "There's no reason to proceed this way. Chaos magic is dangerous under the best conditions. Look what happened to Mother. We need to be careful."

Giselle understood that, but Zara seemed to be stalling for reasons she couldn't figure out. "Our mother was going it alone. We have the power of three. And careful is fine, but the longer it takes us to set this spell in place, the greater chance the fae have of discovering what we're about." Giselle glanced at their third. Ian was beautiful in the dark, dangerous kind of way that made her want to devour him. How nice that her childhood crush, the man her father had kept her from and warned her about, had become such an integral part of her life. His role in their current plan had started as the consecrating of Zara's garden through the Great Ritual, a way to add another layer of potent magic. But it had quickly turned into something far less lofty. And much more carnal. But they were grown women with no living parents. Hell, she was the high priestess of the coven and Zara was her sister. They could do as they pleased. She raised her brows at him. "What say you?"

As if uncomfortable with the new role of decider that had been laid upon him these last few days, Ian shifted, his answer more of a grunt. Not that the tattooed, pierced, eyeliner-wearing wizard was much of a chatterbox anyway. "Zara's right. You lose nothing by slowing down."

Giselle sighed in frustration. Ian was great fun in bed, but that was a small comfort when he was siding against her. She frowned, disappointed in the man she was reluctantly falling for. "The fae have ruled this city—and us—for centuries. I would prefer not to give them a day longer than necessary."

"I understand that." Zara's voice was softer now. "And I feel exactly the same way. But the fae aren't stupid. And you know they work with the human police. I'm just saying we can't afford to bring any sort of attention on ourselves."

If Zara was worried about attention it was best Giselle kept the senator's son's identity to herself. To buy herself a moment of thinking time, she stared out Zara's back windows toward the pond in the garden's center. Zara had created the water feature in the hole left by their mother's fatal attempt at the very same chaos spell they were planning to cast. Zara had since created a second magic space there, a well of souls to hold those they were collecting for their own attempt at the chaos spell. "Twelve souls is going to take forever."

"It's how it has to be. Three is the sacred number and there are four corners to the sacred circle." Zara came to sit beside her. "You've never had any patience, you know. Ever since you were little. Remember that time Mom was making cookies and you ate all the dough before she could bake them?"

Giselle grimaced. "I was sick for two days afterwards."

Zara slipped her hand over Giselle's and meshed their fingers. "This is another one of those times that things have to be done a certain way in order to achieve the outcome you desire. You have no choice but to be patient."

Reluctantly, Giselle nodded. "I suppose you're right. But I'm not going to like a single second of the wait."

"I know." Zara nudged her hip into Giselle's and looked toward the dark wizard filling the room with masculine energy. "Fortunately, we have Ian to occupy us."

He was sprawled in Zara's leather recliner, his leg over one arm of the chair as if he owned the place. Goddess, he was so beautiful he made her heart ache. He grinned as if he knew exactly how she felt about him. "At your service, ladies."

"You *are* reliable." The best Giselle could do under the duress of forced patience was a half smile. She stood. "I should get to the square and get set up for the day."

Zara shook her head. "You're the high priestess of the New Orleans Coven. You don't need to be reading tourists' fortunes in Jackson Square anymore."

"As long as we're filling the well with souls I do. How do you think I've been finding people with little to no family? Luring them here with the promise that they'll have their hearts' desire fulfilled is the easy part. You can't exactly take out an ad for the sort of thing we're doing." It was also a good way to make it appear to fae eyes as though nothing had changed with her or the coven. Although the powers that be would know she'd taken over as high priestess, by showing up in the square she hoped they'd think she wasn't taking her new position with any seriousness.

"True, but slowing down means you could at least take today off." Zara shrugged. "Besides, I don't like you out in the open like that. You're too vulnerable."

Giselle made a face at Zara. "Vulnerable? From whom?"

Zara's mouth dropped open. Then her gaze turned angry. "Have you forgotten what Ogun did to you in this very garden? He nearly killed you."

Ian's eyes narrowed. "He needs to be dealt with. I'm happy to do that."

"Agreed," Zara added.

Giselle huffed out a breath. "You two just complained to me that we've had too many disappearances too fast and now you want to add a death to our list of crimes?" She threw her hands up. "I can't figure either of you out."

Ian leaned forward, his expression deadly serious. "He's threatened you. For that, he should be removed. You're the coven leader now. It's our job to protect the high priestess."

"I appreciate that..."

He cocked one brow. "But?"

"No but. I was thinking maybe you and I should pay him a visit. He has to know by now that his attempt on my life failed. He's got to be expecting some kind of retaliation." She crossed her arms and settled back. "All this talk about not drawing attention to ourselves has made me think we *should* put some distance between us and the process of accumulating the souls. Especially if we can get someone else to do it for us."

Zara frowned. "Are you saying that you're going to force Ogun to do it?"

Giselle lifted one shoulder. "Why not? I could offer him a truce. He brings us the rest of what we need and we forgive his attempt on my life."

Zara seemed shocked. "You would do that?"

"Like you've both pointed out, I'm the high priestess of the coven now. I have to rise above some of this nonsense or no one will take me seriously. And if Ian goes with me, there's no chance Ogun will hurt me. Ian is too powerful and too intimidating."

Ian stood. "I'm game."

Zara nodded slowly. "If you think he can provide us with the remaining souls without causing us further complications, that would be good. However, I don't think he can do anything without creating more complications. I also don't like him knowing what we're about. What's to keep him from telling the fae we're working on a chaos spell?"

"He doesn't need to know the details. Just that we require a few expendable volunteers."

Zara sighed. "You're the high priestess. If you want to do this, I can't stop you, but I'm not comfortable with it. Ogun isn't trustworthy under any conditions." She smiled, but it looked forced. "But perhaps you know him better than I do. And with Ian along, he will see that you have the strength of your coven behind you."

"Thank you." Giselle nodded at Ian. "I want to do this now. Is there any reason you can't?"

He pulled his LMD from his pocket. "Let me check in at the shop, make sure my evening sitting hasn't changed." Ian owned the House of Pain tattoo parlor. It was his business, but the pain he generated was the source of his power. He could also increase another witch's power with his work as he had when he'd tattooed both Giselle and Zara, giving them a nice bump in their abilities. He put the phone to his ear and walked into the kitchen.

Giselle used the moment to confront her sister. "Is there anything you're not telling me? Some reason the spell isn't going to work? Because if that's the only reason you're stalling—"

"No, no, everything's fine." Zara looked away and sighed. "I just don't want to borrow trouble. There's nothing wrong with being cautious and doing things circumspectly."

"I guess." Giselle was starting to have her doubts, but for her sister's sake, she'd let them go.

Zara approached, the worried lines still creasing her brow. "I know you're taking Ian with you, but I still don't believe that's enough to keep Ogun honest. His track record should be enough—"

"Zara, do you think I don't have a plan? I'm only going to tell Ogun we need five volunteers."

"But we need six."

"I know." Giselle smiled. "But that spot is reserved for Ogun when he's brought us the last one. That should tie our loose ends up nicely, don't you think?"

Zara tapped a finger against her bottom lip. "I don't know. We've been careful only to include those who won't be missed. Ogun's disappearance will definitely be noticed."

"And by then, we'll be in charge of the city once again. A missing voodoo troublemaker won't matter."

"What's to stop him from spilling our plans before he brings us a single soul?"

"Besides fear?" She lifted her chin slightly. "He knows our father has passed and that I'm now in charge of the coven. I'll tell him he can have an honorary place at every coven meeting if he does this for us."

Zara's eyes widened slightly. Her smile was genuine this time. "He'd like that, wouldn't he?" She snorted softly. "I don't know why I doubted you. You have my full cooperation."

⚜

Augustine sat across from Grantham as the detective gave him the details of the missing persons situation, including files on the five tourists and Robbie Pellimento, although there didn't seem to be any one factor tying them together. The detective shook his head. "The mayor is leaning on the NOPD hard to get this resolved, supposedly because he doesn't want the tourism industry to suffer. Personally, I think it has more to do with Pellimento's impending visit."

"I'm sure that's a factor."

"It is." Grantham lowered his voice slightly. "And that's where the real suffering will come from. But I'm sure you know that already since you're going to feel her wrath more than I am."

"So I've been told," Augustine said. "Fenton filled me in on her. I promise you have my help." But other than making his lieutenants aware of what was happening, human matters still weren't his main focus. He held the files up. "These copies are for me?"

"All yours. I hope they give you some ideas because we don't have much to go on right now."

"I'll do what I can." Augustine stood. "I'll be in touch." He made his way to the Thrun. As soon as he slipped into the driver's seat, his LMD chimed in his head. "Answer."

"Boss, it's Cy. You're never going to believe this. I followed Harlow like you said and someone else was already following her. Guess who?"

"Maybe you could just tell me." After his discussion with Queen Jewelia, he had too many other thoughts on his mind to play games.

"Father Ogun."

Telling Harlow exactly how he felt wasn't going to be easy but— "What did you say?"

"Father Ogun. The voodoo doctor."

"I know who he is. What the hell has he got to do with any of this? What happened exactly?"

Cy continued. "I located her on Chartres, but he was already trailing her. Not sure for how long but if I had to guess, I'd say he was waiting near the house."

"Has he been camped out for the last three days waiting?" Or maybe he'd done some voodoo thing. "He had no way of knowing when she'd leave. I didn't know he even knew who Harlow was—because that's who he's got to think she is."

"Nothing stays secret in this town for long. Besides, the obit mentioned Olivia's daughter."

"True." And Harlow had advertised her Web design business in the *Picayune*.

"Do you want me to confront him? I could go to his house, maybe rough him up a little, tell him to stay away—"

"No. If anyone does that, it's going to be me. Do you have any idea what he wanted with her?"

"She stopped shopping to get some beignets and that's when he made his move. Sat right next to her. Started talking about clothes and shopping and stuff like that. Then he told her he'd known her mother and that he and Olivia were friends."

"All lies. I would have known about that."

"He also told her not to say anything to you or Lally about meeting him, because you two had never liked him and wouldn't approve."

"He's got that right."

"They talked a little more and she asked him what sorts of things he could do. He said he didn't like to talk about such things openly and they made plans to meet for lunch tomorrow."

"Is that so?" Augustine had a pretty good idea about the kind of thing Ava Mae would want Ogun for. No doubt some sort of ritual to bind her spirit to Harlow's body for good.

There was no way in hell he would let that happen.

Even if he had to kill Ogun to prevent it.

Chapter Four

Giselle and Ian arrived at Ogun's to find him not at home. They drove around the block a few times. Giselle used the time to fill Ian in on her plans to make Ogun the sixth soul. Finally, on the third trip past, his car was pulling into his drive. They made one more circuit before parking outside his yellow two-story and climbing the porch steps.

She let Ian knock. Ogun was quick to answer, his expression immediately angry until his gaze shifted to Ian, but the wizard's presence only took the slightest edge off it. "What do you want?"

"Hello, Ogun." Giselle gave him a moment to process the fact that she was still alive. "Now that you've seen with your own eyes that your attempt on my life has failed, I believe you owe me a conversation." Judging by his velvet suit and the rest of his gaudy outfit, he'd been somewhere more than just the corner market.

His gaze stayed on Ian. "What's he here for?"

"Protection. You can't begrudge me that." But let him try and she would send a shock wave of magic through him that would knock him to the ground.

"Fine." He held the door open wider. "Come in."

She entered, Ian following after her. The ever-present stench of incense assaulted her senses. She wrinkled her nose and waved her hand in front of her face. "I don't know how you can stand the stink of all that."

Ogun closed the door and ignored her comment. "Sit or don't. I don't care." He lit a cigarillo and took a few puffs, unbuttoning his jacket. Maybe that was his answer to her jab about the incense. He sat in the large, kente cloth–covered chair in the center of the crowded living room.

Ian poked at a strand of tiny bones dangling from a lamp, making them jangle. "Quite a collection you've got here."

Ogun pointed the cigarillo at him. "Don't touch those. Or anything."

Ian's fingers lingered on the bones. "Are you threatening me?"

"I'm telling you to respect my things. If you don't, you have only yourself to blame for the consequences."

Ian shot him a dark look. "Now that was definitely a threat—"

"Ian." Giselle wasn't here to play referee. Ian made a face, but kept his hands to himself. She settled in the seat closest to Ogun, the smoke of his cigarillo turning her stomach and making her wish for an extinguishing spell that would go unnoticed. Sadly, there wasn't anything she could do but let the damn thing burn. It was slightly less irritating than the incense. "Ogun, I know you cast the choking spell on me. And I know it was because you were angry over recent events. I'm here, not as the new high priestess of the New Orleans Coven but just as myself, Giselle Vincent, to call a truce between us."

His brows lifted. "Is that so? And just like that I'm supposed to believe you're not here to retaliate?" He laughed. "You just made your new position clear. It seems to me a truce is the last thing on your mind."

She nodded. "It would have been in the past, but things have changed. I have changed."

A look of skepticism crinkled the skin around his eyes. "And I should believe that why? Tell me, Giselle Vincent, how have you changed?"

"As I just mentioned, I'm the high priestess of the coven now.

I have greater responsibilities. My father's legacy to uphold. The coven's welfare to think of. And as always, the weight of the fae oppression on my shoulders. A weight I imagine your people will soon feel."

That got his attention. "What have you heard?"

"What have *you* heard? Because as I understand it, Augustine has taken to the role of Guardian with alarming stringency. He's pushing for more regulations on the witches and due to certain involvements, wants to bring all of your practitioners under the same guidelines."

"What does that mean, certain involvements? Are you sure? He threatened, but I had no idea he was going forward with this." Ogun stood, his hands clenching and unclenching. "He has no right. None."

Giselle held back a smile. She'd been bluffing to get Ogun to help her. That Augustine had actually threatened such action was a bonus. "I agree. Which is why I'm here. The time has come for us to work together toward a common goal."

Ogun stared at her. "What goal?"

"I can't—and won't—reveal details, but I am working on something that would level the playing field. The fae have had the upper hand too long."

He sat slowly. "The only reason for you to tell me about this is you must need something from me. That hasn't worked out very well for me in the past." He glanced at Ian. "I don't want to discuss all this in front of your muscle."

"And I have no reason to trust you alone."

"If we're going to work together, we have to start somewhere."

She glanced at Ian. Ogun didn't know she'd gotten stronger since the last time they'd had an encounter and she needed the voodoo doctor on her side. At least until she could get rid of him. "Could you give us a few minutes alone?"

Ian frowned. "Only if he swears to do you no harm."

Ogun waved him off. "I swear it."

Ian looked at her for approval. She nodded. His frown turned to a hard glare but he left.

She returned her attention to Ogun. "I apologize for what happened in the past. I wasn't as careful as I should have been with the *bokura,* especially with you being so generous to offer it to me in the first place." The words tasted so bitter she could barely form them.

He grunted like it was the least he could have done.

She held back a snort. "I would remind you that I owe you a flesh debt." Something he probably needed no reminding of. "I am trying to repay that now by bringing you into this plan. If you help me, I won't forget it when the witches take their rightful place as the ruling body of this city once again."

His brow furrowed and he shook his head. "You just said you were working on something that would level the playing field. Not raise the witches to power. How does that help my people?"

Damn it, she'd overshared. She scoffed like it was nothing. "We're the same, you and I. Children of the earth. Guardians of the natural magic. When the witches return to power—their rightful place, I might add—your people will never have to worry about the kinds of rules that mine struggle with now. We'll sign a treaty to that effect, guaranteeing your freedom for the life of the city. Those who practice voodoo will never have to feel the kind of oppression my people have. That is my word as high priestess. And that is what we will put in writing."

"A treaty." He snorted. "You think your word in writing means anything more to me?" Laughing, he shook his head. "I don't think so. I need more than that."

"I'm willing to offer you something greater then." She sighed as if she was resigned to the sacrifice she was about to make. "If it would satisfy your desires, I will grant you an honorary place at all coven meetings."

His mouth came open slightly in surprise. He quickly closed it and sat back. She could see the wheels turning in his head by the look on his face. He was considering it. Hard. He ground the cigarillo out. "That's quite an offer."

"It is. But I'm high priestess now and free to make whatever changes I deem necessary. I've learned the hard way you're a better ally than adversary." The dusty lies clogged her throat. "It's time our people worked together, don't you think?"

His eyes narrowed in satisfaction. Smug bastard. He shrugged like he had nothing better to do. "What do you need from me?"

"Almost nothing. A few *volunteers* that no one will miss."

He nodded arrogantly as if he'd sussed out her entire plan from that one detail. "You need lives."

"I need people who won't be missed." She wasn't willing to say more than that. He didn't need specifics. Just to do what she wanted.

He steepled his fingers, a move that reminded her of her late father. He tapped the tips of his fingers against his chin. "I would imagine you also want to remove Augustine's scrutiny."

"I would not be opposed to that, no."

"I'd like him out of my hair as well." For a few moments, he sat without saying anything. At last, he spoke, his eyes narrowing. "How many lives do you need?"

"A handful. Five."

"Five is not a small number."

She shrugged and moved as if to leave. "If it's beyond your abilities..."

"Sit." A hint of anger played in his eyes. "I will help you with one caveat."

She settled into her seat. "And that is?" Of course he had conditions. No one did anything in this town without getting a piece of the action for themselves.

"You will not argue over who I bring you."

What was going on in that mind of his? "I can't blindly agree to that. You could bring me one of my own coven members." Although there were a few she wouldn't balk at adding to the well of souls. "Or one of my clients." She shook her head. "No, I can't give you this."

"The one I have in mind is not a witch, nor one of your coven members." He sat forward, smiling like he was about to give her a gift. "If you..." He swirled his hand through the air. "*Remove* her from this world you could very well set in motion the thing you wish to accomplish without any further work."

She squinted at him. "Speak plainly."

He sighed and rolled his eyes. "I am offering you one of Augustine's inner circle. One who, based on my supernatural perceptions, could count as two lives."

A niggle of suspicion zipped through Giselle's brain. "Who?"

"The woman he shares the house with. Harlow."

Her surprise lasted the briefest of moments, but she knew Ogun had seen her react. How did he know Harlow had another soul within her? Had he been watching that night at the warehouse, too? How did he even know about Harlow at all? "What are you saying? What makes you think she would count as two? And how could you even begin to think you could bring her to me?"

He laughed and pulled a business card from inside his jacket pocket. He held it up between two fingers. "Augustine dropped this a while back on one of his many visits. It seems the late Olivia Goodwin's daughter has not only moved to town but has started a business. I've already met her and am meeting with her again. I will have her under my sway very soon."

"That answers nothing about the two lives."

He pursed his mouth for a moment, thoughts flickering behind his dark gaze. "There is an aura about her." He waved one hand. "A darkness. She is troubled, but not in the way of the grieving. It's as if…she possesses the spirit of another. I expect my next meeting with her will confirm my suspicions. If so, she's worth two souls."

This time, Giselle kept her expression blank, but inside she was reeling over the fact that Ogun had uncovered the same thing she had. Of course, Ogun didn't know that other spirit was Harlow's dead twin, Ava Mae. But then he hadn't been privy to the scene Giselle had witnessed between the girl and her now-deceased father, Joseph Branzino. Ava Mae had laid bare her past in the minutes before she'd slit the man's throat.

Ogun tilted his head. "What say you? Do we have a deal? I deliver the girl and three others, provided she holds two souls, and then we are at peace. Allied, even."

There was no reason not to believe Harlow would count as two. With three more, plus Ogun as the last, they'd have their twelve souls and the *ruina vox* could be cast. Turning Augustine's attention to the missing Harlow would just make their work that much easier. Her plan had become so much more than she'd hoped. "We have a deal. But now I have a condition."

He lifted his head slightly. "What?"

"Bring me Harlow first."

⚜

With Lally and her lemon bars in tow, Augustine hoisted a small bag over his shoulder and took them through the mirror and onto the fae plane. The gloomy gray land was ever the same. Windy, dismal, bleak. No place for the shining source of life that Olivia Goodwin had been. "Livie," he shouted into the wind. "You there?"

"Augie? I'm over here, *cher*."

He and Lally turned toward the voice. Olivia was camped out on a large flat boulder surrounded by several tall shards of rock that formed a natural partial wall. She waved them toward her. "C'mon, it's quieter here. Out of the wind."

Augustine jumped up first so he could give Lally a hand. She settled in beside Olivia and the two hugged each other.

"I've missed you both so much," Olivia said.

"Us, too." Lally handed Olivia the covered plate. "Here you go. I made these special for you because I know you like them."

Livie pulled back the foil. "Lemon bars? These might actually make me forget about being dead."

He reached into the bag and pulled out the bottle of bourbon he'd stashed. "If they don't, this should."

Livie took the bottle, laughing even as tears sparkled in her eyes. "You know, I don't need to sleep or eat or drink anymore, but that doesn't mean I haven't missed certain things. And I'm pretty sure just because I don't need to do something, that doesn't mean I can't." She uncapped the bourbon and took a pull off the bottle, smacking her lips and moaning in pleasure. "Oh, that's the stuff. That might actually bring me back to life."

She and Lally laughed. Augustine shook his head. "I'm surprised to see you up here. It's more of a climb than I thought you could make."

The tears were gone, but the sparkle remained. "I was about to give you grief for not visiting in so long—and I still might— but these treats have me in a good mood, so I'll just give you the update." She leaned in like she was about to tell them a secret. "I'm getting stronger. Not just in whatever form this is, but in other ways, too. Look."

She put the plate and bottle down to pick up the carved wood-framed mirror Lally had given her after she'd first passed over. She held the mirror up and slipped her hand through all the way to her shoulder, then pulled it out. "That's as far as I can get but it's something, don't you think?"

"It's great, Livie. Definitely something." He wasn't sure what it meant that she could only go partway, but it was still progress. Considering that the alternative was her growing weaker and disappearing on this plane, he'd take it. Especially if it kept her focused on something besides being alone out here.

Lally clutched at her necklace. "Oh, Olivia, do you think that means you'll be able to come back to us?"

Livie looked at Augustine before answering. "I have no idea. I hope so." Her gaze shifted behind them. "Say, where's Harlow? Is she still mad at me for not telling her about Ava Mae sooner?"

Augustine had been dreading this. "About Harlow—"

"She is mad, isn't she?" Livie shook her head, her hands fussing with the foil covering the lemon bars. "That child always could hold a grudge."

"No, it's not that. Not exactly." He sighed. There was nothing to it but to dive in. "She was starting to come around, but then she got a hold of Ava Mae's ashes and used the lightning tree to bring her back to life. It didn't go so well and somehow Ava Mae's spirit . . . took possession of Harlow."

Olivia's mouth fell open. She looked at Lally as if for confirmation.

Lally nodded. "I had to tell her about the tree. It was her legacy. She'd figured out something was behind that door in your closet." She glanced skyward. "I shoulda known she'd do the same thing you tried to do."

Olivia shook her head, still speechless. Her hands came up to cover her mouth.

Lally continued. "And after everything that happened, I had to tell Augie."

Olivia slowly took her hands away, but turned to stare sorrowfully into the vast nothing of the fae plane. "Is there any getting her back? Any way to get her free from the tree's clutches? I should have had you bring those ashes to me here." She inhaled a deep, shuddering sigh. "What are we going to do?"

There was nothing she could do, but he didn't want to tell her that. Instead, he reached over to take her hand. "We're all working to figure out how to get Harlow back. Even Fenton. It's our main priority."

She picked up the bottle of bourbon and cradled it in her lap. "I guess I know the real reason you brought me this now."

⚜

Ava Mae hadn't even put her foot on the first stair when Augustine leaned over the upper railing to call out to her. "How was your shopping?"

"Fun." And more productive than she could have hoped. Meeting Rufus Ogun had been a delightful turn of events. "Do you want to see what I bought?"

Harlow sighed. *No, he doesn't.*

He smiled, thrilling her down to her toes. "Sure." He tilted his head to the side. "Come on up and give me a show."

Well, this was a delicious new twist. Lover boy was finally warming up to her version of Harlow. It was about time. "On my way." *See, Sister dear? Boring and dull would have never gotten you this far.*

Harlow went quiet, but Ava Mae could sense her sudden despair at Augustine's invitation. With a smile that was much larger on the inside, Ava Mae jogged up the stairs, shopping bags swinging. She carried them all the way to Augustine's fourth-floor apartment, where he occupied half of the converted attic. The rest was storage, but his side was beautiful, spare and clean and lit by several windows, the largest an enormous leaded glass circle that looked out over the rest of the Garden District neighborhood. The mouthwatering aroma of smoke, his signature scent, perfumed the air and every inch of the space dripped with his masculine energy.

But her favorite feature was the big king bed occupying the far wall when she first entered. With its fluffy down comforter, fat pillows and crisp white sheets, it looked like a nest. The kind she wanted to burrow into with him. Again.

That was if she actually had the first time. Her memory of that evening three nights ago was painfully unclear. It was embarrassing to think they might have already slept together and she couldn't remember it. Was it possible they'd been intimate and it hadn't been memorable? Or had something else happened? Something Augustine had done? The unknowing almost made her growl in frustration.

No matter what her suspicions were, this time it was going to happen for real. And she *was* going to remember it. So was he.

He looked up from where he was sitting on the couch. "That was fast."

She grinned. "I didn't want to keep you waiting."

He sipped a tumbler of amber liquid and smiled. "I appreciate that." He tipped the glass toward another one on the coffee table. Next to it was a tall bottle of bourbon. "After all that shopping, you must be ready to unwind. Fortunately for you, it's cocktail hour." He grinned, almost knocking her down with the brilliance of his smile. "Come join me for a drink and then you can show me everything you bought."

She hesitated. "I don't know. The last time I had a drink with you, I had too much and passed out."

Which was why that evening three nights ago was so cloudy. She couldn't for the life of her remember what had happened after he'd carried her to the bed. She'd tried, but it was almost like the memories were being purposefully suppressed.

Could Harlow be doing that? *Harlow, are you hiding something from me?*

Her sister snapped back. *No, I'm angry at you, you dumb twit. Leave him alone.*

Ava Mae gave a little internal shrug and did her best not to laugh. *Poor Harlow. That's not going to happen. Not when I'm this close to having the night I've been dreaming about.* She wasn't about to be derailed by her sister's sour attitude. She turned her attention back to Augustine.

He held her glass up to her. "Don't worry, I won't let you have more than this one."

She sashayed forward a few steps. "You promise?" She did enjoy the way the bourbon warmed her up inside.

"Cross my heart. This one glass only." His smile was impossible to look away from. "Besides, it's considered impolite in this city to turn down a drink."

She hesitated. There was no way she could say no to that wickedly handsome face. "Tell you what? I will, but I want to put on one of my fancy new outfits first. Okay?"

"Okay." He lifted his glass. "I'll be waiting." He pointed out the door. "Bathroom's right around the corner."

She bit her lip to keep from squealing. Today was going so much better than she could have planned. She turned and took off for the bathroom. It was all white tile, brushed chrome and white marble veined with black. The urge to snoop through his things was strong, but not as strong as the desire to get back to him. She compromised by burying her face in one of his bath towels and inhaling. The intoxicating scent of smoke sent a delicious shiver through her.

She dropped the towel and riffled through the shopping bags, looking for the one from the French lingerie store on Royal. She'd spent almost a thousand dollars there but the bag barely weighed a thing. As she lifted out the emerald silk teddy trimmed in ivory lace and pearls from its tissue paper wrapping, she had a feeling she was about to get her money's worth. She shed her street clothes and slipped into it.

She took a look in the mirror, finger combing her hair just so. The green did amazing things for her eyes. "I look hot."

Yes, you must be the envy of streetwalkers everywhere.

She frowned at her reflection, looking for a glimpse of her sister in her own eyes. "And here I thought you were ignoring me." Poor Harlow. So bitter. "I know you're upset, but you need to see that it's not you Augustine cares about so much as finding pleasure. There's no reason he shouldn't find that with me. Besides, I want to experience everything I can. You're lucky to be along for the ride. You've lived a pretty boring life up until now. You should be thanking me."

Street. Walker. He's never going to respect you. Or love you.

Ava Mae shook her head. "He'll respect me just fine for being the kind of woman you should have been, the one who's not afraid to go after what she wants. As far as loving me, he thinks I'm you. Just new and improved. He'll probably love me more."

Harlow's seething felt like ants crawling on Ava Mae's skin, but her sister stayed quiet. Pity filled Ava Mae, but then she reminded herself that it was Harlow's own fault that she'd missed her chance with Augustine. This was Ava Mae's shot. Her turn to live. And she was not going to waste a second of it feeling guilty. "Try to enjoy yourself, Sister. I know I will."

She traipsed back to Augustine's bedroom and leaned seductively against the door frame. "What do you think?"

His eyes rounded slightly and his jaw went slack. He stared. Then swallowed. "I think...hell's bells." He drained the rest of his bourbon and poured himself another. "That is not what I thought you were going to be wearing."

She came closer and took the glass he'd had waiting for her. "Are you disappointed?"

"That's not the word I'd use, no." He lifted his glass. "Here's to...us."

She smiled. "Us. I like that." She tipped the glass back and drained it. This wasn't the time to sit around sipping her drink and making small talk. She had plans.

"Wow. I didn't think you were going to drink that quite so fast." He stood and came around the coffee table to slip his arms around her waist. "Maybe you should sit down."

The back of her head felt numb. Maybe downing the bourbon so fast hadn't been the best idea, but it was one glass. How much of a buzz could it give her? "I'd rather go to the bed."

"If that's what you want." He bent and scooped her into his arms.

"That's what I..." Her tongue no longer responded to her brain. Darkness was closing in around her. The same kind of darkness she'd felt when she'd first slipped inside her sister's body.

Harlow's spirit rose up inside her.

Ava Mae fought back, but even as she did, her control slipped. The abyss awaited her and as the darkness weighed her down, she slipped into the chasm between soul and spirit, numb to everything around her.

Chapter Five

Augustine laid Harlow on the couch, gently propping her head on the arm. He covered her with a throw, giving the *bokura* a chance to take. "Ava Mae?" No answer. "Harlow? Can you hear me? Are you...in there?"

Her lids fluttered and for a moment, he thought he'd put too much of the powder into her drink. He scrubbed a hand over his mouth. He'd followed Jewelia's instructions exactly, but drugging Harlow felt wrong. The reasoning was right, though. He just prayed it worked.

Her eyes opened to narrow slits, her lids heavy and her pupils wide. "Augie?" Her voice was a whisper. She lifted one hand a few inches off the couch and dropped it right back down.

"Yes, it's me. Is that you, Harlow?"

"Mm-hmm." She licked her lips. "I feel foggy."

It had worked. The thrill of victory gave him a taste of hope. Maybe there *was* a way out of this mess. "You're okay, I swear. I got Ava Mae to drink some bourbon laced with a sort of sedative. Can you sense her?"

Harlow nodded wearily. "It's like she's asleep. Am I free of her?"

"Not yet, sweetheart. I'm working on it, though."

She smiled, but it was halfhearted and sadness filled her eyes to the point that liquid rimmed her lower lids. "Thank you for trying. I'm so sorry I brought her back. I know Lally said to leave the tree alone, but all I could think about was getting my sister back and filling the gaping hole I'd lived with my whole life. I thought she could make it go away." She sniffled. "I guess she did. Just not the way I expected."

"Hey, you did what any of us would do." He wanted to take her hand, but Ava Mae hadn't kept her gloves on with the green negligee and he wasn't sure what a burst of emotion would do to Harlow in this state. "Your mother tried to do the very same thing."

Harlow took a deep breath and blinked a few times. "Olivia tried to bring Ava Mae back?"

He nodded. "Years and years ago. Lally stopped her, though, so that all she managed was to spill a little of Ava Mae's ashes. The tree snatched them up and raised Ava Mae's spirit, but couldn't do more than that. Lally thinks it's part of why Ava Mae is . . . not altogether good."

"Wait, I think Ava Mae said something about that. About how she's been a prisoner of the tree for years. That's how she grew up." Harlow's mouth bent in a bitter frown. "She's not good at all. She plans on seducing you."

He smiled as gently as he could. "I know. She's not subtle."

Harlow turned her head away from him. "She wants to prove to me that you don't . . . care about me. That all you're interested in is a good time. She thinks that will break me."

There was no reason to hold back, but that didn't stop his nerves from tripping over his skin like live wires. Outside of Lally and Olivia, he'd never spoken the words he was about to speak to any other woman. It was both exhilarating and terrifying. "Harlow, that's not going to happen because . . . I love you. Not her. And there is nothing I won't do to set you free. You need to know that."

She looked at him, her lips parted. She stared at him, the liquid forming along her lower lashes again. "You mean that?"

He nodded. "I do."

"You love me." A single tear trickled down the side of her face and ran into her hairline.

He brushed it away with his thumb, hoping that small caress wouldn't overload her with his emotions. "Is it that hard to believe?"

She swallowed. "A little. I'm prickly and difficult and don't like to be touched. I'm really not that lovable."

He laughed. "You're a challenge at times, but it's a challenge I love. You aren't swayed one bit by my charm, which sucks but is also kind of impressive. I can't imagine not having you around. So no matter what you think, that's the truth of it."

She smiled and this time it reached her eyes. "You might need your head examined. Or both of us do because I think I might...love you, too."

"You think you might?" He could live with that.

"No, I do." She blushed, throwing her freckles into sharp contrast.

He winked. "It's only important that you remember I want *you,* not Ava Mae. No matter what she says to me and no matter what I say back to her—because I may have to say things to her I don't really mean in order to free you—you're the only one who occupies this space." He touched his chest. "Got that?"

She nodded, her eyes shining with happiness. "Got it." The happiness disappeared suddenly, replaced by horror. "I just remembered something. Ava Mae met a man today in the French Quarter when she was shopping. A voodoo doctor—"

He held up his hand. "I don't want to tell you too much because I don't know what Ava Mae can read from your thoughts and what she can't, but just know that there is nothing she's done that I'm not aware of. And it will be handled."

"She plans to meet with him again. I know she's going to try to get him to do some kind of voodoo that will give her complete control of my brain and body."

He nodded. "Like I said, I'm taking care of it. You're not in any danger."

That seemed to calm her. "You're sure?"

"Positive."

"You know she killed Branzino."

"I know. Cy, Dulce and Sydra took care of burying his body."

"She's very powerful."

"So are you. Which is why you have to fight."

"I have been. I argue with her constantly and if I try really hard, I can sometimes affect her, sometimes get a second of control back. But she always gets it right back."

"Keep at it. I have it on good authority your efforts will keep her from taking over entirely. Until we can figure out how to get rid of her altogether, that is."

Harlow nodded. "There's something else you need to know. She—I have a new power. Not new, really, just something I didn't know I could do. It's how she subdued Branzino."

He leaned in. "What is it?"

She pulled her hand from underneath the blanket and spread her fingers wide. "The same way that touching someone floods me with emotion, I can force emotion *into* someone. Ava Mae made him feel all the hurt and pain and fear she'd suffered because of him. It paralyzed him."

He took the new information in, turning it over in his head. Had Ava Mae ever used that ability on him? He couldn't be sure. "If Branzino could do it, it only makes sense you and your sister could as well." He shook his head slowly. "It also explains a lot. I couldn't figure out how either of you could overpower him. Not with you being so unused to your abilities."

She slid her hand forward to touch his. She blinked slowly as their fingers intertwined. "I know you're afraid for me. I can feel it. But I can also feel how determined you are to get me back. And how you feel about me. Thank you."

He bent and kissed her softly. The bourbon still lingered on her lips, sugar and smoke. She started to kiss him back, but he broke away, afraid of doing anything that might cause Ava Mae to surface. He ached at how much it hurt that these moments with Harlow were temporary. "I will get you back, Harley Goodwin."

"I know you will." She smiled up at him and he knew that she trusted him implicitly.

He pulled his hand away before she realized what a liar that made him feel like. He had no plan yet, no clear path for freeing her. He couldn't let her know that, couldn't let her lose this new trust.

This new hope.

He made himself smile as he glanced at the time. "The sedative won't last much longer, I'm afraid. In a minute or two, you're going to fall asleep. When you wake up in the morning, I'm not sure how much of this you'll remember, so try to focus on what I've told you, okay? Hold on to it."

She nodded, but her face fell a bit and he could see her struggling not to tear up. "Can you bring me back again soon? Please? I feel so alone when she's got control."

"I will, I promise. As often as I can. Remember to keep fighting."

She nodded, her lids drooping. "You love me," she whispered.

He just nodded. There was no truer statement. Now he just had to figure out how to save her from the demon living inside her. With that thought heavy on his heart, he lifted her into his arms and carried her to her bed to sleep off the rest of the *bokura*.

⚜

Giselle's softly buzzing LMD woke her. Beside her, Ian mumbled something in his sleep and rolled over. She grabbed the device. Ogun's number. She slipped out of bed to take the call in the bathroom. As she closed the door behind her, she whispered, "Hello?"

"Did I wake you, Giselle? The day's half over." Ogun's smile sang through the line.

"No. And the day has barely begun." She didn't care what he thought, she wasn't giving him the benefit of that dig. "I was meditating." That should shut him up. "Why are you calling me?"

"I just thought you should know I plan on bringing Harlow to you this afternoon."

Giselle stilled, shocked by how quickly Ogun had done what she'd asked. "That's... very good."

"Where do you want her delivered?"

She didn't want to do anything that would connect him with Zara's house. "My father's old place in the Garden District. You know it?"

"Yes. Aren't you living there?"

"Not yet, I'm remodeling it. I'll open the garage for you when you get there. We can make the exchange in there. Text me when you're on your way." She hung up and exited the bathroom, plucking her robe off its hook on the way out and slipping into it. Tucking her LMD into the pocket, she headed downstairs to make coffee.

She'd been meaning to get over to the Garden District house anyway to check on the progress of the work. Hard to imagine leaving her French Quarter townhouse behind, but as high priestess, it was only fitting she take over her late father's mansion. She'd need the room for council meetings, coven gatherings, cocktail parties. Things her beloved townhouse just didn't have the space for, although she wouldn't be giving it up entirely. It would still be her retreat.

No, taking over her father's house—her house, she had to stop thinking about it that way—was a foregone conclusion.

Once the work was done and her things moved in, she'd be living there. She'd be able to move forward with her plan of computerizing the coven's records, something she'd begged Evander to do for years, but he'd insisted on keeping records the old-fashioned way.

She scooped coffee into the French press, shaking her head. The thought of going through all those paper records was daunting, but it would have to be done. Just like she'd have to sort through all of her father's things and decide what to do with the warehouse of antiques that filled his house. She poured hot water in, put the lid on and set the timer. The antiques would bring excellent money. But they still had to be inventoried, the contents emptied and sorted through. Not that she expected to uncover anything of any real interest.

Nothing like the candle she'd found at Zara's in their mother's old bedroom, a room Zara had left untouched since she'd moved into the house. Giselle had stumbled upon the room while Ian had been tattooing Zara and in a quest to find something, *anything* that their mother might have left behind specifically for Giselle, she'd cast a seeking spell.

In response, a candle on top of her mother's desk had flickered to life. Upon inspection, Giselle had discovered that the sides of the wide ivory candle were cut with design work and adorned in places with crystals. Only her close family, which at this point was only Zara—and now Ian—knew without a doubt that crystals were her source of power. She couldn't help but think that candle had been left for her by her mother as some kind of message.

What that message was, she wasn't sure. The designs cut into the candle's sides had seemed like sigils, but she'd gotten no further than that. Chaos magic required a sigil to focus it; otherwise the power of the spell would simply disperse and the intended object would remain largely unaffected. If the marks on the candle *were* sigils, had her mother put them there as an example of what to use to work that kind of magic? If so, the candle would be of no help. The chaos spell their mother had tried to cast had ended up killing her.

Trying to cast the exact same spell could lead to the exact same results. The timer dinged. She pushed the plunger down on the press. The coffee's tantalizing aroma would probably wake Ian, which was good. Giselle had things to do. Like taking the candle to Zara and discussing what it might mean. Zara was proceeding like she had everything she needed, but Giselle couldn't help but think her push to slow things down was a stall tactic.

Maybe because Zara didn't have the sigil they needed. Maybe their mother hadn't left it to her in any of her notes. Because she might not have thought Zara capable of chaos magic. Oh, she had the talent, but until a few weeks ago, even Giselle would never have guessed her sister had the backbone necessary for that kind of dark spell.

Or maybe her mother had left the candle for Giselle so that her two girls would have to work together.

Either way, it was very possible the sigils engraved on the candle were the missing piece. If she could just figure out which one to use. She set two cups beside the sugar bowl before going to the refrigerator for cream. She put the small porcelain pitcher with the rest of the coffee service, then leaned against the counter.

Today would be a full day, but a good one. She'd leave in an hour or so to discuss the chaos sigil with Zara and tell her that they were about to have two more souls for the pool, then she'd head to her new Garden District home, check on the work there and finally tackle the enormous project of sorting through her father's things until Ogun arrived.

A slight smile bent her mouth. Delivering Harlow into the

well of souls would be a very rewarding experience, especially when Augustine went mad searching for her, but the real thrill would come from knowing that Augustine's little friend had contributed her life to the downfall of her own people.

Because the chaos spell *would* work this time, and when it was cast it would strip away all traces of fae magic for twenty-four hours, enough time for the witches to rise up and take control. They would have plenty of time to shift the balance of power, something that was centuries overdue.

And then, when the death of the senator's son came to light and Augustine was implicated, disgracing the Guardian and hopefully jailing him, the fae would truly be out of the picture. Not only would New Orleans once again belong to the witches, but the lightning tree Harlow had referred to would be up for grabs.

Giselle's smile widened as she poured a cup of coffee. Today was shaping up to be a very good day indeed.

Chapter Six

Ava Mae woke up feeling like she'd missed something. She was still wearing the emerald-green negligee she'd put on for Augustine, but she was in her own bed. Was this where they'd ended up? Trying to remember the evening was like hitting a wall of fog. She pushed to a sitting position. Other than not being able to remember much about the night before, her head felt fine.

She'd had bourbon, but only one glass, so she wasn't hungover. And she couldn't have gotten passed-out drunk. That much she recalled. She rubbed her eyes and yawned. All her shopping bags were stacked against the wall by her door.

Her romantic evening with Augustine had turned into another vague event. What the hell? Had they slept together? That made two nights she was unclear about. Wouldn't she know if they'd slept together?

Maybe her sister knew. *Harlow, what happened last night?*

Beats me. Harlow sounded snippy, but that was her usual tone lately. Or did that annoyance mean Ava Mae had finally seduced Augustine? Why couldn't she remember?

Frustrated, Ava Mae got out of bed. She caught a whiff of coffee coming from downstairs. Lally must be working on breakfast. That was one woman Ava Mae wanted to steer clear of. She wasn't sure Lally knew exactly what was going on, but something told her that the woman would figure it out soon. She also didn't know the full extent of Lally's powers as a traiteuse but Ava Mae's years of being joined to the lightning tree had taught her that the woman was no one to mess with. Time after time, she'd seen Lally heal people who should have died. And in some way, wasn't Ava Mae inhabiting her sister's body just a supernatural infection?

That thought brought up the truth of what Ava Mae really feared—that Lally might know a way to kick her out of Harlow's skin. No matter, Ava Mae had a meeting with Rufus Ogun today and she would get him to help her. Voodoo was old earth magic, just like the lightning tree. He was bound to know a way to fix her inside this form.

I hope he turns you into a zombie.

Shut up, Harlow. You can't bother me today. I've got things planned. Things you're not going to be able to undo.

Harlow laughed.

The sound echoed through Ava Mae, followed by an over-whelming sense of failure. Was that Harlow's doing? It had to be. The shock of that chilled her to the point of paralysis. She swallowed down a swell of nausea. Harlow might have become quieter lately, but her sudden surges of emotion had begun to affect Ava Mae more strongly.

It felt like Harlow was gaining ground. That she'd figured out how to turn their gift of forcing emotion into a person against Ava Mae. Whether or not that was the case, she didn't know, but if Harlow's strength continued to grow, there was a very real chance she might force Ava Mae out.

That could *not* happen. If Ogun didn't know how to seal her into this form permanently, she'd have to find someone else who could.

She grabbed her shopping bags and dumped them on the bed, rifling through the clothes to find an outfit that would give her a reason to smile and would bother Harlow with its boldness. Outfit in hand, she marched into the bathroom for a hot shower to help prepare her to face Lally at breakfast.

Ogun's help could not come soon enough.

❧

Giselle had dropped Ian at her new house, then gone to Zara's to discuss in private the matter of the chaos spell. She stood now in her sister's kitchen, a cup of coffee in hand as Zara sipped tea. Zara's ever-present youthful glow had dimmed these past few days, undoubtedly a sign of the stress caused by her preparation for the casting of the *ruina vox*. It might be the early hour, but Giselle doubted that. "Everything all right with you? You seem . . . not quite yourself."

Zara held her cup in both hands. She stared into the liquid. "I've been working hard."

"I know. You have been. Which is what I wanted to talk to you about. You haven't said much about the preparation for the spell, other than needing the twelve souls for the well, and I haven't pressed you, but I'm asking you now. What can I do to help?"

Zara shook her head and lifted her gaze to the granite island between them. "Nothing, but as soon as you can help, I'll let you know."

Not enough of an answer. Giselle had no option but to push her. "You have everything you need to make the *ruina vox* work?"

Zara's silent frown was answer enough, but at last she raised her head and after a quick glance at Giselle, looked out toward the garden, a long sigh slipping from her lips. "I'm close but, no. I'm not there yet."

And there it was. "What are you lacking?"

Zara choked out a harsh laugh. "The bloody sigil. The key

to it all. I've spent days casting runes and poring over mother's notes. I can't find it anywhere. I've searched her grimoires, her diaries, her room." Her mouth bent in frustration. "It's part of the reason there's no rush to collect the souls. Until I have that..." She shrugged. "The spell can't be completed."

Giselle smiled. "I think I can help." She pulled the thick ivory candle from her bag and set it on the island between them. The crystals affixed to the wax sparkled in the bright morning light. "See for yourself. Don't those markings look like something more than just a random design?"

"That's the candle you took from Mother's room."

It wasn't a question, but Giselle answered anyway, offering a gentle reminder as to why she'd taken it. "Yes. The one that seemed meant for me because of the crystals."

Zara put her tea down to pick up the candle, her gaze steady on the carvings for a long moment. Finally her head came up. "These definitely aren't random. These *are* sigils."

Giselle nodded. "That's what I thought, too." She covered herself. "I had no idea until I really looked at it this morning. Maybe it was the extra-strong coffee I made, but all of a sudden it just hit me that's what they might be. And that's why I came over here first thing. You hadn't said much about setting up the chaos spell so I had no idea if you had the necessary sigil or not, but—"

"But you think the sigil for the spell might be in these designs." Zara hefted the candle and looked at her sister, the shine in her eyes a welcome sign. She smiled slowly. "I do, too."

Relieved her sister wasn't angry, Giselle jumped in. "How do we figure out what they are? My eyes glaze over if I stare at it for too long. It's too intricate to make sense of."

Zara lifted a brow. "I have an idea." She put the candle back on the counter. "Hang on." She left, returning a few minutes later with a pad of art paper, a tray of watercolor paints and a brush.

Giselle pursed her lips. "It's a little early for arts and crafts, don't you think?"

"Just watch." Zara flipped the pad to a clean sheet of paper before filling a glass with water. Then she popped open the paint tray, picked a brush and wet it. She swirled the brush in green paint and began to cover the candle with paint in long, sloppy strokes.

"Hey, what are you doing? You're ruining the candle."

"No, I'm not." The candle's sides were swathed in green. Zara put the brush down and held the candle by the top and bottom, careful not to touch the paint. She turned the candle longways, laid it on the paper and rolled it from one end to the other. Returning the candle to the counter, she pushed the paper toward Giselle. "There are your sigils."

Giselle looked closer. The designs on the candle had left behind a print like a rubber stamp. "Unbelievable." Seen on paper like that, the confusing markings made sense. There, in the green paint, one sigil stood out. She pointed at it. "This has to be the one. It's the only sigil that's repeated."

Zara seemed to almost tremble with excitement. "I was wrong not to share more about the process of preparing for the spell with you. I'm sorry about that. I was a little ashamed to tell you I didn't have everything I needed."

"Zara, we're a team. Or at least we should be. It seems that's what mother wanted. I want it, too. I want to help."

"I agree that mother intended us to do this together. Why else would she divide the parts this way?" She smiled. "I'm happy you feel that way. I do, too. We're so much stronger together."

"Good. Then that's settled." Giselle glanced at the sigil again. "You think that's the right one for the chaos spell?"

"Absolutely."

Giselle wasn't so sure. "If this is the right sigil, why didn't the spell work when Mother cast it? It ended up turning inward and destroying her."

Zara's happiness faded a bit. "I...I don't know." She studied the candle. "And if it is the same one, it'll kill us, too."

"Maybe she thought it *was* the right one. Look, as much as I want to break the fae's grip on us, I don't want you casting this spell if it could...hurt you." A rare ache of emotion filled Giselle's gut. "I can't lose you, too, Zara."

"You won't. I'm more powerful than Mother, especially thanks to Ian's ink work. And while I'll be casting the spell, there will be three of us controlling it." She paused for a moment, hefting the candle. "I think I know a way to test it. Won't take me long."

"That would be great. Then we can go back to filling the well with souls and preparing to cast the *ruina vox*."

"About that." Zara set the candle down. "That's not exactly the spell we're going to cast."

That was news. "What have you been working on all this time then?"

"The information in the grimoires Mother left me was for something...stronger. From her notes, it seems the spell she cast was meant to be more of a test run. The one she was practicing for, and the one we're going to cast, is the *ruina vox totem*."

"Which is what?"

"The *ruina vox* was meant to temporarily disrupt all fae magic throughout the city."

"Right. For about twenty-four hours. Just long enough for us to cast a few more spells that would destroy the fae strongholds and take out a few of their key people. What's the new spell do?"

Zara's eyes took on an unusually brittle light. "The *ruina vox totem* won't just work for twenty-four hours. It will destroy the power of any fae on Orleans Parish soil for good."

⚜

Augustine was sitting at the breakfast table with Lally when Ava Mae walked into the kitchen. Being unsure about last night made her even less certain about how to greet him. She kept it simple with a smile and "Good morning."

He nodded. "How'd you sleep?"

Was that supposed to mean something? She had no idea. "Fine. You?"

He smiled and nodded. "Good. Really good."

She bit her lip. That sounded like something had happened last night. She tried to think, but again came up empty. Feeling utterly foolish but not wanting him to know, she smiled right back as she made her way to get coffee. "I'm happy to hear that."

Lally shot her the same questioning side-eye she'd been giving Ava Mae every morning. "Where you off to all dressed up like that? The circus in town?"

Harlow's laugh echoed in Ava Mae's head. *She's right, you know. Only clowns wear that many colors.*

Ava Mae wanted to snap and snarl. Instead she smiled at Lally. "I doubt anyone would wear something this expensive to the circus." She took her coffee to the table.

Lally snorted as she got up. "If that's expensive, then you got ripped off, child."

Augustine shook his head. "I don't know much about fashion but I think the colors are very nice."

Ava Mae sat down catty-corner from him. "Thank you."

"I still think she looks like a Mardi Gras float. And Mardi Gras is over." Lally brought over a serving platter of pancakes and bacon before joining them at the table.

"That's enough now." Augustine held the platter for Ava Mae. She helped herself as he asked, "Where are you headed? You must be going somewhere special to be fixed up like that."

She reached for the syrup. "Just meeting a new friend for lunch." Before he could ask anything else, she changed the subject. "What are you doing today?"

He passed the platter to Lally. "I'm helping the police investigate some missing tourists."

"I read about that," Lally said. "It was in a real tiny section of the paper, in the back pages. You can always tell when the tourism board wants to keep something on the down low."

He nodded. "I'm sure they do. They've had six tourists go missing in the last three days. It's practically an epidemic."

"Probably some folks still sleeping off Mardi Gras." Her head came up sharply. "Unless you think it's vampires again."

"Not a chance. I thought it might be the aftereffects of Mardi Gras also, but Detective Grantham said it's too many." He grabbed another piece of bacon. "Hey, that reminds me, you know his grandmother, Jewelia?"

Lally's face brightened into a smile. "Queen Jewelia? I sure do. Me and her go way back."

"That's what she said, too."

She turned so that her brown eyes pierced straight into Ava Mae. "Now there's a woman with some power."

Ava Mae refused to be intimidated. "What's that supposed to mean? And what kind of a name is Queen Jewelia anyway?"

"Queen Jewelia's one of the most revered voodoo mambos in this town."

Augustine sipped his coffee, his gaze filled with a strange curiosity. Ava Mae was dying to know what was going on in his head. She sniffed. "Most revered? Why?"

Lally lifted her chin slightly. "Because she's a good woman who uses her gifts to do good things."

Augustine nodded. "Unlike some of the other voodoo practitioners in town." He held a hand up. "Not that I know much about any of that. We fae tend to keep our distance from anything related to voodoo, just like they keep their distance from us."

Ava Mae stuck her fork into some eggs. "Why's that?"

He sat back. "We have our magic, they have theirs. It's just our way to keep to ourselves." He stared at her for a long moment. "Maybe because of what happened with the witches all those years ago."

"You mean when that witch fell in love with a fae man and he broke her heart so she cursed the city? The reason vampires can daywalk if they're within parish boundaries." She'd read through everything of Harlow's she could find, including some journal entries she'd found on the computer in a file called Recipes.

He nodded, his mouth quirking up in a half smile. "Yes, exactly that."

She crossed her arms. "What? You look surprised that I remembered. It's not like the vampires were here that long ago."

"Not surprised. Happy you're learning. Or maybe *retaining* is a better word." He tossed his napkin on his empty plate. "I have to go in a few minutes. Grantham's got a lead on one of the missing tourists. I'll see you ladies for dinner, though." He glanced at Ava Mae. "Enjoy your lunch with your friend."

She kept her eyes on him. "I will, thank you." Something was odd with Augustine but she couldn't tell if that was just because they had slept together and she hadn't acknowledged it or for some other reason. If only she could remember last night. Add to that the quiet, almost passive attitude Harlow had suddenly adopted and things seemed...off. Harlow being silent would have pleased Ava Mae if not for the seething undertone that poured off Harlow like a dark fog.

Something was going on. She pushed her chair back and stood. "I think I'll head out early myself, maybe wander around the Quarter a little before my lunch date."

Lally picked up the plates and took them to the sink. "Sounds good to me. I got gardening to do anyway."

Ava Mae didn't wait for Augustine to answer. She darted up the steps to her room for her purse and keys. Whatever weirdness she was feeling would all be swept away soon enough. Rufus Ogun would see to that.

Chapter Seven

Lally stared after Ava Mae. "I'm glad she's going out." She shook her head. "I don't like being alone in the house with that creature."

"I know." Augustine got up and kissed her cheek. "She'll be gone as soon as I can make it happen."

Lally leaned against the sink. "What are you going to do about this lunch date of hers?"

"I'm meeting with my lieutenants this morning. Call me when she leaves the house and I'll have Cy track her again." Ava Mae might be expecting Augustine to follow her and Ogun definitely knew his face. With Cy's mimicking abilities, he was the best one to tail her. "Once he confirms she's headed to Ogun's, I'll take care of it."

Lally nodded. "Good. I want my girl back."

"Me, too. See you later." He headed out to the Thrun, his head full of the day that lay before him as he drove to the Pelcrum. Once inside the underground headquarters, he entered the war room. Everyone was there but Beatrice, the late Guardian's pregnant widow, and Dulcinea, who was helping take care of her.

"Sydra, Fenton, Cy." He greeted his team as he took his place at the table.

Fenton pushed a piece of paper toward him. "Grantham sent this by messenger this morning, along with a few other things. I sent a few things back I thought might be helpful, but you need to go see him as soon as you're done here."

Augustine read the note. "I will, thank you." He looked up at his waiting lieutenants. "Cy, I need you to follow Ava Mae again today. Lally's going to call me when Ava Mae leaves the house to meet with Ogun. Keep your distance and don't use any of the same forms you did yesterday. All I need to know is if they head to his house. If that happens, you call me and I'll take care of it."

Cy nodded. "What do you think he's going to do to her?"

"If he's smart, not much and they won't even leave the restaurant they're meeting at." Augustine scratched one of his horns. "I'm hoping he's just working a scam on her. He had to have seen the money she was spending when she was out shopping. He's probably going to sell her some bogus spell or candle or tonic or something and then when it doesn't work, tell her she didn't believe hard enough."

Sydra tapped her fingers on the table. "And if it's not a scam and he does plan on taking her back to his place to work some actual voodoo?"

Augustine's jaw tightened. "Then Ogun's going to have a very bad day."

The doors to the war room opened and Dulcinea and Beatrice came in. Dulce gave a nod. "Sorry we're late."

Beatrice was showing fairly well. She lifted her hand in greeting.

Augustine stood. "Beatrice, I didn't expect you. I take it your morning sickness is behind you?"

Beatrice waved her hand back and forth, but Dulcinea answered. "She's pretty much over it but her voice is completely gone. Khell was only part wysper but enough that the baby is affecting her. Otherwise, she's good."

"Happy to hear that," Augustine said. "You're here so I assume you want to get back to work?"

Beatrice nodded.

Augustine hesitated. Beatrice could take care of herself for the most part, but not being able to communicate meant she'd have to be paired up. "Let me think about it." He gestured for them to take their places, then went on with the meeting. "As you know, a large number of tourists have gone missing." He held up the piece of paper Fenton had given him. "Latest tally is six. Detective Grantham has asked me to meet him at the station as soon as I'm done here, because unfortunately one of the missing includes Senator Pellimento's son."

Fenton interjected, "She already doesn't like othernaturals. Her son going missing could tip things against us in a way you can't imagine."

Augustine nodded. "Which is why I've told the NOPD we'll help them with this issue. Consider this missing tourists business a fae concern until it's solved."

Beatrice held up a hand and frowned, then quickly scribbled something on the tablet she'd brought and held it out to Dulcinea. She read it, then looked at Augustine. "Bea wants to know if you think an othernatural is responsible for the missing tourists."

"I have no reason to think so right now, although one of the missing tourists was seen talking to Zara Vincent at the farmer's market."

Dulcinea snorted. "I've talked to her there, too. I get tinctures from her. She's nothing like Giselle."

He shrugged. "I'd agree, but if being Guardian has taught me anything it's that nothing is guaranteed."

The group nodded. Sydra spoke up. "You want us to ask around? See what we can find out?"

"Anything you can do would be a help. The police are questioning relatives and the like but so far, there's not been much useful information turned up."

Cy made a face. "Have they checked security cams?"

"That's being done but there's a lot of footage to go through."
Cy crossed his arms and frowned. "Harlow could get it done."
The room fell silent.

Slowly, Augustine nodded. "Yes, she could. Which brings me to my next topic. As you all know, Harlow has been, for lack of a better term, possessed by the spirit of her dead twin, Ava Mae." He held a hand up. "I know you're going to have questions, but I don't have answers. Not many anyway. What I can tell you is that while Ava Mae seems to have taken over, Harlow is still in there. And until I tell you otherwise, I want you to treat her like you normally would. Like you have no idea Ava Mae even exists. Cy's been working with me on this and hopefully we'll have Harlow back soon."

Lines furrowed Dulcinea's forehead. "I'm really sorry to hear that. If there's anything we can do, you know we'll do it."

"I know. Thank you." He looked around at the others, seeing concern and wishing he could do more to reassure them. "Beatrice, as far as putting you back to work—"

Fenton straightened. "If I may?"

Augustine raised his brows. "Go ahead."

Fenton tugged at his jacket. "I'm sure Augustine would rather you not be in the field if you can't communicate, but if you're willing, I could use some help here. Detective Grantham has delivered copies of all the files they've collected on the missing tourists. I've been combing through them for anything that might offer a clue, but…" He sighed. "It's an enormous amount of work."

She nodded eagerly, holding her hands out.

Fenton smiled. "Thank you. I don't mind telling you I'm a little relieved I won't be tackling the job by myself."

Augustine kept his smile to himself, but he was grateful to Fenton for helping out like that. Beatrice could be useful but out of harm's way. It was a perfect solution. "I'm headed to the police department. Cy, you're on call as soon as I hear from Lally, and Beatrice is here with Fenton. Sydra and Dulcinea, I want you two on patrol together in the Quarter. That's where all the tourists that have gone missing have been staying so there could be a connection. Let yourself be seen. Go armed up. Take pictures with the tourists if they want them. I want a visible fae presence there."

Dulcinea rolled her eyes and started to say something.

He cut her off with a look. "I can answer your question without you even asking it. Yes, you have to be nice to the tourists. Report back on anything or anyone you think is out of place or unusual. Feel free to swing by Belle's and see if Renny has any info we could use." The gator shifter was Dulcinea's on-again, off-again beau and a bartender at the Quarter's oldest other-natural bar. If anyone had his ear to the ground, it was Renny. Augustine stood. "All right, we've all got our jobs. Let's get out there and get them done."

He took off for the police station. When he arrived, a handful of reporters were milling about in the lobby.

One of them pointed at him. "Hey, you're the fae Guardian, right?"

Augustine stopped short. It wasn't often humans knew his position. "Yes. What can I do for you?"

"Why are you here? Are you helping the police find the missing tourists? How are the fae involved in this?" An LMD got shoved in his face, most likely to record his answers. "Is this a fae crime? Are the police not doing enough?"

Damn it. He hadn't anticipated this. "As Guardian of the city, it's my job to protect all of its citizens, so I'm here to offer whatever help I can to the very capable officers of the New Orleans Police Department."

More questions got lobbed at him, but he ignored them and shoved through the group to make his way toward Grantham's office. Even as he left the reporters behind, the questions kept coming. He knocked on Grantham's door before entering. "This a good time?"

Grantham looked up from a file. "Robelais. Thanks for coming. Yeah, it's a fine time, come in. Shut the door behind you."

Augustine did as he was asked and took a seat across from Grantham's desk. "I didn't know there'd be reporters here."

Grantham grimaced. "Parasites. These disappearances might have stayed quiet if not for Robbie Pellimento." He turned the file around. "There he is in all his glory."

The picture clipped to the file was of a handsome twenty-something with perfect teeth, an aura of money and a kind of know-it-all gleam in his eye. "Looks like a fancy college boy."

"Which is pretty much what he is." Grantham dropped the file flat on the desk and sat back. "And we still have no leads. His mother—"

"The infamous Senator Pellimento."

"Yes. She arrived late last night. As you know, she's not exactly othernatural friendly. She's brought in a group of recovery specialists to help search for her son. If this doesn't end well—"

Augustine frowned. "Recovery specialists?"

"Mercs, if I had to guess. Soldiers for hire. She's supposed to be calling me with a time and location to meet them. She's requested the Guardian's presence, so I'm hoping you'll go with me. Some positive fae interaction with her could be a good thing."

"And it could be a really bad decision." Augustine's stress notched up a level. "Hired soldiers make things a whole lot more serious. But at this point, there's no othernatural link that we know about so Pellimento can pound sand for all I care. This is still a human issue. I know I said I'd help you, and I will, but I'm not interested in meeting with her goons."

"I'm not, either, but Pellimento's let it be known that if we don't play ball, she's going to lock the city down. No one in or out until her son is found. If that happens, the mayor isn't going to be happy with either one of us."

Augustine frowned. "*Sturka.*"

"I feel you, but…" Grantham tapped the file on his desk. "You need to be here." He sat back. "Besides that, it's an election year. Pellimento is already riding a wave of anti-othernatural sentiment that's been building since the covenant was broken and humans suddenly discovered we're not alone in this world."

"I get it. I need to be some kind of fae example." That was so not his wheelhouse.

"That and Pellimento doesn't need any more ammunition. In fact, I was hoping—" A knock on the door interrupted Grantham. "Come in."

A young woman stuck her head in. "Sorry to interrupt. We found Pellimento's hotel. He was staying at the Sonesta, using the alias Bobbie Palomino."

Augustine laughed softly. "Probably didn't want Mommy to find him while he was getting his party on in the Big Easy."

The woman continued. "Tech put together a vid of the last time he left the hotel. They tracked him as far as they could by camera. I sent the important part to your tablet." She tipped her head at Augustine, but kept her eyes on the detective. "Good thing you brought him in."

"Thank you, Sasha. I'll pull it up now."

She crossed her arms and leaned against the door. Grantham brought the tablet to life, then tapped the screen a few times until a holoscreen opened above it. The video played.

Robbie Pellimento stumbled through the Quarter, clearly intoxicated, if his movements were any indication. He wandered into an open space.

Augustine edged closer. "That's Jackson Square."

"It sure is," Grantham said.

Robbie ducked beneath a familiar white pavilion. Augustine held his tongue until a little more of the video played out. It skipped ahead to a different location. The time stamp showed it was several hours later. Robbie left his hotel and got into a cab. The cab drove out of range and the feed went blank.

Augustine sat back. "She's finally done it."

Grantham turned the tablet off. "Who's done what?"

"That pavilion belongs to Giselle Vincent. That's her fortune-telling stand in Jackson Square. She's finally gotten herself into a mess she can't get out of."

Sasha shook her head. "We talked to a few of the other vendors in the square. They said Giselle doesn't work there anymore since her father died."

"If that was true, why is her pavilion still there?" Augustine shook his head. "It's more likely the vendors are scared of her. She's probably threatened them to keep them quiet."

Grantham tapped his desk. "You should know the NOPD consider the witches othernaturals since they fall under fae rule and I have no doubts the senator will also." He looked at Sasha. "Any luck tracing the cab?"

"We have a call in to the dispatcher now to check the driver's records."

Augustine shifted in his chair. "The cab was headed out of the Quarter."

Grantham turned his attention back to Augustine. "You think Pellimento was going to Giselle's house?"

"Not if the cab was leaving the Quarter. She lives there. Her father's house is in the Garden District, but to my knowledge she's not living there yet. Although I'm sure she will be soon." Augustine thought for a moment. "Her sister, Zara, lives in the Garden District, too, but this has Giselle's stink all over it."

"As soon as I hear from the cab company, I'll let you know." Sasha turned to go. "There's also a crew headed to his hotel room. They'll let you know about whatever evidence they find."

"Thanks." Grantham kept his gaze on Augustine as she left. "I should know by tomorrow morning if the room search turns up anything interesting. I'll keep you posted on it all the same. In the meantime, I need some more coffee if I'm going to make it through the rest of these files."

"I hope you find something that ties Giselle into all this." Augustine stood as Grantham did the same. "Let me ask you— if you consider the witches othernaturals, does that mean I have jurisdiction?"

Grantham answered right away. "So long as any guilty parties are properly dealt with, yes."

"And if witches are othernaturals, what do you consider those who practice voodoo?"

Grantham rubbed one hand over the fight-scarred knuckles of the other. "Your people don't regulate voodoo like you do witchcraft."

"We've never had a reason to, but that might change depending on a few factors."

Grantham's dark gaze held both distress and a sense of helplessness. "Then I guess we'll cross that bridge when we come to it."

He made to leave but Augustine stopped him. "I'm not talking about Jewelia, just so you know. I'm talking about Father Ogun."

"But what affects one, affects all." Grantham sighed, then raised his head to look at Augustine straight on. "Tell you what. Ogun gets in your way, whatever happens, happens."

"I take it you don't like him any more than I do."

"He gives those who do good with the practice a bad name. Like my grandmother." He raised his brows. "I want her kept clean of all this, you hear me? I know she's helping you with something, but if that help drags her into some kind of mess..."

"You have my word. She's got nothing to fear." Augustine gestured toward the door. Jewelia's *bokura* had made it possible for him to talk to Harlow. He wasn't about to do anything to hurt the mambo. "Good luck with those files. I'm going to go see a certain witch and see what information I can get out of her."

Grantham gave him a stern look. "You give me your word you'll be back to speak to Pellimento's recovery team?"

"I'll try, but I've got other fae business to deal with. That has to take precedence."

"That's not good enough. You don't show for that meeting and the senator is going to be all over you like stink on a pig."

"I'll deal with her if and when the time comes. But that time might not be today." He wasn't about to abandon Harlow for the senator's missing kid. Not when Augustine had a pretty good idea Robert Pellimento was already dead.

⚜

Ava Mae strolled toward St. Jacques Bistro for her lunch date. She spotted Rufus Ogun immediately. He was inside and already at a table, reading the paper. Waiting for her. Her pulse jumped a tick at the thought that very soon, with the help he was about to give her, she would permanently reside in this body.

Not if I have anything to do with it.

Settle down, Sister. This is for the best.

Ditching me is for the best? Like hell. It's my body!

You had your chance to behave but your constant bitterness and fighting is too much. You brought this on yourself.

I wish you were still dead!

Harlow's shout spiked anger through Ava Mae, causing her arm to jerk and her purse to slip from her shoulder. She glanced around to see if anyone had noticed. She closed her eyes for a moment and concentrated on pushing Harlow down.

Harlow barely budged.

Ava Mae ignored the twinge of panic her failure brought on. She fought harder and this time succeeded in wresting back control. With a shuddering breath, she yanked the strap of her purse onto her shoulder and hurried into the restaurant. There was no time to waste. She smiled brightly as she approached the table. "Rufus, you beat me here."

He looked up from his paper and met her smile with one of his own. He folded the paper and set it aside. "Don't you look lovely. I'm so glad you could join me. I've ordered a couple of Sazeracs. Have you had one before?"

She sat, shaking her head. "No, what is it?"

"My dear, it's the signature drink of New Orleans. It was invented right here in the French Quarter. I thought it might be a nice way to celebrate our new friendship."

She struggled to hold on to her smile. Her past experiences with alcohol weren't very good. What if something bad happened this time? What if he was trying to get her drunk? He wouldn't do that, would he? He had no reason to. Plus it would be rude to turn down the drink. And she needed his help. "I agree. To new friends."

A server arrived with the drinks. She stared at hers.

He picked his up to toast, then hesitated. "You seem nervous."

"I think I'm what you'd call a lightweight."

"I see." He put his glass down, his smile gentle and warm. "Then why don't you skip it? I don't want to make you uncomfortable."

"You don't care if I don't drink it?"

"Not at all." His smile widened. "Although, if it's all the same to you, I'm going to drink mine." He laughed. "In fact, I'm probably going to have another."

She was making a big deal about nothing. She picked up her glass. "Here's to friends."

He lifted his as well. "All right then. To friends and a future that brings us both what we desire."

She sipped the tawny liquid, the sweet but bitter taste swirling over her tongue. "Not bad."

"You'd probably like something more fruity."

She shrugged. "I don't drink enough to know, really. My mother liked mint juleps. That's not a bad drink." She quickly put her hand up like a stop sign. "Not that I want one."

He chuckled and leaned forward. "They make a great raspberry tea here. Let me get you one of those." He waved the server over and ordered.

Lunch was as light and pleasant as she'd hoped. Rufus knew everything there was to know about the city and told the most amazing stories. By the end of the meal, she felt like she'd known him for years. But they still hadn't talked much about her problem and what he could do to help. Every time she brought the subject up, he danced around it.

Finally, lunch was over, the bill paid—something she'd argued with him about, but he'd insisted on picking up the tab—and it was time to go. Other than Harlow's silent irritation, her presence had been almost forgettable. Ava Mae and Ogun left together.

As they hit the sidewalk Ogun tipped his hat back, a straw fedora with a bright blue band, and took a long look around them, eyeing each passerby with suspicion. "I know you want to talk about your situation, but I don't trust open spaces. How about we go for a walk to somewhere I like better?"

"Okay." Anywhere he felt comfortable was fine with her. She matched his pace.

"We're not far and it's a spot you should see anyway. Lot of history in where we're headed."

"Is there any place around here that doesn't have history?"

He laughed. "No, I guess not." They walked a few blocks, finally approaching a large compound surrounded by a high plastered wall. Behind the wall, the second and third stories of a large, rectangular building were visible. He pushed open an arched wooden gate for her to go through. "Here we are. The Ursuline Convent."

She paused, her feet still on the sidewalk. "Can you...that is, your...people, can they go in places like this?"

He snorted. "Child, I'm a voodoo doctor, not a vampire. We hold dear to the church." He waved a hand through the air, pushing her comment away. "But I suppose this is all new to you. Even your Augustine's a religious man. Well, he was. Not sure about that lately. His mother, now there's a woman who clings to the cross."

Ava Mae walked through the gate. "Really?" This was interesting. Anything she could learn about Augustine that might bring them closer was a good thing. Perhaps Harlow felt the same way, as she'd gone oddly quiet. Like she was listening intently.

Rufus followed her, then took the path leading to a small shop. "Oh, yes. His mother hates all things fae. But then I'm sure he's mentioned that."

"Not much." Not at all that she could remember.

Rufus paid the admission then led her into the main building, the huge white rectangle she'd seen outside the wall. It was a simple, austere building. The third story's windows were shuttered. The building's inside matched its exterior, with crisp white walls and dark wood floors that were beautiful but restrained. Their steps echoed on the thick planks, but upstairs the voices of children and adults could be heard. He gestured around the space. "They keep the convent open to the public, but it's a working school so the only areas we can access are the grounds and the path to the chapel, which is fine. That's the place I want to show you."

He led the way until they came into a huge open space with a soaring ceiling painted with a blue sky complete with angels. White marble columns surrounded the altar, gilded here and there with touches of gold and more intricate painting. The quiet was so profound it pressed against her ears.

She took a few steps in, immediately ill at ease for reasons she didn't understand. She had as much right to be here as the next person.

He walked them back a few pews and gestured for her to sit. She slid across the polished wood until she was under one of the large crystal chandeliers hanging from the ornate ceiling. Even with the chandeliers, the space beyond the altar was dim. It felt...sacred. Cool, quiet. Nothing like the space the lightning tree inhabited. Nothing like being part of the tree. She shoved those memories down and took a breath. The slight smell of something perfumey lingered in the air. Incense maybe?

Rufus sat beside her and spread his hands wide. "See," he said softly. "Not a soul. The perfect place to talk."

"It's very pretty." And it was, despite the way the small hairs on the back of her neck had raised the moment they'd entered. She tucked her hands under her thighs and stared at the altar and the two large angels flanking it.

A small noise near the entrance captured their attention. A wizened nun in white and blue robes made her way to the altar gate and kneeled to pray. Ava Mae looked at Rufus, tipping her head toward the old woman.

He smirked. "Nothing to worry about." He kept his voice to a whisper as he sat back. "What kind of help do you want from me? What exactly is going on?"

She had no choice but to trust him if she wanted to accomplish her goal. With that in mind, she told him exactly what she wanted. "I need some kind of spell or potion or whatever you can do to make sure my soul stays in my body." She watched him, waiting for the look that told her he thought she was insane. It never came.

He nodded, squinting off toward the distance. "That seems like it might be an issue, does it? Keeping one's soul in one's body isn't the type of request I usually get."

"Does that mean you can't help me?" Panic edged along her spine.

Harlow latched on to that feeling. *Nothing good can come of this.*

"No, but knowing a little more will help me create the spell. Why do you feel like this is something you need help with?"

She took a breath. "Because mine is not the only soul in this body."

That's right, tell him how you're an interloper.

He nodded again, appearing unshaken by what she'd said. "I see." He was quiet a moment. The old nun kept her place at the rail, her head bent. Rufus turned in Ava Mae's direction. "That other soul giving you trouble?"

"Yes."

Hah! You're the only soul in trouble. Messing with voodoo is going to come back to haunt you. Just like I will if you try to ditch me.

His brows lifted knowingly. "Because it was the original owner of the body?"

She stared at him, a little unsettled by what he'd surmised. Harlow's bitter laughter rang in Ava Mae's ears. "Can you help me or not?"

"No." He held up a finger. "But I know who can." He kept his gaze on her. "I'm your friend, child. Whatever you say to me, stays with me. I want you to know that and trust that."

"Thank you." But words were easily broken. She'd believe him when she got what she wanted. "This person you know who can help me, who is it?"

"A friend." He smiled coyly. "I can take you to her, if you like."

A woman? That was somewhat reassuring. "When?"

He looked at his watch. "She should be home. Let me text her and see if she can meet us now. If that works for you."

Ava Mae smiled, mostly out of relief that Ogun hadn't told her what she needed was impossible. "That works perfectly."

The sooner, the better.

Chapter Eight

Giselle looked up from a set of blueprints to see Augustine stomping through the demolished insides of her house. How he'd known to find her at her father's old place, she had no idea. Wretched fae intuition. She had to get rid of him before Ogun showed up. "What are you doing here?"

The angry glitter in his stormy eyes told her it wasn't a friendly visit. Typical. He only came to see her when he wanted to accuse her of something. "You're lucky I don't haul you in for questioning. Actually, I might, depending on how things go."

"What now, Guardian? I'm busy. And not with anything that needs fae interference." She put a hammer on one side of the blueprints and a level on the other to keep the paper from rolling back together, then crossed her arms and glared at him. "Someone put a curse on you and you need me to remove it? I have to say I'm surprised it's taken this long."

His expression didn't change. "What do you know about the missing tourists?"

Her smile almost faltered. "I didn't even know there were missing tourists. A little too much Mardi Gras fun, perhaps?" She reached for the blueprints. "That's neither a crime nor witchcraft, so if you'll excuse me—"

He smacked his hand down on top of them, six fingers splayed against the blue and white drawings. "Do not play cute with me, witch."

Cute was the last thing she wanted to be with him. She stopped smiling and brushed an errant fleck of sawdust off the sleeve of her white linen jacket. "I've answered your question. What else is it going to take to get you out of my house?"

"The last tourist that went missing was seen getting his fortune told by you in Jackson Square." He lifted his hand from the blueprints to jab his index finger at her. "And before you try to tell me you don't work the square anymore, I already know better, so save your breath."

She crossed her arms again. It helped keep her fingers still, which were itching to fling spells at him. "No, I do still set up shop there on occasion, but not with the same regularity that I used to. I'm high priestess of the coven now, you know."

He snorted. "I'm aware."

She waved her hand toward the pile of discarded lumber in one corner. "Plus, as you can see, I'm busy remodeling this place and—" Her LMD buzzed. She pulled it out and looked at the screen. Incoming text from Ogun. Damn it. He must be on his way. "Just a moment, I have to deal with this."

Her fingers flew over the screen. *Change in plans. Take the package to Zara's.* She sent that text, then sent another to Ian, who was currently upstairs overseeing the installation of the granite countertops in the master bath. *Augustine is here. I sent Ogun to Zara's. Text her, then get over there. Will join you as soon as able.*

Ogun's reply came first. *Will do.*

Then Ian's. *Done. On my way. Will wait on your arrival.*

She tucked the LMD back into her pocket and smiled. "You know how remodeling is, all the contractors need an answer at the same time. So if you'll excuse me, I really should get back to work. Besides this job, I still have a coven to run."

He pulled his own LMD out, flipped it around and showed her the screen. "Do you recognize this man?"

She studied the face of the last tourist they'd fed to the well of souls. The one she'd known was a calculated, but brilliant risk. "He looks vaguely familiar." She nodded and pointed at the picture. "That's one of the missing tourists, I assume? I guess he looks familiar because I either saw him in the square, on one of the news reports or I could have even read his fortune. I can't really say which."

He tucked the LMD into his pocket. "Try harder. We have the two of you on video together."

"Then I guess I did read his fortune, but I can't give you more than that. I don't ask for the names of those I read for. I prefer to let the crystals speak for themselves." She held back the curse prying at her lips. Those damn surveillance cameras. They infested the city like a plague. How much could they have really gotten? "Let me see the picture again."

He showed her the photo a second time.

She stared at it, buying herself some time to think. She squinted as if recalling even a few details took effort. "I can tell you from what I read off him and the way he was dressed, he comes from a family of money and influence."

Augustine nodded. "Good read." He lifted the LMD higher. "This is Senator Irene Pellimento's son."

She leaned forward, the buzz of a saw in the next room causing her to raise her voice. "Why should that mean anything to me?"

Augustine shouted over the din. "If you don't know, maybe we should go somewhere you can think better. One of the holding cells at the Pelcrum should do nicely."

"On what grounds? I've done nothing." The saw went mercifully quiet.

"On the grounds that you're a witch and I don't give a *fet'ka* what you think. I'm so tired of dealing with the problems you create. You're a thorn in my side and I'd like to yank you out and be done with you."

Taking the senator's son had created exactly the pressure and distraction she'd hoped. Augustine's patience was thin. He could be pushed even further with a little more effort. But all she really needed to do was leak a little misinformation to the right sources and he'd have his hands too full to bother her and her sister until it was too late. Not to mention she was about to double his stress by making his little girlfriend disappear, too. "Are you threatening me?"

"Yes." His eyes sparked with dark intent. "You witches are a boil on the ass of this town."

"A thorn *and* a boil?" She clutched at an imaginary set of pearls. "You know how to cut a girl to the quick." She dropped her hand. "Funny, I feel the same way about the fae." The sawing started again, this time from somewhere upstairs. She narrowed her eyes at him. "So I read the kid's fortune. That's not a crime."

"Maybe it should be."

She scowled at him. "I had nothing to do with him going missing. If he's the senator's son, maybe you should figure out who her enemies are and start there. But that list certainly doesn't include me."

He shook his head, the anger in his eyes building.

She spoke before he could, trying to look as innocent as possible. "I get that you have a job to do, but do it somewhere else. Not only does this not involve the witches, but I've got nothing to do with it. I'm a little busy with running the coven, which is more work than I anticipated. On top of that, I'm trying to fix up my dad's house and live my life. I'm tired of all this bad blood between the witches and the fae. If I hear anything, you'll be the first one I contact."

The anger in his eyes died a little, but his scowl stayed put. "You do that." He dug out his LMD again and glanced at the screen. Something was flashing. A message. Thank the goddess someone else needed him. He looked at her. "Today's your lucky day. I have more important places to be. But don't think for a second I'm not watching everything you do." With one last glance, he strode out.

He was going to have a hard time watching her when the senator was watching him. She went to the window, waiting until his car pulled out of the drive before she acted. Ian would be halfway to Zara's by now. She'd pick him up when she passed him. She grabbed one of the construction walkie-talkies off the makeshift table and yelled into it. "Trent!" No immediate response. "Trent, where the hell are you?"

"Right behind you, Ms. Vincent."

She turned to see the foreman she'd hired, some beefy kind of varcolai, but what kind of shifter he was exactly, she couldn't tell. Maybe wolf? Bear? Who knew. Who cared. He was a foot taller and wider than she was and as dark as one of the Houma tribe, which he probably was. "Trent, I have to leave, but that doesn't mean anyone gets to slack off. This job is running behind and I—"

He frowned, his gold eyes judging her. "It wouldn't be running behind if you'd stop changing things. My men are hard workers and fast, but that only goes so far when they have to start from scratch on something because you got a new idea."

Today was not her day. "It's my house. My money. And you work for me. I'll have all the new ideas I want, understand?"

He smiled like he was staring at a petulant child. "Completely, but you can't expect us to keep the same work pace." His smile disappeared. "Understand?"

"I could replace you tomorrow."

This time he laughed. "I'm not so sure about that. I'm the third foreman you've had in less than two weeks. The union probably won't send you any more."

She snarled at him, grabbed her bag and stormed toward

the garage. "I better see progress by tomorrow." She slammed the door behind her for good measure and stalked to her white Mercedes sedan, something else she'd inherited from Evander. Once inside, she took out her LMD, fired up the app that would make her number untraceable and her voice unmatchable, then dialed the number she'd been holding on to for just this occasion.

It rang twice. "Senator Pellimento's office."

"The senator's son was kidnapped by the fae Guardian of New Orleans, Augustine Robelais."

"Who is this?"

"The Guardian plans to kill the senator's son in retaliation for the anti-othernatural bills she's pushed through."

"Give me your nam—"

Giselle hung up and smiled. That should keep Augustine occupied. She peeled out of the driveway and headed for Zara's. A few minutes later, she spotted Ian on the sidewalk. She pulled over and unlocked the car so he could jump in.

He climbed in and shut the door. "What did Augustine want?"

"Nothing, just to hassle me. You know how the fae are." Ian and Zara didn't need to know that the missing tourists had become an issue. The senator's son was her own little insurance plan. One that had just been put into place.

She stomped on the gas and threaded through the remaining streets until she pulled into Zara's drive. "Ogun should be here any moment."

Zara opened the front door as they were getting out. "I got Ian's text. What's going on?"

"I had to divert Ogun because Augustine showed up at the house."

Zara's eyes rounded in panic. "What did he want?"

"Coven business. Some issue with registrations. Nothing to

worry about." She made herself smile as she and Ian entered. "Are we ready for two more souls?"

Zara took a breath and nodded, but the tension didn't quite leave her face. She shut the door. "Yes, I've prepared everything."

Ian shucked his leather jacket. "If we added Ogun now, that would only leave us three more to go."

"No," Zara said. "We should be even more cautious than before if Augustine is poking around."

Giselle held her temper. Her anger wasn't at her sister anyway; it was at that damn fae. "I told you it had nothing to do with the souls we've already collected. There's nothing to worry about. In fact, if his constant presence is a sign of anything, it's a sign we should cast the spell as soon as we can. I'm fine with adding Ogun now and collecting the rest of the souls ourselves."

"I'll bring you three tonight, if you want." Ian's sly smile warmed Giselle's belly. "Bourbon's full of drunken idiots just looking to get lost."

"Then it's settled." Giselle nodded. "We add Ogun now and Ian supplies us with the last three we need."

Zara twisted her hands together. "I don't know."

Giselle grabbed her sister's hands to keep her from knotting them together anymore. "Zara, the sooner we do this, the sooner we're free. We have the sigil. There's nothing to stop us. Think about it. The power we've been forced to restrain because of the fae laws could finally be let loose. The city would swarm with witches if they knew they could live here with one of their own in power. No rules, no registrations, no restrictions. We can own this city the way our ancestors once did."

The light in Zara's eyes strengthened. "I know you're right. I'm just...I'm a little scared. Not of the fae, but of casting this spell."

"That's natural. After what happened to Mother, how could either of us not be afraid? At least a little." Giselle squeezed her sister's hands. "This time is going to be very different. We're prepared and we're stronger. And we're going to succeed." She wanted to say more, but the doorbell rang. "That'll be Ogun. I'll get it since he knows me."

She ran to the door and opened it. There stood Ogun in one of his usual outlandish getups. Harlow stood beside him, her eyes wide but full of hope. Her fingers wiggled. "Hello. Rufus said you could help me."

Ogun pointed his hand at Harlow. "Giselle Vincent, this is Harlow Goodwin, my friend that I called you about? She's in need of your particular brand of help."

"Ah, yes, please, come in." Giselle motioned toward the interior of the house, watching Harlow for any indication that the woman remembered Giselle from the time she'd read Harlow's fortune. So far, nothing. "Any friend of Father Ogun's is a friend of mine." She stood to the side until they'd entered the foyer, then shut the door and led them into the living room, where Zara and Ian awaited. "Father Ogun, my sister Zara and our paramour, Ian."

Ogun stopped in the hall. A bead of sweat trickled down from beneath his hat. "Why are they here? You didn't say they'd be here."

She put her hands on her hips. "When I said to meet me at my sister's, did you think she wouldn't be home?" She tilted her chin down and smiled. "What's the matter, voodoo man? The presence of three powerful witches make you uncomfortable?"

"No." He straightened, putting Harlow before him slightly. "Harlow, tell them about your...situation."

Harlow's shoulder jerked, pulling out of his grasp. "Why am I—" Her eyes rolled back for a moment, then she shook herself and put her hands out. "Did you see that?" She pointed at herself, then to Giselle. "For reasons I don't care to explain, I do not have full control of this body. Rufus said you could secure me inside it. Possibly get the other soul inside me out. I want you to use your magic to do that now. So I can be who I really am. Ava Mae."

Giselle held her hands up. "Ava Mae, hmm? What you're asking is no small task but not impossible. It's a good thing there are other witches here. As this is my sister's house and she is a green witch, we'll go to the garden and prepare the necessary things. Her garden is a magic place with the capacity to grant dreams and desires." She looked at Ogun. "You will wait here until we're ready. Understood?"

"Yes." He made a face and shifted nervously, his hand coming up to rest on the little red pouch hanging around his neck.

She turned before he could see the smile on her face. He should be nervous. No matter what voodoo he'd done to protect himself before coming here, he was about to die.

⚜

The iron cuffs bit into Augustine's wrists like bone saws. Every nerve in his body hummed with low-level pain, but the worst was that the iron made it impossible for him to shift into either of his shadeux or smokesinger forms. Which was no doubt exactly why Pellimento's recovery team had clamped them on him after they'd dragged Grantham off to another part of the warehouse where the team had set up their headquarters.

The attack had happened so quickly, Augustine had to wonder if some of the team weren't secretly othernatural. Of course, if they were, it shouldn't have taken seven of them to get the cuffs on. None of them smelled like varcolai or vamps, either.

The leader of the team, a man named Sutter, cracked his

knuckles. Blood crusted at the corner of his mouth where Augustine had landed his last punch. "Now that you're feeling a little more cooperative, someone would like a word with you."

From out of the shadows walked a slip of a woman, her short gray hair and wire-rimmed half spectacles giving her the appearance of a very stern grandmother.

Augustine stared at her. "I was wondering when you'd show. Call your dogs off or you can forget getting any help from me."

Senator Pellimento smiled. "Is that any way to talk to the woman who holds your life in her hands?"

Augustine popped an incredulous brow. "My life? I think you overestimate your power, lady."

Her smile turned into a menacing grimace. "I could say the same about you, Guardian. Where is my son?"

"How am I supposed to know? We just started looking for him. We have some leads but nothing—"

"Again," she said, motioning to Sutter.

Sutter's fist connected with Augustine's jaw.

Fresh blood spilled across Augustine's tongue. He spat out a mouthful of it. "Really? This is how you want to do this?"

Pellimento tugged on leather gloves, then took hold of one of Augustine's horns, forcing his face up to look at her. "I know you took my son. If you don't give him back to me, alive, I will cut one of these off and shove it into your heart."

He jerked his head away, ripping the horn out of her grip. "I don't have your son. I didn't even know who he was until a couple of days ago."

"Liar!" she screamed, sending droplets of spittle across his face.

Rage smoldered in his belly, sending wisps of heat through his bones. With the shackles on, there was no outlet for it, making him wonder if a smokesinger had ever spontaneously combusted. "Why would I take your son?"

She tipped her head. "Don't play coy with me. We both know there are many reasons you'd want to hurt me."

"You mean because you're a bigot?"

"You and all those like you are an abomination. You're unnatural. You should be exterminated."

This time he smiled. "You know I've got a little human in me. There's a very good chance you've got a little fae in you."

She slapped him but the blow barely made an impact. "If my son isn't returned to me by this time tomorrow, I will have the governor, who owes me a wealth of favors, declare martial law and lock this city down."

He tsked. "The tourism board isn't going to like that."

"You have twenty-four hours." She snapped her fingers at Sutter. "Give him a taste of what will happen to him if my son isn't standing beside me tomorrow."

As she walked away Sutter rolled his shoulders like he was loosening up for a big fight. "I've been looking forward to this, fae."

The remainder of the team lined the perimeter of the gloomy space, assault weapons at the ready. What exactly did they expect to happen? Augustine glared at Sutter. Too bad fae powers didn't include death by thought. "You don't get out much, do you, human?"

Sutter's stony face didn't move. "You're going to regret your involvement in the disappearance of Robert Pellimento."

"I already told the senator I have nothing to do with—"

Sutter's fist connected with Augustine's jaw. Pain ricocheted through his skull. He hoped Grantham wasn't taking the same kind of beating. Humans didn't have the same kind of resiliency that fae did, but then, Grantham had done his time in the ring. If anyone knew how to take a punch, he did.

Sutter leaned in. "If the fae didn't bring tourists to this town, Senator Pellimento would have run your kind out of here a long time ago. Now tell me what you know about her son's disappearance, or I'll introduce you to another more intimate pair of iron shackles."

The guy apparently had a hard-on to please his boss. Maybe there was more going on between Sutter and the senator. As gross as that thought was, Augustine managed a grin. "I pegged you for the kinky type as soon as I saw you. Is that how the senator likes it?"

Sutter punched him again. "Tell me what you know."

Augustine spat blood onto the concrete then sighed like he was bored. "I already have. Robbie was last seen getting into a cab. Based on what Grantham found out on our way over here and what I suspect he's already told you, the cab company has no record of the fare."

Sutter growled and leaned in. "I don't like your kind any more than Senator Pellimento does."

"Really? I never would have guessed." A chime rang through Augustine's head. *Sturka*. Not the best time for an incoming call. "Answer," he mumbled.

"Boss, you'd better get here now. Something weird is about to go down." Cy sounded rattled, a rare thing for the big fae.

Sutter barked in Augustine's face. "Did you just take a call while I'm talking to you?" He shoved Augustine's head back.

Augustine ignored Sutter. "Cy, are you at Ogun's?"

"No, boss. He took her to—"

Sutter slid his fingernail beneath the com cell stuck behind Augustine's ear and flicked it away.

Heat waves edged Augustine's vision, narrowing his line of sight until Sutter's ugly face was all he could see. He unclenched his jaw enough to speak and lowered his voice. "There is one thing I forgot to tell you." He made his voice even quieter. "One...very...important...thing..."

"What?" Sutter leaned in to hear.

Augustine rammed one of his horns into Sutter's forehead. Blood poured from the split. With a howl, Sutter jerked his arm back and threw another punch at Augustine. He ducked, causing Sutter's fist to connect to the steel pole behind Augustine. Bones crunched.

A few of the team members rushed toward Augustine. Rifle butts slammed into his head and body. Blow after blow rained down, cracking bone and causing pain until everything went black.

Chapter Nine

Harlow drew on whatever strength she could muster. Without knowing exactly what was about to happen, she didn't know how to prepare for what lay ahead. Except to expect something really, really bad.

Ava Mae had nodded and gone along with whatever Ogun and the witches told her to do and now stood in the garden quietly waiting, but Harlow wasn't so easily fooled. She knew *why* Ava Mae was here. To get rid of her. Fear almost numbed Harlow to the point of inaction, but she gave herself over to her anger instead and clung to the fact that Augustine had promised he knew what Ava Mae was planning and that he'd protect Harlow.

Any minute, he'd show up. Any minute, he'd make everything right.

But the minutes were ticking by and there was no sign of him. Or anyone who might help her.

She steeled her entire being, such as it was, and geared up to fight in whatever way she could, waiting and watching for some kind of opening, some chance to make her move.

After some final preparation, Giselle's sister, Zara, and the sorcerer Ian positioned themselves around a large pond in the center of the garden. Giselle gestured to the stone path beside her. "Come stand with me, Ava Mae."

Ava Mae looked at Ogun. He nodded, encouraging her. Idiot. But Harlow restrained her temper so as not to give Ava

Mae any indication of what she was feeling, saving it for the moment she'd need to strike. Ava Mae took her place beside Giselle.

Movement pulled at the edge of her vision. Everyone turned to look as a nondescript man vaulted over the high wall surrounding the property. Human, maybe. Except Harlow didn't think humans could jump like that or move with that kind of speed or agility.

He charged toward them. "Don't touch her—"

Giselle's hand shot forward as a single word left her mouth. The man was immobilized. Holding her hand out toward the man, she looked at Ava Mae and raised an eyebrow. "A friend of yours?"

Ava Mae shook her head. "I've never seen him before."

Neither had Harlow. Could this man be working for Augustine? Her panic level jumped a notch.

Giselle's mouth was tight. "Enough of this. Let's get to why you're here, shall we?" She seemed to be holding the spell on the intruder without effort. With her free hand, she pointed to the pond. "This water has the power to grant your deepest desire."

"So it will bind my soul to this body?"

Giselle's frustration showed in her eyes. "If that's your deepest desire, then yes."

"It is." Ava Mae's eagerness washed through Harlow. "So what do I do?"

Giselle smiled but it was plainly forced. "Just walk in and submerse yourself. The water will do the rest." She took a few steps back until she was equidistant from her sister and Ian, then nodded. "Whenever you're ready, but sooner rather than later." She tipped her head toward the intruder. "I can't hold this spell forever."

"I have to get my clothes wet?"

Giselle's smile thinned. "You may remove as much or as little as you like."

Ava Mae nodded and toed off her shoes, then stripped down to her underwear. "This outfit was very expensive. I don't want to ruin it. Or go home soaking wet."

Giselle's sigh was audible. "The sooner you get in—"

Ava Mae put a foot into the water. "I'm in." She pulled her foot back out. "Are you kidding? It's freezing."

Giselle glanced at Zara. "If you could help?"

Zara's returning glance was strained. "I'm already *helping.*"

"I can do it," Ian said. He lifted a hand over the water and mumbled something. "Try it now."

Ava Mae stuck her foot back in the water. "It's warm now, thank you." She gave him a sly smile and put her other foot in, too. Harlow couldn't believe her twin was flirting at a time like this, but then again, maybe she could. Ava Mae took a few steps and was waist deep. "I never would have guessed this pond was so deep."

Harlow planned on throwing every bit of anger into Ava Mae to shock her out of control as soon as she submerged. She hoped Ava Mae would be concentrating on holding her breath and not on what her sister might do.

Giselle nodded wearily. "Please, all the way under. I can't hold this spell much longer."

Ava Mae waved her hand. "All right, I'm going. I hope you have a towel." She took a deep breath and ducked under.

A flash of light and an audible crack of sound followed, rending Harlow senseless and blind for a moment. Ava Mae was oddly silent. And still.

Harlow's awareness returned. There was no water. Not exactly. She lay on her back on hard, damp earth, but the ceiling above her danced and rippled like a sheet of water. Light filtered through, illuminating the space with a faint, diffused glow.

She pushed to her feet, aware that she was at least partially in control of her body again. A look around told her she wasn't alone. A few others shuffled around her like they were sleep-walking. Some sat against the sloped walls, hunched in the fetal position. Six in total. Another clap of light and sound, and a body fell through the ceiling, landing beside her, head cracking hard on the ground.

Ogun. The man who'd gotten her into this...whatever it was. He lay still. She nudged him with her foot. "Hey. Get up. What have you done? Where the hell are we?"

Another flash of light and sound. She ducked as yet another body fell into the pit. One she recognized. "Oh no." She forgot Ogun and sank to her knees. "Cy?" She grabbed his shoulders as his lids flickered open. "Are you okay? How did you get here? Were you that intruder in disguise?"

He sat up. "That was me." He rolled his shoulder and winced. "Damn witches. I'm okay, but my shoulder is killing me."

"Please tell me Augustine is on his way and that you know what's going on."

He stared at her. "Are you...you again?"

"Kind of. I don't know if it was the fall or what, but Ava Mae seems to be taking a breather."

"Glad to hear that." He stood, helping her to her feet. "About the other stuff, I have no idea what's going on and that includes with Augustine."

"What do you mean?" That wasn't what she wanted to hear.

"I was on the phone with him telling him what was hap-pening, but we got disconnected and...then nothing." He shrugged, then grimaced in pain. "I think my shoulder's dislocated."

"I'm really sorry about that. If I knew how to help you, I would." No Augustine? And Cy was injured. They were in deep trouble.

"I can fix it." He went to one of the walls, clenched his teeth and then jammed his shoulder into it. He cursed loudly as he worked the joint. "It's back in."

Okay, maybe not *that* deep. "You're hard-core, you know that?"

He snorted. "Not hard-core enough to keep myself out of here."

"What on earth just happened to us?"

He glanced up, shaking his head. "That spell paralyzed me, but I could hear everything. Before they forced me into the water, Giselle said something like, 'Ten down, two to go.'"

"Ten down? With you here, there are nine people in this... whatever this is."

"Some sort of holding cell. Maybe you counted wrong." He looked around. "No, I count nine, too." His gaze stuck on her. "You're Harlow again but you say Ava Mae's still with you?"

"Yes, I can still feel her in me. But it's like she's knocked out."

His eyes widened. "There's two of you. That makes ten souls." He scrubbed a hand across his face and looked around. "There's no way this could exist below the pond without some sort of spell. This must be a kind of magical holding tank."

"For people?"

He frowned. "I guess. No doubt the witches are planning something big. No clue what, but it can't be good. Not if they need souls to make it happen."

The thought made Harlow shiver. Then something else disturbed her. Someone else. Ava Mae was awake.

What's going on? Where are we? Why are you still here?

Harlow smirked. *Not the end result you were hoping for, hmm, Sister?* If anything, the fall into the witch's holding pit had stripped Ava Mae of some of her power.

No! Ava Mae yelled. *I was supposed to have control of the body now, not you. You're supposed to be gone!*

Harlow grabbed Cy's arm. "Ava Mae's awake and angry."

"Fight her," Cy urged. "You're stronger. You can do it."

Harlow nodded as Ava Mae screamed in frustration. The emotion ripped through Harlow like a shot of electricity, frying her nerves. She gasped and fought back, calling on her anger and her years of loneliness, letting Ava Mae feel everything that had built up over time.

Ava Mae shrank back. *Stop fighting me. Let me have the body. It's supposed to be mine.*

Like hell it is. I was born into it, remember? You lied your way in. Harlow shoved more emotion at Ava Mae, then added to it the rage accumulated from every time Ava Mae had tried to take Augustine to bed. *You can dish it out, but you can't take it, can you?*

Ava Mae whimpered. She sounded far away now, like she was in a deep well. *You're hurting me. I need the tree. I'm too far away.*

You've been hurting me since you lied and took over.

But I'm your sister. I love you. You love me.

Harlow snorted. *I loved the idea of you, but you're not really my sister, you're the lightning tree's idea of my sister. My twin died at the hands of our father. There's so little of her left in you that you've become a monster made of dark magic and witchcraft. Get out of me.*

Ava Mae went still. She was there, but so diminished Harlow had to work to feel her. Harlow reached for Cy again. "I think I did it. She's not gone but she's barely hanging on."

"Good. Now we get you out of here."

"Shouldn't we wait for the others to come?"

"What others?"

"Augustine and the rest of the lieutenants? Won't they show up eventually?"

He took a long breath. "I have no idea. I honestly don't think anyone knows where we are." He stared at the ground like he was embarrassed to have to tell her this. "Like I said, I was trying to tell Augustine where I was when the line went dead. And I was about to call the others when you, or Ava Mae rather, walked into the pool. You looked like you were in danger. I couldn't wait. I jumped the wall and that's when she froze me." He frowned. "So like I said, we need to get you out of here."

And just like that they were back to deep trouble. "How exactly are we going to do that?"

He cocked one brow. "Remember the *Star Alliance* episode where the crew was being held prisoner in the Rathian slime pit?"

Her mouth opened slightly. "It's not that I doubt your strength but your shoulder is hurt and...are you serious?"

"Do you see another way?"

She looked at the watery ceiling above them. It was at least fifteen feet over their heads and the walls were too slick with pond scum to be climbable. "Assuming I make it, what if the witches are still up there?"

"You'll have the element of surprise on your side, but otherwise...run like hell. You're the only chance any of us has of getting out of here alive."

A small knot clogged her throat for a moment. He'd risked his life to try to save her. She wasn't about to let him lose it because she was too chicken to try this. "Okay, that's the plan then." She took a breath. "I'm ready when you are." She glanced at the ceiling again. "You sure about aiming and everything? I don't want to fall back through."

"I've got this." He laced his fingers together, then bent down, holding his hands out. "Put your hands on my shoulders."

She put her foot into the step he'd made and braced her hands on his shoulders. The amount of muscle beneath her palms was nothing short of astonishing. There was no doubt he had the strength to get her out of here. She smiled down at him. Of all Augustine's lieutenants, she felt the most connected to Cy. "Whatever happens, thank you. For everything."

He gave her a nod. "Just get us out of here."

"I will." She hoped.

"Ready?"

She nodded. Ava Mae moaned distantly. Harlow prayed that her twin wouldn't revive when Harlow got home and close to the lightning tree again.

"Make yourself stiff like an arrow, arms at your sides. Stay that way until you're through, then roll like a ball to land."

She positioned herself as he asked, tensing in preparation.

"Here we go." He sank into a deep bend, counting as he hit the bottom of each squat. "One...two...three." On three, he exploded upward and hurled her through the air.

She pierced the waterline a second later. A cold shock ripped through her, leaving her breathless and hurting to the point she almost forgot Cy's instructions. She managed to wrap her arms around her knees just before she landed. She hit grass with a thud, one arm awkwardly bent beneath her. She bit down to keep the yelp of pain to herself.

She lay there, for how long she wasn't sure. A numb, empty feeling spread through her. Like she'd lost something. At last she pushed to her elbows.

The garden was dark and deserted, but lights blazed in the house. How long had she actually been in that pit? Shivering in her underwear, she crouched behind a few plants bordering the pond while she got a better look at the house. There was movement inside, but she couldn't be sure who it was. Water trickled off her hair and down her back. The clothes Ava Mae had left at the pond's edge were gone. *Damn it, Ava Mae. Why did you have to get undressed?*

Harlow waited for her twin to snap back with some comment, but the response never came. Frowning, she pulled her focus inward. The hollow place Ava Mae had once filled was empty again. Ava Mae seemed to be well and truly gone. Had she gotten stuck in the pond? Was hers the soul that the witches' magic had stolen? Was that the icy shock she'd felt as she'd been thrown back through the pond? Cy *had* said it was a holding pit for souls, after all.

Harlow leaned forward to gaze into the pond. The water was black and glittering beneath the newly risen moon. Here and there a few koi swam lazily. Nothing indicated the pond was anything more than a pond but somewhere under there, Cy was trapped.

With a sigh, she sat back and stared at the house once more. Three figures were visible through the sheer curtains, so all the witches were in there. And judging by the fact that her clothes were gone, they probably felt confident she wasn't getting out of their trap. She lifted her chin. Let them think that. It meant she had the upper hand.

She tried to focus on that as she kept to the shadows and made her way to the garden wall. Gaze still on the house, she reached for the latch on the garden gate. The metal burned her fingers. She yanked them back, hissing softly. Wearing gloves all the time had made her forget that iron hurt. Getting through the gate wasn't going to be fun. She took a deep breath, yanked the gate as wide open as she dared and slipped through. Welts swelled on her fingers where she'd made contact. The gate clanged shut behind her.

Startled by the noise, she ran into the darkness, hoping she'd see a street she recognized or a patrolling police car, anything to guide her home.

⚜

Zara's head jerked up. "What was that?"

Giselle frowned. "I didn't hear anything." Holding the necessary spells for the chaos magic was wearing Zara's nerves threadbare. Giselle worried the work required for the *ruina vox totem* was too much for her sister.

Ian tucked his hands behind his head where he lounged on the couch, watching some game on the holovision. Thankfully, he'd kept the sound low. "I didn't, either."

Zara went to the window and pulled back the sheers to stare into the darkness of the garden. "I heard *something*."

"Maybe it was the holovision," Ian said.

Zara needed comforting, assuring. Anything they could do to keep her stress free. Giselle motioned at Ian. "Make Zara a cup of tea, would you?"

"On it." He got off the couch.

Giselle turned to her sister. "Please rest. You've had a long day and there are more long days to come. I'll check the garden. It was probably just a neighbor's cat getting into your catnip bed again."

Zara turned away from the window. "Maybe you're right." Her shoulders dropped and the creases in her forehead smoothed out. "Thank you." She went back to her chair.

Giselle opened one of the French doors. Ian shot her a concerned look as he went into the kitchen. "I won't be long."

She closed the door behind her and let her eyes adjust to the dark. What she could see of the garden looked just as they'd left it. She strolled the stone path that led to the pond. The water rippled in the breeze, but was otherwise undisturbed. A few of the koi surfaced as she neared, their mouths gaping for food.

Ignoring them, she surveyed the whole of the property, her gaze finally stopping on the gate. The tall rectangle of wrought iron sat oddly. The swirls and twists of the metal were so thick and intricate, there was little space for anyone on the outside to see through. Still, she went to inspect it. And found it unlatched. From the inside.

She slipped through and checked the street in both directions. Nothing. Back inside, she studied the pond and garden again. There was no way anyone could get out of the pool once they'd gone through. Was there? She couldn't imagine how. After Zara had designed the pit, Giselle had overlaid a numbing spell on it so that anyone inside would become too lethargic to attempt escape. She stared at the pond. She'd created that spell for humans. She hadn't considered how long it might take to affect a fae.

Regardless, it *would* work. None of their gathered souls had escaped. The gate was merely an oversight. Zara was so tired lately, she'd probably left it unlatched herself. Or maybe Ian had done it. Giselle brought the bar down into the slot, secured the door and made her way back to the house.

They only had two more souls left to gather and by tomorrow, they'd have them. Now was not the time to become scared of their shadows. None of them, Zara included, needed the pressure of paranoia. One more added stress and Zara might crack. Then there would be no chaos magic at all and their hard work would be for nothing.

She went back into the house, locking the French door behind her.

Zara looked up from her tea. "Did you find anything?"

Giselle gave her a warm, reassuring smile. "Nothing at all."

Chapter Ten

Augustine came to with every inch of his body throbbing in pain. He blinked, trying to get his bearings. Not in the warehouse anymore—

"He's awake! Thank the Lord, he's awake." Lally leaned over him. "Lay still, Augie, you're hurt bad."

Two more faces appeared behind hers. Fenton. And Grantham. The scent of old paper and leather told him they were in the library. Being back on home turf was good, but not enough to quell his anger.

"You." Augustine jabbed his finger at Grantham. The small movement created a wave of pain that rippled through him. "What the hell happened back there? Did you know what they were planning?"

"Look at me," Grantham said. His right eye was swollen and his lip was split. "Do I look like I knew what they were planning? Damn Pellimento's thugs."

"I will *kill* Sutter the next time I see him. Maybe the senator, too." Augustine swung his legs off the couch and onto the floor. New pain erupted as his feet touched down. A wash of nausea caused his mouth to water with the urge to vomit. He took a deep breath and dug his fingers into the couch cushions until it passed. Rings of red, blistered skin encircled his wrists where the iron shackles had been.

Fenton shifted nervously. "Augustine, I understand you're upset. And with good reason. What those men did to you and

Detective Grantham was abhorrent. We will find a way to make them pay, but killing one of Pellimento's men, even threatening to kill Pellimento—"

Lally stepped in front of Fenton, hands on her hips. "Lay *down*, Augustine. Near as I can tell, you've got a couple of broken ribs, one of your horns is chipped and your face is swollen up like a birthday balloon. Fenton called the fae doctor."

Fenton nodded. "Yes, Dr. Carlson is on his way."

Lally pursed her mouth. "And you ain't going nowhere till he sees you."

Augustine stood, creating more nausea and freshening the pain that had begun to subside. "I'll heal, Lally. Right now, Harlow's in trouble." He looked at Fenton. "Cy was tailing her. He called me to say that something bad was going down, but Sutter skinned my com cell off and I lost the call. Have you heard from him? What happened?" He dropped his head to look Fenton straight in the eyes. "More importantly, where is Harlow?"

"I haven't heard from him." Fenton paled. "And I have no idea where Harlow is. I didn't know any of this was going on."

"There was no way you could." He looked at Lally. "Any sign of her?"

Lally shook her head. "She hasn't been home all day. With Ava Mae acting all uppity, I just figured she was out doing who knows what." She covered her mouth with her hand. "That poor girl."

Growling in frustration as much as pain, Augustine patted himself down. His coat and sword had been removed. "Where's my coat? My LMD was in the pocket and I need it. I've got a chip on the Bentley. I can at least track the car. Fenton, call Cy."

Fenton nodded and pulled out his LMD as he moved to a corner of the library.

Lally ran out of the room and came back with his coat. She

dug in the pocket and fished out his LMD, handing it to him. "Here. Find our girl."

"That's the plan." He listed to one side, righting himself with a small effort that made him wince. He definitely had at least one broken rib.

She tipped her chin at the couch. "Sit down before you fall over."

"Augustine." Fenton pushed his glasses up, the hand holding his LMD trembling. "Cy's not answering."

Augustine slumped onto the couch, his pain numbed by the soul-deep feeling that something very bad had happened. "Call Dulce. Call Sydra. Call—"

"I have," Fenton said. "I've sent a text to all of them."

A noise sounded from the back of the house. The kitchen door maybe. Lally patted Augustine's arm. "That must be the doctor. I'll bring him right in."

As she left, Augustine checked the tracker he'd put on the Bentley. "The car is parked in the Quarter." He looked up at Fenton and Grantham. "Harlow was meeting with Ogun today. You can add him to the list of people I'm going to kill if—"

"Augie! Augie! Come quick!" Lally's joyous shrieks tore through the house. "Praise the Lord, she's home!"

Augustine didn't wait for further explanation. He leaped off the couch and sped to the kitchen, Fenton and Grantham behind him. He skidded to a stop, the pain catching up to him a moment later. Ava Mae stood in the middle of the room in nothing but a purple lace bra and underwear, hair wet, makeup smeared.

Lally came back into the room with a bathrobe. "Here, let's get this on you."

Fenton and Grantham both made awkward noises and turned around.

Augustine was as done with Ava Mae and her antics as a

person could be. He was also done pretending he didn't know that Ava Mae had taken over Harlow's body. Anger fueled his words. "Listen to me, Ava Mae. I don't know where the hell you've been or what you've been up to, but coming back here like this is unaccepta—"

With a soft whimper, she lunged for him, catching him off guard as she wrapped her arms around him. "It's me, Harlow. I swear it. Ask me anything, but I promise Ava Mae's gone. At least I think she is. She might still be in the witch's pond with Cy and Rufus. I'm pretty sure the witches tried to kill me. Either way, they're up to something bad. Very bad." Harlow looked up at him, her amber eyes filled with emotion but not a trace of the bottomless black he'd come to associate with Ava Mae. "It's so good to be me again, but it's even better to be me again with you." She sighed wearily. "Did that even make sense?" Her face screwed into a questioning expression. "What on earth happened to you? You look like you were in an accident."

Harlow was in his arms. He smiled, despite the pain her hug was causing him. Hell, he'd stand this way for hours if she wanted, even if she did smell like an old mud puddle. "Yes, it made sense. I'm thrilled you're you again. I'm not sure I understand about Cy and the witches' pond, but we can figure that all out. What happened to me is not important. You're home. *You're* back. That's what matters. Although, I'd love to hear how you got rid of Ava Mae. Queen Jewelia said it would take dark magic to free you." He bent to kiss her, but reeled back as the pain almost blacked him out.

She pushed him into a chair. "Sit down before you fall down." She cupped his face gently and kissed his mouth. "I missed you so much," she whispered.

"Me too you," he whispered back, the pleasure of her mouth a fair trade for the throbbing ache of his body.

"As soon as you feel able, I need to hear more about what

Queen Jewelia said about dark magic." She shivered. "That falls right in line with what—"

The doorbell rang.

Harlow looked toward the front of the house. "Who's that?"

"Probably Dr. Carlson." Fenton cleared his throat. "I'll bring him in."

"Doctor?" Harlow let Augustine go and stepped back. "I assume that's for you?"

Lally pushed a chair next to Augustine and directed Harlow toward it. "Yes. Sit, child. Augie's in a bad way. As you can see."

"I'm not—"

Lally didn't let him finish. "We think he's got a couple of broken ribs from the beating he took. And you can see his face."

"Beating?" Harlow's eyes widened as she sat beside him, her hands soft on his thigh. She seemed incapable of not touching him. If he felt better, he'd be reciprocating. She leaned in. "Who beat you? No discussion later. I want to know now. Then we need to figure out what to do about Cy and all the other souls trapped in that pond."

While the doctor examined him, Augustine explained about Pellimento, her loathing of all things fae, her missing son and how the police weren't getting very far with any of the missing persons cases.

Lally sat nearby while Fenton stood, both allowing enough space for the doctor to work. Harlow listened intently. "How many tourists have disappeared?"

Before Augustine could answer, Dr. Carlson pulled out a tablet from his bag, then gestured at him. "Shirt off, please."

Augustine shook his head. "Getting my arms over my head isn't currently an option. Cut it off me." He went back to Harlow's question as the doc set the tablet down, took out scissors and went to work. "At last count, six."

Harlow's mouth opened slightly and she shook her head, her

gaze drifting to the silver brand on his chest that marked him as Guardian. "I know where they are."

A hush fell over the room and everyone except for Dr. Carlson looked at her. He was busy scanning Augustine with the tablet, making little noises and nodding.

"Where?" Augustine prompted. His patience was thinning, but that was because of the pain, not Harlow.

"They're the souls in the witches' pond. In the holding pit. There were six people already in there when I fell in, then they threw Rufus Ogun in after me and then Cy, but Cy said he heard one of the witches say something about ten down, two more to go. Whatever they're planning, they need twelve souls for it."

"Father Ogun. That stupid fool." Augustine thought a moment. "Sounds to me like the witches knew you had Ava Mae inside you somehow."

Harlow looked appalled. "Because that's what Ogun took Ava Mae there for—so she could get rid of me and have my body to herself."

The doctor shot a quick glance at Harlow, then went back to work. Let him wonder. He didn't need to know what had happened. Augustine growled in disgust. "Unbelievable. They were all working together. Although Ogun got the short end of that deal. Not surprisingly." He glanced at Grantham. "We might need Jewelia again. And now we should be able to return Pellimento's son to her and get her men out of our city." He tried to turn to see Fenton and groaned.

Dr. Carlson shook his head and flipped the tablet around so Augustine could see the bone scan. "You have one broken rib and two cracked ones. I need to bind them but they're still going to hurt until they heal. Even with our fae metabolism, that will take two or three days. Bed rest would be—"

"Out of the question. I've got too much to do to lie around.

I can handle the pain." Augustine held his arms out as far as he could without passing out in agony. "So bind me up. I've—" He grinned at Harlow. He was done leaving her out of anything. "I mean, *we've* got some planning to do. After we rescue the people from that holding pit, our next job is to put these witches in their place once and for all."

Fenton chimed in as Dr. Carlson started wrapping a mesh bandage around Augustine's torso. "I won't argue about including Harlow, but we've got to be smart about this, Augustine. There are human lives at stake. If this isn't done right, there's no telling what the witches will do."

"Agreed," Grantham said. "I want to rescue those people as much as anyone else, but I'd like to get a team together, maybe call in SWAT."

Augustine considered it. "So long as the fae play lead on this. The witches are human, but they're still more powerful than your guys." He lowered his arms as Dr. Carlson finished the binding.

Grantham nodded. "I'm sure that'll be fine. I know the fae have an understanding with the NOPD about these kinds of things."

Harlow raised her hand. "I feel horrible about this with Cy trapped in there, but if I don't get a few hours of sleep, I'm going to be worthless. Being stripped of Ava Mae has left me feeling..." She shook her head. "I'm just worn-out. Having said that, if you think it's best we go now and try to take advantage of the element of surprise, I'm there."

"I know you are." For the first time since she'd returned, Augustine took a hard look at her. Dark circles sat beneath her eyes and her usual spark was missing. "But a couple of hours of sleep isn't going to cause us to lose that advantage. We both need the sleep and I can do a lot of healing in a few hours. Who

knows, Cy might have this whole thing wrapped up by then."
Although Augustine doubted that. Cy was good, but none of
them had ever gone up against three witches at once.

"Excellent," Dr. Carlson said. He whipped out a short, silver
wand and tapped the blunt end into Augustine's naked shoulder.

It stung like a mother. "What was that?"

"Painkiller and a sedative." Dr. Carlson tucked the high-tech
syringe back into his bag. "You'll thank me when you wake up."

Fenton smiled conspiratorially. "And while you two are sleeping, Detective Grantham and I will make plans."

"I feel like I'm being ganged up on, but I'm going to let it
slide considering the circumstances." Augustine pushed to his
feet and offered his arm to Harlow, who took it to stand beside
him. Smiling down at her, looking into her eyes, the sense that
all would be right washed through him. He kept his gaze on her
as he spoke. "Besides, I have more important business."

⚜

They were on the second floor landing before either of them
spoke. Harlow started at the same time Augustine did. She
laughed softly. "You first."

"No, you." He nudged her with his elbow, then winced.

"You hurt pretty bad, huh?" She was thrilled to be reunited
with him, but ached that he was in so much pain. Her anger
at the men who'd done this to him simmered inside her like a
pot forgotten at the back of the stove. If she didn't deal with it
soon, it would boil over. Fortunately, dealing with Ava Mae had
schooled Harlow enormously about controlling and using her
emotions.

"Not as bad as I did before. Whatever the doc gave me has
taken the edge off." He grinned and his voice came out a husky

whisper. "I'm so glad you're back, sweetheart. I missed you so much. I love you, you know."

"I know. I remember that." She nodded, tickled by his drug-induced gushiness. "I love you, too. Which is the only reason I'm not going to give you grief about drugging me."

"I did it for your own good."

"I know that, too." She grinned, unable to contain the happiness of being beside him again.

His expression shifted toward sternness. "Those witches are going to pay." He shook his head. "None of those people deserve to be trapped in there. Cy especially."

"No, he doesn't. Maybe he and Ogun will come up with a way to get themselves out before we do."

"Ogun's a snake. A worthless, lying piece of garbage."

"Shh." She stroked his arm. "No point in getting yourself worked up right before you're supposed to be resting and healing. Save that for the battlefield."

As they rounded the landing toward his attic room, his brows knotted in surprise. "Are you sure you're the same Harlow you used to be? Because that Harlow never talked about battlefields unless it was that online game thing."

She laughed. "That was me, but so is this. The new me, I guess." Her smile faded. "Having Ava Mae inside me and in charge of things definitely changed me." She walked him to the bed. He sat and she kneeled to help him take off his boots.

He put a hand on her shoulder. "Changed you how?"

She looked up. Concern etched his face. She leaned back on her heels. There were no pretty words for the truth of what had happened. "Augie, I killed a man."

"That was Ava Mae."

"It was both of us." She turned away, feeling the sting of tears threatening to spill.

He patted the bed beside him. "Come sit, beautiful."

"Beautiful is sweet, but hardly accurate. I'm wearing Lally's old robe and smell like a fish tank." She took the spot he'd indicated anyway.

He stared into her eyes and nodded. His pupils were wide with the effects of the meds. "You don't smell good, but you're still pretty."

She laughed. "I feel like I should be asking you all kinds of things right now since the drugs he gave you apparently double as a truth serum."

Augustine shrugged lazily and lifted his hands. "What do ya wanna know?"

She rubbed her thumb over the broken tip of his horn. "Do you think you can stay awake long enough for me to take a shower?"

"Are you going to keep doing that?" His eyes took on a wicked glint.

"I might."

"If it means you're coming back here afterwards, all cleaned up, then yes, I can stay awake."

Barely suppressing another laugh, she answered, "Yes, all cleaned up. I just... want to be close to you."

"Oh yeah." He grimaced from the effort of nodding. "I'll be bright-eyed and... awake."

She doubted that.

He raised a finger. "On one condition."

He was really slurring his words now. "What's that?"

The finger went to his cheek. "Kiss me."

She played coy. "On the cheek?"

"No," he growled, struggling to move his finger to his lips. "Here."

"I can do that." She leaned forward and took his hand, lacing her fingers with his as their mouths collided. His raw emotion spilled into her through his skin, a sweet fog of love and happiness laced with threads of pain and anger that he hadn't done more for her. She almost lost it right then. She pressed her mouth to his and like a thirsty woman finding water, she drank him in, this man who loved her. This man who'd fought for her. This man she was about to fight beside.

He kissed her back with the eager sincerity of a teenage boy in love for the first time, no doubt brought on by the drugs, but in the moment, it was the perfect kind of response. She needed to be wanted with that kind of abandon, to know that she was his whole focus, the center of his world. He didn't disappoint.

Those emotions flowed into her, suffusing her with a pure, bright joy and making her whole again. The emptiness that had plagued her life was gone. She was no longer the wounded child who feared being touched and shied away from interaction. For all of Ava Mae's destructiveness, she had made Harlow stronger.

With a soft nibble on Augustine's bottom lip, she gently broke the kiss, but held the contact by touching her forehead to his. "Thank you," she whispered.

"For what?"

"For not giving up on me." She pulled back to see his face.

His lids were heavy, but his face shone with happiness. "I would never give up on you." His smile broadened. "Or us."

She returned his grin. "We do make a great team." She eased him back until his head hit the pillow, then she stood and hoisted his legs onto the bed. She unlaced his boots and pulled them off. "I'm going to shower, but I'll be right back, okay?"

No answer. He was already asleep.

She kissed him one last time, then slipped out to her room on the floor below. The clothes that Ava Mae had purchased lay in piles here and there, but otherwise, everything was pretty much the same. She'd return most of it, but that could wait for a day when Cy and the rest of the trapped souls were freed and there was peace in the city.

She reached for one of the nighties Ava Mae had picked out. This one wasn't too bad, a slip of teal green that was as soft and light as a feather. Might be nice to sleep in something like that. Not as nice as Ava Mae being gone. She started for the bathroom, ready to stand under a long, hot shower when a thought struck her immobile.

Ava Mae was out of Harlow's body, but chances were good she was still stuck in the well of souls. And if they freed the souls trapped in the pond and Ava Mae was still down there, what did that mean for Harlow?

The shower would have to wait. Harlow needed to talk to the only person she could think of who might have the answer for that.

The keeper of the lightning tree. Lally.

Chapter Eleven

Fenton and Grantham were still in the library talking and from the sounds of it, Dulcinea and Sydra had joined them. Plans were being made. That made Harlow happy, but she'd be happier when she had a few of her own in place.

She rapped softly on Lally's door. "Lally? You still up?"

The door opened a few seconds later. "Child, what are you doing not in bed? You should be showered and asleep." But Lally moved to let her in anyway. "What can I do for you? Does Augie need something?"

Harlow entered and shut the door behind her. "He's passed out cold, he's fine. I need to talk to you because honestly, I don't know who else to go to."

Concern creasing her forehead, Lally nodded. "Of course. I'm always here when you need me. C'mon and sit down." Lally led her to the small sitting area near the window and sat. Harlow joined her. "What's troubling you?"

Harlow quickly explained her theory about Ava Mae being in the holding pit. "She was already weak, so I don't know if it's possible but if it is..."

Lally's hand went to the charms around her neck. She caressed the locket, rubbing it between her fingers. "She was far away from the tree. Weak enough to lose her grip on you. But that doesn't mean weak enough to fade away." Lally took a slow breath. "As much as I know about the tree and its power, I'd say she's still in that pit. The shock of going through that magic was enough to make her lose her hold on you and from what you were saying, she was already slipping."

"So freeing everyone inside it would free her, too?"

Lally tipped her head to one side like she was considering that. "It could. And that would not be good. She would find her way into someone else. Force that person to make their way back here, back to the tree."

"What if that person was one of the witches?"

Lally's brows rose. "That would be especially not good."

"So how do I fix this?"

"We, child. You're not alone in this." Lally smiled. "I have an idea but it's not going to be easy. Dangerous, in fact."

"I don't care. I would do anything to keep her from taking over another person. I want to be done with her." Harlow leaned forward. "What do I have to do?"

Lally lowered her voice and her gaze shifted toward a door on the far wall. "I'm gonna have to get a piece of the tree, but that's not the hard part." She took a breath. "You're gonna have to go back to the witches' and put that piece in the pond."

Harlow sat back, her body tensing. "I don't know if I can go back there." The thought of ending up back in that pond, or worse, with Ava Mae inside her again, sent a shudder of fear through her. But Cy needed her. All those other people trapped in that well of souls needed her. And if putting a piece of the tree into the pond meant she'd never have to deal with the twisted thing the tree had turned her sister into, then Harlow was just going to have to dig deep and find a way to do it. She lifted her head to look at Lally.

Lally's gaze held compassion. "It's a scary thing, ain't it? Returning to a place where so much bad happened to you. I understand not wanting to go. I guess I can—"

"No, Lally, you can't do this." Harlow blew out a breath, forcing the fear out of her system. "I can do it. I don't want to and

I don't like the idea, but if it's what has to be done...I'll find a way. Can you explain why?"

"Sure. Putting a bit of the tree in there should take care of things. Ava Mae is weak right now—she ain't got you and the tree is too long a way off to help her. She's nothing but a loose spirit looking for a new home. We're going to give it to her. That way, if she breaks free of the witches' magic, the branch will act like a magnet, drawing her to it and containing her the way a new body would. It should last until you and Augie can retrieve it."

"Then what?"

A dark light shone in Lally's eyes. "Then we burn it, child. Then she can't be a bother to anyone ever again."

"And if it doesn't last until we can retrieve it?"

Lally stared at her hands for a moment. "That's the downside. It might give her enough strength to get back inside someone else, but I have a feeling you and Augie are going to keep those witches from getting any further with whatever it is they're planning."

Harlow stood. "Get me that piece. I'll do whatever I have to do to get it into the pond."

Lally got to her feet. "Going to take me a few. Go have your shower if you want." She glanced at the robe Harlow still wore. "At the very least, get yourself some clothes on."

⚜

"I know she's gone. That's the reason I came down here." Augustine tried to temper his anger, but the doctor's meds had given him a nightmare. Bad enough to wake him. When he'd realized Harlow wasn't beside him, he'd gone to look for her and found she wasn't in her bed, either. "Lally, where is she? Why do I feel like you're purposefully keeping something from me?"

"I'm not keeping anything from you. Harlow had to take care of something important."

"And she went alone?"

"Yes." Lally crossed her arms.

"Why?

"Because she didn't need an old woman tagging along and you sure weren't in any shape to help her."

He shoved a hand through his hair. The drugs were still in his system, but fading fast. His anger had probably amped up his metabolism. Both were contributing factors to the fresh pain throbbing like a second heartbeat in his body. "Lally, I'm in no mood for this. Where is she?"

Lally sighed and pursed her mouth in a resigned sort of way. "She's gone to the witches' to—"

"What? Why the hell would she go back there?"

Challenge filled Lally's gaze. "I sent her. And if you'd let me finish, I'll tell you why."

"I wish you would." He couldn't believe that Lally, of all people, had done something so stupid. If there wasn't an amazingly good reason, he was going to lose it.

Lally filled him in on the particulars.

It didn't help his mood. "She's going back to the pond."

"Yes. You gonna yell at me?"

"No. I don't have time. I'll be back when I'm back." He brushed past her and slipped into his half form as soon as he stepped outside of the house. His half form was a creation more smoke and shadow than flesh and blood. In the dark of night, it rendered him nearly invisible, but even better, it allowed him to move silently and right now, he needed quiet speed. It also seemed to take the edge off his pain.

He took off toward the witches' house, slowing only as Harlow came into view. She'd flattened herself against the high stucco wall that surrounded Zara's property and contained the garden. He sidled up beside her, shifted back into his solid form and slipped his hand over her mouth while whispering in her ear. "Harlow, it's me. Don't make any noise. I'm here to help."

Eyes wide, she turned to see him, her pulse thumping in his ears. As soon as her gaze landed on him, she relaxed.

He pulled his hand away, careful to keep his voice low. "What the hell are you doing here?"

"I should ask you the same thing," she whispered back. "You're supposed to be all drugged up and resting. I guess Lally told you what I was doing."

"She told me enough."

Harlow sighed and tipped her head back against the stucco. "What happened to the drugs the doctor gave you?"

"I have a fast metabolism." Made faster by his ill temper. "They're mostly gone." His ribs were killing him and the pain had been amplified by the running he'd just done. But he wasn't about to let her do something like this on her own. "Lally said you had to get back in the garden to drop the branch into the water and keep Ava Mae from hurting anyone else."

"That's the short version." She explained further what it might mean if Ava Mae really was still in the well of souls. "Lally thinks putting a piece of the lightning tree into the pond will draw Ava Mae like a magnet and then we can recover the piece when we take the witches down. Lally will take it from there."

"That's all well and good, but there's got to be an easier way. One that doesn't involve sneaking onto Zara's property."

"You can't just fling the branch over the wall and hope for the best. The only way to make sure it's in the water is to go into the garden and do it properly." She frowned at him. "I'll give you thirty seconds to come up with something better, then I'm headed in." She edged toward the tall iron gate. Even from here, it made his skin crawl.

He ground his teeth together. "No."

She stopped and looked back at him. "No what?" she hissed.

"You're not going in." He glanced at the top of the wall. "I am." He held out his hand. "Give me the branch. Look, I can easily jump that wall, then make myself virtually invisible once I get on the other side. I'll drop the stick in and be back here before you know it."

She looked like she was about to argue.

He sighed. "You should have let me do this in the first place."

"I was trying to let you heal."

He softened his tone. "I appreciate that, but you're also at risk here—what if Ava Mae was just waiting for you to come back so she could slip inside you again?"

Harlow's eyes rounded slightly as if that possibility hadn't occurred to her. "I'll let you do this on one condition."

"What?"

"We get home, you're going right back to bed. You need to heal."

That he did. "Agreed." He'd expected more of a fight, but then maybe Zara's pond wasn't a place Harlow was eager to visit again.

He must have been right because her shoulders dropped like a weight had been removed from them. "Lally wants a soil sample, too."

"For what?"

Harlow shrugged. "Said she wanted to know what she was dealing with." She reached into her jacket and pulled out a long narrow thing tied up in an old scarf. "Here's the piece of the tree." He reached for it but she pulled it away before he could grab it. "Do *not* touch it under any circumstances."

"Got it." This time she let him take it. He stuck it in the back pocket of his jeans.

She handed him a little plastic sandwich bag. "For the soil."

"Thanks." He tucked that in a front pocket. "Anything else?"

She made a strange face. "Yes." Then went up on her tiptoes and kissed his mouth. "Be careful. Remember Cy's in there."

"I know. That part's killing me."

"Me, too."

"Okay." He gave her a little nod goodbye. "I'll see you at home."

She frowned. "You'll see me right here. I'm not going anywhere until you're done."

"Stubborn as your mother," he muttered.

She squinted at him, the moonlight turning her eyes almost colorless. "I heard that."

"Back in a few." He took a couple of steps away, then sprang over the wall.

He bent his knees as he landed, but the impact, even on grass, forced him to stifle a groan as his ribs protested. He fell forward onto his knees and stayed there, waiting a few breaths to make sure he hadn't tripped some kind of witchcraft alarm system. The house remained dark.

He returned to his transparent half form and crept toward the pond, keeping in the tree shadows as much as possible for good measure. The moon wasn't full, but it was bright enough to see by and he didn't want to risk it. When he got to within feet of the water, he dropped to the ground and crawled the rest of the way. His ribs made it slow going, but he gutted it out.

At the pond's edge, he stopped behind a clump of tall, feathery grasses. He stared through them into the water. Slivers of white and orange undulated beneath the surface. Koi, he realized. Hard to imagine that this pond was really more of a hellmouth and that somewhere under that water was one of his lieutenants.

He took the branch from his pocket and unwrapped it until he held it in two scarf-draped fingers. It was black and sooty and smelled of ash and dark magic. He tossed it into the pond. With a small splash it hit the water and sank. Little ripples rode toward his hiding place. He stuffed the scarf back into his pocket.

Not wanting to be there longer than he had to, he used the dagger in his boot to pry up a chunk of earth, bagged it and made his way back to the wall. He leaped over, and again the landing sent new jolts of agony through him. He hissed out a breath and leaned back against the wall until the pain dissipated, somehow managing not to pass out.

"Are you okay?" she whispered.

He nodded, trying to breathe through the dull ache that had taken hold of his entire body. If she thought he was going to put up a fight about going back to bed, she was dead wrong. He might fall asleep before he made it to bed. He slumped against the stucco wall. Exhaustion and pain had begun to shut his body down. "Dropped the stick in. Dirt's in the bag."

"You look like crap."

He felt like crap. The best he could do was nod.

Without another word, she looped his arm around her shoulders and started walking him back to the house.

Chapter Twelve

Morning light spilled through the door as Ian came in from the garden. Giselle was just pouring her first cup of coffee. They'd both spent the night at Zara's. With them being so close to finishing the preparations for the *ruina vox totem,* it made sense. And if she was truthful, she worried that leaving Zara alone would cause her sister to crack under the pressure of maintaining the ancillary spells necessary for the chaos magic to be viable.

Wiping out all fae magic would be a triumph, but not if she lost her sister in the process.

He lifted his gaze toward the ceiling. "She still sleeping?"

"Yes. I thought it best to let her get as much as possible."

He poured a cup of coffee. "It's wearing on her, isn't it?" He shook his head. "And that's wearing on you."

She stirred in a spoonful of sugar. "She'll be fine and so will I." Becoming close to Zara again had made Giselle protective of her, like when they were children, but they weren't children; they were adults. Giselle couldn't force Zara to do anything she didn't want to. Like admitting the strain of the spellwork was too much. Although, it wasn't like Ian couldn't see it for himself. "I hope."

"I could give her some more ink. Increasing her power couldn't hurt."

Giselle sipped her coffee. "You can ask her, but she's already stressed with maintaining these spells...I don't know if adding pain, however brief the duration, would be the right thing to do."

"Maybe not." He set his cup down. The black liquid gleamed with his reflection. He hooked his thumb toward the garden. "We're ready as soon as she's up."

"Who'd you get?"

"Couple of transients camped out by the river. No one will miss them."

Giselle straightened. One of the reasons they'd been selectively choosing people was to not only pick those who wouldn't be missed but also those who were of sound mind. "You're sure they're in good shape mentally?"

He shrugged. "A soul's a soul, right? Does it matter if the gray matter is fully functioning?"

With a sigh, she shook her head. "Actually, it might, but at this stage of things what matters more is getting this spell cast so Zara can rest."

"What's your plan after the fae are powerless?"

She took another long, slow sip, buying herself some time. Her plans were numerous, but for the most part, they'd only been shared with Zara. And they'd both agreed not to tell Ian about the lightning tree, which would be their first stop. Every witch in the parish would want a piece of that tree for themselves. It was imperative that she and Zara take control of Augustine's house and secure the tree as soon as possible. She smiled. "Getting rid of the Guardian will be our first priority."

Ian smirked. "You think he's noticed his little girlfriend is missing yet?"

"It's not much past dawn. Augustine doesn't strike me as an early riser. I'd say not yet." Besides that, she suspected the senator might be keeping him busy with some issues of her own.

"What's not yet?" Zara leaned against the open doorway into

the kitchen. Dark smudges shadowed her eyes. For a green witch who spent most of her time outdoors, she was terribly pale.

Giselle turned. "We were talking about Augustine figuring out Harlow was missing. How are you? I thought you'd sleep longer."

"I tried." Zara smiled weakly. "Holding this spell is like having a loose tooth. It's impossible to ignore for any length of time."

"I got the last two souls," Ian offered. "We can cast them in whenever you're ready."

She yawned and nodded. "That would be good. Once that's done, I can lock the pit. That'll take some of the pressure off." She glanced at Giselle. "I know you're eager to cast the *ruina vox totem,* but I worry that if I don't sleep before we do that, I might make a misstep and that could be fatal."

"Agreed. You should sleep. In fact, I insist. We'll get these last souls in, then you can go back to bed for the rest of the day. Casting the spell at twilight will only strengthen it. Chaos magic thrives on the in-between hours anyway. How about that?"

"That sounds great." Zara tightened her robe. "Let's go do it."

"Don't you want a cup of coffee or anything?"

"Not if I'm going back to bed." She slipped on the shoes she kept by the French doors and headed for the garden.

Giselle and Ian followed. Two men lay on the stone path at the front edge of the pond, struggling as if bound with rope, but Ian had used magic so nothing physically held them, making their struggles oddly comical. If not for the terror in their eyes, they would have looked like Jackson Square mimes. "Ian, would you do the honors?"

"Of course." He positioned himself by the two men, taking the spot that would also allow him to toss the men into the pond, since they obviously couldn't walk in on their own power.

She and Zara moved around the opposite sides until they were as far from each other as they were from Ian. Zara yawned as she spread her arms, then began the incantation to open the mouth of the pit. As she worked, Giselle inhaled the morning air. Zara's garden always had the most pleasurable aroma of earth and flowers. The sweet olives were in bud, adding to the honeyed perfume surrounding them. Something splashed near her feet. A frog, probably. She glanced down but all that remained were a few ripples.

She narrowed her focus. Something had dug into the dirt beside the pond. A chunk of soil was missing in a purposeful shape. Not like something left behind by an animal.

The sharp pull of magic brought her head back up. Faint lines of power danced blue and purple and green off Zara's body, connecting her to Ian and Giselle. The pull increased as the lines flowed through both of them and connected, completing the circle.

At last, Zara's attention shifted from the heavens to the water's surface. "Ready," she whispered, the strain of the spellwork evident in her thready tone.

"Hurry, Ian," Giselle said. Zara needed to rest.

With a nod, he used one hand to raise the first bound man into the air. The man went still as he hovered in the air, then his struggling resumed with great force. Ian guided him to the pond's center, then jerked his hand closed, breaking the link.

The man plunged into the pond. His head disappeared below and the now-familiar flash of light filled the water as though the sun had exploded in the depths of the pond.

Ian wasted no time in doing the same with the other man, who whimpered and moaned until he too vanished into the pond.

They held the spell as Zara uttered the final phrases to close the well of souls. As the last words left her mouth, her eyes rolled back into her head and she collapsed.

Giselle and Ian ran to her, meeting on their knees at Zara's side. Ian scooped her into his arms. Her head lolled to one side. "I'll carry her up to bed."

Giselle ran ahead to open the door. "I wish there was something I could do." Zara was as pale as ashes. Casting the *ruina vox totem* tonight might not be an option if she didn't have the strength.

"You could smudge her room. Clear out any lingering stress from these past days. Other than that, she just needs to rest." He started for the stairs.

"I'll get some sage." She followed him up but veered off into the altar room to collect her things. She bundled the sage, her thoughts returning to the divot by the pond. It was nothing to worry about. There were lots of explanations for a hole like that. Things like... nothing she could think of.

Maybe the stress of preparing for the chaos spell was getting to her, too. Or maybe it was the worrying over Zara.

"You okay?"

She jumped. "Ian, you startled me."

He frowned. "You followed me up here." He came to her side, taking the sage out of her fingers and holding her hands between his own calloused ones. There was comfort in the roughness of his skin, his familiar scent and willing spirit. "Hey, we're all a little on edge. I know you're worried about Zara, but she's going to be okay."

She wanted to agree, but that would be a lie. "You know our mother died performing chaos magic."

Sympathy filled his gaze. "I had no idea. The coven was told... well, you know what the coven was told."

She nodded. Her father had covered their mother's death by telling everyone it had been suicide. "I don't want to lose Zara the same way."

He lifted one hand to cup her cheek. "You won't. There are

three of us and we are strong, powerful spell casters. We've done everything right in our preparations and will continue to do everything right. The risk has been minimized." He smiled broadly and her fears retreated. "An hour after the sun sets, the fae will be running scared and the witches will once again be in control."

"I hope you're right. Perhaps I should work on the sigil." It had to be drawn perfectly. In their blood, on virgin unbleached paper. A single error or wobbled line could throw the whole spell off.

"There is time for that." He brushed his lips against hers. "You are about to become the Queen of New Orleans, my Lady."

Despite what she'd been feeling a moment ago, she smiled. "What does that make you? The prince?"

His grin turned wicked. "I would much rather be your consort than your prince. My talents deal with pleasure, not diplomacy."

"I'm aware of your talents."

He laced his fingers with hers and brought the back of her hand to his mouth. "Then you should also be aware that they are *always* at your disposal."

His warm breath on her knuckles raised goose bumps on her skin. "I am."

"Are you sure?" He nipped the skin on her wrist, causing a soft moan to escape her lips. "I'm worried you may have forgotten everything I'm capable of doing for you, my Lady."

"Maybe you should remind me after I smudge Zara's room."

"Maybe I'll remind you first, then we'll smudge her room together." He kissed his way to her elbow.

Every pleasure point in her body came alive under his touch. It was hard to remember why she'd even come in here. "I... think that would be okay."

"It will be more than okay, my Lady."

She smiled as he led her out of the altar room and down the hall to the guest bedroom, but her attention was pulled briefly toward the closed door of Zara's room. She sobered a bit as they passed it.

She might as well take her pleasure now. Come twilight, she and Zara could very well suffer the same fate their mother had. Death by chaos magic.

Not even Ian's willing mouth and skillful hands could erase that thought from her mind.

⚜

The kitchen was empty when Harlow came down, but the coffee was brewing and there was a pan of sausages in the oven, so Lally was definitely awake. The only other indicator that Lally had been in the kitchen was that the bag of dirt from the witches' garden was no longer sitting on the counter where Augustine had dropped it on their way in last night.

Harlow was getting eggs out of the fridge when Lally walked in. "Morning."

"Morning, Harlow. I was just checking on Augie, but I'll get to the rest of breakfast now."

Harlow wasn't that hungry, but her body needed the fuel. There was too much to do today to run on empty. The smell of the sausages baking was helping her work up an appetite, though. "How's he doing?"

"Still asleep." Lally moved to the stove and took out a pan. "Go sit, I've got this."

But Harlow didn't move. "How can he still be asleep?"

"I made him some tea."

"Yeah, but the doctor gave him drugs and they wore off in a little over an hour."

Lally smiled. "The doctor gave him something to *help* him sleep. I gave him something to *make* him sleep."

Harlow suppressed a grin as she took her coffee to the table. "He's not going to like that."

"I don't care." She started cracking eggs into a bowl. "I'm his elder and a traiteuse. I know what's best for that boy and right now, it's to sleep and heal. He's going to be worthless otherwise, and there's a war coming." She stared out the window for a moment. "I can feel it in my blood."

Harlow cupped her hands around her mug but even the heat coming through the ceramic couldn't shake the chill of Lally's words. "I'm sure you're right. Unfortunately, I have no idea how to prepare for it. I've only just learned how to control my gifts beyond the most basic of ways. I'm not sure I'm going to be any help to Augustine when it comes to fighting the witches."

Whisk in hand, Lally nodded. "I worry about that for all of us. The witches are powerful. Too powerful, I think. And they've never had anything but hard feelings for the fae."

Harlow sipped her coffee, her thoughts spinning through her head faster than she could grasp them. "There's got to be something we can do. Some way to figure out what the witches are up to. Are there any witches who are friendly with the fae?"

Lally dumped the eggs into a pan and stirred them. "None who're gonna tell us what's about to go down." She shook her head. "It's never been that way between the witches and the fae. No cooperation. Just bad blood for a long, long time."

"What about the woman Augustine mentioned, the detective's grandmother?"

"Queen Jewelia?" Lally stopped stirring to look at Harlow, a strange light in her eyes. "What about her?"

"Maybe I should go see her." The idea of visiting a woman who was supposed to be a powerful voodoo sorceress intimidated

Harlow a little. Rufus Ogun had been ready to serve up her soul to the witches without any compunction. "If Augustine was going to talk to her, there's no reason I couldn't. Right?"

Lally nodded slowly and went back to stirring the eggs. "Sure enough."

"No reason I should be afraid of her, either. Right?"

Lally pursed her lips. "She's an extremely powerful voodoo mambo, so there's plenty reason to be afraid of Jewelia, but none that should be of any direct concern of yours."

"Well, that's...reassuring." Except that it wasn't. But help was help and any edge they could get would be valuable. "I guess I should call Fenton."

"Why's that?"

"So he can set things up."

"No need. I know Jewelia. We'll go see her after breakfast."

"That's great, but shouldn't we still call or something?"

Lally set plates out. "I can if you'd like, but there's no reason. For one thing, she'll be expecting us."

"She will?"

Lally pulled the sausages from the oven. "She knows things like that."

"And? I feel like there's a second thing."

"There is." Lally divided the scrambled eggs between the two plates, then went back for the sausages. "Jewelia's my niece and family doesn't need an invite. Now eat your breakfast and then we'll go."

She'd said it as if being related to a scary voodoo sorceress wasn't any big deal. Typical Lally. "So the detective is your great-nephew? And Jewelia is your sister's kid?"

"She's my mother's brother's child. Well, more removed than that, but close. Eat your breakfast before it gets cold."

Harlow smirked. Lally loved her murky details. Harlow spent the rest of the meal mulling over what meeting Jewelia would be like. Then a thought occurred to her. "Ava Mae can't get too far away from the tree unless she's got a body to host her."

Lally kept eating. "Mm-hmm."

"You said something about that once. Not being able to get too far away from the tree or you'd get sick."

"That's right." She drank some coffee, then added more hot sauce to her eggs.

"So how are you…" Harlow gestured toward the door. "I mean, are you going to be okay leaving the—wait a minute, you *are* going with me, right?"

"Yes, child." Lally set her fork down, then reached to her necklace and tapped a finger on the locket dangling from the gold chain around her neck. "I carry a little piece of the tree in here when I have to leave the house. I don't do it often, though. Even that tiny bit could cause trouble if it fell into the wrong hands."

"Does Jewelia know about the tree?"

"She does."

"Don't you worry about that?"

"No."

"Because she's family?"

The strange, hard light returned to Lally's eyes. "Because she knows the tree brings death and destruction. And she knows that I will level that same force against anyone who attempts to use the tree for their own purposes." Lally tipped her head to one side in a kind of nod. "Also because she's family."

"Okay then." Harlow finished her breakfast in silence. When she'd moved into the house after her mother's death, she'd thought Lally a kind, caring woman who'd not only befriended Olivia but put her own life on hold to look after her. And Lally remained that. She'd been Olivia's best friend, and still was, judging by the way the two had acted when Harlow had watched them reunite on the fae plane.

But the more Harlow came to know about Lally, the more she realized that Lally was much, much more than just her late mother's companion and housekeeper. So much more, Harlow's admiration for the woman had turned into what she imagined would be considered a "healthy fear." It made her wonder what would have happened if Ava Mae had tried to carry through with her threats to harm Lally.

Harlow could only guess that Ava Mae would have been the casualty of that conflict, not Lally. She took her plate to the sink. "I'll be ready in about ten minutes."

Lally nodded. "Sounds good to me. You'll have to drive, but I can show you the way."

"Not a problem." Lally was the last person Harlow was going to argue with.

Chapter Thirteen

Jewelia's house was a cute little place located in a neighborhood Lally called Treme. Harlow liked the house's soft blue exterior finished with white and the front porch with its squared columns. The yard was tidy and pots of flowering plants swung between the columns. The place had a welcoming air that eased her nerves but she was still glad she'd put gloves on. Who knew what she might touch in a mambo's home?

She stood at Lally's side and let the older woman ring the bell. This was her family, after all.

The door opened shortly and a much younger-looking woman than Harlow had expected stood on the other side of the screen. "Well, Tante Eulalie, as I live and breathe." She pushed the screen door wide. "Come in. I had a feeling you'd be stopping by."

Lally nodded. "I thought you might." She rested a hand on Harlow's shoulder. "This here's my friend Harlow Goodwin. Harlow, meet my grandniece, Queen Jewelia."

Jewelia's eyes lit up. "Well now, it's a true pleasure to meet you, Harlow. Come on in, I've got coffee cake and a fresh pot of coffee."

Harlow followed her into the house as Lally shut the front door. Cake was the last thing she wanted after a breakfast she hadn't been hungry for, but she got the sense that you didn't turn down that kind of offer in this kind of situation. The warm aroma of cinnamon and sugar that greeted her made the prospect a little less daunting. "That sounds lovely, thank you."

Jewelia guided them toward the kitchen table, which was already set for three. "You're the one that fae boy is in love with. He's a nice fellow. Very sincere. I take it you being here means your *problem* is resolved? The one with your sister?" She stared deeply into Harlow's eyes. "I can't sense anything improper going on inside you so I'd say yes."

Trying to hide her astonishment, Harlow nodded and took a seat. "You're right, my twin sister's spirit isn't possessing me anymore, thanks." Jewelia was definitely related to Lally.

Jewelia glanced at Harlow's gloves. "You've got the touch, too, I see. Best you keep those on in here."

Harlow tucked her folded hands onto her lap.

Lally swatted the younger woman on the shoulder. "Jewelia, enough. You're scaring the child." She took up the silver carafe and began filling cups. "Don't mind her, Harlow. She's trying to impress you right from the get-go. That's what mambos do so they can charge you extra based on how impressed you turn out to be."

"Now who's spinning yarn?" Jewelia sliced the crumbly, glazed Bundt cake working overtime as the table's centerpiece. "You're far scarier than I am, Tante." She added a thick slab of cake to Harlow's plate before dishing one out for Lally and then herself. At last, she sat. "So, Harlow, what sort of help do you need that brings you to my house?"

Harlow hadn't said anything about needing help, but the woman before her was clearly astute. She stuffed a bit of cake in her mouth to buy some time.

Lally rescued her. "The witches are planning something."

Jewelia nodded as though she was contemplating that bit of news. "So I've heard."

"The cake is delicious," Harlow piped up.

Jewelia smiled, taking another few years off her already impossibly young face. "Thank you."

Harlow took a breath and plunged in. "Have you heard anything else about what the witches might be planning?"

"No, but I'm guessing you have." Jewelia stirred sugar into her coffee. "What do you know?"

Harlow put her fork down and explained what had happened to her, about the souls, about the number being collected and about the others still trapped beneath the pond. There was no point holding back information now. "We've got to rescue those poor people."

"Ogun can stay in there for all I care, but the rest don't deserve it. One is fae, you say?"

"Yes. He's one of Augustine's lieutenants. And a good friend." She ached to think of Cy stuck down there.

Jewelia tipped her head to the side, her eyes narrowing slightly. "He may not be affected by the witches' spell, or at least not affected as greatly, but the humans…" She shook her head. "I'm not sure they can be saved."

Harlow leaned forward. "Why? What do you think the witches are going to do?"

Jewelia went quiet.

Lally folded her hands in her lap. "Out with whatever it is you're not saying, Jewelia. This is not a time to hold things back, girl."

"I'm not. Just trying to suss it all out." Jewelia sighed. "It doesn't sound good. For witches, a well of souls is a kind of battery. It's meant to power something greater. A spell they wouldn't otherwise be able to cast on their own. There's three of them, you say?"

Harlow nodded. "Two sisters and a man."

Tension pulled at Jewelia's mouth. "The power of three," she whispered. Her gaze went to Lally. "You know what this might be?"

"I have my suspicions." Lally reached into her purse, took

out the sandwich bag of dirt that Augustine had collected and dropped it on the table in front of Jewelia. "I thought maybe you could confirm them."

Harlow got the feeling that Lally would have made this visit with or without her. "What can that dirt tell you?"

"Maybe a lot." Jewelia picked up the bag. "Maybe nothing." She opened it and stuck her nose in, inhaling deeply. Her mouth went slack and she froze for a moment. Then her gaze lifted and she dropped the bag like it was poison. She crossed herself. "I never thought this would happen again so soon."

Desperation ate at Harlow's bones. "What is it?"

Jewelia's eyes flashed with anger. "Chaos magic."

"What does that mean? What will it do?" Panic echoed in Harlow's voice, but she couldn't help herself. Not knowing what a thing was capable of made it that much more frightening.

Jewelia breathed openmouthed. "It's bad business. It could strip the magic from the city."

"From the city?" Harlow sat back, the cool air of relief washing over her. "That's not so bad, is it?"

Jewelia looked at her. "Not if you're one of the witches, who will be protected from it. But all the rest of us, fae, varcolai and voodooer alike, will be powerless. All your fae abilities, gone. The varcolai won't be able to shift into their animal forms and none of my spells will mean a thing. The witches will take control of this city and they will wipe out all traces of the rest of us."

"You're sure about this."

"No."

Harlow took a breath, clinging to the hope that had just been offered.

Jewelia canted her head to one side. "Could be the witches are only after one thing: settling the score between them and the fae. Could be the fae will be the only ones stripped of their magic."

Harlow's panic returned with a vengeance, clawing at her throat until breathing was an effort. "They'll kill Augustine."

"Child, they will kill us *all* if they get the chance."

⚜

Ian had been a pleasurable distraction, but by the time Giselle was done smudging her sister's room, all she could think about was what else remained to be done. The difficult, important task of drawing the sigil. She went back to the altar room, collected the necessary things and then, with her bloodletting kit in hand, she returned to Zara's room. She whispered the same sleeping spell she had before smudging the room, then opened the door and slipped in.

Even in sleep Zara twitched and moaned softly as if the burden of it all was too much. Maybe she dreamed about what was to come. Or maybe the efforts of her spellwork bore down on her regardless of what state her body was in.

"It'll all be over soon, Sister." Giselle pulled a glass vial and a silver needle from the kit's wooden box and pricked Zara's finger, catching the blood in the vial. Drop after ruby drop filled the glass. It was a fair amount of blood, but this wasn't something Giselle wanted to do twice. Zara mumbled a few incoherent words, but stayed asleep thanks to the spell meant to keep her that way. Vial filled, Giselle stoppered it, pressed a bit of gauze to the tiny wound to stem the bleeding, then slipped out as quietly as she'd entered and shut the door.

She returned to the altar room, where Ian now waited. "Did she wake up?"

"No, the spell did its job." She lifted the kit. "Your turn."

He held out his hand, watching her while she went to work.

She glanced up at him. "I was about to ask why you didn't care that I'm about to stick you with a needle, but then I realized that's sort of your job. You must be immune to needles at this point."

"No, they don't bother me. And I know you're not going to hurt me." He wiggled his brows. "In fact, you can stick me with anything you like."

"You're a little twisted, you know that?" She laughed as his blood trickled into the tube. He was probably making her laugh to keep her mind from everything else. He was sweet like that.

"Admit it, you love that about me."

"All done." She capped the vial, her smile still in place. "You're not boring, I'll say that much."

He sucked the bead of blood off his index finger, then pinched it against his thumb. "Are you worried about getting the sigil right?"

"Yes, but who wouldn't be?" She opened an empty vial and tried to stand it upright in the wooden box but it tipped over. She sighed in frustration and tried again.

"Your hands are shaking." He took the vial from her. "Let me do this."

She handed the silver needle over and held out her finger. She looked at him. Really looked at him. Not through the eyes of her lovesick teenage self, but through the eyes of the woman she'd become. Yes, she'd been sharing him with Zara, but it was clear Ian's heart lay with her first and foremost. She couldn't imagine doing this without him any more than she could Zara. "Thank you."

He shrugged. "Like I mentioned, sticking people with needles is kind of my job."

"I meant with everything. With getting me through my father's death, with the way you've supported me as high priestess, with your willingness to help Zara and me cast this spell... just with everything."

He stilled, the needle above her fingertip, and brought his

gaze to meet hers. "In case you haven't noticed, Giselle Vincent, I am deeply, madly in love with you. I have been ever since you were legally old enough for me to do something about it."

"Then why didn't you?"

"Your father." Ian shook his head, the tiniest spark of anger in his eyes. "He was the high priest of our coven. Going against him would have meant losing what little contact I had with you. It would have jeopardized my mother's place on the Circle of Thirteen as well." He bent his head back to his work. "I wasn't willing to risk either of those things, but especially not losing contact with you."

Her heart filled her throat. She winced as the needle went in but was glad his concentration was there and not on her face, which was undoubtedly showing every emotion currently coursing through her. He held her finger over the glass tube. Her finger throbbed as the blood trickled out and at last she found her voice. "I had no idea."

He looked up and smiled. "Now you do." He held up the vial, filled with her blood. "All done."

Her position as high priestess dictated certain things be done certain ways, and while Ian was a member of the thirteen, she was still his superior.

He brought her finger to his mouth and kissed the remnant of blood away. "Anything else I can do for you?"

"Yes." Emotion thinned her voice to a whisper.

His brows knotted as though he sensed the seriousness of what she was about to ask. "Anything. Name it."

She swallowed and found her courage. Casting the chaos spell was nothing compared to this. "Marry me."

His mouth curved into a warm smile and his brows lifted almost imperceptibly. "Are you trying to make an honest man out of me?"

She laughed. "I'm not that ambitious."

He kissed her, then tipped his forehead against hers. "I would say yes in a heartbeat…"

"But." She pulled away, preparing herself for rejection. "But what?"

"You're under a lot of stress right now. I want to know that this is what you really want and not a reaction to everything else happening around you."

"It's not. Just because I'm stressed doesn't mean—"

He put his finger to her lips. "If that's true, then great. But there's no reason we can't get through this and then talk about it some more." He took his hand away. "Besides, if this is going to happen, things between us have to change."

She stared at him, unable to fathom what he meant. "How?"

"For one thing, you need to stop trying to do everything yourself and let me truly be your partner. I have abilities, talents that…" He started to say more, then closed his mouth and shook his head.

"How are you not my partner?"

His eyes narrowed. "Let's start with the fact that you're preparing to draw this sigil yourself."

She looked at the paper and quill she'd laid out. "How is that you not being my partner?"

He frowned. "Do you know what a tattoo artist does all day?"

"Tattoo people?"

"I *draw*." He tapped the desktop. "I am far more equipped to trace out the sigil than you and yet, you never even thought about asking me to do it, did you?"

She twisted a strand of hair around her finger and stared at the desk. "No, I didn't." She dropped the hair to look at him again. Goddess help her, she needed to learn to let go. "I'm not only a bad high priestess, I'm a bad girlfriend. I'm sorry."

He took her shoulders, forcing her to meet him eye to eye. "Hey, you're just stressed. And used to doing things alone. Let me do the sigil and you . . . get out of this house for a while and do anything but think about casting this spell."

"Get out of the house? Where am I supposed to go? The new house? Visiting that place only makes me crazy when I see how much work there is yet to be done. Visiting the old one makes me sad."

"Neither. Go for a walk. Get some fresh air. Just go. I know you're not a green witch, but it'll still do you some good. Let me draw and your sister sleep."

"Are you ordering me?"

A rebellious light gleamed in his eyes. "Yes, as a matter of fact, I am."

Chapter Fourteen

As a way of offering Harlow some help and protection, Queen Jewelia had offered to make her a *gris gris*. The cake and coffee had been cleared and Queen Jewelia was now positioned directly across from Harlow. In the center of the table sat an old family Bible, the gilt worn off its edges and the leather cover cracked and shiny with use. On top of the Bible lay a small, red leather pouch. It reminded her of the one Rufus Ogun had worn around his neck. Which brought to mind a new question.

Harlow lifted her finger. "I don't mean to interrupt, but how is this going to protect me? Ogun wore one of these around his neck and he's stuck in the well of souls just like everyone else."

Jewelia made a face. "I can guarantee that man's *gris gris* wasn't for protection against the witches, although it shoulda been. His was probably for the drawing of wealth and the influencing of strangers." She waved her hand. "Nothing like what I'm about to make for you."

Satisfied, Harlow nodded and went back to watching.

Jewelia situated four small dishes around the Bible. One held salt, one water, one a lit candle and one a cone of incense.

Jewelia nodded at Harlow. "All right, child. Put your hand on the Bible, over top the bag."

Harlow did as she asked, but her face must have showed her surprise.

"Still don't believe, do you?" Jewelia looked at Lally. "If the child doesn't believe—"

"It's not that," Harlow interrupted. "I've seen enough these past weeks to believe in almost everything at this point. I just didn't expect you to use a Bible."

Jewelia's smile was thin but it reached her eyes. "Voodoo, like any religion, requires a lot of faith. Most of us who practice go to church and pray just like the rest of you. Maybe more than the rest of you. Now, for some, it's just show. For others, like myself, it's not. Which is also why I will not do many of the rituals Father Ogun considers normal practice."

Harlow smiled. "Thank you for explaining." She sat up a little straighter. "What do you need me to do next?"

Jewelia struck a wooden match, then lit the incense cone. A thin stream of smoke spiraled up, filling the room with a woodsy scent. "As the incense burns, we will consecrate the charms that will go in your *gris gris*. Hold out your other hand." Into Harlow's palm she placed a dried mushroom, a small piece of bark, another bit of some kind of root and a pinch of salt. Then she closed her hand over Harlow's and placed her other on the Bible. "Hear my voice, O God. Hear my prayer. Preserve Harlow's life from the fear of the wicked."

She lifted her hand and added more things to Harlow's palm: a tiny metal cross, a coiled length of black thread, a shard of bone or shell, a tiny slip of paper with a pentagram drawn on it and lastly, a pinch of the earth collected from the witches' garden. She covered Harlow's hand again and put her other one back on the Bible. "Hide her, O God, from the secret council of the wicked. Keep her from the insurrection of the workers of iniquity. Your will be done. Amen."

Harlow whispered, "Amen."

Lally said it as well, then Jewelia nodded her approval. "Put all those things into the pouch."

Harlow emptied the bits and pieces into the little red bag, then looked at Jewelia expectantly.

Jewelia dipped her fingers in the bowl of water, then marked a cross on the bag as it rested in Harlow's palms. "Close the bag between your hands, bring it to your mouth and breathe on it."

Harlow followed her instructions.

"Very good." She took the bag from Harlow. "Now I'll string it on a cord and you must wear it around your neck, under your clothes. Don't let the witches see it." She hesitated. "Either way, they may figure out you're being protected if they attack you, but I don't care. It's high time those spell casters learned they're not the only ones with power in this town."

⚜

After walking for only a few minutes, Giselle knew that Ian had been right. Getting out of the house had been the perfect solution to her frenzied brain. Already she was starting to feel more at peace and more prepared for the work that lay ahead. In her heart, she knew they were ready. There was no reason to fret about it so much.

Lost in her thoughts, she paused to figure out where she was, only to realize she was standing beside the gate that led into the backyard of Augustine's house. She stared up at the house. It was easily one of the most impressive in the neighborhood, not just for its sheer size but for its history. The house was basically a fae landmark.

And now that she knew it contained the lightning tree... She smiled. This might be her chance to see if the tree really existed—the house began to waver before her eyes, making it impossible to focus on. Every time she looked at it, her gaze slipped across the street or to the neighboring house. Testing an idea, she forced all thought of the lightning tree from her mind and focused only on how beautiful the house was.

The image cleared enough to prove her theory. The house was warded. Of course, it was fae magic. How could she break through that ward? Keeping her thoughts pure was nearly impossible. Maybe it wasn't worth the effort of trying to get in. She whispered a seeking spell, sending it through the house to find out if anyone was in it. The spell found one life. Had to be the housekeeper. No doubt Augustine was out scouring the city for his precious Harlow. Or being interrogated by the senator's people.

Either way, he wasn't having any fun. And if the housekeeper was the only one home, there seemed no better time to do a little investigating. But how to get in? She leaned against the gate and pulled out her LMD so that anyone watching her would think she was just taking a call or checking email.

Think, think, think. If keeping her thoughts pure could get her in, maybe she could cast a temporary spell on herself? Something that would convince the ward she had nothing but good intentions. It was worth a shot.

She sketched a quick sacred circle in the air, knowing it would be thin without the proper preparations but hoping it would be enough to achieve the desired effect. "Bind my thoughts of their true goal until I slip inside these walls." She chanted the phrase three times.

As the last word left her lips, she blinked and looked at Augustine's house. What had she come here for? Had he called her here? Something to do with coven business? More regulations, no doubt. Damn those fae, always interfering.

With an odd determination to get inside, Giselle lifted the latch and slipped through the gate, careful to close it behind her. Maybe the housekeeper would know what Augustine wanted.

She climbed the steps to the back porch and raised her hand to knock. When no one answered, she tried the knob instead. To her delight, it turned effortlessly. She quietly called out, "Hello," and waited. The scent of coffee lingered in the empty kitchen.

No response came. She stepped into the house and closed the door behind her. A flush of memory hit her, the spell she'd placed upon herself. Now she knew why she was here. Smiling at her own cleverness, she sent out another seeking spell, this time to determine where the life source was.

The information it brought back told her whoever was in the house was several floors above her. She smiled and her thoughts turned to the lightning tree, but her smile faded fast. How could there be a tree in this house? It couldn't be a large tree. She walked through the kitchen and into the foyer, one part of the house she'd been in before.

Her fingers grazed the enormous gilded mirror hanging on the wall. The last time she'd been in this house had been to deliver a list of coven members to Augustine and he'd been fixated on this mirror. She'd sensed some kind of magic about it, but nothing concrete. Could it have some connection to the lightning tree?

She peeked behind it. Just the wall, no secret portal or hidden door. She started past it, walking toward the library, and got the distinct feeling she was being watched. Turning back to the mirror, she looked into it again. Nothing. Except she couldn't shake the feeling that there was something more to it than a valuable antique. She coasted her fingers along the antique frame. "My father would have loved you."

Focusing on the task at hand, she left the mirror behind and strolled into the library, the only other room in the house she'd been in. It remained as filled with treasures as the last time she'd been here, including a rare and ridiculously valuable Gutenberg

Bible. A single page from that book would bring in a hefty sum. But she wasn't here for something as fleeting as money.

She wanted proof of the tree.

She searched the rest of the rooms on the first floor, coming at last to a room at the rear of the house. She opened the door and frowned in disappointment. Looked like the housekeeper's room. She glanced up. What were the chances she could search the rest of the house before the housekeeper found her?

Pretty good if she took the housekeeper out of the picture.

Giselle sent the seeking spell out a third time, adding a small spark to it that she could follow. It floated down the hall and up the stairs. Giselle crept after it. Step after step, the spark led her on until she arrived at the top floor. There was nowhere left to go.

It hovered outside a closed door for a moment, then vanished. The housekeeper was in that room. Giselle put her ear to the door but heard nothing. Was *this* the housekeeper's room? Or had she fallen asleep in the attic? Giselle eased the door open, expecting to see the woman dozing in some dusty rocking chair.

Instead, she found Augustine.

He was sprawled on his back in a king bed, a sheet covering most of him and white linens surrounding him like a cloud. She wrinkled her nose at the aroma of smoke that perfumed the space. His scent. The smell of his kind. She studied him. Other than the gentle rise and fall of his chest, there was no movement. The room was certainly not what she'd expected, either. It was a sparse but gorgeous space with an enormous window that looked out over the expanse of the Garden District. Sheers covered it at the moment.

She'd always pictured him in some claustrophobic nook filled with cobwebs and old furniture. How wrong she'd been.

The diffused lighting shadowed his face like bruises. She crept closer to the bed. The marks on his face weren't shadows after all, but the remnants of what must have been a horrible beating. He had cuts on his brow and cheekbone, healing but still visible, and the end of one horn was chipped off. Apparently, the senator's team had already been to see him. Or had the police finally found the address she'd planted on the senator's son? If so, why wasn't Augustine in custody? If he'd been released because of his position as Guardian . . . she snorted in disgust, then stilled in sudden panic at the noise she'd made, but he didn't stir.

Was he unconscious? On a hunch, she leaned over him and inhaled. He was unconscious all right. She straightened. Someone had dosed him with a sleeping potion.

How convenient. She tipped her head. Killing him would be so simple, but really, what would be the point? She'd only be robbing herself of the pleasure of seeing his face when he realized what she'd done to him and all his people.

"You poor, sad thing," she whispered. "Might as well stay asleep because in a few hours, you're going to be just as powerless."

Of course, this *was* the perfect opportunity to put an end to him without all the fuss. She lifted her hands, the words of a suffocation spell forming on her lips. He shifted, startling her.

She dropped her hands and fled the room before the pounding of her heart woke him. She leaned against the closed door as her stomach soured with the knowledge that she wasn't as brave as she'd like to believe. She stood as still as a statue while her nerves settled. Her disgust at her actions made her grimace. No matter, the chaos spell would change everything and that was all that mattered. *Focus. Find the tree. Get out before you're caught.*

Where would the tree be? Zara would probably have found it already, being a green witch and all. Giselle's pulse was back to normal and her bravado with it. She straightened. If the tree was in the house, wouldn't it be hidden in some way? Otherwise, anyone who visited the house might find it. The house was steeped in fae history, so if there was magic hiding the tree, it must also be fae. With that thought, Giselle unclasped her crystal pendulum necklace, held it out before her and whispered, "Show me the greatest source of magic in this house."

The tip of the crystal moved, pointing toward the door on the other side of the landing. She followed it, going into the room with no expectations of any kind this time. High transom windows on one side shed enough light to see boxes and bins lining the walls, all marked with odd phrases like *autographed scripts* and *misc. good wigs*. Beyond those containers were stacks of things wrapped in muslin, odd pieces of furniture, what looked like a taxidermy porcupine and an honest-to-goddess throne. "What on earth is this place?"

If there was a tree hidden in here, she was going to have to move a lot of rubbish to get to it. The crystal drew her in deeper and as she rounded a towering pile of ancient vinyl records, she saw just how big the room was. It had to run the length of the house.

The necklace suddenly swung out at a right angle, quivering as it pointed at the wall. "End spell."

The pendulum dropped, lifeless. She gathered up the chain and crystal, then stuck it in her pocket so she could examine the space. There was nothing remotely treelike. She moved a coatrack complete with coats, an easel and three giant paintings. Flocked wallpaper covered the wall, so old and hideous it was probably from the days when the place had been a whorehouse.

Still no tree—or magic, despite what the pendulum had indicated.

Dust covered her hands in grime. She brushed them off. Her cleanliness spell would be working overtime trying to keep her ivory trousers and blouse from getting soiled in this grubby old space.

A thin breeze teased her ankles. She glanced around but none of the windows were open. They were all too high up anyway. The breeze drifted over her skin again. It was coming from down low. She studied the wall she'd just cleared. The wallpaper, besides being about as ugly as wallpaper could be, curled up from the bottom seam.

Giselle grabbed the edge and tore a long strip off. Dust flew everywhere. She held her breath and backed away, trying hard not to sneeze. As the dust settled, the outline of a door became visible. Excitement tripped over her skin. Forgetting the grime, she scoured her fingers along the edges, looking for a way to open it. Near the bottom, she found an indentation. She pressed it but the door was locked. She almost laughed. Locks were no match for a practiced witch. She muttered a spell to free it, then pressed the indentation again. This time it released with a sigh.

Almost trembling now, she pushed the door open and stepped through onto a balcony. The aura of magic danced over her skin instantly. Light filtered through a large skylight, illuminating the most amazing thing she'd ever seen. Black and twisted, gnarled in an unnatural way and reeking of soot and smoke, the lightning tree stood before her.

Beckoning her.

She walked to the edge of the narrow balcony, her gaze following the branches as they disappeared into the structure of the house. The tree had grown *into* the house, which meant this thing before her was alive. But then, she could feel it—in her bones, in her blood—the magic vibrated through her.

There were more balconies below her and a set of stairs that wound around the outside of the tree's enclosure. She leaned over the railing to see where the tree came out of the ground. Its trunk was thick enough that two people could circle it with their arms and still not meet. How long had this tree been here? Before the house, it seemed.

Charred leaves sprouted in clusters, most of them closest to her where the branches grew thin and whiplike. Everything about the tree, the bark, the knots, the leaves, was burnt black with soot. If only Zara could see this.

Giselle smiled. After tonight, she'd be able to bring Zara here. After tonight, this city would belong to them. This tree would belong to them. She reached up and stroked one of the branches. The unmistakable tingle of power shot through her fingertips, causing her to gasp out loud.

She snatched her hand back out of shock. Something about the tree had changed. Awakened. The air around it shifted and wavered with magic so strongly that Giselle had no doubts it would be plainly visible to anyone, witch or not. But more than that, the tree wanted her to touch it again.

It *needed* her to touch it again.

She placed her palm flat on the nearest section of trunk. The swell of power made her eyelids flutter and her heart palpitate. No, it was best if Zara didn't know about the tree just yet. Zara might be a green witch, but the tree was speaking to Giselle.

Protect me.

"I will," she whispered.

Keep me close to you.

She nodded and, intoxicated with the tree's powerful voice, snapped off a cluster of leaves and started to stuff them into her purse.

Closer.

She hesitated. The leaves pulsated with life in her hand. No, these shouldn't go in her purse. They needed to be on her. On her skin. She tucked them into her bra, against her heart.

She nodded. That felt right.

Yes.

Chapter Fifteen

Augustine nodded toward the car coming through the gate. "They're home now." He'd had hours of sleep and was in much better shape than before, but couldn't shake the feeling that he'd missed something while he'd been out. One thing he knew without question—those hours of sleep hadn't come naturally.

"Ah, very good," Fenton said. "We'll see if they know anything."

"I have some personal business to discuss with them first."

Fenton's brows rose. "Do you want me to leave?"

"No. You can stay." Augustine waited until Harlow and Lally were in the house and the kitchen door was shut before he said another word. "Which one of you did it?"

Harlow jumped as Lally flipped the light on. "You scared me."

Lally frowned at him. "You know very well I did it, Augie." She moved to the stove and turned on the burner under the kettle. "Mr. Welch, nice to see you again. Can I fix you a cup of tea?"

Fenton shook his head nervously. "No, thank you, I'm fine."

Augustine stared at her. "Lally, you can't just drug me and act like it's no big deal."

Harlow, who'd been standing motionless by the door, stepped in front of Lally. "She did it for your own good. So you could heal. Which I'm guessing is what happened because you look a lot better."

He wasn't going to be swayed that easily. "Something could have happened."

"He's right," Fenton said. "You never know."

Harlow made a face at Augustine. "Oh, the two of you. Augustine, stop being so grumpy. And Fenton, you sound like an overprotective parent. Get over it, okay? Lally did what she thought was best for you. You needed to sleep and heal more than you needed to be awake. Plus the house is warded. What could have happened?"

He closed his mouth. Lally was smiling. The two of them had ganged up on him. Not something he was used to. It didn't bode well for the future, either. He shoved a hand through his hair. "Don't ever do it again. Either of you."

Harlow grabbed a bottle of cola from the fridge. "I'd do it again in a heartbeat if I thought it was the right call." She pried the top off and sat at the table. "How are your ribs?"

He sat down beside her, frowning. When had she become so...sure of herself? He liked it. Mostly. "Much better. Still some pain—hey, where were you two?"

Harlow took a slug off the bottle. "We went to see Queen Jewelia."

Not the answer he'd expected. He glanced at Lally. "Is that a joke or did you really?"

Lally nodded. "We did."

He leaned back in his chair, trying to get a handle on what had happened. "So you drugged me, went to see the only voodoo practitioner who can rival Father Ogun and Harlow came back with a new attitude?"

Harlow wiped her finger through the condensation on the bottle. "I got the new attitude after I survived being possessed by my sister, but otherwise, that about sums it up."

He stared at her. "Queen Jewelia perform some sort of sass spell on you, too?"

She looked at Lally. "Can I tell him or will that make it not work?"

"You can tell him. It's the witches you need to hide it from."

Harlow grinned at him. "Jewelia made me a *gris gris*. For added protection against the witches."

He wasn't quite sure what to do with that, but since Harlow seemed happy about it, he took that direction. "That's great. Do anything else while you were there?"

Harlow nodded. "We had coffee cake. And talked to Jewelia about what the witches might be doing. She's pretty sure it's some kind of big spell that could potentially wipe out all magic from the city, except the witches, of course. She called it chaos magic."

Fenton's mouth fell open.

Augustine's gaze narrowed. "*Sturka*. Are you sure?"

Lally joined them at the table. "Yes. You know what that means."

"I'm not sure I do entirely." He looked at Fenton. "You're the historian."

"Yeah," Harlow said. "Queen Jewelia answered my questions as best she could, but even she wasn't entirely sure that's what the witches were up to. Do you know anything more, Fenton?"

"I do. At least, I can tell you what I know and what I think." With a soft exhale, Fenton began. "According to myth, legend and rumor, none of which can be proved, Giselle and Zara's mother died trying to cast a chaos spell. There were no witnesses and the ruling fae never did anything about it, because her husband, Giselle and Zara's father, Evander, refused to say it was anything other than a suicide. He and Vivianna had been divorced for some time, but it was clear he had never fallen out of love with her. Her death nearly killed him."

"What about the chaos spell?" Augustine needed to know what they were up against.

"It's not really one spell, it's a type of magic like white magic or green magic or whatever kind a witch might do, although it's clearly on the dark side of the spectrum. Chaos magic is the most unpredictable by its very nature. Something obviously went wrong with the spell Vivianna was trying to cast, and it killed her."

Augustine tried not to get frustrated with Fenton but the man kept skirting around what Augustine really wanted to know. "That's not really what I'm asking. Can this magic really destroy other magic? Is that what Vivianna was trying to accomplish by casting the spell in the first place?"

Fenton shook his head. "We don't know. Not exactly. After it happened, the Elektos ruled that any witch caught performing chaos magic would be banished from the city. Chaos magic was already forbidden. There wasn't much more that could be done without proof. We consulted with some weaver fae and the best we could determine is that Vivianna was trying to alter the power system in the city. Possibly to make the witches invincible."

"Or the fae vulnerable." Augustine glanced at Lally. "If Branzino was working with Giselle, it's possible she knew what he was after and is now after the same thing. With Zara's help. Which would make sense considering Zara's a green witch and the... *thing* they're after used to be green." He didn't want to mention the lightning tree in front of Fenton, but he figured Lally and Harlow would know what he was referring to.

Lally jerked back like she'd been struck. "That can't be..."

Fenton raised a hand. "Before you carry on with this vague, roundabout sort of conversation again, let me just say that I did some research and I'm pretty sure I know what you're talking about. The same thing that caused all the trouble with Ava Mae."

They all turned to look at him.

He stared right back. "I have access to every fae record ever written down. All the histories. All the transactions." His expression turned smug. "You should be more astonished you kept the tree from me this long."

Lally stood to take the whistling kettle off the burner, then faced them again. She didn't seem too surprised by Fenton's announcement. "If you think that's what the witches are planning, to knock out all other magic so they can come into this house and take control of the lightning tree, then we need to be prepared. If you'll excuse me for a moment." She didn't wait for a response, just left and by the sound of it, went to her room.

Harlow's eyebrows shot up. "What was that all about?"

Augustine shook his head. "No idea." He looked at Fenton. "You think Nekai knows anything about chaos magic?" The weaver fae wasn't one of Augustine's favorite people, but help was help. If the witches were coming against them, they needed every soldier they could muster.

"If anyone does, it would be him."

"As soon as you can, fill him in and see what he thinks. We're going to need all the help we can get."

Lally rushed back into the room, panic dripping off her like bad perfume. "Someone was in the house."

Augustine's hand went for the hilt of his sword even though he wasn't wearing it. "How do you know?"

She swallowed, her brown eyes filled with a mixture of fear and anger. "The tree's been touched. Worse'n that. Whoever was here helped themselves to a piece of it."

⚜

While Augustine and Fenton waited for Nekai, Harlow decided to spend her time in a different way. She got up and took Lally's hand but spoke to Augustine. "We'll be back in a bit."

Augustine's forehead furrowed. "Where are you going?"

She tipped her head toward Fenton. "Somewhere Fenton doesn't need to know about."

"I heard nothing." The cypher fae gave her a knowing glance as he stood. "If you'll just excuse me, I'll be on the porch for a moment."

As soon as he stepped out, Augustine spoke. "Are you telling me you're taking Lally through the mirror to see Olivia?"

Harlow nodded. "You have a problem with that?"

"Not at all." He liked Harlow's new confidence. "You okay to go through the mirror by yourself? I mean, I have no doubt you can do it, you just haven't before."

"I can handle it."

"Yes, you can. And good for you." Augustine waved a hand. "Olivia needs to see you and know that you're all right. Last time we were there, we had to tell her what had happened to you and she was pretty destroyed by it. She'll be thrilled to know you're okay. Give her my love and let her know I'll come visit again soon."

"You know that won't be good enough. She'll want to know why you didn't come this time."

He nodded. "I know. Tell her what we're dealing with. That should buy me some slack."

"Okay. Back in a few. C'mon, Lally." She pulled the woman into the foyer. "You're not scared to do this with just me, are you?"

Lally tugged back on Harlow's hand. "Not one bit." She pointed at the enormous gilt frame mirror in the foyer. "If I ain't scared of traveling through that thing, then why should it bother me who I go through with? You're as fae as Augie."

"I don't think that's exactly true. But he says I can do it, so... why not." Traveling by mirror alone was a little daunting, but it was just another part of being fae. And since her mother was trapped in the fae plane as a result of dying as she was trying to pass through, visiting her there was the only way Harlow *could* see her. "Besides, I haven't seen my mother in a while. Last time we left things sort of...rough between us. I don't want that anymore."

"I agree. That's not how it should be between a mother and daughter." Lally's upset over the tree being touched seemed at least partially forgotten. Or she was hiding it. She smiled. "You got your mirror for the return trip?"

Harlow patted her pocket. "I do. Ready?"

"Ready." She squeezed Harlow's hand.

"Okay, here goes nothing." But how hard could it be? She'd traveled by mirror with Nekai and Augustine and they'd both explained it. You just imagined the place you wanted to go was in the mirror and there you were. She could do this.

Lally winked at her. "We all gotta start somewhere."

Holding tight to Lally, Harlow reached out with her other hand, touched the mirror and imagined she could see the part of the fae plane where her mother now existed. Her vision swirled like she was having a dizzy spell, but that only lasted an instant and then it was gone.

The fae plane lay before her, bleak and gray and as dismally windy as the last time she'd been here. In the distance rose the Claustrum, a horrible fae prison. Sadly, her mother was stuck here but not because she'd done anything worth punishment. The Claustrum and the chance Augustine might be sent there had been the last thing on her mind when she'd died, her body stretched out on the very mirror they'd just passed through.

"Olivia!" The wind tore Harlow's shout from her lips.

Lally shielded her face against the scouring grit. "I don't like this place much."

"Me, either." Harlow tried again. "Mother, are you there? It's me, Harlow."

The wind calmed a bit as Olivia came toward them, appearing out of the swirling dust like a phantom. "Harley!" Then her face darkened. "Is that really you? Or are you Ava Mae in disguise?"

"No, it's really me. Ava Mae's gone. Long story, but she is." Harlow held back, not sure how her mother would receive her after the last visit.

"Oh, *cher,* my darling, I'm so glad. I was sick with worry." She clasped her hands to her face. "I'm so glad you came. I saw someone in the house. Through the mirror. A woman. I didn't recognize her."

Lally squeezed Harlow's hand hard. "What did she look like?"

"Long dark hair, thick bangs, all dressed in white."

Harlow's belly went cold. "Giselle. We have to go back and tell Augustine."

Lally nodded.

Olivia angled her head to one side, her hands reaching out. "Please stay a few minutes. I haven't seen you in so long. I'm so sorry for everything that's happened between us. For everything I didn't tell you until it was too late. I know you're mad at me, but please, forgive me. I don't want things to be so awful between us."

A few minutes wouldn't make much difference. Harlow fell into her mother's arms. "I don't want it to be awful between us, either. You're forgiven. But you have to do the same for me." She pulled back to look into her mother's eyes. "I was a horrible daughter. I treated you terribly. And now that you're . . . here and not at home, I feel even worse about all that." She swallowed. "All those years I wasted."

"We both wasted them." Olivia cupped Harlow's face in her hands and smiled. "Let's put all that behind us and focus on moving forward, shall we?"

Harlow nodded. "I'd like that."

Olivia gave her another quick hug before releasing her, then hugged Lally. "I wish I hadn't greeted you with such terrible news, but it's good to see you again and so soon! I'm getting spoiled."

"Not that spoiled." Lally held out her hands. "I didn't bring you anything this time."

Olivia put her arm around Harlow's shoulders. "You brought me my daughter and that's the only present I need. Let's go sit and catch up."

Harlow hesitated. Telling her mother that Giselle had stolen a piece of the lightning tree would only upset her. "Just for a little bit. We have to tell Augustine about Giselle being in the house. The witches are trying to cast some big spell to knock out the magic in town, so we've got full plates, as you can imagine."

"Oh my." Olivia's mouth bent in a frown. "Maybe you shouldn't stay after all."

"A few minutes won't hurt anything." Harlow wasn't sure that was true, but spending some time with her mother felt more important.

Olivia nodded. "Well, then, I'll take what I can get." She led them to a flat rock surrounded by a few other jagged pieces, helping to shield it from the wind. They climbed onto it and sat.

Harlow leaned against one of the tall slabs of black rock. "It's nice to be a little more protected from the wind. Although it's already started to die down."

Olivia nodded. "I agree, but near as I can figure the wind only kicks up like that when someone enters the plane. It's kind of like an early warning system, letting me know there's someone at my door. Although I have to say, it's been windier than usual lately."

"Do you just sit here all day?" Harlow didn't like the idea

of her mother alone in this vast wasteland of a place, the ever-present shadow of the Claustrum a constant reminder of all that was wrong with their world.

Olivia shook her head. "No. I wander around, practice trying to travel back through the mirror, this and that." She leaned in. "And I only keep this form when y'all are here. Otherwise..." She vanished.

"Mom!" Harlow's heart lurched. "Where are you?"

Olivia reappeared smile-first like the Cheshire cat. "I never left. I'm just not visible unless I want to be. It takes some effort being visible *and* solid."

The realization of what Olivia was saying struck Harlow hard. "You're a ghost, aren't you?" Why that made her eyes burn with tears, she couldn't say. Maybe it was how fine a point it put on her mother being dead.

Sadness took the shine off her mother's smile. "I guess you could say I am."

Harlow turned to Lally, anger creeping into her gut. "Is there nothing we can do to help her? Something we could use the tree for?" She scrubbed at the threatening tears. "I don't care if she's a ghost. I just want her back and out of this place." She stood up. "I hate this place." The wind kicked up. She thrust her chest out and screamed it into the air. "I *hate* this *place*."

Olivia reached up to her. "Harlow, darling, there's nothing we can—"

Two figures stepped out of the air. The man Harlow recognized as Hugo Loudreux, the father of the girl she'd helped rescue right before Ava Mae had taken control of her body. The woman was Blu, Loudreux's personal security and Augustine's half sister. Loudreux snapped his mirror case closed and stared at her.

A very bad feeling overwhelmed Harlow. She stepped in front of Lally. "Prime Loudreux. I didn't expect to see you here."

"I'm sure you didn't." He looked around. "I suppose Augustine is here with you somewhere?"

"No, he's at the house. Do you need him? Is Rue okay?"

Loudreux's expression soured further at the mention of his daughter's name. "She's fine."

"That's good." Harlow wanted to ask if Rue's finger and ear tip had grown back yet, but considering Harlow's late father, Joseph Branzino, was the one who'd cut them off in the first place, she kept quiet. "Anything else I can do for you?"

He motioned to Blu and she took a step forward. "Yes. You can come with me."

Harlow jumped down off the rock. "I thought you didn't need help with anything."

Blu grabbed her arm. "Sorry," she whispered.

Harlow glared at her. "What are you doing?"

Loudreux's smug expression made her want to punch him. "I'm arresting you. For transporting a human to the fae plane."

Chapter Sixteen

Augustine's new com cell had synced just fine based on the buzzing in his head. He held up his finger to Fenton and pointed at his head. "Answer."

"Augustine, it's Yanna, something terrible has happened. Loudreux just arrested Harlow for—"

"What? Wait, I'm putting you on speaker." He jabbed the button on his LMD to get the call out of his head and make it available for Fenton. "Go ahead, Fenton's here."

"Loudreux just arrested Harlow for transporting a human onto the fae plane. Your housekeeper, I believe."

"*Fet'ka*. That piece of garbage. I'm going to kill that *bala'stro*." Augustine moved to get up, but Fenton clamped a hand on his arm.

Fenton's eyes held an unfamiliar anger. "Yanna, how do you know this?"

"Because Loudreux called a special council. A few of us, myself and Salander Meer, were not included—"

"Nor was I," Fenton snarled. "Continue."

"Another Elektos alerted us, one who was called in but sides with us. Word is Loudreux plans to hold a tribunal to sentence Harlow to the Claustrum."

"How the hell does he think that's fair?" Augustine didn't care if the man was Prime. Augustine would forcibly retire him. "He owes Rue's life to Harlow. She was instrumental in getting Rue back after she was kidnapped."

"Yes," Yanna said. "Kidnapped by Branzino. That's the sticking point. Loudreux blames you for setting the whole chain of events into action, but he blames Harlow for bringing Branzino to New Orleans and for what happened to Rue."

Fenton stiffened. "That is ludicrous." He shook his head. "And so typically Hugo. That man is a cancer."

Augustine's vision narrowed to the point that all he could see was Loudreux's face. "The best way to remove a cancer is to cut it out."

Fenton's fingers squeezed harder. "Yanna, how did he know Harlow had gone to the fae plane?"

"Apparently, he'd posted a few of his own men in rotating shifts. He'd kept them on the other side of the Claustrum."

"He planned this." Fenton's voice cracked with a shard of icy rage. "Yanna, is the meeting still going on?"

"Yes. Salander and I are almost there."

Fenton looked at Augustine as he spoke. "Augustine and I are on our way, but keep that to yourselves. I prefer to take Hugo by surprise, just as he took Harlow."

"Absolutely," Yanna replied. "And so you know, Fenton, Salander and a good handful of the other Elektos stand with you and Augustine on this."

Fenton stood. "I appreciate that, but even if you didn't, it wouldn't stop what I'm about to do. This day has been a long time coming." He tapped the button on Augustine's LMD, ending the call. "Get the car. We have a visit to make."

Augustine nodded. "On it. Maybe we should get Dulce and Sydra there, too. For backup."

Fenton shook his head slowly. "We won't need them. Not for what's about to happen."

"You seem awfully sure of yourself." Augustine frowned. "What aren't you telling me?" He'd never seen Fenton like

this—angry but in a calm sort of way that made it far worse
than if he'd been screaming and yelling.

Fenton pushed his chair in and headed for the door. "You'll
know soon enough."

Augustine wasn't sure what Fenton was planning, but it
didn't matter. There was no way Harlow was being shipped
off to the Claustrum. He'd kill Loudreux to keep that
from happening. At the very least, that way they'd get to go
together.

⚜

"You can't just leave Lally there, you idiot." Harlow tugged at
the restraints securing her hands behind her back, but they
weren't budging. At least Loudreux had dismissed Blu after he'd
instructed the shadeux fae to put Harlow in restraints. Apparently, he didn't think she was enough of a threat to keep his
personal security on hand. "She's not fae. She can't get back on
her own." Lally must be freaking out. At least she had Olivia to
keep her company. That didn't keep Harlow from being wicked
pissed at Hugo Loudreux for hauling her off the fae plane like a
low-rent criminal.

Loudreux glared at her. "I guess you should have thought
about that before you took a human to the fae plane." His scowl
made his pinched little face uglier than usual. "Don't worry. A
few formalities and you'll be back there. As a permanent resident
of the Claustrum."

"What?" Fear chilled Harlow's bones. She couldn't imagine
a more awful place. "For taking Lally to see my mother? You're
insane. Augustine won't let you do that."

"Augustine has no say in this. In fact, your precious Guardian doesn't even know this is happening."

"He's not *my* Guardian, he's the city's Guardian. He protects all of us. Moron."

"Whatever." Voices drifted up from downstairs. He rested his hand on the bolt stick hanging from his belt. "The tribunal is about to begin. Let's go."

"Release my hands."

"Why? So you can run? No." He grabbed the restraints and forced her out the door ahead of him.

"Who runs with their hands?" She shook her head. "You're as dumb as you look. How did you ever become Prime?"

He shoved her forward. Apparently, he didn't find her funny. "Walk."

She almost stumbled on the first few steps, but caught herself. It gave her an idea. She slipped on purpose this time, tumbling onto her side and sliding almost to the bottom step. Her shoulder throbbed like she'd seriously bruised something but she breathed through it. "I told you to take off those restraints. I think I dislocated my shoulder."

"You're fine. Get up."

"I can't without my hands, you twit."

He cursed in words she didn't understand, then waved the key at her like a weapon. "One wrong move and I'll zap you with my bolt stick, understand?"

She nodded and tried to look sufficiently intimidated.

He bent to unlock the restraints. As soon as her first hand was free, she latched on to his wrist.

"Hey," he grunted in surprise. He went for the bolt stick.

Before he made contact with it, she shoved him back against the stairs and kneeled her full weight on his arms. She didn't weigh that much, but cyphers tended to be on the slight side so holding him down wasn't hard. His skin was clammy beneath her touch.

She grabbed the fingertips of her glove with her teeth and

yanked it off. Then, using what she'd learned, she fastened her hand around his wrist and began to thread emotions through him, starting with fear. "You hate Augustine. I get that. And I guess you hate me by association."

"Your father," Loudreux mumbled through a mouth twisted in fright. "He hurt Rue."

"Yes, he did. *He.* Not me. I helped find her, you idiot. If I'd wanted her hurt, why would I have done that? Now Branzino is dead and Rue's on the mend." She poured weakness into him, doing her best to make him feel small and helpless so he wouldn't attack her back. "You're trying to punish me for something I didn't do. That ends now, understand?"

He nodded submissively.

"And you know what else?"

He looked like he was about to cry.

She leaned in a little. "Get off Augustine's back. He's killing himself to be the best Guardian he can be and all you do is make his life miserable. Leave him alone and let him do his job or I will give you a real reason not to like me."

His nostrils flared.

"Am I getting through to you?"

More nodding.

"Now we're going into that tribunal and you're going to tell everyone what a mistake you made—"

The front door flew open. Yanna burst in with Salander behind her. Even though Yanna was the only ignus fae, they both looked like were about to set something—or someone— on fire. "Hugo, where are you? What's the meaning of—" She turned toward Harlow, her gaze flicking from Loudreux to Harlow and back again. Sparks flew around her, evidence of how angry she was. "What's happened? What's going on?"

Harlow held fast to Loudreux. "He's trying to send me to the Claustrum."

"We know." Behind Yanna, Salander nodded. Yanna moved closer to Harlow. "That's why we're here. To keep that from happening."

"You can't," Loudreux wheezed. He lifted a trembling hand to point down the hall. "I've already called them."

"Call it off." Harlow pushed another wave of emotion into him.

Loudreux whimpered.

Yanna's expression turned curious. "Harlow, what are you doing to him?"

Before she could answer, Augustine and Fenton ran into the house. Both looked like they were on the verge of murder. "Harlow, are you all right?"

She nodded at Augustine. "I'm okay. You know what he's trying to do to me?"

Augustine's lip curled. "Yes. But it's not going to happen."

"He says it will." Anger swelled inside her and Loudreux cried out.

Augustine glanced at Loudreux. "Harlow, let him go. As much as we both might want him dead, killing him in front of all these people isn't something I can defend you against."

"I'm not going to kill him. I was just trying to defend myself." She moved her weight off him to kneel on the step, but kept her hand on him. She was trembling with adrenaline and the effort of using her skills.

Fenton came forward, grabbed Loudreux's bolt stick from his belt and pointed it at him. "You can let go. I've got him covered."

Harlow released him and slumped onto the bottom step. Her shoulder was killing her. She exhaled with the effort of forcing emotion into Loudreux. Or maybe it was the weight of the Claustrum hanging over her. Either way, she was spent.

It took Loudreux a moment, but he snapped back to his old

self. He climbed to his feet, shaking and growing visibly angrier by the second. He jabbed a finger toward Harlow. "How dare you lay your hands on me? I am *the* Prime. Do you understand what that means?"

Fenton raised the bolt stick. "It means nothing if you lose that position."

Loudreux's face blanked. He turned to look at Fenton. "What?"

"In accordance with the Codex, amendment two, section one, subsection A, any Prime deemed unfit to continue service may be redacted by a quorum of the Elektos or by three or more members having served a greater term than the Prime."

Movement caught Harlow's eye. The other Elektos who'd gathered for the tribunal had begun filtering out into the hall, no doubt drawn by the noise.

Fenton lifted his head, seemingly unfazed by his new audience. "Yanna Quinn, Salander Meer and I have each been members of the Elektos since before you, making each of our terms greater than yours. Perhaps that has something to do with why you failed to invite us to this tribunal? Regardless, we deem you unfit to continue service and call for a vote to redact you and a special election to replace you."

"You fool." Loudreux's anger returned. "You've wanted this job ever since I've known you."

"As always, Hugo, you are wrong. I am very happy in my position as liaison to the Guardian."

Yanna stepped forward to stand beside Fenton. "I, however, would be happy to take your place. You're a bully who shows favor only to those who stay firmly in your pocket. We have one of the best Guardians we've ever had and yet you've done everything in your power to hinder him. You are not the Prime this city deserves."

"And you are?" Loudreux spat the words.

She nodded. "Yes, I believe I am."

One of the Elektos in the crowd raised his hand. "I believe she is, too."

"That settles it then," Fenton said. "As we're all assembled, we can move forward with the recall vote of the Prime and the special election to replace him." Fenton held out the bolt stick and looked back at Augustine. "If you would keep an eye on Hugo while the Elektos adjourns to the living room to work this out?"

"Happy to." Augustine took the bolt stick. "Maybe you could pardon Harlow on special circumstances or whatever while you're at it, too."

Fenton nodded, the first hint of a smile cracking his face. He shot a quick look at Harlow. "There's a section in the Codex that covers that." Then he scowled at Loudreux. "Something you'd know if you ever bothered to study the book that has guided us for centuries."

Augustine's expression was priceless. "Is that so? You couldn't apply that section to me when I was in trouble for the same thing?"

Fenton shrugged. "Harlow was directly responsible for the Prime's daughter being rescued. Such an act grants her a one-time boon of leniency. You didn't have that. Then."

Harlow smiled. "Thanks, Fenton. I don't have any idea what this Codex is, but I'm glad you know it so well."

Yanna laughed softly. "Fenton knows more about the Codex than most of us know about being fae." She clapped him on the back. "We should get this meeting going."

"You're all going to pay for this," Loudreux muttered.

Fenton shook his head and walked with Yanna and Salander into the other room.

Augustine closed the gap between him and Harlow. "You sure you're okay?"

"I banged my shoulder up, but it'll heal."

"Yep." His eyes gleamed with something dark and fierce, his look suddenly more appropriate for the bedroom than hostage holding. "I really want to kiss you right now."

Loudreux made a gagging noise. "You two disgust me."

Harlow kept her eyes on Augustine, but wiggled her fingers in Loudreux's direction. "Say the word and I will make him a lovesick teenager."

Augustine's eyes narrowed. "You can do that?"

"No idea, but I'd be willing to give it a shot."

Loudreux snarled. "Touch me again and I'll—"

Augustine turned on him. "You'll do nothing, Loudreux. And speaking of touching, you ever lay a hand on Harlow again, and I will bring the full weight of my wrath against you. Understand?"

Loudreux nodded.

Augustine sighed as he looked at her. "I am damn tired of people trying to hurt you."

"That makes two of us." She grabbed one of his horns, pulled him in and kissed him on the mouth.

Chapter Seventeen

With the warmth of Harlow's mouth still lingering on his, Augustine unlocked the shackle from her other hand, then hoisted Loudreux to his feet.

"What are you doing? Unhand me."

"Relax. We're going into the kitchen. Unless you'd rather sit on the steps?"

Loudreux frowned. "No."

"Great. Lead the way." Augustine tapped the bolt stick's trigger, making it buzz. Loudreux jumped.

Harlow snorted as she walked alongside him. "I really want one of those."

Augustine gave her a look. "Judging by what you did to Hugo, I don't think you need one. You've mastered your powers pretty well, huh?"

"I wouldn't say mastered, but Ava Mae gave me a crash course."

"I feel like I've barely seen you since you became you again. How are you doing?"

"I'm good." She shrugged and winced. "Okay, my shoulder's not good."

"I'll get you some ice." He shoved Loudreux into a kitchen chair, then attached one of his hands to it with the restraints. "You." He pointed at Loudreux. "Stay there."

Loudreux yanked on the restraint. "Like I have a choice."

Augustine grabbed a towel, went to the dispenser in the fridge door and started filling the linen with ice. He tied it in a knot, then sat beside her and held the bundle up. "Left shoulder?"

She nodded, tipping her head to the right to make room for the ice pack.

He placed the bag against her shoulder, positioning it so it would stay in place. "Let that sit for a few minutes." Unable to resist the smooth expanse of her neck so exposed to him, he kissed her there, just below her ear.

She gasped softly, an intimate sound that made him hate Loudreux even more. She followed it with a long sigh. "Thanks. I'm sure it's just a bruise. Lally will probably have some ancient remedy to—Lally!" Harlow twisted toward him, knocking the ice pack loose. She caught it in her lap. "Lally is stuck on the fae plane. I have to go get her."

Augustine pulled his LMD from his coat pocket. "I'll send Dulcinea to do it." He sent her a text explaining what was going on, then put the LMD away. "I'm sure Lally will fill her in on what happened."

"Won't Dulcinea end up coming over here then? She'll think Hugo's trying to put me away."

Loudreux grunted and looked out the window.

"No," Augustine answered. "I told her it was handled."

"Something the situation with the witches is not. Which reminds me, Olivia says she saw someone in the house, through the mirror. The description fits Giselle." Harlow put the ice back on her shoulder.

He ground his teeth together. "So much for Nekai's ward. I'd love to know how she got around that." He shot her a look. "We'll discuss the details of her visit when we're alone." Because he certainly wasn't about to discuss the lightning tree in front of Loudreux.

"Agreed." She sighed. "What are we going to do? We've got to get Cy out of there."

"And Pellimento's son."

Loudreux perked up. "Senator Pellimento?"

Augustine nodded. "Yes."

"Where do you have to get him out of?"

Augustine shifted his gaze to Harlow. They hadn't talked about how much anyone outside of their immediate circle needed to know. The look she gave him in return said she understood completely.

Loudreux leaned toward them as if sensing their reluctance to talk. "Senator Pellimento hates the fae. If her son is in trouble, I say let him rot."

Augustine turned to look at him. "So she can bring a world of hurt down on us? Yeah, that sounds like something you'd like." His LMD chimed. "Hang on a sec." He checked the device. "Dulce says Lally's home. Do we need her for anything else?"

"We might," Harlow said. "Considering what we were just talking about."

"I'll tell her to stick around. Knowing Lally, she'll enjoy the company."

"You mean having someone to feed."

Augustine laughed. "That, too."

Loudreux tipped his head back and sighed in frustration. "I'm still Prime. I demand to know what's going on."

Augustine snorted. "You might still be Prime, but—"

Fenton pushed the kitchen door open as Augustine was speaking. "He's not Prime anymore." He looked at Loudreux. "You were recalled by a majority vote. And Yanna was elected by the same margin. She's Prime now."

Loudreux's face drained of all color. "You piece of . . . *sturka*. How dare you do this to me? To my family?"

Fenton shook his head. "You did this to yourself, Hugo."

Yanna stepped into the room behind him. "Harlow, your indiscretion has been forgiven." She smiled. "For my first act as

Prime, I've granted Lally Hughes honorary fae status with all rights and privileges forthcoming. Obviously, she still won't be able to travel via mirror solo, but anytime one of you wishes to take her through to see Olivia you may without repercussions."

Harlow jumped up and hugged Yanna. "Thank you. That's amazing." Harlow released her. "I didn't even know you could do that."

Yanna grinned at Fenton. "Neither did I, but once again, Fenton knew."

Augustine nodded. "That's great, but one question."

"Yes?" Fenton's brows lifted.

Augustine jerked his thumb toward Loudreux. "What do we do with him?"

Fenton looked to Yanna. "Madame Prime?"

She took a breath. "As this was unexpected—although I must say it should have at least been anticipated considering your actions, Hugo—I will grant a grace period of three months for you and your family to find a new place to live."

Loudreux sputtered. "B-but—"

"Hugo," Yanna interrupted. "This house belongs to the Prime, as do the services of your head of security, Blu. She will be coming to work for me immediately, but as for the house, I'm being considerate giving you three months. Leave with your dignity intact while you still can or we'll forgo the three months and I'll have our very capable Guardian escort you out now."

Loudreux's mouth shut in a hard line.

Augustine nodded in approval. That was the smartest move that man had made in a long time.

⚜

Giselle walked the garden, trailing her fingers through a patch of tall ornamental grass. Everything had changed. The air smelled cleaner, colors were more vibrant, sounds vibrated through her body. The lightning tree had not only filled her with power but connected her to the earth in a way she'd never been before. Was this what it felt like to be a green witch? Was this how Zara experienced life, as part of the world and not just a spectator?

She stretched her arms out and embraced the sun's dying rays. It was glorious. Like she'd been reborn. Like she'd been freed from a cage she hadn't even known existed. And soon she would have an opportunity to put her new power to use as she took over the city. The tree would belong to her. It wanted to belong to her. She heard it in her blood.

"You look like you're enjoying yourself."

She turned to see Ian had joined her. "It's beautiful outside, isn't it?"

He nodded. "It is." He swatted at something. "I could do without the bugs."

She frowned at him. "The hum of the insects is like music to me."

One of his brows quirked up. "Have you been into the wine? I'm not sure that's a great idea before we attempt this spell."

"No." She inhaled and let his accusation slide over her. "I am completely sober." She smiled as she realized how she must look. "I might be a little drunk on power. We are about to own this city, after all."

He laughed. "That's true." He took her hand, pulled her close and began to sway side to side with her in his arms.

"What are you doing?"

"Dancing. Can't you tell?" He kissed her jaw. "You said the insect noise was like music, so..."

She smiled. "You're the right man for me."

"I couldn't agree more." He moved them around the pond in a slow, waltzing circle. "Zara's awake and taking a ritual cleansing bath. We're about an hour from showtime."

"I'm ready. I couldn't be more ready."

"Good."

She canted her head and looked at him. He would do whatever she wanted him to. No matter what that was. The growing sense of power within her blossomed. "Do you love me?"

"You know I do." He spun her out and back in again. "Have I given you any reason to think otherwise?"

"No. I just wanted to hear it." She stroked her fingers down his cheek. "I could have killed Augustine today."

"Why didn't you?"

She smiled as sweetly as she knew how. "Because after we cast this spell, I want you to do it." The lightning tree leaves fluttered against her chest. "And I want you to get rid of that busybody housekeeper of his, too."

Ian bowed low. "Your wish is my command, my Lady. So mote it be."

⚜

Augustine shut the Thrun's engine off, but instead of getting out, he turned toward Harlow. "Dulcinea's in the house. We can't discuss Giselle taking a piece of the lightning tree in front of her."

Harlow nodded. "I know, but keeping something this big a secret isn't going to be easy. At what point do we share everything? Giselle having that piece of the lightning tree could be crucial."

"Or it could mean nothing. She probably doesn't even know what she has."

Harlow looked out the window. Pink and orange streaked the sky as the sun set. "She's a witch. How hard could it be to figure out?"

He sighed. "It's not my place to tell Dulcinea about the lightning tree."

She glanced at him, frowning. "Are you saying it's mine? Because to me, it feels like Lally's decision. She's the most involved." She shook her head. "I say we talk to her first, see what she wants to do."

"Okay, that's our plan then." He reached over and rested his hand on her arm, the fabric of her long-sleeve tunic preventing anything other than his warmth from getting through. "I know I've already said it but I am so glad you're you again."

"Me, too. More than I can tell you."

"Whatever happens with the witches, with Senator Pellimento, with any of this, nothing pulls us apart again. As much as we can help it."

"Agreed." Her heart did a strange, fluttery thing and she knew she was about as deep in as a woman could get. She loved him. Without a shadow of a doubt. "Let's go figure out how to rescue Cy and the others, huh?"

"You got it."

They walked to the house hand in hand, separating as they entered the kitchen.

Dulcinea greeted them. "Hey, Lally's resting, so don't make too much noise."

"Thank you for taking care of her." Harlow smiled. She was completely over whatever tension remained between her and the changeling. So what if she'd slept with Augustine years ago when they were kids. So what if she'd flaunted her faeness when Harlow had first arrived. She was a kind, generous, powerful woman who never refused to help, no matter what the situation, and for that, Harlow was grateful. "That was very kind of you. I really appreciate everything you've done. Not just for Lally but for me, too."

Dulcinea's bicolored eyes widened a bit. "Um, sure."

Augustine stood at Harlow's side, a curious look on his face.

Harlow shook her head. She knew her words must seem odd.

"I mean it. You're a valuable member of Augustine's team and I hope we can be friends. Not the kind that just tolerates each other, like we have been, but real friends."

A huge smile lit Dulcinea's face. She gave Augustine a look before answering. "You get hit on the head or something?"

"Something like that." Harlow laughed. "We're on the same side. We should act like it."

"Cool." Dulcinea nodded, the beads in her dreads rattling against each other.

Augustine took off his leather coat and draped it over one of the kitchen chairs, then sat. "As much as I hate to break up this rather interesting moment—which has my total approval, by the way—we have the matter of the witches to deal with."

Harlow flopped into a chair between him and Dulcinea. "I wish we could just kill them all with fire. My shoulder hurts, I'm still cranky from being arrested and I could eat a horse."

"I can't do anything about your shoulder or your crankiness, but Lally made brownies," Dulcinea said. "You want some?"

"How many ways can I say yes? And actually, that might take the cranky down a notch." Harlow straightened. "I'm surprised you didn't eat them all."

Dulcinea retrieved a pan from the counter. "I did. This is the second batch." She put the dish in front of Harlow, then took her seat. "Fill me in on the witches? I know Cy's trapped in their well of souls, but beyond that I'm a little in the dark."

Augustine explained what they knew as best he could. "Also, Harlow talked to Queen Jewelia—"

"Lally mentioned something about that." Dulcinea lifted one shoulder. "To be honest, that only added to my confusion. Where does she fit into all this?"

"We went to her for information. She thinks the witches are planning a chaos spell," Harlow mumbled around a mouthful of brownie.

Dulcinea's jaw went slack. "A chaos spell?"

Augustine nodded. "You know about that?"

Her chest rose and fell with a long breath. "I do. Some. Enough to know that it's not something you mess around with. That kind of magic goes wrong and there's no recovering from it. Because you're dead."

Augustine snagged one of the brownies. "Fenton told us that's what Vivianna Vincent—"

Dulcinea held her hand up. "Giselle and Zara's mother, right?"

"Yes. That's actually what killed her. She didn't commit suicide, she died trying to cast a chaos spell."

"And now her daughters are trying to re-create it. I guess stupid is hereditary." Dulcinea's jaw worked. "You know how I feel about Giselle, but Zara always seemed so...decent."

Harlow wiped her mouth. "Yeah, well, so much for that. They're in this together. Plus there's some guy helping them out. He's all inked up and wears eyeliner and dresses in black leather. Ian, maybe."

"Ian Dufrene?" Dulcinea scratched her ear. "Lots of silver jewelry. Longish hair. Rides a motorcycle?"

"Yes on the hair, but I don't know his last name or what he drives." Harlow reached for a third brownie. "The silver jewelry part is right on, too. I think his nails might have been painted black also. My memories of when Ava Mae was in charge are a little hazy. It was kind of like looking out through rainy glass."

Augustine snapped his fingers. "That guy was at Evander's funeral ceremony. He was one of the coven members in the circle with Giselle and Zara. He seemed pretty friendly with both of them."

Dulcinea nodded. "I know this guy. Ian owns the House of Pain tattoo shop." She sat back. "So that's their third, huh? Strong spells are best cast by three. Even better if the three are linked somehow. Giselle and Zara share blood, obviously, but if I had to guess I'd say they've both probably slept with Ian in order to bond with him."

"Gross." Harlow got up and grabbed milk from the fridge, then poured herself a big glass. She held the jug up toward Augustine. "You want some?"

"Sure, thanks."

She poured a glass for him, then put the jug away. "So we know what kind of spell they're going to cast, who they're casting it with, what the spell might do to them—"

"What the spell might do to us." Augustine pulled the glass of milk toward him but didn't drink it. "If that spell is really capable of rendering all fae magic useless, we will be as defenseless as humans against the witches."

"Jewelia thought it could take away the voodooers' power, too," Harlow added.

He slowly tapped his finger on the tabletop in time with his words. "We must find out when this spell is going to happen."

"Agreed," Dulcinea said. "I can shift into one of my animal forms and stake the place out."

Harlow washed down the last of the brownie with the milk. "Just be careful the witches don't know what you're up to. That's kind of what Cy was doing and look what happened to him." Poor Cy. "You think he's doing okay stuck in that pit? I hope he knows we're working on a way to get him out."

"He knows. And I'm sure he's doing fine. Probably bored, but fine. I'm more worried about the senator's son." Augustine lifted a hand. "Hang on, I've got a call coming in. Answer."

While he talked, Harlow contemplated another brownie. Dulcinea seemed to be thinking the same thing as they reached for the same one. Harlow laughed. "I should probably stop at three."

Dulcinea shrugged. "If the witches have their way, we'll all be dead soon, so I say eat as many damn brownies as you want."

"That's not exactly a happy thought, but it does put this thing in perspective." Harlow took the brownie.

Dulcinea took a different one, tipping her head toward Augustine. "You're good for him, you know. But if you break his heart—"

"You'll kill me?" Harlow bit into the brownie.

Dulcinea laughed. "No, I was going to say I'd understand. He can be a real pain sometimes."

Harlow smiled, lips closed to keep from sharing the crumbs in her teeth. "He's all right."

Augustine stood. "We need to go now."

Harlow stared at him. "Why? What's happened?"

"Fenton said two more people have gone missing."

"The witches think the well is full then." Harlow dropped her brownie and got to her feet.

Augustine pointed at Dulcinea. "What's the most powerful time for a spell like this to be cast?"

She tilted her head in thought. "Witches favor dawn, twilight or midnight."

Augustine nodded. "If it's midnight or dawn, we have a long stakeout ahead of us." He glanced at the window. "If it's twilight, we're almost out of time."

Chapter Eighteen

Giselle watched as Zara lit the last of the fire bowls nestled into the points of the pentagram she and Ian had drawn around the pond, then Zara walked toward them. She stopped in front of where the paper rendering of the sigil lay on the ground and lifted her hands. "Let us charge the sigil."

Giselle held out her hands to Zara and Ian. Excitement coursed through her. They were finally casting the spell that would change everything. They formed a tight circle around the sigil Ian had drawn beautifully. The blood had dried to a brownish red, the intricate lines so perfect the sigil looked like it had been created on a computer.

Bodies cleansed and dressed in their ceremonial robes, they now had to prepare their spirits. Heads down, eyes focused, they all stared at the sigil as they filled their minds with their desires for the spell they were about to cast.

The lines wavered in Giselle's vision, blurring and dancing on the page. She held her gaze. She needed to stay in this state where the sigil ceased being lines drawn on paper and became a living tool of magic, alive with the power necessary to animate the chaos spell. Being here felt effortless, perhaps because of the help of the lightning tree.

To indicate she'd reached the desired state of being and further charge the sigil, Giselle began to softly chant the first line of the chaos spell. "With this sigil, we summon chaos."

Over and over, the words slipped from her mouth until

the phrase blurred into a sound of power. Ian joined her next, blending his voice with hers. Then Zara finally. Together they chanted the line three more times, then stopped.

Silence pervaded the garden. They lifted their heads. They'd decided early on that as the green witch among them, Zara should be the one to lead the spell. Giselle bristled at this now, the leaves at her breast burning her skin with their urgings. She should be the one to lead.

At that moment, Ian softly squeezed her hand and smiled at her. She found herself again. No, Zara had to be the one to do it. Zara was the most tuned in to the earth. Giselle took a breath and wondered if she should give the leaves to her sister.

No.

It echoed through her like a shout. One leaf, perhaps.

No.

Giselle held still, happy to keep the leaves to herself as Zara picked up the sigil to continue the casting.

Zara lifted the sigil skyward, holding it high above her head. The sleeves of her ceremonial robe slipped down to her elbows. "Let this seal of power guide our spell. Let this sigil focus our work and bind our intent."

Giselle and Ian repeated the phrases, then with Zara in the lead the three of them walked to the pond. Zara stood in the middle. She gently eased the sigil onto the water's surface, careful to keep it afloat. With a slight breath, she propelled it toward the center.

Giselle and Ian left her to position themselves equidistantly away, bringing the new circle into being.

Zara raised her hands again and continued the casting. Thin lines of power, green and purple and orange, darted out from Zara and connected her to Giselle and Ian. Giselle felt them as they wound through her, tremulous and buzzing like bees. The leaves against her breast joined in, humming with power.

Zara began. "Oh, goddess of all that is earth and life and per-fection, I ask that you stand aside this hour so that our casting may be unhindered. Oh, spirits of all that is broken and dying and chaotic, come to us now." She lowered her hands to point to the pond. "Read this sigil. Feast upon these souls. Grant us our desire."

New lines of power leaped from Zara and traveled the circle, ropey strands of angry red that dug into Giselle's skin and made her bones ache. Ripples spilled across the pond, churning the surface.

Zara continued. "Now I call my circle back to me."

Giselle and Ian returned to Zara's side. The lines of power crackled and thickened until a halo of light surrounded each of them.

Zara pointed her hands toward the pond. "By the power of all that is dark and broken, by the strength of three, and by the desires set before us in the sigil, I call forth chaos!" She bent her head and thrust her hands forward. New power burst off her fingers and shot into the water as the lines of energy drained off Giselle and Ian and into Zara.

The pond frothed and boiled as though something might erupt from it. "Something's wrong." Zara twitched like she was being shocked. "This isn't how it's supposed to be." She moaned and her eyes rolled back in her head. "Something's wrong."

"What? Tell us," Ian said.

Giselle knew she should have led the casting.

Zara shook her head and spoke with obvious effort. "There is a hole in the spell. There aren't twelve souls. I can feel one is missing. The spell is trying to pull me in. Trying to use me to replace it. Grab hold of me."

Ian took her right arm as Giselle took her left. The drag of the spell became immediate. Giselle dug her feet in. Ian braced one foot against the low rock wall bordering their side of the pond.

Zara leaned back. "It's not working. It's going to take me." She grimaced and turned to look at Giselle, her eyes filled with grief and regret. "I'm so sorry. I love you, Sister, but there's no other way." She wrenched free of Ian, clasped Giselle's arms with surprising strength and thrust her into the water.

⚜

Giselle's scream rent the night, covering the gasps of the two women flanking Augustine. Even he hadn't seen that coming. Zara had actually just shoved her sister into the well of souls. There was no denying it. From their vantage point on the roof of Zara's house, he, Harlow and Dulcinea had front-row seats to the madness below.

"Whoa," Dulcinea whispered. "So much for Zara being the nice one."

Harlow nodded, her hands gripping the roof so hard her knuckles were white. "You can say that again."

Augustine responded, his voice just as quiet. "One less witch is one less witch."

"Do you think the spell will work now? With Giselle as the twelfth soul?" Harlow asked.

He hoped not. "I don't—"

Water spewed up from the pond like a geyser.

"It's like Vegas," Dulcinea muttered.

It was, kind of. The water glowed, making the gushing explosion look very much like a casino fountain.

"There's nothing Vegas about *that*." Harlow inched closer to Augustine.

If he hadn't been using both hands to secure his position on the roof, he would have crossed himself. A figure rose up from the center of the water.

He cursed.

Harlow nodded. "It's Giselle. Or what's left of her."

The figure was indeed the sacrificed witch. As she appeared, the water smoothed but continued to hold her aloft. Her hair floated around her, borne on an invisible current.

Harlow's gloved hand grabbed his arm and squeezed tight. "Her eyes...look at her eyes."

Giselle's eyes were solid black.

Harlow dug her fingers into his arm. Her pulse kicked up, beating in his ears like a warning drum. "Ava Mae had those same eyes. Do you think—"

"How dare you, Zara," Giselle bellowed. Her voice sounded not altogether hers. "I am not a pawn to be sacrificed, I am your sister." Her robes drifted around her when they should have been wet and clinging. "I am your *high priestess.*"

Zara held her ground even though her voice wavered with fear and unshed tears made her eyes luminous. "And I am a green witch. The one most capable of carrying out this spell. I did what had to be done for the good of our people, not because I wanted to. Isn't that what you would have done?"

Giselle smiled, confirming what Harlow had just hinted at. Giselle's mouth held rows of sharply chiseled teeth. The same as Ava Mae's had when she'd been angry.

"No," Harlow whispered. "It can't be. How did this happen?"

Giselle walked across the surface of the pond. Bodies floated up in her wake.

Augustine cursed a second time as Cy came into view. He looked so peaceful, eyes closed, body relaxed, mouth slightly open as if he might be about to smile. Dulcinea muffled a sob and tensed like she might do something. He grabbed hold of her. "Not yet, Dulce. Not yet."

Her nod was slight but enough that it registered. From the hard set of her mouth and the mournful depth of her eyes, he knew she was in a dark place. They all were.

Giselle spoke again. "We should thank you, Zara. By throwing me into that pond, you did me a great favor." Seeing her standing there on the water's surface only added to her overall creepiness. "You brought us new power." She lifted her arms toward the sky. The five flames surrounding the pond flared to double their size, spilling flickering shadows over the entire garden. "We have been reborn!"

"We?" Zara shook her head and backed away. Ian did the same. "I don't know what's happened to you, Giselle, but if you try to interfere with this spell—"

"Interfere? You think the spell is still viable?" Giselle waved her hands toward the water. "The souls are gone. Used up." She tapped her chest. "We are all that remains."

"What? No." Zara's chest rose and fell like she was panicking. "The chaos spell—we were so close to completion."

"And then you threw me in." Giselle spread her arms. "These souls might be used up, but one of them..." She ran her hands down her body. "One of them is very much still alive inside me."

"Ava Mae," Harlow whispered.

Ian shook his head. "What are you talking about?"

"That's not possible," Zara spat.

"Oh, but it is, Sister dear." Giselle reached inside her robe and extracted a handful of black leaves.

Augustine narrowed his eyes. Sick to his stomach, he leaned toward Harlow. "Are those what I think they are?"

"I think so."

Dulcinea shot him a questioning look. He shook his head. This wasn't the time or place to tell her about the lightning tree.

"You see?" Giselle held the leaves up. "Leaves from the tree you desired to control. Leaves that drew the soul of Harlow's sister to me. A soul that is now as bound to me as she is to the lightning tree. I am Giselle. But I am also Ava Mae. We have become one."

Dulcinea's brows lifted and this time, the look she gave Augustine said he *would* be explaining. So much for keeping the cat in the bag.

Giselle stepped off the water and stalked toward Zara. "And you...you are no longer necessary for our plans."

Ian moved into her path. "What are you doing, Giselle?"

"Ian." She caressed his face. "Sweet, pliable Ian. You are still necessary for our plans." She laughed and grabbed him, kissing him roughly. When she released him, his mouth was bloody. "Now be a good boy and stay out of our way."

He stood his ground. "I can't let you hurt Zara."

She tipped her head and smiled at him. "Sweetheart, you can and you will if you want to reign beside us. The power you have now pales in comparison to what we can give you. You will be our right hand. In all things. Or...we will remove you, too."

A moment passed. Indecision swirled around him like a cloud of mosquitoes. He stepped out of Giselle's way.

"Ian!" Zara screamed. She jerked like she was going to turn and run.

Giselle pointed a finger at her. "Hold still, Sister."

Zara froze from the waist down. She grabbed her leg, tried to move it and failed.

Giselle walked to her, shaking her head in obvious disappointment. "All this time, we were thinking what a burden you'd taken upon yourself. How dear you were to shoulder the weight of prepping for this spell. All the while, you were ready to serve us up if that's what it took."

"No." Zara shook her head frantically. "It was a mistake. I'm sorry. I never planned for this to happen. If I hadn't given your soul to the pond, we all would have died."

"You're only saying you're sorry because you think it's what we want to hear." Giselle wound her hand into Zara's hair, pulling her head back. "Too little, too late. You've proved you're of no use to us. And since we can't trust your disloyal ways, you must be dealt with." Her black eyes gleamed. "We hate traitorous sisters."

A low keening poured from Zara's lips. Branches swayed toward the pair. "Don't do this, Giselle. Forgive me. Let me live. I'll never go against you again. I promise to serve you and do whatever you want."

"You had already promised those things when you said you'd support us as high priestess, and look how that turned out." Giselle sighed. "No, I'm sorry. You are a traitor, just like father was. He had to die and now, so do you."

Perhaps fear gave Zara courage because she seemed to stiffen with defiance. "Did you kill him, too, Giselle? Did you drown him in his own pool?"

Giselle smiled that horrible, toothy grin. "We helped him in that direction, yes."

Zara said something Augustine didn't understand, a spell in Latin maybe. Vines burst out of the ground around Giselle's feet. They crawled up her body, binding her.

Giselle spoke a single word and the vines withered and fell away. She looked at Zara and shook her head. "You tire us." In one swift move, she snapped Zara's neck.

Zara's body fell lifeless to the ground. Giselle turned to face Ian. "Drag her body into the house."

He nodded like an automaton, eyes as blank as a doll's. It was as if fear had rendered him numb to everything else.

"Good." Giselle started for the house. "As soon as you've done that, you will come with us to the French Quarter house. This property must be destroyed."

"Wha-what about the bodies in the pond?" he managed to gasp out.

She whipped around. "What about them?"

"Aren't you concerned that they'll be traced back to you?"

"No. This will all be on Zara's head. It will be clear that she was attempting something she shouldn't and died as a result of it. Her body will be found in the ashes of the house and that will be that. Are you concerned for another reason? Something we should know about?"

He shook his head but looked utterly unconvinced. "No."

"No, what?"

"No, my Lady?"

"Very good, Ian." With that horrible, toothy smile stretching her face, Giselle strode out of Augustine's sight and into the house.

Chapter Nineteen

Harlow's heart ached with the horrifying loss of Cy, but along with that ache came anger. The kind that made her care not about the consequences, only the results. "We can't leave Cy's body here," she whispered. "He wouldn't leave one of us."

"Agreed," Dulcinea replied, the cry in her voice echoing the pain in Harlow's soul.

"As soon as Giselle and Ian leave," Augustine added.

"She's going to set the house on fire," Harlow hissed back. Below, Ian lifted Zara and carried her into the house. Her head lolled at an unnatural angle.

"I know, but we'll have time. There's no way it'll reach the second floor before we can get down." His gaze was fixed on Ian as well. "Once we're on the ground I'll get Cy and the senator's son out of the pond while you and Dulce see if you can put out the fire."

Dulcinea pulled her LMD out. "We should call the cops."

"So Giselle can kill them, too?" Augustine shook his head. "We've had enough death. Let her and Ian leave, *then* I'll call Fenton and Grantham."

Dulcinea tucked her LMD back in her pocket. "You're the boss."

"I smell smoke," Harlow said. She looked at Augustine. "And for once, it's not you."

The sound of doors closing, first the house, then the car,

reached them. Augustine shifted, lifting up slightly, his gaze tracking something down below. "And . . . they're gone. Let's go."

She and Dulcinea followed him to the edge. Thin streams of smoke curled over the guttering. He jumped down first, then reached his hands up to her. "Dulce, give her a hand down."

"I can do it."

"C'mon," Dulcinea said softly. "Now's not the time to break something. Grab hold of my wrist." She held out her hand.

Harlow took it, clasping her gloved fingers around Dulcinea's wrist as Dulcinea did the same to her, then Dulcinea lifted Harlow and lowered her over the side until Augustine caught her around the thighs.

"Got her," he called up.

Dulcinea released Harlow and jumped down next to them.

Harlow planted her hands on Augustine's shoulders and looked down at him. He still held her around the waist. "You can put me down now."

"I know." He loosened his grip so she slid down his body. "I just don't want to." He looked toward the pond. "I'm tired of losing people."

She held on to his arm. "We all are. Look, you call Fenton. Dulcinea can look after Cy and I'll see what I can do about the fire, okay? After you fill him in, come help me in the house." Bright orange fire danced behind the sheers covering the windows. "You're part smokesinger. You should be real comfortable in all those flames."

He nodded, a gentle smile forming on his face. "All right then." His serious demeanor took over as she walked toward the house and heard him say, "Call Fenton."

She tried the door. Locked. She picked up a rock and smashed one of the French door's panes, then reached through and unlatched the door. As she pushed it open, a wave of heat hit her. Inside, flames licked the walls and smoke pooled on the ceiling. She blinked and got her bearings.

Plants filled the house. The kitchen was off to the left and to the right was the sitting room. Zara's feet were visible on the other side of a large leather sofa.

Harlow almost felt sorry for her, but the woman had tried to kill her and planned to kill Augustine. She'd gotten what she'd deserved. Harlow made a run for the kitchen and started digging under sink cabinets for a fire extinguisher. She found it behind a stack of towels. The crackle and thrum of the flames grew louder. She grabbed the extinguisher and stood, about to run down the source of the fire, when Dulcinea dashed into the house.

"We've been calling you. Forget the house." Her face lit up. "Cy's *alive*." With a tip of her head toward the garden, she left as quickly as she'd come in.

"What?" Harlow dropped the extinguisher and ran after her. As soon as she got outside the house, she realized how much smoke she'd been breathing in. Augustine crouched by the edge of the pond, obscuring Cy's body, which didn't look any more alive than the last time she'd seen it.

She jogged to catch up with Dulcinea, trying to ignore the bloated, floating corpses of those who hadn't made it. As they rounded the tall growth of reeds and grasses on the pond's backside, she realized that while Cy was still lying down, he was talking to Augustine.

She fell to her knees beside him. "Cy! How are you still alive?"

A massive smile greeted her. "You're not going to believe this, but I think Father Ogun had a lot to do with it."

"Really? After he sold me out to the witches?"

"But he didn't know they were going to turn on him, too. He had no love for them, I promise you that." Cy coughed, spitting up a little water. "Once he came to, he spent the rest of our time down there chanting spells over both of us and drawing lines of protection around us in the dirt. Did he make it?"

Harlow looked at Augustine. He glanced toward the pond for a moment, then back at her and shook his head.

"I think you're the only survivor," Harlow said. "Queen Jewelia, a voodoo mambo I talked to, said you might not be affected by the witches' spell the same way as the humans because you're fae. Ogun's voodoo doesn't seem to have had the same benefit." Harlow grabbed Cy's big hand and squeezed it. Sirens pealed through the air. The good guys were on their way. "Whatever the reason, I'm so happy you're still alive."

"Might need a few days of recovery." He smiled weakly. "Feel like I've been run over by a jun-jun."

She laughed, knowing she was the only one who'd get his reference to the enormous, armor-shelled beast that roamed the badlands of the RPG they both played. "At least you don't smell like one."

He nodded, then went serious. "I guess you managed to get rid of Ava Mae?"

"Yep. When you tossed me out of the pit, she got stuck behind. Although, she didn't entirely disappear." She glanced at Augustine before answering. "There was a lot of other stuff that went down first, which we'll explain later, but the wrap-up is Ava Mae seems to have taken up residence in Giselle, the witch who tried to kill you."

"Wow." He stared at the sky, his face illuminated by the fire now engulfing the first floor of the house. "I guess we're not rid of her yet."

"Nope." A loud crack erupted behind her. She turned. Firemen had smashed the garden gate off its hinges and were dragging hoses through the yard. Augustine and Fenton, heads bent in deep conversation, stood halfway between the house and the pond. Emergency pole lights, set up by the firemen, flared brightly turning the night into day.

Dulcinea was directing two paramedics toward Cy's location. She ran along beside them. "He's right here." She pointed at Cy but looked at Harlow. "They're going to take him to the hospital, check him over, probably keep him the night. Make sure Cy knows."

"You hear all that?" Harlow asked Cy.

He nodded. "I'm not much on human hospitals but considering how I feel, I'm not going to argue."

The paramedics lowered the stretcher. "Excuse us, ma'am, we're going to need you to give us some space."

Harlow gave Cy's hand a final squeeze, then pushed to her feet and backed up. "You take good care of him."

"Yes, ma'am." They went to work doing whatever paramedics did. Dulcinea helped them lift Cy's enormous bulk onto the gurney, then they wheeled him across the grass and into the waiting ambulance.

Harlow walked to Augustine's side, but it was Fenton's attention she wanted. "They're taking Cy to the hospital." She nodded at the ambulance. "Are those human doctors going to have any idea what to do with him?"

Fenton smiled. "Not sure, but there are fae doctors there, too. Always have been. They'll take good care of him."

"Thanks, that's reassuring."

Grantham joined them. Behind him, uniformed police were trickling in. "You people don't do anything on a small scale, do you?" He glanced at the house. The firemen seemed to have the fire under control. He shook his head as he pulled out his tablet and stylus. "Want to give me the short version?"

Bits of soot and ash floated down onto them. Harlow flicked a piece off her arm. "People are dead, the house is on fire and our witch problem is not yet solved."

Grantham looked at her. "Maybe not that short."

Augustine nodded. "Robbie Pellimento's body is in the pond, along with nine others including Rufus Ogun. One of my lieutenants was in there, too, but he's the only one who survived and the EMTs are taking him to the hospital. Zara Vincent's body is in the house. Killed by her sister. Who is now most likely at her house in the Quarter with her boyfriend, Ian, but she's got a little possession issue that's going to make it tricky for you guys to handle. Probably ought to leave her to us."

Grantham stared at him for a moment, then slowly started to shake his head. "Damn." He scratched his forehead. "Pellimento's dead, huh? That is not going to go down well."

Augustine held his hands up. "His blood is on the witches, not the fae."

Grantham sighed. "I wish I thought that was going to matter."

Fenton pulled off his glasses and wiped them clean with a hanky. "What sort of fallout should we expect exactly?"

"I'll assume you've been monitoring the senator's track record?"

Fenton slipped his glasses back on. "We have. We're well aware of her hatred for othernaturals despite her clever attempts to hide the actions she's taken against us through her shell corporations and connections."

"Then it won't come as a surprise to you that she'll use her son's death to make some public noise about this." Grantham brushed a piece of ash off his suit coat. "My guess is she's going to try for something big, like all othernaturals have to be registered, that sort of thing. Or..."

When Grantham didn't immediately finish, Harlow spoke up. "Or what?"

"She threatened me with martial law," Augustine offered.

"That." Grantham took a deep inhale. "Or she'll keep to her usual MO and try to force her will upon the fae in private."

"In what way?" Augustine asked.

"Blackmail. Extortion. Something of that nature." Grantham frowned. "She's a senator. That's just business as usual for her."

Augustine put his arm around Harlow's shoulders. "Let her try. We've got bigger issues right now than a racist politician."

Grantham nodded. "I hear you. Just let me know if I can help." He pointed at them. "And watch your back. Her goons are still in town."

Augustine snorted. "I can assure you they will not get the jump on me twice."

The coroner arrived. Grantham gave him a wave. "If you'll excuse me, I better get to work. I'll let you know if anything interesting turns up."

Harlow spoke up. "Zara's neck is broken." Grantham looked back at her. She shrugged. "Just thought you should let the coroner know."

"Will do. You take care now." He took off, leaving the three of them alone.

Fenton put his hands on his hips. "This is a mess." He looked at Augustine. "You have a suggestion on what to do next?"

"Yes," Augustine said. "But not here. We need to regroup at the Pelcrum."

Fenton nodded. "All right. Do you and Dulcinea want to head over there? I can run Harlow home."

Augustine pulled Harlow a little closer to him. "About that." He looked at her. "I can't do this without you, but I'd like to make it official. How'd you like to be one of my lieutenants? You're doing a good part of the job already without the title."

"Well, when you put it that way..." The idea scared her witless, but she grinned anyway. "I thought you'd never ask."

❧

Sydra and Yanna were waiting for them when Augustine entered the Pelcrum's war room.

"This place is so cool," Harlow whispered. She ran her hands over the huge table that hosted their meetings. The large fleur-de-lis inlaid in the center gleamed, the wood polished to a high shine.

Augustine grinned at her. Hell's bells, it was good to have her back and at his side. "You don't have to whisper, babe."

Her cheeks flushed, making her freckles pop. She looked down and a curtain of hair swung over her face. If that's the response "babe" got him, he was going to have to try out a few more terms of endearment.

"Yanna— I mean..." Augustine hesitated. "I guess I should call you Prime Quinn now."

She smiled at him. "I think we're past that, Augustine."

"Whatever you're good with, so am I. How's Blu working out?"

Yanna tipped her head back and forth. "She's adjusting. I don't need the level of protection Loudreux did, but I think she's pleased not to be working for him anymore." Her gaze shifted to Harlow. "I'm not opposed to Harlow's presence, but isn't it a little unusual to allow someone into the Pelcrum who hasn't been sworn in?"

"It is, but she'll be sworn in soon." Augustine took his seat. "She's agreed to become one of my lieutenants, and in light of recent circumstances, I felt we could use all the help available. Hell, I would have brought Lally in if I'd thought about it sooner."

Yanna nodded. "I see. And I approve." She leaned forward. "Now that I'm Prime, I have no intentions of turning into

Loudreux. I'm not going to cramp your style as Guardian. It might be a bit unorthodox at times, but you're doing a good job. I would ask that you keep me informed, however. I want to help. I'm not interested in the disdainful, hands-off approach of my predecessor."

"Good." Augustine spread his hands on the table as the others took their places. "Cy is in the hospital. Fenton, they sent you a report, didn't they?"

The cypher cleared his throat and pulled out his LMD, swiping his finger across the screen. "Yes, here it is. Cylo is dehydrated and suffering from what the doctor is calling blood poisoning." He looked up from the screen. "Dr. Carlson took on Cylo's case and he'll be scheduling the shift nurses assigned to Cylo as well. For those of you who don't know Dr. Carlson, he's fae. He believes this blood poisoning is a result of Cylo's system fighting off the witches' magic."

"It's my fault," Harlow muttered. "He was only in there because of me."

Augustine shook his head. "He was in there because he was doing his job, which just happened to be protecting you. Someday, as a lieutenant, you may do the same for him."

She nodded solemnly. "With pleasure."

Augustine looked at Fenton. "Thank you for the update. Let us know if there's any change."

"I will," Fenton answered.

"Now," Augustine said. "We need to focus on the issue at hand. Giselle Vincent. Based on what we saw happen at Zara's house—"

"They were trying to perform chaos magic, correct?" Yanna asked.

"Yes. Fortunately, they failed. As soon as it became clear the spell wasn't going to work, Zara shoved Giselle into the pond holding the sacrificial souls."

"They also floated a paper with a strange design onto the same water," Harlow added.

Yanna's brows lifted. "Did it look as though it was drawn in blood?"

"Maybe." Harlow looked at him, then Dulcinea. "What do you think?"

Dulcinea nodded. "Definitely could have been blood."

"It was a sigil," Yanna said. "They would have used one to focus the spell and direct the chaos energy toward their goal." She frowned. "I wonder why the spell didn't work."

"Because," Harlow said. "Cy got me out of the pond without the witches knowing about it. They thought they had the right number of souls."

"So that's why Zara pushed Giselle in? To add the soul they needed?" Yanna clucked her tongue. "Those witches are a cold, calculating lot."

"It gets worse," Augustine added. "Adding Giselle to the pond didn't work the way Zara had hoped. Something went wrong. Giselle emerged from the pond with one of the sacrificial souls melded to hers." Explaining this without mentioning the lightning tree was growing more difficult. "It seems to have grown her power exponentially. She killed Zara like it was nothing. She also set fire to the house. And she's got another wizard working for her, under fear of death most likely, by the name Ian."

Yanna's expression held many questions. "How do you know she has this other soul? Why would that give her more power? I don't understand how this all happened. A failed casting of a chaos spell should have killed them all."

Augustine glanced at Harlow. The look she gave him in return said she understood what he was struggling with.

She swallowed before addressing the table. "I know I'm not officially one of you yet, but—"

"Yes, you are," Dulcinea interjected. "Don't worry about what's official and what's not."

Augustine smiled at her. He loved that she and Harlow had come to this new understanding, loved they were acting like a team and not competitors.

"Thank you," Harlow said. "With that understanding, I assume anything said here can be kept in confidence?"

He knew what she was leading up to. "What you're about to tell us won't go beyond this room." He glanced around the table, taking a moment to pause on each face. Yanna, Sydra, Dulcinea and Fenton all gave him a nod in return. "Go ahead, Harlow. Your words won't go beyond these walls."

She took a deep breath. "Inside my mother's house, my house, I mean, the house that Augustine and I share, inside that house there is a very powerful thing called a lightning tree. It's been there longer than the house."

Yanna gasped. "I thought that was a fae legend. That's real?"

Harlow nodded. "I wish it wasn't."

Fenton spoke up. "If you go back far enough in the archives, you'll find sealed records of the deal made between Lally Hughes's mother, the original owner of the land the tree was on, and the fae Elektos at that time. They built the house around the tree, weaving in protective and secretive magic to keep the tree hidden and to cause its memory to fade from people's minds. Lally Hughes was granted immunity from this magic and as caretaker was promised the right to stay with the tree her entire life. Which she's done."

"It's not like she has much of a choice," Harlow said. "She can't get too far from the tree for too long or she gets sick." She sighed. "Anyway, I did something stupid. I tried to use the tree to bring my dead twin sister, Ava Mae, back to life. I poured her ashes onto the tree and she did come back to life, just not the way I expected. The tree turned her into a kind of spirit that was warped with the tree's magic. She possessed me and it wasn't until the witches threw me into the pond that I was able to get free of Ava Mae."

Yanna made a bleak face. "I can already see where this is going. Ava Mae is the soul that melded with Giselle, isn't she?"

"Yes. Worse, we're pretty sure Giselle broke into our house, stole a piece of the lightning tree and had it on her. That's how Ava Mae was drawn to her and able to take control of her."

Sydra shook her head. "Unbelievable."

"Tell me about it." Harlow made a face. "We actually tried to recapture Ava Mae by sinking a piece of the lightning tree into the pond after I escaped, but I get the sense that the combination of Giselle's living body and the leaves overrode that. Which means there's still a piece of the lightning tree in the pond we need to recover." She raised her hands. "Whoever tackles that task must be sure not to touch the piece with their bare hands."

"*Sturka*." Yanna looked at Augustine. "Giselle being possessed by Ava Mae is a very different kind of problem than just dealing with the witches. Power that old and that strong isn't going to lie down and give up."

Augustine took a long, slow breath. "No, it's not. Which is why we're in this war room. We have to come up with a way to stop Giselle before she destroys everything we've worked for."

Chapter Twenty

A va Mae tucked one arm between her head and the pillow. The witch's house wasn't as comfortable as Harlow's but it would do for now. Or at least until she took control of that house once again. First she had to solve this issue of the body once and for all.

Her time in the well of souls hadn't been wasted—suffering had a way of putting a fine point on things. While she'd been in there, she'd had an idea about what might secure her in whatever body she could find, but it meant getting back to the tree. She had to have a body. She'd been trapped in that tree for so long, years of being filled with the tree's own desires to escape the confines of the house, that attaining a body was all she could think about.

That meant getting back to the house, preferably without being noticed. How that would happen she wasn't sure, but it had to happen soon because possessing the witch was nothing like possessing Harlow had been. Giselle had no hollow place in her, no rent in her soul that Ava Mae could slip inside and fill like she had with her twin. Harlow had been her blood, her body double, her twin. Their powers had meshed, making them a force to be reckoned with, but this witch...Ava Mae tensed as the body she inhabited tried again to reject her.

The aftershock passed. A tiny, metaphysical tremor that turned Ava Mae's stomach with a few seconds of nausea.

The witch had a very different set of powers. She was human,

not fae, and she hadn't welcomed Ava Mae's invasion so much
as allowed it to spare her own life.

Fortunately, the witch still slumbered, the fall into the pond
and her brief dance with death enough to keep her subdued.
But that wouldn't last and Ava Mae knew it. Her struggle for
control was about to become a war, but she had a plan.

Until then, she would enjoy the calm before the storm. If
she couldn't have Augustine, she would continue to amuse herself with the male witch. He lay beside her in the bed, the rise
and fall of his chest finally returning to normal levels. Humans
were not as resilient as fae, but she felt certain her use of him
wasn't going to do him any permanent harm. And if it did,
well, she had no intentions of keeping him alive that much longer anyway. He was wary of her and had too much rebellion
in him.

"Ian," she whispered.

He swallowed. "Yes, my Lady."

She turned on her side and stroked her fingers down his
naked, tattooed chest. She stopped where the face of a snarling
devil breathed fire, then traced the whorls of red and orange
and black until goose bumps rose on his skin.

"You've had enough rest."

He shifted very slightly away from her. "Again? I don't think
I can. I'm spent."

That was not the answer she wanted to hear. She straddled
him, staring down into his face. "Find a way."

He shook his head. "It doesn't work like that. I can't just snap
my fingers and—"

"What good is your magic then?" She could feel the tree
manifesting itself in her appearance. "What good are *you*?"

His eyes reflected how black hers had gone. How wide and
toothy her smile had become. He nodded, fear and tension tugging his mouth open slightly. "Of course, my magic, I was just

too tired to think." He lifted a hand to caress her cheek and smiled. It didn't reach his eyes.

She didn't care. She wanted obedience, not sincerity. "I'll let you sleep after this, I promise."

But not for long, because after they were done, they were going to Harlow's house. Her house. The home of the tree that had given her life. And then, with the help of that tree, she would finally become truly whole. No other soul inside her, no sharing a body. Just her, in control.

Then she would deal with Harlow. Despite the pleasure from Ian's efforts, Ava Mae's lip curled in anger and fear. Because having been inside Harlow, Ava Mae knew what her twin was capable of.

Even if Harlow didn't.

⚜

Giselle had never experienced fear like she had after being pushed into the pond. She'd felt the crush of the spell, her breath leaving her lungs. Her soul leaving her body. Terror had clawed through her like the will to live. She'd cried out for help. Any help. Her last memory had been a mouthful of water and a plea to be saved.

She'd awakened expecting to find herself in the Summerlands. Instead, she found herself alive and no longer alone. The tortured soul who'd come to her for help, the one she and Zara and Ian had tossed into the very same pond, now possessed her.

Ava Mae. Having her inside Giselle's body felt like wearing a coat two sizes too small.

As the effects of the failed chaos magic wore off and Giselle's memory became clearer, she understood how it had happened. Ava Mae had wrenched control from Giselle in those last dark, breathless moments after entering the pond. When Giselle's instinct had been survival at any price. When Giselle had clutched at the lightning tree's leaves and cried out for the tree to save her.

This was not what she'd had in mind.

This is my body.

Ava Mae laughed. *I see you're awake. You're welcome, by the way.*

For what?

For saving your life, of course. Now if you could hold it down. I'm in the middle of something. Or perhaps I should say someone's in the middle of me.

As the scales fell away from Giselle's eyes, she realized what she was seeing. Ian. On top of her. No, not her. Ava Mae. Did he know? Based on the numb look in his eyes, she guessed he did.

Ian, help me.

He can't hear you, witch. I'm in charge now. Remember? It's what you asked me for.

You? I asked the tree.

More laughter. *I am the tree. The tree and I are one.*

The leaves burned against Giselle's breast like a reminder. If that was true, if Ava Mae and the tree were one and the same... *Goddess grant me the strength to free myself.* Giselle focused every ounce of power and energy she could scrape up into a single move.

What are you doing?

Giselle answered Ava Mae with a burst of power, throwing Ian off as she tore the leaves from her skin and hurled them to the floor. The moment the contact was broken, her control steadied.

No, Ava Mae cried. *What have you done? You stupid, stupid woman. Don't you know what I can do for you? The power we can have together? We can rule this city—*

"*Mortus sonus.*" The silencing spell did more than shut Ava Mae up. It affirmed that Giselle was truly in charge again. She exhaled with relief at the sound of her own voice. "At last."

Ian looked thoroughly confused. He opened his mouth to speak, but nothing came out. He frowned.

"Sorry," Giselle said. "That wasn't meant for you." She released the spell and held up a finger to Ian. "Just a moment, my love." *Ava Mae, if you try to take me over again, I will do more than silence you. I will exorcise you. Understood?*

Understood. The voice that answered her was half the volume it had been before. Being relegated to the position of second fiddle had taken the wind out of her parasite's sails.

But the power that coursed through Giselle verged on the euphoric. She wasn't about to exorcise Ava Mae. Not if she could help it.

"What's going on?" Ian asked. "Aren't you Ava Mae?"

"No, I'm back to being me. Giselle." She patted herself down. Everything felt as it should have.

Ian slumped against the headrest. "Thank the goddess. If I had to have sex with you again, I thought I'd die." He shot her an apologetic look. "Not you. Ava Mae."

"I knew what you meant." She rolled her shoulders, happy to be in control of her body again. "My memory of what happened is pretty fuzzy in some spots. I know we didn't make the chaos spell happen, did we?"

"No."

"Where's Zara? Recovering? I imagine she'll sleep for a few days after—"

"Giselle."

She looked at Ian. His face held a deep seriousness. "What?"

"Zara's dead. You... or Ava Mae, I guess, snapped her neck."

His words brought the memory of what Ava Mae had done back with a cold, hard shock. Giselle nodded stiffly as the scene played out in her head. It might have been her body, but she had definitely not been in charge of it. "I remember that now." She crossed her legs and hugged a pillow to her chest in an attempt to stifle the pain. She almost broke, then reminded herself, "It's no different than what she planned for me."

Exactly, Ava Mae whispered.

"I don't think she had it planned. More like it seemed the best way to fix the spell in the moment." Ian shook his head sadly. "I had no idea she would even try something like that. If I had, I would have stopped her."

"I know that." Giselle lifted her chin, her chest aching with the loss as much as from the betrayal. "I *am* sorry she's gone. We were just reconnecting. And she was the only close family I had left." She swallowed down the emotion clogging her throat. "But if she'd had her way, I wouldn't be here."

"That's right." Ian nodded, moving to be next to her. He wrapped his arms around her. "I'm so glad you're the one who made it."

She rested her head on his shoulder. "Having Ava Mae's spirit inside me is a little overwhelming, but the possibilities of what this new power can do for me—for us—are too great to ignore. I feel almost invincible. Like I've been surrounded by an impenetrable shield." There was nothing that could hurt her. *Us.* Nothing that could stop her from accomplishing whatever it was she desired.

Us! Ava Mae shouted.

"So what now?" Ian asked.

Giselle ignored her to answer him. "Now we do exactly what we intended to do with the chaos spell. We find a way to take over the rule of this city just as we were meant to. The way our ancestors did."

We will rule together, witch.

"Yes," Giselle whispered. "Together."

Ian pulled back to look at her. "Were you talking to Ava Mae?" She nodded. "It must be confusing for you."

"I don't really understand it, but if you want to keep her inside you then I'm willing to go along with whatever you think is best."

"What's best is for me to rest." She lay down on the bed and pulled the sheet over herself. "I am exhausted from all the preparations for the chaos spell, from almost dying and from having a very demanding voice inside my head. A few hours, that's all I need." Ian didn't know about the lightning tree and she didn't have the energy to explain that this spirit that had come to live inside her was the soul of that tree. She welcomed Ava Mae as a gift from the tree, but Ava Mae's desire to be the one in charge was something she was going to have to get over. That was never happening.

I am stronger than you, witch. I am older. I know what needs to be done.

Ian kissed her cheek. "Get all the rest you need. I'll be downstairs, working on a plan."

Giselle closed her eyes and feigned sleep. *I am the high priestess. I am the most powerful witch in this city. You either work with me or I will remove you.*

I am the one with the power. Ava Mae's anger manifested like an itch on Giselle's skin.

She smiled. *You have your own power, yes, but the tree gave you to me. To use as I see fit. And right now, I don't need you.*

You needed me at the pond.

You did save my life. I owe you for that. But you took my sister's life, so I consider us even.

She needed to be taught a lesson.

I don't know about that, but as she was going to kill me anyway, I'm letting it go. Now stop your incessant chatter or I'll bespell you again.

Ava Mae went quiet.

Satisfied that her parasite was taking her seriously, Giselle asked her a question. *What do I need to do to take over the city?* She already had a good idea but she wanted to see what Ava Mae's approach would be.

A moment passed without a reply and Giselle got the distinct impression that Ava Mae was pouting. At last, she answered. *For us to take over the city, we need to remove the fae. It's that simple.*

And how would you propose doing that, since the chaos spell didn't work?

Ava Mae laughed. *Further proof you have no idea how powerful I am. The tree, witch. The tree can do anything you desire.*

Giselle's eyes opened. *What do I have to do?*

Easy. Offer it a sacrifice, then ask for what you want. The tree will do the rest.

What kind of sacrifice?

Ava Mae answered her question with another one. *What is your greatest desire?*

To destroy the fae and their Guardian.

And who represents that desire best of all?

Augustine.

NO! Ava Mae's scream raked pain through Giselle's body. *You will not touch him.*

Giselle cringed as she replied, *Who then?*

Ava Mae paused. *Harlow.*

Chapter Twenty-one

Harlow entered the house ahead of Augustine and Fenton, calling out for Lally as soon as she was in the kitchen. "Lally? Where are you? We need to go see Queen Jewelia." She pulled her gloves off and tossed them on the counter. She'd almost progressed to the point that she didn't need them, but they'd become something of a safety blanket.

Lally came in from the foyer, the serious set of her mouth a sign that all was not right. "We got something else to deal with first."

Fenton and Augustine walked in behind Harlow. Augustine shucked his coat. "What's going on?"

Lally looked older than she had when they left. She pointed to the front of the house, her voice solemn and quiet like she was fighting tears. "Detective Grantham is here to see you, Augie."

Fenton looked at Augustine. Augustine shrugged. "Then let's go see him."

"He's in the library."

"After you." Augustine followed Lally, leaving Fenton and Harlow to trail behind. The tension in the house was palpable, causing her stomach to knot.

Grantham wasn't alone in the library. Two uniformed police officers stood with him. He didn't look any happier about being there than Lally had. "Robelais, I'm sorry about this, but my hands are tied."

Augustine stopped short. "Sorry about what?"

Harlow stayed by his side, nerves turning her insides to mush. Something bad was about to happen. The air reeked of it.

Grantham wiped a hand over his mouth. "Augustine Robelais, you're under arrest for the murder of Robert Pellimento. Anything you say can and will be—"

"What?" Harlow felt like punching something. She stepped in front of Augustine. "The witches killed the senator's son. The witches killed all of those tourists."

"—used against you in a court of law." Grantham had handcuffs out, but the set of his face showed the effort it was taking him to do his job.

"This is preposterous," Fenton sputtered. "On what grounds is he being charged? On what evidence?"

"Yeah," Augustine said. "I'd like to know that myself."

"You have the right to an attorney. If you cannot afford an attorney, one will be provided for you." Grantham reached for Augustine's arm.

Harlow smacked him away.

The uniformed officers lunged, grabbing her and pulling her to the side. Grantham scowled at them. "Let her go."

She jerked away from them to grab Grantham's bare hand. She felt how sorry he was, how angry, how helpless. Then her anger returned. She forced it away and focused on Grantham. She pushed into him the desire to help, her need to protect Augustine making her reckless.

"I'm sorry," he said. He shook his head slowly. "There's nothing I can do. This was all the senator's—"

"Harlow, enough." Augustine pulled her away by the hem of her tunic. "I appreciate what you're doing but this clearly isn't Grantham's idea." He looked at the detective. "Is it?"

Grantham blinked like he was clearing his head. "No." He paused a moment, then looked at the officers. "Wait outside."

The pair hesitated.

He repeated his command. "Wait outside. There won't be any more trouble." He glanced at Augustine and Harlow. "Will there?"

Augustine shook his head. "No."

Harlow crossed her arms. She wasn't going that easy. "We'll see."

Augustine put his hand on her shoulder. "Harley," he muttered.

She ground her teeth together and gave the answer she knew Augustine wanted. "Fine. No trouble."

The officers left. As Lally slid the library doors shut behind them, Harlow turned on Augustine. "Why are you so calm about this?"

He shrugged. "Because you're not?" He winked at her, infuriating her a little, but that was probably what he was going for. "Because I'm sure it's just a misunderstanding."

Grantham exhaled, then shook his head. "It's not."

Lally clutched at her throat and muttered a soft prayer.

"What do you mean?" Fenton asked.

Harlow nodded, unable to form words to adequately express what her insides were doing.

Grantham swallowed. "The coroner found a slip of paper in the pocket of Robert Pellimento's shorts. It had this address on it."

Augustine's hand tightened on her shoulder. She narrowed her eyes at Grantham. "That means nothing. His mother could have given him that."

Grantham's brows quirked up. "Why would she have given him this address?"

"As a place to avoid?" But it sounded thin even as it left her mouth. "What about the fact that he died in that pond? That's proof Augustine didn't have anything to do with it. The water in Pellimento's lungs is all the evidence you need."

Grantham sighed. "That's part of the problem. There is no water in his lungs. There's no water in any of the victims' lungs. It's like they died somewhere else and were tossed into the pond postmortem."

A chill sucked all remaining hope out of her. Augustine was going to be taken away from her and there was nothing she could do. She shook her head. "The spell killed them, not the pond. They didn't drown in the water. Their souls were ripped from them by magic."

Lally crossed herself and sank down on one of the couches. She looked up at Fenton. "Mr. Welch, there's got to be something you can do."

Fenton approached Grantham. "Surely we can work together on this. You know as well as I that these poor souls are dead because of the witches. Augustine had nothing to do with this. You were at Zara's house. You saw the aftermath of that chaos spell with your own eyes."

Grantham shook his head. "We may know the truth, but the senator doesn't care. She's pushing this hard. If I don't take Augustine in, they'll call SWAT to do it." He sighed, his eyes heavy-lidded. "They'll tear this house up. You don't want that."

"No, we don't." Augustine stepped forward. "I understand. You're just doing your job."

Fenton shoved his glasses back on his nose. "We'll post bail immediately."

Harlow's heart ached like it was being clawed apart. "What? We're just going to let him go like that?"

Fenton's eyes held anger and pain. "We have no choice. This may be a Haven city but we are still ultimately subject to human law." He turned back to Grantham. "Where are you taking him?"

"Orleans Parish Prison. Bail could take up to seventy-two hours." He shrugged. "With the senator involved, it could move a lot faster. She'll want him charged immediately." He exhaled like the weight of the world pressed down on him. He shifted to look at Augustine. "You ready?"

"Can I have a minute?"

"Sure, but clock's ticking. I'll be in the foyer."

Augustine didn't wait until Grantham had left to pull Harlow into his arms and kiss her. "This is going to be all right. The man's just doing his job. In the meantime, I need you"—he looked at Lally and Fenton, too—"all of you, to work on a solid defense."

Fenton nodded. "We have a criminal defense attorney on retainer. I'll get him there immediately."

Augustine took Harlow's shoulders and bent to look her in the eyes. "Don't worry about me. I'll be fine. Human jail is a cakewalk. It's not like I haven't been there before, although it's been a few years."

"Just because you spent time in juvie doesn't make this all right." She clenched her hands so tightly they throbbed. "I will find a way to prove your innocence *and* take the senator down."

"I know you will." He kissed her forehead. "Sun's up in a few hours. You should get a little sleep."

She snorted. "I'm not about to sleep while you're locked up."

"Try. You're going to need it." He shrugged one shoulder. "As soon as I'm processed, that's what I'll be doing."

Lally sniffed and wiped at her eyes. "I don't like this one bit." She stood and walked over to Augustine. "Imagine if Olivia knew."

Augustine slanted his eyes at her. "Under no circumstances is she to know about this. You got it?"

Lally frowned but nodded. "I got it."

Augustine hugged her. "I'll be home soon. I promise. Right after Fenton bails me out." He let her go and strode to the door like he was about to go meet a friend, not be booked for murder. He slid the library's pocket doors back, gave them a little salute, then walked toward Grantham, hands out in front of him.

Harlow turned away. "I can't watch this. It makes me want to kill someone."

Fenton stood beside her, stiff with obvious anger. "In light of the current circumstances, perhaps another choice of words would be in order. But I know how you feel."

Harlow crossed her arms, the click of metal against metal ringing in her ears as Grantham put the cuffs on Augie. The crack in her heart widened seeing him shackled like that. "You just worry about getting him out." She stared out the library windows into the darkness. "I'll worry about keeping him free."

⚜

Augustine sat in the back of Grantham's police-issued sedan, one leg sprawled out on the hard plastic bench seat. The other two officers flanked his vehicle with their patrol cars as they traveled the dark streets of the Garden District. Grantham kept glancing at the closed-circuit screen that showed everything going on in the rear seat. Augustine slouched against the window. "You can stop checking on me. I'm fine."

Grantham frowned and shook his head, shifting his gaze back to the street. "This is a damn travesty."

"But one that neither of us has any say about, so stop beating yourself up over it." They passed into a lower-rent area and the streets got darker. "Besides, I'll be out as soon as bail is set."

"Could be two, three million if the senator has a say. Which she will."

Augustine shrugged. "Doesn't matter. Fae pockets are deep." He glanced forward. "Fenton will take—hey, what the hell?"

Two black SUVs barreled toward them. The lights on the vehicles switched off.

"No idea." Grantham straightened, all business.

Sparks erupted as the first SUV rammed the patrol car in front of them, sending it into one of the live oaks lining the street. Grantham swerved around the wreck and sped past. "Hang on."

"I am." Augustine put both feet on the floor and braced himself. These had to be Pellimento's men. No wonder she'd pushed for the arrest so hard. She'd planned it to draw him out.

Behind them, the second SUV sideswiped the rear patrol car, pushing it over the median and rolling it onto its side. Grantham cursed but kept going. "I have no idea what the hell's going on."

"I do." Augustine swiveled to see out the back window. Both SUVs had turned around and were following them. "They want me. That's why they're still coming after us."

"I see them." Grantham whipped down a side street, fishtailing the car around the turn. The man might have been a boxer, but he drove like he'd retired from Formula One.

The SUVs were on their tail, so close Augustine could see the driver. "*Sturka*. That's Sutter and his boys."

"Damn Pellimento." Grantham sped up but the SUVs stayed glued to them.

Augustine pulled against the cuffs, snapping the links between them with little effort. He was pretty sure Grantham knew they'd just been for show anyway. He leaned over the seat. "What's the plan here? Being Sutter's guest again isn't high on my list."

Grantham glanced in the rearview camera. "Mine, either."

Augustine looked behind them again. "Backup has to be on the way, right?"

"In theory." Grantham handed him a nightstick. "Maybe you should take this."

Augustine held his hands up. "I don't need it." He'd never used his fae talents to kill a human, but tonight might change that. "If we get out of this car alive, I'm going to disappear. I'll still be here, just in a form you won't be able to see. I'll take out as many as I can." Which should be most of them.

"Sounds like a plan. Son of a—"

Ahead of them, a third SUV careened out of a side street to cut them off. Grantham jerked the wheel, but it was too late. His sedan plowed into the side of the new SUV, throwing him and Augustine up and forward. The air bags deployed with a loud pop as the sedan flipped onto its side and slid to a stop in the middle of the street.

Grantham shifted, cursing softly. He tapped something and the air bags deflated. "You still alive, Robelais?"

Wheels squealed not far away. Augustine pushed an air bag out of the way to grunt a response. He got his bearings a second later. The SUV they'd hit was parallel to them and dented but otherwise hadn't moved much. "Three coming out of the SUV on the side."

"And behind us?"

"Half a dozen more. All heavily armed. And all in night vision goggles." He had no idea if that would allow them to see him in his half form or not.

Grantham unholstered his gun. He was bleeding from the side of his head and his nose looked broken.

Augustine grabbed his arm. "Listen, all they want is me. You can't take out nine guys before they can hit you. Just surrender and let them have me. At least then you can get word to Fenton and Harlow, let them know what happened."

The thugs were getting closer. Grantham shook his head. "That's not my style."

"I know. You're a fighter. But I need you to come out of this alive."

With a disgusted but agreeable look on his face, Grantham holstered his weapon, kicked the cracked windshield free and crawled out. He got to his feet and put his hands up as the mercs approached. "Let's do this easy, boys."

Augustine worked his way toward the gaping exit of the windshield.

Sutter headed for Grantham, assault rifle pointed directly at him, but his gaze seemed to be aimed at Augustine. Hard to tell with the night vision goggles. He jerked his chin at Augustine. "Give yourself up and the cop goes free."

Sirens whined in the distance. Backup? Augustine had no way of knowing. He pulled himself free of the car, turned around and put his hands up.

Sutter smirked. "That's a good little fairy."

Augustine would kill this guy. He made himself that promise. "Let Grantham leave now."

"Or what?" Sutter snorted. "You think you call the shots?"

"Grantham leaves now and I go easy." He moved slowly forward on an angle, trying to put himself between Sutter and Grantham.

"The cop is fine where he is." Sutter cocked his head back. "Garcia, Nguyen, get the shackles on him."

Behind him, Grantham whispered, "I could take at least three."

Augustine slowly shook his head. "No." Sutter looked way too trigger-happy.

Sutter's men came forward with the hellish iron cuffs. They spun Augustine around and yanked his arms back. Augustine looked Grantham in the eyes and mouthed silently, "Tell Harlow."

Grantham frowned, but nodded. Had to love the guy's warrior soul.

The iron clamped around Augustine's wrists, gnawing into his flesh like hot metal teeth. A second later, the pain traveled into his bones. His teeth clenched of their own accord and for a moment, every muscle in his body went taut. He took a hard breath and forced himself to relax.

"Prisoner secured, boss," one of the men called back to Sutter.

Someone, Sutter, checked the restraints, giving them a good tug that brought the metal into greater contact with Augustine's skin.

He ground his teeth together to keep from reacting.

Sutter moved to stand beside him, his face inches from Augustine's. "This is going to be fun, fairy boy."

Then he pulled out his sidearm, leveled it at Grantham and shot him in the chest.

Chapter Twenty-two

"Y ou should sleep, child." Lally shook her head at Harlow. "Just lie down there on the couch and close your eyes a bit."

"I can't." She was exhausted but wired.

Fenton nodded from his chair. "I can't, either."

Lally stood. "Well, then, I'm going to make some coffee." She left.

Harlow tipped her head back against the couch and stared at the ceiling. "Why is it taking so long? It's been two hours. Shouldn't we have heard something by now?"

"I would have thought so. The lawyer's there, waiting on him." Fenton sighed. "I'll call Augustine's lieutenants, let them know what's going on."

She moved into a different position so she could see him. "I hate everything about this."

He nodded. "So do I."

She leaned forward. "Why can't you write up a report on everything the senator's done against othernaturals, then take it public?"

He grimaced, his mouth pulling to one side, before looking at her. "I thought about that, but there are several factors going against us."

"Such as?"

"There are a lot of people out there who would side with her. We're inured from much of the anti-othernatural sentiment because of where we live." He paused. "Do you remember when the covenant was broken and suddenly the humans knew we existed?"

"Of course." That had been the last day she'd been able to pass as human.

"And do you remember all the stories in the media about what celebrities and other public figures were othernaturals?"

"Sure, the Web was plastered with them." She nodded, remembering the stories about her mother. "Some thought it was exciting, but there was a lot of backlash."

"There still is. But in New Orleans, home of the fae, land of voodoo and witchcraft and a slew of varcolai clans—"

"Varcolai are shifters, right?"

"Right. With all of us here, the way tourists flock to this city to get a glimpse of the fae, we've earned a kind of immunity to the sort of bias that for some of our kind is an everyday thing. The *Picayune* doesn't put othernatural crimes on the front page like most newspapers." He shrugged. "The tourist board has something to do with that, too."

"I never really thought about it, but I know you're right. After everything happened and people knew they weren't alone in this world, there were protests in the streets in Boston. And not just handfuls of people. Hundreds and hundreds." She wrapped her arms around herself. "I never considered myself fae then." She smiled sadly. She'd been so foolish then. So trapped in her own world. "Funny how things can change."

He smiled brightly. "You've come a long way, Harlow. A long way. You should be proud of yourself. You've done things that have required incredible amounts of courage."

Lally came through the doors carrying a silver tray laden with coffee, sugar, creamer and a plate of biscuits and jam. "Thought we might as well fortify ourselves."

"Coffee smells wonderful." Fenton got out of his seat to help her with the tray.

"Thank you." Lally handed it to him as the house phone rang. "Lands, that phone never rings. Hardly anyone's got that number." Her face brightened. "Maybe it's Augie." She answered it, lifting the old-fashioned handset from its cradle on a far table.

"Goodwin-Robelais residence." Her happy expression didn't last long. "Slow down, Jewelia. What now?" She clutched at the apron she'd tied on, her mouth coming open. "Lord Jesus, have mercy. Where? All right. I'll tell them. Yes, child. I'll be praying, too." She hung up and turned toward Harlow and Fenton, tears in her eyes.

Harlow stood. "What happened?"

"I'm not sure but there was a car accident on the way to the police station and Augie's gone and J.J. was shot. Bad." She sobbed once. "He's in the hospital."

Fenton was already headed for the door. "I'll get the car."

Harlow made her way to Lally's side and hugged her close. "I'm sure your nephew will be fine."

She pulled away, tears gone. "That boy had Jewelia's *gris gris* round his neck. I'm sure he'll be fine, too. Hurt, but he'll heal. It's Augustine I'm worried about."

Harlow swallowed, trying to find her voice. Her hand went to the *gris gris* bag hidden beneath her tunic. "That makes two of us. C'mon, let's go see what we can find out."

Fenton drove like a madman, getting them to the hospital in fewer minutes than Harlow thought possible. He dropped Harlow and Lally off at the doors. "You two go inside, I'll park."

She and Lally raced in. The hospital was busier than she expected but then it was almost 7 a.m. Lally went to speak to someone at the information desk while Harlow waited but when Lally returned, she was shaking her head.

"Visiting hours don't start till nine and they ain't gonna let us in. She said they might make an exception for me being family, but not you. Not until nine o'clock."

Queen Jewelia came in from the parking lot with Fenton a few steps behind her. The two women embraced.

Lally sighed and gave the woman behind the desk the stink-eye. "They're not letting us in, Jewelia."

"That so?" Jewelia marched over to have a talk with the receptionist herself.

"I overheard." Fenton looked at his watch. "We can't wait that long to find out if Grantham knows anything about Augustine."

"Agreed." Harlow was already antsy. She flexed her fingers. "Can't you pull some strings?"

He frowned. "This is a human hospital first and foremost. My pull here is not great."

"What about Dr. Carlson? He's one of us."

Fenton nodded as he pulled out his LMD. "It's worth a shot. If you'll just excuse me." He walked to a quiet corner to make the call, coming back a minute later. "All right, some good news. Dr. Carlson is sending word down that we're to be allowed up. They're only going to let us up for fifteen minutes and only two at a time, however." He nodded at Jewelia and Lally. "Despite the urgency, you two should go first. The first faces he sees should be family."

Jewelia's expression grew a little less anxious and she smiled. "You're a good man, Mr. Welch."

"Yes." Harlow nodded. "He is."

The pair went back to the information desk, got Grantham's room number and into the elevator they went.

Fenton's brows lifted slightly. "I hate feeling useless."

"You're not useless. But I know what you mean." She took a deep breath, wishing there was a simple way to make this all right.

He shifted once, his eyes scanning the room. He nodded toward a vending machine. "Would you like some coffee? I'm sure it's terrible, but—"

"No, that would be great." Harlow found a couple of seats in the waiting area away from the rest.

Fenton returned carrying two small cups of coffee. He grimaced as he handed one to her. "I don't have much hope it's drinkable."

She took her cup and smiled. "That's okay. It's hot and caffeinated. Two out of three ain't bad." She wrapped her hands around it while he sat beside her. They stared straight ahead, but she had the feeling all he could see was the same thing as her—Augustine's face. She sipped the oily black liquid. "Ugh. You're right. That's horrible."

He set his cup on the arm of the chair. "I'm rarely wrong."

She took a long breath. "Then what's your best guess as to where Augustine is?"

He bent his head, his gaze on his hands, which were now folded in his lap. "I'm afraid my best guess is not good news."

She put her cup on the floor. "The senator?"

He nodded slowly. "And my intel on her is fairly limited due to the heavy security that always surrounds her. I don't know where she's staying—not that she'd be foolish enough to hold Augustine there."

"Maybe I can help with that." She wiggled her fingers. "With my computer skills, I mean."

He nodded. "You might."

"What do you think she wants with him?"

He glanced at her, a brief, apologetic smile disappearing as quickly as it had appeared. "Most likely to make an example of him."

"To show the world just how bad the fae really are?"

The apologetic smile returned. "Yes."

Lally and Jewelia were headed toward them. Lally pointed at the elevators. "Go on, you two. Get up there and find out what you can." She shook her head. "He's in an awful lot of pain."

"He's in room 315," Jewelia added. "I'll carry Lally home. I'm sure you all are going to have more work to do after you leave here."

"I'm sure we are, too, so that would be great, thank you. Get some sleep, Lally," Harlow said as she and Fenton got up and headed toward the elevator bank. Lally gave a little wave.

In a few minutes they were walking into Grantham's room. A nurse was taking his pulse. She finished up, then gave them a stern look. "No more than fifteen minutes. I *will* kick you out."

"They're all right," Grantham mumbled.

Fenton nodded at her. "Yes, ma'am."

Harlow bit her tongue and focused on Grantham instead. His lids were at half-mast. "How are you feeling?"

"Like I just fought Ramon Rivera all over again." Grantham frowned. "I've got a chest full of cracked ribs and a bruise that feels like there's an elephant sitting on my lungs." He managed a half smile. "But I'm alive."

Harlow smiled. "We're all really glad about that."

"Me, too." He rested his fingers on a small device affixed to the bed rail. "Self-dispensing pain meds."

She stood at the side of his bed, the soft beeping of a monitor a reminder the accident could have gone differently. "Which you're going to get to use in a few minutes. I don't want this to take long, so forgive me for getting right to it, but do you have any idea what happened to Augustine?"

He nodded. "Pellimento's men took him."

"How many total?"

"Nine." He paused. "Yeah, nine. They're mercenaries led by a man named Sutter. Probably took Robelais to the same place we met them, especially if they think I'm dead. A warehouse near the CBD. Talk to someone at the station, they can log into my GPS, get the address."

"Is it registered in your name?" Harlow asked.

"Yes." He coughed and his face contorted in agony, his hand slipping off the medication button. "I'm sorry I can't be more help."

"No, you've been a lot of help," Fenton said. He lifted Grantham's hand back onto the pain dispenser. "Now go ahead and push that button."

But Grantham hesitated. "These are trained mercenaries. They had serious firepower on them. Enough bullets and even a fae stops breathing. Be careful."

Fenton dipped his head. "Thank you."

Grantham nodded, pushed the button and a few seconds later, his lids drifted closed. Fenton and Harlow made their way out. She waited until they were in the car to speak. "I can hack into his GPS and check that address faster than waiting on the police to get it for us."

He pulled the car into the street. "I thought you might. Can you use the system at the Pelcrum or do you need me to take you home?

"Is it fairly current?"

Fenton made a funny smile. "State-of-the-art. That contact lens you used at the Exemplar Ball, the one that had the facial recognition software embedded into it? That was built in the Pelcrum's computer lab."

"Then I'm sure it's more than adequate. Let's go straight there."

"Wonderful. While you do that, I can assemble what's left of the team at the Pelcrum. I have a few favors and friends I can call in to bulk up our numbers."

She sat back. "Sounds like a plan."

He glanced at her. "You know it's highly unlikely the senator will be wherever they're holding Augustine, right? Just her men?"

Harlow let out a long, slow breath. "All I care about right now is Augustine."

✧

Finally, the witch was awake. Ava Mae couldn't wait to be rid of her. The more time she spent in the witch's body, the more she realized that she had to be back inside Harlow. And by telling the witch they needed to sacrifice her sister to the tree, Ava Mae had a plan in place to make it happen.

Then she would finally be complete.

Now all she had to do was live long enough to get to that point. Since the witch had gotten rid of the leaves, Ava Mae had begun to weaken. Her only chance was to get the witch in the house, close to the tree. That should give her enough power to take control again. If not, she had another idea about how to make it happen.

Either way, she wanted back in her sister's body. It was the only place she would be able to comfortably inhabit for the rest of her days.

Get up, Ava Mae urged Giselle. *We have work to do.*

And I have coffee to drink. I've only had a few hours of sleep. Calm down.

The longer we wait, the more advantage Augustine and Harlow will have. They'll be prepared for us. We should have gone to the house immediately, while they were still asleep.

Giselle sighed. *I may be a witch, but I'm also human. I have to have sleep.*

Ava Mae was aware of just how human her new host was. *We should go now. Augustine usually leaves the house right after break-fast. Chances are good he won't be home for a few hours.*

"Ian, my love." Giselle shook his shoulder gently.

Ava Mae wanted to throttle her. *Are you paying attention to me? We need to go now.*

Ian turned to face Giselle, blinking. He stretched and the

sheet fell away to reveal his naked torso. For a moment, Ava Mae considered staying in bed awhile longer. He yawned. "It's too soon to be awake."

"I agree, but my parasite wants me up."

Don't call me that.

"She's insisting I go to Augustine's house and take possession of the tree now."

He pushed up to his elbows. "I'm not sure I'm ready for a confrontation with two fae."

Giselle sighed. "She says Augustine won't be home right now."

He shrugged. "Can I at least get some coffee first?"

We don't need him. This is something you and I must do alone.

Giselle hesitated.

Ava Mae pushed harder. *Do you want him to know all the secrets of the tree that I'm about to reveal to you?*

She leaned in and kissed Ian on the cheek. "I'm just letting you know I'm going out. It's nothing I can't handle. I'll be back before you know it."

He gave her a strange look. "You're sure?"

"I'm sure." Giselle smiled. "If I'm not back by twilight, come look for me."

"That's a long time."

Some of the rituals I'm going to show you take time. The power ceremony cannot be rushed. Ava Mae was making stuff up as she went along, but Giselle seemed to be buying it.

Giselle shrugged. "It's just one of those things. It takes some time." She slipped out of bed, showered and got dressed.

What's with the white all the time? It's so boring and dull.

It's not boring and dull. It's sophisticated and it sets me apart.

You sound just like someone else I know. Ava Mae sighed. *Hurry up.*

I'm walking out of the house. I can't go faster than that. Giselle missed the click of her heels on the cobblestones but for breaking into a house, flats were more appropriate. She unlocked her car and slid behind the wheel.

Nice car.

"Thank you." Giselle preferred speaking out loud to her parasite. All that conversation in her head was making her queasy. "It was my father's."

The one you killed?

Giselle stiffened. "I did what I had to for the good of the—"

Hey, I get it. I killed my father, too. I guess we're more alike than I originally thought. Dead fathers, sisters that betrayed us, the desire for power... But the witch was still human and living inside her still felt like a slow death. *Now let's get to Augustine's so we can get things under way.*

Giselle sped away from the house.

Ava Mae kept quiet until they were close, more to conserve her energy than to give the witch a break. As the neighborhood vegetation turned green and leafy and the houses grew palatial, Ava Mae relaxed. *Almost there. Park a couple blocks away.*

"I know," Giselle snapped. "I'm not an idiot."

No, you're not. Otherwise I wouldn't have bothered with all this. Your cunning and intelligence is the reason I think a great partnership lies ahead for us.

Ava Mae could feel Giselle calm at the lies she'd just been told. Humans were so gullible.

Giselle parked the car. "I may have some trouble getting to the house. It's warded against anyone intending harm."

How did you get in to get the leaves?

"With a spell that forced me to believe I was there to see Augustine about a business matter."

Interesting. You won't need to do that this time. My presence should negate the ward.

"We'll see." Giselle got out and started walking. The house came into view with a block left to go.

If Ava Mae could have inhaled, she would have, sure that she would have been able to detect the soft, smoky scent of the tree that had given her life. Already her energy was kicking back up.

You were right, Giselle said. *I can see the house no problem. Last time it wavered and disappeared when I started thinking devious thoughts.* She opened the side gate and walked right through.

Of course I was right. New life coursed through Ava Mae as Giselle's feet made contact with the grass surrounding the house. Beneath that layer of green coiled the roots of the lightning tree. Ava Mae was home. *Now get inside, find Harlow and let's get to that tree.*

Chapter Twenty-three

Four minutes, thirty-two seconds." Harlow dropped the scrap of paper onto the table in front of Fenton. "Not bad, huh?" She pointed at the address scrawled on it when his brows knit together. "That's how long it took me to pinpoint the warehouse in the CBD that Grantham and Augustine went to."

"Nice work." Dulcinea had arrived at the Pelcrum a few minutes ago.

"Yes." Fenton nodded. "Very impressive. We've never had a lieutenant with your set of skills. We could have used you a long time ago."

"Thanks." Harlow sat at the round table in the war room, the satisfaction of being useful and appreciated warming her. She preferred the computer lab with its slight scent of ozone and the subtle hum of the equipment, but the war room was a close second. There was so much history in this room; it hung in the air like a comforting presence. She looked at Fenton expectantly. "What's next?"

"Sydra should be here shortly and at some point, we may see Cylo. Dr. Carlson said he's releasing Cylo early because our ethos fae isn't exactly being the easiest of patients."

"I'm here." Sydra walked in, her flaming red hair braided into a tight plait in sharp contrast to her deep green leathers. She looked like a wild forest elf. The thought made Harlow smile as Sydra jerked her thumb over her shoulder. "And look who's with me."

Behind her, the enormous ethos fae lumbered in. Cy grinned. "Dr. Carlson said I was the worst patient he's ever had."

Harlow laughed, mostly because Cy seemed so proud of that designation. She jumped up and hugged him. "I'm so happy to see you."

He hugged her back. "Me, too, you." The joy left his face. "I'm really sorry about Augustine. You know we'll find him."

She nodded. "I know." She looked at Fenton. "Are we all here?"

He shook his head. "Nekai will be joining us at some point and I've got two more coming, goblin fae associates of mine. They're strong as oxen and built for this kind of assault." He looked at the time on his LMD. "They should be here soon."

Harlow remained standing at Cy's side. "My house isn't far from here, right?"

"No." He seemed puzzled by her question. "Have you changed your mind about going with us?"

"Hell no. I just want to run home and get Augustine's sword."

"Ah." Fenton's mouth pulled at the corners. "I appreciate your bloodthirstiness, but that sword will only work for the Guardian. In your hands it will be more of an anchor than a weapon."

"I don't want to use it. I want to bring it to him." She shrugged. "I thought I'd give Lally a quick update, too."

He smiled. "In that case, it's a marvelous idea. On both counts. By the time you get there and back, I'll have everyone up to speed, Guz and Rat will be here and we'll be ready to go."

She started for the door, then stopped. "Hey, I can't get back in here by myself since I don't have the fleur-de-lis brand, right?"

"Yes, we must rectify that." He tipped his head toward the hall. "You've seen me turn the sconce to open the door. Just repeat that. It won't work, but it will set off a small alarm." He smiled. "Close enough to a doorbell."

"Okay, got it. See you in about fifteen minutes."

"Harlow?" Fenton's voice stopped her a second time.

"Yes?"

"Any reason you don't just go by mirror?"

"Hmm. Only because I hadn't thought about it. It's not quite part of my thinking process yet. I mean, I know that's how I go visit my mother, but to just go places...I'm not thinking that way yet."

"Understandable. But the more you do it, the more comfortable with it you'll be."

"Totally agree." She held out empty hands. "Except that I don't have a mirror."

He smiled as he stood and went to a nearby cabinet. "I can remedy that right now. Which reminds me I haven't done my duty as the Guardian liaison and outfitted you with the things I typically give each lieutenant."

Harlow lifted one shoulder nonchalantly. "I'm not actually a lieutenant yet, so don't worry about it."

"You are a lieutenant for all intents and purposes, you merely lack the official seal, as it were." He slid out a drawer and took something from it, then offered it to her. "Standard issue for all lieutenants."

In his hand was a small silver compact, a simple but elegant fleur-de-lis embossed on the front. Harlow took it. "It's beautiful."

"And functional. Keep it with you always."

"I will." She opened it, just to look at the mirror, then snapped it shut again.

"I'm not quite done yet." Still smiling, he opened a second drawer and removed a slim, sheathed blade. He pulled it from its nylon covering and showed it to her. The metal was worked in an elaborate design.

"That's beautiful."

"And sharp enough to cut bone in the right hands. Such as

our Cylo's. When it comes to blade work, he is our most skilled lieutenant. I'm sure he'd be happy to give you a few lessons."

She glanced at Cy, who nodded and gave her a big smile.

"Anytime," he said.

Harlow took the blade and tucked it into the back of her waistband, beneath her tunic. "Thank you." Then she held up the silver compact. Traveling by mirror alone was one thing. Traveling by mirror in front of an audience was something else entirely. "If you don't mind, I'll do this out in the hall."

He nodded. "I understand."

She gave them a wave, then walked out into the long hall for a little privacy. She considered traveling to the kitchen, but if Lally was in there, she didn't want to scare her by just suddenly appearing. The foyer was a safer bet. She'd be quiet regardless, in case Lally really was sleeping, but she had a feeling that wasn't going to be the situation. It was hard to rest when someone you loved was in danger.

Flipping open the compact, she looked into the mirror and focused on the entrance to the house, imagined herself standing before the ornate gold mirror. A half second later, the magical pull she'd come to expect tugged at her. She blinked at the slight dizziness and opened her eyes to find herself standing in front of the mirror she'd just been thinking about. She smiled. It was good to master a new skill. Even better, it was good to be fae.

Lally's voice sounded from the kitchen, the smell of vanilla cake and rum permeating the whole house. Whatever Lally was baking smelled good enough to eat. Mouth watering, and eager to explain they'd found the warehouse where Augustine was probably being held, Harlow headed in. "Hey, guess what—"

"Well, isn't this convenient. Just the fae we were looking for." Giselle stood over Lally, who sat in a kitchen chair. Anger shone in Lally's eyes, despite the butcher knife Giselle held to her throat. "And you said she wasn't home."

Mixing bowls sat on the counter while two buttered cake pans awaited filling on the kitchen table. "She wasn't," Lally snapped.

"Get away from her, witch." Rage replaced every thought in Harlow's mind. Her fingers tingled with the urge to grab the blade hidden at her back, but what were the chances she could get to it before Giselle harmed Lally?

"Now, Sister dear, is that any way to talk to us?" Giselle's lids fluttered and her eyes once again held the solid black of Ava Mae's possession. Harlow's fingers twitched as Giselle kept talking. "We have every right to be angry with you after you left us in that pit."

"I didn't leave you there. You were too weak to make it out." Not that Harlow would have had things go differently. "What do you want with Lally?"

The knife moved dangerously close to Lally's skin. Giselle smiled, revealing a mouthful of tiny, razor-sharp teeth. "We're so glad you asked. We don't want anything of Lally. What we want is for you to come to the tree with us."

"The tree?" That couldn't lead to anything good. Harlow turned slightly so that her right hand was hidden. The blade was tempting, but not something she felt secure using. Instead, she eased the compact open. She wasn't going to get a second chance at this.

Giselle screeched at her. "Don't play dumb with us. You know what tree we mean."

Harlow nodded. "The lightning tree, right, of course. I don't know what I was thinking." She inched closer. "Put the knife down and I'm happy to go with you. I've wanted to get a better look at that tree for a long time but this old woman won't let me."

Giselle narrowed her eyes. "Why should I believe you?"

Harlow frowned and stuck her bottom lip out, pretending to be hurt. "Have I ever lied to you before? Give me a chance. I want to know about that tree just as much as you do. Besides, Mother would want us to do this together, don't you think?"

For a moment, Giselle's black gaze muddied with uncertainty. "I...guess..."

"Good." She looked at Lally, prayed she could read between the lines, and made a very cross face. "Don't you dare tell Fenton or Olivia where we've gone, you understand me?"

Lally's eyes widened and she nodded.

Giselle pulled the knife back and raised her hand like she was about to knock Lally out with the blunt end.

That was the only signal Harlow needed. She opened the mirror as she lunged forward, latched one hand on to Giselle and with the strength of a single thought, took them both through to the fae plane.

⚜

Augustine's last memory was everything going black and a sharp pain in the side of his neck. As consciousness returned, he understood that pain was from being injected with a sedative as soon as Sutter's men had loaded him into the SUV. The blackness was from having a hood yanked over his head.

The hood was gone now and whatever had drugged him worn off, the remnants of it lingering like ashes on his tongue. But the biting pain of the iron cuffs remained, digging into his skin and making the back of his skull ache like he was in the throes of the world's worst hangover.

Shadows moved across the wall. It was morning, but not super-early. Still, for him to have been out as long as he had they must have given him an extremely high dosage of something. An animal tranq, maybe.

He kept his head down, and only moved his partially opened eyes as he scoped out his surroundings. From the looks of the place he was in the bedroom of a hotel suite. A nice one if the elaborately dressed four-poster bed was an indication. Nearby sat a desk and chair. He leaned to the side to get a better look at the pad by the phone. The Ritz-Carlton. Hell's bells. He was in the heart of the French Quarter. Not that he could do anything with that knowledge.

He tested his bonds, but succeeded only in causing himself more pain. The chair he was tied to was pitted metal with a cheap vinyl seat and looked more like it had come from the hotel's employee lounge than been part of the suite's furnishings. Judging from the plastic tarp under the chair and covering several square yards around him, there was probably a reason for the grungy chair.

They didn't want to get blood on anything in the suite.

His coat was in a heap in the corner and from what he could tell, his weapons had been stripped from him. He flexed his ankle. Yep, the blade in his boot was gone, too. Damn it. He was about as vulnerable as he could be: unable to use his powers, weaponless and restrained. There weren't enough curse words, fae or human, to express how he felt. Weak heat tingled along his spine, the best his body could manage with the iron suppressing his abilities.

He listened hard, but the iron kept his senses too dull to make a solid determination about who else was in the suite. The heartbeats in the other rooms were so muddled and indistinguishable, it was hard to say if there were two or four. Two things were certain: The place reeked of humans and he was not alone.

As if on cue, the door to the bedroom opened. He kept his head down, eyes closed, and feigned unconsciousness.

"Still out," a male voice said. Not Sutter, but familiar. One of the men from the abduction.

"Wake him. She's on her way up," replied another, also familiar but not Sutter.

The door closed. Footsteps approached. Combat boots came into view. A rifle butt jabbed his shoulder. "Rise and shine, princess."

Augustine made a show of coming to. He lifted his head slowly, blinking and acting like he was trying to focus. "Where am I?" he mumbled.

"Don't worry about where you are." The man in front of him wore black tactical gear. Augustine didn't recognize him from earlier, but if he wasn't one of Sutter's guys, he had to be part of Pellimento's personal security detail. But wouldn't they wear suits? How big a crew did Sutter have? The man went to stand by the open door, then spoke to someone outside the room. "He's awake."

"Good." That voice he recognized and the woman belonging to it walked in a moment later.

The senator had arrived.

Tablet in hand, she strode toward him, stopping at the edge of the tarp. "You killed my son."

Augustine picked his head up a little more to give her the full benefit of his stare. "The witches killed your son. I tried to save him."

"Your lies won't help you." The man pulled out the desk chair and moved it to the edge of the tarp. Pellimento shook her head. "No, not here. Further back." He moved the chair as Pellimento indicated and the senator sat. "No, Mr. Robelais, the only thing that will save you now is your confession."

Another man Augustine recognized came in carrying a camera and tripod setup. He was also dressed in the same black tactical gear.

Augustine snorted. "I'm not going to confess to something I haven't done just so you can use it to further your anti-othernatural campaign."

Her hair and makeup were done, her suit pristine. Was today

the day she'd been scheduled to dedicate the statue in Audubon Park? Had she still done that knowing her son was dead? If so, the woman was colder than he'd imagined.

She crossed her legs and continued to stare him down. "You will do exactly that." She looked at her watch. "You have until five p.m., which is when I'll be announcing my son's murder and airing your taped confession at my news conference. After that, it will come as no surprise when I use martial law to lock the city down until my new othernatural identification program goes into effect."

"You're never going to get that approved."

For the first time, she broke into a thin smile. "You really have no idea what I'm capable of, do you? Now I'll give you one more chance to say yes to my very generous offer." She turned the tablet around so he could see the screen. "I've already written your confession for you."

From his position, he could make out only a few phrases. *My evil nature... uncontrollable desire to kill... hatred of humans.* A muscle in his jaw twitched. "There's no way in hell I'm reading that."

"Interesting choice of words." She sniffed. "Very well. But remember, this is the path you chose." With a shrug, she placed the tablet facedown on her lap, then tipped her head to look down her nose at him. "I do think you'll change your mind sooner than expected." She snapped her fingers. "Mr. Sutter, we're ready for you."

Wearing the same black gear as his men, Sutter entered the room. Two more mercs followed him. He pointed at Augustine with the iron bar he held in one hand. "Haul him up."

"You piece of garbage," Augustine spat. "You killed a good man today."

The men grabbed Augustine's arms and lifted him to his feet. Sutter approached, twirling the iron rod like a baton. "Grantham was collateral damage."

"You'll pay for his death." Augustine glared at him, wishing he could take the man on one-on-one, no restraints, no weapons, just some good old-fashioned hand-to-hand. They'd see who was collateral damage then.

Sutter stepped onto the tarp, but the senator lifted her hand. "Remember, not the face."

Sutter smacked the bar against his open palm and cocked his head to one side as if assessing Augustine's vulnerable areas. "That still leaves a lot to work with." He pulled back and swung, smashing the bar into Augustine's ribs.

Augustine bent with the blow in an attempt to lessen its force, but the pain that shot through him told him it hadn't done much good. The iron only added to the impact, leaving behind a welt that seared like a third-degree burn. Despite the pain, he straightened. He'd endured worse on the streets in order to make enough scratch to buy dinner. The stakes here were much higher—the liberty of all New Orleans's other-naturals. With as much nonchalance as he could muster, he smiled at Sutter. "Anyone ever tell you that you hit like a girl?"

Scowling, Sutter drew back again.

Augustine braced himself. All he had to do was hang on until his lieutenants figured out where he was.

How hard could that be?

The bar slammed into his ribs again. The crack of bone seemed to ring in his ears. Maybe a better question might be, how long could that take?

Chapter Twenty-four

Giselle landed on hard, rocky ground. With Harlow on top of her. Wind swirled around them, tugging at their clothes and hair and scouring them with grit. They tussled for a moment until she got enough leverage to shove both hands against Harlow's shoulders. "Get off me or I'll put a hex on you."

"Hex this." Harlow slugged her across the mouth. "Never touch Lally again. Do you hear me?"

Giselle put her hands in front of her face to block the next blow and cast a protection spell at the same time. Harlow's fist connected with Giselle's stomach, forcing the air from her diaphragm. So much for the protection spell. She coughed, twisting to her side and finally dislodging Harlow. She found her breath, taking in a mouthful of dust with it. She coughed some more. "What the hell? Where are we?" Nothing looked familiar. "Why isn't my magic working?"

Harlow had already gotten to her feet and now stood over Giselle, glaring down at her. "Maybe because you're on the fae plane."

Giselle wasn't even sure what that meant. *Ava Mae, where are you? Why aren't you helping me?*

Ava Mae's response was feeble and distant. *We're too far away from the tree.*

Harlow leaned down, fists raised and eyes angry. "Are you Giselle or Ava Mae?"

Giselle pushed to her feet. Her mouth tasted of blood and

dirt and her jaw ached. She spat as much of the mess out as she could. "Both."

"You don't seem like Ava Mae. Your eyes aren't black and your teeth look normal."

Giselle glanced down. Her clothes were filthy. She brushed at them while she glared at Harlow. "What is this place?"

Ava Mae moaned. *I don't like it here.*

Shut up. This is your fault.

"I told you," Harlow repeated. "This is the fae plane."

Giselle backed away, almost stumbling over the hardscrabble ground. There was a nothingness about the place she'd never felt before. Everything was gray as far as she could see. Gray skies, gray earth, gray rocks, gray mountains on the horizon. It even smelled gray. Like an old dusty attic. "Is this fae hell?"

"No, but it might be your hell. I'm guessing your magic doesn't work here because you're human and not supposed to be here anyway." Harlow still had her fists raised. "I want to talk to Ava Mae."

I can't. Too weak.

"You can speak to her through me." Giselle was barely holding it together. If this was the fae plane, how was she going to get back to New Orleans? She didn't even know where that was from here.

Harlow scooped a silver disk out of the dirt and tucked it into her pocket. "Tell Ava Mae that it's over. One way or the other, she's not leaving here. Even if I have to kill you."

Giselle stiffened. "Lay a hand on me and I'll…" She really had no recourse.

"You'll what? Fall down again?"

Harlow's mocking tone was interrupted by Ava Mae's whine. *I'll die if I stay here. Tell her I'll die, witch.*

Giselle put on her best I-couldn't-care-less face when she replied. "She says staying here will cause her to die."

"I'm okay with that."

But we're family.

"She says what about your family connection?"

"She's not my sister any more than she's yours. She's an abomination created by the lightning tree."

Giselle pursed her mouth. "I have no idea what you're talking about."

Harlow barked out a rough laugh. She dropped her hands to pull a small blade from behind her back. "One, you just told me in the kitchen that you wanted me to go to the tree with you. Now you're telling me you don't remember that? Two, I watched you come out of that pond and pull leaves from the tree out of your robe. And three, I know they were lightning tree leaves because I also know you were in my house. My mother saw you."

How was that possible? Giselle scoffed. "Your mother? Your mother's dead."

A woman materialized at Harlow's side. "Not quite, witch."

Giselle jumped, immediately angry at herself for reacting, but damn, this place was getting weirder by the minute. "Who in the name of the goddess are you?"

"Not a movie fan, hmm? Philistine." The woman crossed her arms and looked at Harlow, nodding. "That's the one I saw skulking through the foyer." She pointed at Giselle. "I'd recognize that dyed black hair anywhere."

"My hair is not dyed." It was henna and indigo, but those were natural and totally didn't count. "Are you...Harlow's mother?"

The woman spread her arms. "Olivia Goodwin, Oscar winner, philanthropist and mother of the world's greatest hacker, at your service."

"Mom." Harlow shook her head, a tiny smile turning up the corners of her mouth.

"Well, you are, *cher*," Olivia started.

Giselle rolled her eyes. "Why don't you spare me the motherly pride and instead tell me how you're not dead? I didn't see you in the foyer. And besides, there was only one other heartbeat in the house and it was Augustine. I checked."

"I *am* dead, but I'm here because I'm fae." Olivia walked toward her. "And of course, I don't have a heartbeat, you silly twit. That's what being dead means." Before Giselle could move, Olivia sailed right through her. A chill zipped from the top of her head down to her toes.

Mama! Ava Mae cried.

Olivia gasped as she exited behind Giselle, putting her hands to her chest. "Oh my dear sainted Elizabeth Taylor. Ava Mae's inside her."

Harlow nodded. "It's a long story, but basically this witch broke into the house and stole leaves off the lightning tree, which caused Ava Mae's spirit to possess her after she left me."

Olivia scurried back to Harlow's side. "There's only a little bit of Ava Mae left in there. The tree has warped her, turned her into a monster of its own doing." She shook her head and pointed at Giselle. "You're in trouble, witch. You have no idea what you've done."

Giselle stalked toward the old woman and Harlow. "I'm not the one in trouble." She pointed at the pair. "You are if you don't get me out of this goddess-forsaken place. Get me home now or I will call up the power of the tree and destroy both of you."

A thin man in glasses stepped out of the air, the housekeeper at his side. "I don't think so, Giselle."

Olivia clapped her hands. "I haven't had this many visitors in ages."

"Mom," Harlow said. "This is not exactly a social event."

"I don't know about that." The man in glasses stared at Giselle. "For one of us, it might qualify as a going-away party."

⚜

The arrival of Fenton and Lally took some of the pressure off
Harlow. She shot him an appreciative look. "I hope that means
what I think it means. Thanks for showing up, by the way."

"You're welcome." He answered her without taking his eyes
off Giselle. "I came through by mirror to check on you when
you didn't return in a timely manner and Lally informed me of
what had happened and where you'd gone."

"I knew you'd get it." Harlow smiled at Lally. She was carrying a cloth shopping bag.

Lally smiled back. "My mama didn't raise no fool."

"No she did not." Harlow motioned with her free hand for
Fenton to continue. "So you grabbed her and came here."

"Something like that. I made a few arrangements first, which
is why we weren't along immediately."

Harlow jabbed her blade in Giselle's direction. "Let's deal
with her then."

Fenton held up a finger. "First things first. Which would be
Ava Mae."

Harlow nodded. "Apparently she's still inside Giselle but
pretty weak."

"She should be," Lally said. "She's about as far away from
the tree right now as a person can get." She tipped her chin at
Giselle. "You still hear her voice in your head?"

Giselle nodded, looking very much like she wasn't entirely
sure what was going on. "She's faint, but still there." She crossed
her arms. "Although she seems to be perking up, so if one of you
doesn't take me back home in the next few minutes, things are
going to get ugly."

"Shut up, you stupid cow." Olivia ignored Giselle's shocked
look to clasp her hands and address Fenton. "Please don't hurt

Ava Mae. I know some of what's in the witch is the lightning tree, but some of what's in there is still my child. I felt it. I felt *her*."

"We planned for that." Fenton smiled at Olivia before he spoke to Giselle. "Sit on the ground, witch, and don't move."

Giselle's lip curled at his suggestion. "I think not. This place couldn't be filthier. And besides, what's to stop me from running?" She narrowed her eyes. "Or turning Ava Mae on you?"

Fenton laughed, a sound Harlow wasn't that familiar with. "Ava Mae is most likely still too weak, but go ahead and run if you feel that's in your best interests." He stretched out his arms. "You might want to consider just how vast this part of the fae plane is. And then there's the fact that you're human. You still need to eat and drink. Do you know what fae plants are poisonous? Which fae streams hold restoring waters and which ones hold those that diminish? How many creatures there are in the distant forests that would consider you a succulent morsel?" The smile left his face as his expression became stony. He pointed to the ground. "Sit. Or I will let Harlow assist you."

Giselle sat.

"Good witch. Now stay there and don't move." He punctuated the sentence by placing his hand on the bolt stick hanging from his belt. Then he nodded at Lally. "All right, go ahead."

Lally pulled an oddly shaped package from the shopping bag and unwrapped it from what looked like a length of fae leather. On closer inspection, it was fae leather. A pair of Augustine's new pants, actually. And they'd been concealing a thick, black branch that Harlow knew instantly.

Giselle's lids flickered as the whites of her eyes disappeared. She moaned, hands outstretched toward the branch. "Give me the lightning tree. I need it. I'm dying."

Lally held the branch out and nodded. "Come get it, Ava

Mae. Leave that witch and sink yourself into this tree. I'll carry you home and you can be whole again."

Giselle began to tremble. Her eyes rolled back in her head for a moment. She cried out, the wind whipping up to carry her voice away. "Get out of me, Ava Mae. Get. Out." She lurched to her feet. One eye had returned to its normal state, but one had remained solid black. Whatever was happening inside her wasn't pretty.

She stumbled toward the branch, muttering and moaning and talking under her breath like a crazy person. "Get to the tree. Leave me alone! I need the tree. I need to be home…" Giselle and Ava Mae were fighting for control, but Ava Mae was too weak to take it fully. She reached a hand toward the branch, fingers inches from touching it while half of her seemed to be holding back.

Lally jerked the branch away as Fenton shot forward and zapped Giselle with the bolt stick.

With a guttural howl, she shuddered and fell to the ground. Lally crouched over her, holding the branch above her like a divining rod. A few seconds later, Lally's sharp intake of breath announced something had happened.

She stood up, holding the branch away from her body. "She's in there."

"Who's in there?" Harlow asked. "Ava Mae?"

"Mm-hmm. She slid right in after Mr. Welch zapped Giselle. The stress was too much. She needed a safe place." She looked at Fenton. "You were right, but we gotta act fast."

"Yes." Fenton dug into the shopping bag and pulled out a lighter and a bottle of butane. "Ready when you are."

"What are you doing?" Olivia looked on the verge of tears. "You're going to kill her."

"No, Livie," Lally said. "We're going to set her free. You'll see." She dropped the branch onto the ground.

Fenton sprayed butane all over it and clicked the lighter. The branch went up in a whoosh of flame. The wood popped and whistled, but burned hot and bright. Within seconds, it was ash. Lally went back into the shopping bag, this time pulling out a little cloth bag. She emptied the bag onto the ground, adding what looked like a teaspoon of more ashes.

"Are those Ava Mae's?" Harlow asked.

Lally nodded. "What I was able to scrape up from around the tree." She kept her eyes on the ground, watching the pile as expectantly as Fenton.

"Is something supposed to be happening?" Olivia asked.

"I thought so," Lally replied. "Looks like I was wrong."

A soft breeze drifted past. Giselle moaned. They turned to look at her.

She rolled her shoulders like she was stiff. The wind picked up for a moment, then went still again. "That hurt. What the hell did you zap me for?" She blinked and her gaze shifted to a spot behind them. Her eyes rounded in fear as her jaw went south. She scrambled backward on her hands and feet. "Goddess, help me."

They looked at the pile of ash, but it was gone. In its place stood the somewhat transparent mirror image of Harlow.

Harlow gasped, but before she could do anything, Olivia rushed forward and pulled the figure into her arms. "Ava Mae."

"Mama," Ava Mae cooed.

The two seemed to blur into one another, their individual lines hard to distinguish from the others. Harlow shook her head. "Mom, I don't think you should do that."

Ava Mae looked up from Olivia's embrace. "Mama."

Was that all she could say? There were no scary sharp teeth, no eyes like black pits. Harlow wasn't entirely convinced, though.

Lally reached out and put her hand on Ava Mae's arm. Her

fingers passed through the woman's form and Harlow realized that's why Olivia had blended into Ava Mae. Neither one had a solid form, although Harlow knew her mother could manage that if she wanted. Lally nodded. "That's Ava Mae all right. No tree at all." She smiled at Fenton. "It worked."

He looked pleased. "Yes, it did. And all your idea, Eulalie." He smoothed the collar of his jacket. "You would have made a very fine lieutenant, you know that?"

She laughed. "Minding that tree is all the work I need."

Harlow walked past them to join her mother. She studied Ava Mae, trying to see her with new, unbiased eyes. "You're really my sister? No games?"

Ava Mae shook her head and smiled wistfully. "Sister."

Olivia glanced at Ava Mae. "It's her, Harlow, I promise. She feels... new to me, innocent again. I think she's reverted to being a baby in some ways." Olivia wrung her hands. "I'm sure she's sorry for all the trouble she caused you and Augustine, aren't you, Ava Mae?"

Ava Mae nodded. Tears welled in her eyes.

"There, there," Olivia soothed her. "No tears now, it's okay. Everything's right as rain again, *cher.*"

Harlow froze. "No, it's not." She turned around. "Fenton. *Augustine.*" She pulled out her mirror. "We need to go now." There would be plenty of time to figure out this new Ava Mae later.

Giselle shook her head. "You can't leave me here. I'm starting not to feel so good."

Harlow rolled her eyes. "That's the least of my worries."

Fenton raised his hand. "Go, Harlow. I'll secure the witch—"

"Secure me? What does that mean? Like hell." Giselle scrambled to her feet, her malaise apparently forgotten.

Fenton zapped her with the bolt stick again. She fell to the ground in a heap. "Like I was about to say before I was so rudely interrupted, I'll secure the witch until we have a better idea what to do with her. I'm sure Lally will assist me. Then I'll bring her home." He smiled. "I understand there's a rum cake to finish making."

Harlow grinned. She had a deep admiration for Fenton's no-nonsense side as well as his way with Lally. "That would be great, if that's all right with Lally."

Lally slanted her eyes at him, the coyest smile playing on her lips. "Sure, that'd be fine with me."

"It's settled then," Harlow said.

Fenton adjusted his glasses. "Be sure to go straight to the Pelcrum, Harlow. The others will be waiting for you there." He bent and hoisted Giselle up under her arms. "Eulalie, if you would be so kind as to take her feet."

Lally bent to help, lifting Giselle with one ankle in each hand. "Like a sack of potatoes," she muttered.

With a wave to her mother and sister, Harlow slipped through the mirror and back to the Pelcrum, her mind solely occupied with Augustine.

Chapter Twenty-five

Augustine's insides were a throbbing mass of pain. His leathers had held thanks to the fae craftsmanship, but he was sure his skin was a road map of welts, bruises and iron burns. He teetered on the edge of consciousness, aware that slipping over the side into the nothing would probably buy him a reprieve. Perhaps it was for the best. The abyss looked so comfortable...

Sutter waved an ammonia tab under Augustine's nose, pulling him off the ledge of darkness and bringing him back into the cold light of day. Augustine muttered a curse.

Sutter hoisted the iron bar again.

Pellimento hadn't moved an inch the whole time he was being beaten, but at last, she lifted her hand. "That's enough, Sutter. Let me speak to him again." She twisted to look over her shoulder. "Nguyen, get that set up back there."

"Yes, Senator," the thug answered, and busied himself with something Augustine didn't have the energy to care about.

He exhaled slowly, trying to control his movement to lessen the pain.

Sutter leaned down. "Still think I hit like a girl?"

Augustine hung his head, relief flooding him at the chance to rest. "No. At least not a fae girl. They hit way harder."

Sutter dropped the bar, grabbed Augustine's chin and jerked his head up. His other hand was pulled back, fingers curled into a fist.

"Sutter." Pellimento's voice cut through the air like a steel blade. "I said not the face. I also said that was enough. Leave us for now." She pointed at the two men holding Augustine upright. "And you two, put him back in the chair."

With a wet snarl that would have put a rabid dog to shame, Sutter released Augustine and stalked out of the room, slamming the door behind him. The two holding Augustine dropped him into the banquet hall chair. Blood rushed back into his shoulders, causing the pins and needles from lack of circulation to sting deeper, the pain a reminder of just how long he'd been unable to move.

She tipped her head at the two thugs and raised her brows. "*Go.*"

They left, closing the door much more quietly. Only the senator and the lower-level merc remained in the room, but he stood behind her, near the camera on its tripod.

She stared at Augustine for a moment without speaking, then shifted to cross her opposite leg over the other and spoke. "Why do you antagonize Sutter? You know it's only going to make him hit you harder."

He lifted his head to make eye contact. He thought about telling her the truth, that being fae meant he could take a beating no human could ever endure, and that Sutter's temper meant goading him could cause the man to make a mistake, but Augustine knew neither of those things would win him any points with her. Instead, he kept his mouth shut and dropped his head again, just to see how she dealt with being ignored.

He felt her gaze on him awhile longer as the silence stretched between them. When he finally lifted his head again, she looked back at Nguyen, gave him a subtle nod, then returned her attention to Augustine. "Did you kill my son simply to strike at me or did you have a greater plan? Were you going to hold him hostage until I met some sort of demands? Was the death accidental? I'm curious, as the autopsy has turned up no clues about how you murdered him."

"I did *not* kill your son." He exhaled slowly, but nothing lessened the constant knife-sharp ache of his numerous broken ribs. They wouldn't begin to heal in a meaningful way until the iron was no longer in contact with his skin, something he had begun to realize might not ever happen.

It was very possible he could die in this room. The finality of that filled him with a recklessness that was both calming and freeing.

Pellimento sighed like she was bored. Or perhaps just tired of his refusal to capitulate to her request for a confession. "Then why was your address in his pocket?"

"Because someone put it there, most likely to make it seem that I was involved." The realization of what he'd just said came to him as he spoke the words. "*Someone.*" Of course. Giselle.

"Is that also why I got an anonymous tip telling me you were responsible for his disappearance?"

"Yes." Augustine narrowed his gaze on her. "No one reaches a position of power without accumulating some enemies. At the very least, those who are jealous of your power. In my case, it's a woman by the name of Giselle Vincent, the witch who killed your son. You of all people must understand what it's like to have enemies."

She laughed bitterly. "Ah yes, that's good, show me how we're alike. Perhaps that will earn you my sympathy, hmm?" Her twisted smile straightened into a hard, unforgiving line. "We are nothing alike, you and I."

"My mother was half human. *Is,*" he corrected himself.

The senator's eyes darkened with pain and anger. "Mentioning your mother won't help your case, either. All that serves to do is remind me that *her* son is still alive." She raised a single finger. "But that is something I have the power to change."

He snorted and shook his head, the reality of his impending death loosening his tongue. "If you think she cares for a second what happens to me, you're wrong. She's probably one of your biggest supporters. Not that anyone outside the fae world knows what you really intend to accomplish with all those shell corporations and private interests."

A spark lit in Pellimento's gaze. He'd piqued her curiosity but with what? Knowing about her shell corporations? "Is that so? Your mother, who is half fae, isn't your greatest fan?"

His mother. He almost laughed. His least favorite subject. But since he'd finally found a topic that got Pellimento off the matter of her dead son, he decided to answer. "No, she's not. She hates my fae side. Put me on the streets when I was thirteen because she couldn't deal with how fae I am. After that, I'd certainly have a reason to hate humans, but I don't. When I took the job of Guardian, I knew it meant protecting all the citizens of this city, not just the fae. Not just the varcolai. *All* the citizens. Humans included."

"And yet you continually blame the witches for my son's death."

Back to the topic he'd been trying to steer her away from. "Because they're guilty. Giselle Vincent killed her own father." He shook his head. "If you think I killed your son, who do you think is responsible for the other victims found floating in the witches' pond?"

She smiled. "I would imagine you killed them as well."

"What's my motivation for all these killings?"

"They were all human." She shrugged. "My people have worked it out." She planted her elbow on the arm of the chair and pointed lazily to the camera over her shoulder. "Like I said, we've written your confession for you. You simply have to read it and all this will be over."

"Except it won't be over for me."

"No, obviously not. I can't let a killer free just because he confessed." She laughed like that was the craziest idea she'd ever heard. "You'll be executed. Publicly, of course. After the atrocities you've committed, I think the people deserve that, don't you?"

His bones prickled with heat again and anger filled his body with the kind of heady need to act that left him almost mute. That need mixed with the recklessness he'd already been feeling and gave him his tongue again. He spoke slowly and distinctly, but schooled the anger out of his expression, instead pretending to be defeated by the inevitable. "Turn your camera on."

Surprise and delight dancing over her features, Pellimento snapped her fingers. "Nguyen, you heard him."

"Yes, ma'am." The merc fussed with a few buttons, repositioning the camera slightly. "Good to go."

She held her hand out. "The floor is yours, Mr. Robelais."

He stared directly into the lens. "Senator Pellimento is a vile bigot and should be impeached before this city pays the price for her lunacy. Furthermore—"

"Sutter!" She shot to her feet, knocking her chair over. "You shut your mouth, fae." She charged forward and slapped Augustine across the face.

He almost laughed at her feeble attempt to inflict pain. If he died here, which seemed more and more likely, maybe they'd find that footage. Or maybe they wouldn't. Either way, he'd gotten to say what he'd felt. Almost. In case the camera was still rolling, he shouted, "Harlow, I love you."

Pellimento slapped him again. "You dirty fae bastard." She turned to Nguyen. "Did you get what I needed?"

He nodded. "I think so. You might want to review it."

Sutter charged in.

She pointed at Augustine, lip trembling with barely controlled rage, and simply said, "Again."

❧

Harlow appeared in the hallway of the Pelcrum, exactly on the spot she'd left from. She ran into the war room. All the lieutenants were there plus three new fae. One of them, Nekai, she recognized. "Hey, Nekai. I was afraid the rest of you would be gone." The other two she'd never seen before but guessed they were the pair Fenton had mentioned. They had squat muscular bodies and dusty skin that looked like they'd rolled in gray flour. "You must be..." She bit her lip. What had Fenton said their names were?

"Guz," one rumbled.

"Rat," the other grunted.

Cy stood up. "They're goblin fae. Not much for words. But super-strong, very loyal and basically indestructible. Guz once took two bullets in his left shoulder." Cy shook his head. "Never even knew it until he tried to go to the aquarium a few weeks later and set the security scanner off."

Guz grinned, showing off teeth that looked like slightly sharpened sugar cubes. "Like fish. Fish good."

"Fish are great." Oh-kay. Harlow gave the curious pair a little smile. "Nice to have you on the team." She gave Cy a questionable look.

"They're fine, I swear," he whispered.

With a nod, she addressed the rest of the group. "Can we hit that warehouse now? Get Augustine out of there?"

"About that," Dulcinea started. The hesitant look on her face gave Harlow a sinking feeling. "Right before he went to check on you, Fenton had me call in a backup request to our contact at the police department. They sent a few unmarked cars to the location. Got fidgety while they waited and decided to do a little recon."

Harlow leaned forward when Dulcinea stopped talking. "And?"

Dulcinea sighed. "They searched it top to bottom. It's empty. No sign anyone's been there in a few days."

Harlow sank into the nearest chair. The air in her lungs no longer sufficient, she opened her mouth and tried to breathe. The loss of the lead hit her like a punch to the gut.

Cy sat beside her. "We'll start patrols, we'll canvass the streets, talk to anyone who—"

"What about security cameras?" Dulcinea asked. "Augie said you'd set up some kind of thing to search for Rue using facial recognition and security feeds?"

Harlow looked at the changeling. "Genius."

Dulcinea nodded. "Augie said it was good—"

"No. You. That idea." She pushed back to her feet. "I need to get back to the computer lab." She jogged down the hall and to the room that held some of the most amazing equipment she'd ever laid hands on. She pushed the door open, stripped off her gloves and threw herself into the chair at the station she'd used to hack Grantham's GPS.

"What are you going to do?" Cy asked.

"Hmm?" She looked behind her, only then realizing the whole crew had followed her in. They stared back at her. Except for Rat and Guz, who seemed mesmerized by some of the blinking lights. "I cloned Augustine's phone not long after I moved in. I used it to track him once when the vampires were an issue. Watched him kill one right in front of me."

"Cool," Sydra whispered.

"I didn't exactly think so at the time." But things had changed a lot since then. She pulled out her LMD, set it on the remote access port and logged into its memory through the computer's mainframe. She maneuvered her way through the data, calling up the clone she'd installed and transferring it to the monitor in front of her. A moment later, the monitor flickered to life and a map appeared, a single blinking red icon lighting the black-and-white schematic. She pointed to it. "There, what's that?"

Dulcinea leaned in. "Nine Twenty-one Canal Street." She thought for a second. "That's the location of the Ritz-Carlton."

Harlow zipped through the Web to the Ritz-Carlton's servers, finding her way into their system without a snag. The screen shifted to reflect her activity. She pushed her way into the guest registry, filtering the names with a single mental command.

The name she'd been looking for flashed on the monitor. A few softly muttered curses from those behind her filled the air.

"Are you kidding me?" Dulcinea stabbed a finger at the monitor. "Does that mean what I think it means?"

Harlow stood. "Yes. Augustine's being held in the Ritz-Carlton." She glanced at the name listed next to the Grand Presidential Suite. "And Senator Pellimento didn't even bother to register under a fake name."

Cy whistled. "She thinks she's untouchable, doesn't she?"

"Yes." Harlow looked around. "Anyone ever been to the Ritz? Because I haven't and I don't think we can get there by mirror if we haven't actually been there, right?"

"Right," Cy answered. "And no, not me."

"Not me, either," Dulcinea said.

"I'm out, too." Sydra shrugged.

"I have," Nekai said. "My sister is on the housekeeping staff there. Or was." He frowned. "They fired her after the covenant was broken. They cited some bogus reason, but I'm sure it was because they thought their guests would freak out if they saw someone so blatantly fae on staff."

Harlow snorted. "No wonder Pellimento stays there. They're her kind of people." She shook her head. "Nekai will take us through to the hotel then. What kind of weapons do we have? From what Grantham told us at the hospital, Pellimento's got at least nine hired men, all with guns."

Nekai put his hands on his hips, the silver runes covering his midnight skin catching the light in a very reassuring way. "I can help with that, too. I have a spell in my repertoire that renders firearms useless for twenty-four hours."

"I'm hoping we don't need more than a few minutes," Harlow said. "That will do nicely. They have the advantage in numbers, but I'd take seven fae against nine human mercs and a senator any day."

Sydra snorted. "With Cy and the goblin boys, I'm pretty sure the advantage is ours."

"Better," Rat said. "More kill."

"Maybe less kill, more rescue." Harlow shot him a smile. "All right then, let's grab our gear and storm this joint. It's time to bring Augustine home."

Chapter Twenty-six

Harlow and the lieutenants Nekai had yet to take through to the Ritz-Carlton were still in the computer lab when Fenton stuck his head in. She tipped her head at him. "Hey." She knew him well enough by now that if he needed to tell her something, he wouldn't hesitate, so if he didn't stop her, she'd assume he hadn't had any issues taking care of Giselle or getting Lally home.

His brows rose as Nekai popped back in from transporting Cy and Guz. "Headed to the warehouse?"

"No, there was no one at the warehouse. We're headed to the Ritz-Carlton," Harlow answered. "Pellimento's holding Augustine there."

Nekai took Sydra and Rat through next.

Fenton's brows lifted a little farther. "Ballsy move on the senator's part. I'll call in a request to get backup there."

"Thanks. I'd totally forgotten about that," Harlow said.

He shrugged. "That's what I'm here for. I'm sure the NOPD wants those mercenaries in custody as much as we do."

Dulcinea chimed in. "Give them my number, tell them to text me when they've arrived and I'll text back when we're ready for them to take custody of the suspects."

"You got it," Fenton said.

Nekai returned and looked at Harlow. "You and Dulcinea ready?"

"Yes." She nodded at Fenton. "See you later."

Pride shone in Fenton's eyes as he looked at her. "May fate fight with you." He lifted his chin a little, the set of his jaw giving him an air of great seriousness. "Bring our Guardian home safe, Lieutenant."

"I will."

Nekai stuck his hand out and she and Dulcinea grabbed hold of it. Harlow hadn't expected Fenton's words to put a lump in her throat, but as they joined the other lieutenants in the hotel, she swallowed, pushing the emotion down. There was nothing she wouldn't do to bring Augustine back, a sentiment shared by the crew around her. She wasn't alone in this.

Enormous barrel-shaped machines lined the walls, most of them humming away. The noise level was substantial but not deafening.

"Are we in the laundry?" she asked.

Nekai nodded. "I thought it was better than dumping everyone into the lobby."

"Agreed." She looked at the faces around her. "What's our plan? We know he's being held in the penthouse. How do we get up there?"

The door opened and they ducked behind the last row of machines. A uniformed housekeeper came in, gathered a few towels off a shelf and left again.

Cy grinned. "I know how we're getting up there." He looked at Nekai. "Do you need a special key to get to the penthouse in the elevator?"

Nekai nodded. "And I don't have one."

"I bet we don't need one." Cy's attention shifted to Harlow. "Can you do your computer thing and override the mechs to get us up there?"

She smiled back. "Absolutely."

He spoke to the rest of the group. "Harlow and I will run up there. I'll get in the room and do what recon I can, count the guys in there, see if I can get eyes on Augustine, that kind of thing. Once that's figured out, we'll come back down, grab the rest of you and storm the place."

"Sounds like a plan," Dulcinea said. Behind her, Sydra nodded.

Guz chimed in with a guttural "Plan."

Nekai gave Cy an odd look. "How are you going to get in the room?"

Cy winked at Harlow and a second later she was looking at the housekeeper who'd interrupted them a few minutes ago. He put a hand on one hip. "How do you like me now?"

"Damn, man." Nekai shook his head, but his eyes were full of laughter. "I knew you were an ethos fae, but for some reason it never occurred to me you might do...this. It's good, but I don't think they're just going to let you into the room because you're housekeeping."

"I'll take some towels."

"Towels aren't going to cut it." Nekai looked around the room. "That cabinet over there holds the incoming dry cleaning. Find something that looks like what the senator might wear and take that."

"I'll find something," Dulcinea said. She went to the cabinet and started digging.

Cy pointed at Harlow. "You get me up there, then stay in the elevator. There's a good chance she'll have at least one guy posted in the hall."

Harlow nodded. "Agreed."

Dulcinea returned with several hangers' worth of women's clothes. "There's even a slinky nightie in here. I don't think it's something the senator would actually wear, but it might be good to have something her thugs won't want to be responsible for."

Cy said his thanks and took the clothes.

Harlow glanced at Nekai. "Which way to the elevators?"

"Down the hall and take a right."

"Great. Don't get caught while we're gone."

"You, either," Sydra said.

She and Cy the housekeeper left the laundry behind. She looked at him as they walked through the hotel hall. "You better do something about your voice or they're going to know something's up."

"How's this?"

His voice had become girly, but with a little edge. She made a face. "Are you imitating me?"

"I can only replicate people I've seen and heard. The housekeeper didn't say anything so..." He shrugged. "Is that okay?"

"Sure." She thought about it a moment. "But what if Augustine hears it and calls out to me?"

Cy was quiet as they rounded the corner to the bank of elevators. "Or what if he hears me, thinks it's you and realizes we're there to get him out? It might give him hope."

She punched the up button. "I hadn't thought about it like that. Do whatever you want."

"Okay." He got on the elevator beside her.

She pulled off one glove and pressed her palm flat to the touch screen. She closed her eyes for a moment as she steered through the maze of circuitry. Finding the floor she needed, she bypassed the key code and gave the elevator the command to rise. As it moved, she put her back against the panel, where she'd be less likely to be seen when the doors opened. In that position she was able to keep her hand pressed to the controls.

The elevator stopped. Cy had the dry cleaning over one arm, looking as perfectly like the housekeeper as was possible. The doors slid apart, then he whispered, "Wish me luck" and was gone.

She let the doors close about six inches, then held them there with a mental command to the circuit board. She listened as hard as she could.

"What's your business?" a gruff voice asked.

Her own voice said, "I'm bringing up the senator's dry cleaning."

A grunt was the only answer returned. A moment later, she heard three short knocks followed by "Housekeeping."

A brief pause, then a door opened. Cy spoke again. "I have Senator Pellimento's dry cleaning."

"I'll take it," a male voice answered.

"I don't think so," Cy said. "There are some...delicate items in here. I'm not turning them over to someone I don't know."

More grunting. Then the sound of the door shutting. She tipped her head back. Unbelievable. He'd gotten inside. Several long minutes passed. A single bead of sweat inched down her spine.

Footsteps. She twisted toward the opening between the doors, waiting, anticipating what to do if it wasn't Cy. Her free hand moved toward the blade secured in her waistband.

"Just me," Cy whispered as he stuck a hand through the doors.

She exhaled her relief and commanded the doors to open all the way.

He walked on and gave her a nod, his voice still quiet. "Let's go get the others."

As soon as the doors were shut, he turned back into himself again. "I counted four guys, but only heard the senator. She was in another room on a phone call. There were a lot of computers and some camera equipment. I tried to take the clothes into the bedroom, but the guy blocking the door wouldn't let me. I smelled smoke."

"Augie." The knot of emotion had once again clogged her throat. She forced it down.

Cy nodded as the elevator doors opened. "He's definitely in there."

They made their way back to the laundry room. Cy stuck his head in. "All clear." He held the door for her.

She gave the group a nod. "We need to get him out now."

Dulcinea looked at Cy, who was shutting the door behind them. "Augie's there?"

"It smelled like a smokesinger was in there." He leaned against the door. "Four guys plus the senator. No idea where the others are."

"Maybe they're working in shifts," Nekai said.

"Wait," Harlow said. "Is that including the one in the hall?"

Cy frowned and shook his head. "Five."

"Either way it's fewer than we thought. Guns?"

"Yes," Cy said. "Big ones. Assault rifles."

"Then I'll go first to knock out the weapons. After that…" Nekai shrugged. "I'm not much of a fighter."

"I am." Dulcinea pointed at the goblin fae. "I'll go in behind Nekai and you two come in behind me. Guz, you take the one in the hall. Rat, you find and subdue the senator."

Rat nodded fast.

Dulcinea narrowed her eyes at the goblin. "Subdue does not mean kill. No blood. No death."

Rat heaved out a sigh. "No blood?"

Harlow almost laughed at his utter disappointment. "*Very little* blood, Rat."

"Okay. Small blood okay." His grin returned.

Dulcinea looked at Cy, Sydra and Harlow. "Sydra and I can handle the other three in the penthouse, especially if they don't have operational weapons. Nekai can keep watch in the hall for more of her men. That leaves Cy and Harlow to take out the guard on the bedroom door if he hasn't already left his post to help the others. By then Guz should be in the penthouse, too. If there's another merc in the bedroom guarding Augustine, we'll be able to handle him no problem." She pointed at

Harlow. "Chances are real good they've got iron cuffs on him. If you can't find the key…"

Harlow held up her hands. "I can get them off."

Cy looked at her. "You sure your ability to manipulate metal extends to iron?"

She nodded. "Yes. I'm sure it won't be fun, but I can do it. And for Augie, I'd do anything."

"That's for damn sure," Dulcinea said. "And by the time we've got the mercs and the senator secure, the NOPD should be ready to cart them away. Although I think we might have a little conversation with the senator first."

"Sounds like a solid plan." Harlow itched to get things under way. "I say we're ready to go. Everyone knows their job. Let's move."

⚜

Giselle awoke with the strangest feeling of itching all over, not just her skin but somehow also beneath her skin. She stretched and sat up, running her fingers through her hair and raking her nails over her scalp. Scratching did no good. It wasn't that she itched exactly; it was more like a full-body rash. She felt her face and neck, but her skin was just as smooth as it had always been—no bumps or welts.

Weird. She blinked, trying to get her eyes to adjust. Nothing around her looked familiar but it was hard to make out much in the dark space. Was it night? How long had she been out? Where was she? Last she remembered, she'd been on the fae plane.

Unable to see more than dim shapes, she reached out to the ground around her. There were none of the small rocks and expanses of dirt that she recalled. Instead everything was smooth. Almost polished. Like concrete maybe. She lifted her hand and called fire, but nothing happened.

Damn it. She must still be on the fae plane. That would explain the moaning of the wind she heard, although she couldn't feel it. Was she inside a building? Again she tried to call fire and again she failed. Shoving to her feet, she grunted in frustration. Having no magic made her feel vulnerable. Naked. Angrier than she had words for.

Slowly, her eyes adjusted. She tipped her head back. Definitely a building. The ceiling of wherever she was glowed softly. Some kind of phosphorescent paint maybe. Although on the fae plane, who knew what it might be. Algae. Bugs. Anything.

She shuddered and scratched at her head again, squeezing her eyes shut. Still no relief. She opened her eyes and shuffled a few steps forward. Lines came into focus ahead of her. Behind those lines seemed to be a path. Lines? She put her hands out and continued moving forward, scuffing her feet on the ground as she walked to avoid a misstep.

Her hands connected with the lines. They were *bars*. What the hell? She grabbed them and shook just to be sure. They were solid under her fingers. And they didn't budge. She was in some kind of cell. "You stupid fae!" she screamed. "Let me out of here!"

Outside the wind picked up, the howling and moaning almost deafening. Then she realized the howling and moaning wasn't the wind. Those sounds were animal or...fae. She shivered and backed away from the bars. The noise was coming from the cells around her. "Goddess help me," she whispered.

Grunts and cries punctuated the howling. She turned away from the bars and went farther back into the cell. She could make out the walls now. They seemed to have a slight glow to them also. Or maybe it was just the reflection of the ceiling, as the glow only lasted a few feet down the walls.

Blocks of a softly colored, translucent stone made up the rest of the cell walls. A small bench hugged one side. Judging by the

thin mattress, slim pillow and blanket, it was supposed to be a
bed. She swallowed and cocked her jaw to one side. She would
not cry. Especially if there was a chance they were watching her.

She looked around, but saw no cameras. Nothing that
remotely resembled technology. Was this whole place run by fae
magic then? She knew enough about magic to know there were
often loopholes. Maybe she could find a way out.

The moaning had died down a bit. She glanced at the bars.
If this place had guards or wardens, she'd yet to see any. Which
was fine with her. She looked at the walls again. The stone
blocks didn't look like they'd been set with any kind of mortar,
just laid on top of one another until they reached the ceiling.

The idea that one might be movable intrigued her. She
latched on to it like a life vest. She wasn't a weakling. Maybe
she could loosen one enough to dislodge it completely. And if
she could manage that, she could certainly manage another one.
And then another. Enough to make a hole to escape through.

True, she had no idea where she'd go on the fae plane, no
idea what was edible and what wasn't, but she'd figure that out
when the time came. All that mattered was getting free of this
place.

She studied the lines between the stone blocks, looking for
one that might have a chip or a tiny gap. Her gaze snagged on
one. A hairline crack ran through it from top to bottom at one
end. That was something she could work with.

Kneeling beside it so her body was parallel to the wall, she
clenched her hand into a fist and wrapped her other hand
around it to make both hands into a battering ram. The itching
was so intense she wanted to rip her clothes off and scratch until
she was bloody. Instead, she made herself focus all her strength
and energy into what she was about to do.

She pulled her hands back and swung with all her might.
The side of her palms struck the stone hard.

The stone didn't budge, but her skin felt like it was on fire. Painful heat shot through her from her hands, radiating such agony into her body that she almost vomited.

She dragged herself away from the wall, staring at the blocks with a fresh new hatred. No wonder there was no mortar. They weren't made of stone after all. They were made of the one thing that could cause a witch the most harm. The thing that in great enough quantities could incapacitate a witch without any further effort.

She spat the word out, as poison on her tongue as it was to her magic and her body. "Salt."

Chapter Twenty-seven

Harlow and the rest of the lieutenants waited in the elevator while Nekai, Dulcinea and Guz stepped out into the hall. Guz followed Dulce, his lumbering gait almost comical behind the long, leggy stride of the changeling. The trio disappeared from view, but their voices carried as they approached the guard at the door.

"I'm sorry, can you help us?" Dulcinea asked. "We seem to be lost."

"You do not have authorization to access this floor," the guard said, his voice gruff.

"I believe my friend Nekai has your authorization right here," Dulcinea replied.

The faint smell of ozone, a sure sign of Nekai's magic, reached them a moment later, while Guz's incomprehensible grunts followed next. The guard managed half a curse. The final sound was a soft thump.

A few seconds later, Dulcinea stuck her head around the side of the elevator, her dreads swinging past her bright smile. "All clear. Let's take the hotel room!"

Harlow and Cy went after her, with Sydra and Rat behind them. Nekai stood poised at the hotel suite's double doors. He glanced at Harlow, leaning his head toward the door.

She nodded, stripped off one glove and quietly pressed her fingers to the lock. A moment later, the green indicator lit up.

Unlocked. They only had a few seconds before the light went red again.

Dulcinea and Cy each took one door, grabbing the lever handles and watching for Nekai's signal. He lifted his hands and nodded. They shoved the doors open. His hands began to move, weaving the spell necessary to render the weapons useless.

The thug closest to the door whipped around, hoisting his rifle. Guz charged the man. He got off a single round. The bullet sank into Guz's thick body as he attacked but didn't stop him. The goblin took the thug down, flattening him on the carpet. Guz followed with a massive fist to the man's jaw, and just like that, the odds started to shift.

Two more mercs came out from another room, guns raised, but nothing happened when they pulled the triggers. Sydra and Dulcinea attacked.

Harlow took off on her own, searching for Augustine. Halfway down the hall, she found an unguarded door. She opened it and almost retched. The room stank of blood and smoke and human body odor.

One of the hired soldiers stood over Augustine's lifeless body, a bloody iron bar raised over his head like he was about to strike again. Augie was sprawled on a tarp, his face bruised and swollen to the point of almost being unrecognizable. Both horns were broken off and blood soaked his leathers.

The man began to bring the iron bar down on Augie again. On a hunch, Harlow yelled, "Sutter."

He stopped mid-swing to look at her. "What the hell?"

She charged him, her anger coming out in a soul-deep cry. She knocked him down but he turned on her in an instant, elbowing her across the cheek.

Adrenaline took care of the pain. She planted her bare hand over his face and squeezed, pouring as much hurt and suffering into the man as she could manage while fighting the ugliness coming off him. He lashed at her, but within a few seconds began crying out, his struggle to be free forgotten. A few seconds more and he wept softly. Finally, he went limp, the emotional overload more than his human system could bear.

She released him and crawled over the bloody tarp to Augie. It hurt just to look at him. Her strong Augustine, so brutally beaten. If he didn't survive, she would kill Sutter herself. She touched the side of Augie's head that seemed the least bruised. "I'm here," she whispered. He was breathing, but it was more like a shallow wheeze. His lids twitched, maybe in response to her voice, maybe because of the pain he was in. She prayed it was her voice, prayed that he knew she was there.

"I'm going to get that iron off you now." Even if he wasn't hearing her, she would keep talking to him, keep letting him know he wasn't alone anymore. She moved to his hands and the shackles. She could feel the iron at this range, her fingers stinging with the metal's irritating power. Beneath the cuffs, raw, oozing blisters covered Augie's skin. Angry tears clouded her vision. "It's okay, baby," she said. "You're going to heal up just fine."

She wiped at her eyes with the back of her hand, pulled off her other glove and went to work, grabbing hold of the first shackle. The shock of iron on her bare skin dug knives into her flesh and made her gasp. She closed her eyes, gritted her teeth and forced the metal to bend to her will. It bit back, but slowly, the tumblers aligned. The shackle fell open.

"One down." She yanked it off Augie's wrist and took a long, shuddering breath in an attempt to alleviate her pain. It failed. Her hand looked like she'd dipped it in hot oil. The skin on her fingertips puffed with burns and the lingering pain sparked stars at the edge of her vision. She sucked in another breath and fought the urge to cry out. Augie didn't need to know she was in pain. He had enough to deal with.

Beside her, the merc moaned, prompting her to get the second shackle off. With her unaffected hand, she latched on to the remaining cuff and fought through the pain to unlock it as well. Once it was off Augustine's wrist, she sat still for a moment, letting her head drop as the pain caused a swell of nausea that almost knocked her unconscious. All ten fingertips were now equally blistered. She breathed through her mouth, bending one leg to touch her knee to Augustine's thigh. She couldn't stand not to touch him. Couldn't bear the idea that he might think she'd left him.

The merc moved his head to the side. His fingers stretched like he was feeling for that damned iron bar. "Cy, Dulcinea, someone help me!" Ignoring her injured hands, she dug the blade from the back of her waistband. The blood weeping from her burned fingers made the dagger's grip slippery. She tightened her grip. Pain screamed through her. She rose to her knees, nudging Augie behind her, and aimed the weapon at the merc. The blade seemed insignificant in light of the situation.

Dulcinea came charging in, Cy behind her. "What do you need—never mind." Dulcinea jumped on the merc, rammed her fist into his head and knocked him out. She started stripping the weapons off his prone form. Cy kicked the iron bar away and used zip ties from the man's own utility belt to secure his wrists.

Augie moaned and tried to move.

"Stay down, Augie." Harlow jerked the weapon toward the mercenary. "Get him out of here." She tucked the blade away, then eased Augustine onto his back. His leathers were sticky with blood.

Dulcinea wrapped a hand in Sutter's belt and lifted him. "We'll add him to the rest."

"Get Dr. Carlson here *now*. I'm not sure we can move Augie just yet." Harlow glared at the downed merc. "And keep a close eye on that one. I'm pretty sure that's Sutter, the one in charge. The one who shot Grantham."

"You got it," Dulcinea said. She pulled out her LMD with her free hand and used her thumb to tap at the screen. "Sent Carlson a text." She tucked the phone away. "We're almost done searching the suite. Five guards in total. Rat's dragging in the one from the hall." She glanced at Augie, her jaw popping to one side in clear anger. "We're going to spend a little time interrogating them, if you don't mind."

"No, I don't mind at all." Harlow shook her head. "Do whatever you want." She wasn't sure what there was to be gained from questioning the soldiers but she certainly didn't care if it happened.

Dulcinea's gaze shifted to Augustine. "You think he's going to be okay?"

"Absolutely. Although it's going to be a long recovery."

Dulcinea slung Sutter up and over her shoulder like he weighed fifty pounds, not two hundred, muttering something in faeish that sounded like curses. "I should get back..."

"Go ahead, I'm fine." Harlow tipped her head toward Augie. "I'm going to stay here with him." Even if they needed her, she wasn't leaving Augie's side.

"Yeah, cool. Good." Pride shone in Dulcinea's eyes. "You stay with him as long as you like. As long as he needs. If something changes, we'll let you know."

"Yeah." Cy nodded. "We've got things under control. And we'll send the doc in as soon as he gets here."

Harlow glanced past them toward the door. "What about hotel security?"

Cy looked at Dulcinea before shrugging. "I haven't heard anything."

Harlow nodded, thinking. "Augustine's in no position to be moved just yet. I mean, we can if we have to but—"

"It wouldn't be the best thing for him," Dulcinea finished.

"No, it wouldn't." Harlow tempered the ache in her heart at Augustine's condition by focusing on the bigger picture. She needed to buy him some time. "Cy, can you mimic one of the mercenaries and stand guard at the penthouse door just in case someone comes up?"

He smiled. "That's a great idea. Will do." He jogged out of the room.

Dulcinea bounced once, adjusting the weight of the man on her shoulder. "I'll let the others know what's up. You take all the time you need. Well…" She hesitated. "Not all the time. We should get out of here as soon as reasonably possible."

"Agreed." Harlow rested the back of one hand on Augie's shoulder. Her fingertips had stopped bleeding and the pain had lessened to the point that she no longer felt like passing out or throwing up. Amazing how quickly the fae body healed. An idea started to form in her head. "I might be able to speed things up."

"I'll leave you to it then." Dulcinea started for the door, stopping a moment later. "One small bit of bad news I forgot to mention."

Harlow looked up. "And that is?"

"The senator has yet to be located, so there's a pretty good chance she left before we got here."

"That sucks."

Dulcinea frowned. "Maybe we'll get lucky and she'll return before we leave; otherwise…" She shrugged.

"We'll figure something out."

"Yep." With that Dulcinea spun on her heels and took off with the merc. She closed the bedroom door behind her.

"Hi." Augustine's raspy whisper caught Harlow by surprise.

She glanced down at him. His left eye was swollen shut, but his right eye was open a slit. The white was bloodshot and glassy. Her heart clenched but it was good to hear his voice. "Hi. I'd ask you how you're feeling but I think I can guess."

He tried to smile but only got halfway before it turned into a grimace. That's when she saw his broken tooth.

She looked toward the wall, taking a moment to rid her face of the bitter desire to kill someone on his behalf.

"Yeah," he said, the word whistling over the jagged edge of his incisor. "I'm not great."

She forced herself to smile. "But you will be. The iron cuffs are off, so you should be able to heal now." That and the fact that she was about to try something she never had. "The suite is secure but we're not ready to move you yet, so close your eyes and rest. You're going to need your strength."

He did as she asked. Or perhaps he'd passed out again, she wasn't sure. Either way, she had to help him in any way she could.

Gently, she placed her damaged hands on top of his, careful not to touch his wrists where the skin still looked like it had been scrubbed with a wire brush dipped in acid. She took a breath and opened herself to him.

Pain flooded her system so hard she jerked back, breaking the contact. What she'd felt touching the iron had been nothing compared to what he was still enduring. Fighting her natural instinct to avoid pain, she put her hands on his again and with a little more control this time, allowed his pain into her body.

She closed her eyes and rocked back on her heels as it hit, but managed to hang on. Bit by bit, she took on more of his agony. New feelings layered over the pain. His fear of dying without seeing her again almost undid her. His anger at being helpless made her want to rip Sutter's heart out. His grief at Grantham's death tore at her. She moved her hands so she could gently curl her fingers under his as she opened her eyes and found her voice. "Augie, if you can hear me, move your fingers against mine."

His fingers pressed against hers. She inhaled as the touch

caused her new pain, but this time she was able to smile without effort. "Grantham isn't dead. He's in the hospital with some cracked ribs and a pretty nasty bruise, but he's going to be just fine. He had a vest on. And Jewelia's *gris gris*."

Augie's grief disappeared like a shot and a sense of joy spilled into her.

"Now stay still," she reminded him. Then she went back to work, pulling as much of his pain and suffering into her as she could handle. Some she was able to disperse but the bulk of it stayed with her. Still, she continued absorbing what she could, eyes closed, head lowered in concentration, until she finally had to sit back and take a breather. The hurt was intense, but her pride at being able to help him with her gift, something she'd always considered a curse until these past few weeks, helped take the edge off her distress.

"What did you do to me?"

She glanced up to see him looking at her. "Just siphoned off some of your excess pain." She shrugged, then wished she hadn't. With every breath, she felt his broken ribs; with every facial movement her body knew his bruises; with every bend of her wrists her skin burned. She tried to hold on to her smile but the pain was ebbing slower than she expected.

"I feel a lot better." He blinked hard, finally able to open his other eye. Suspicion filled his gaze. "You feel it, don't you? The pain you took off me."

She couldn't deny it. "I only took what I could handle. We need to get out of here soon. Get you home."

"I know. Trust me, I'm ready to get the hell out of here." With a great amount of obvious effort, he pushed to a sitting position, muttering quiet curses as he finally got upright. He let out a long exhale. "You're something else." He shook his head slowly. "Harley Goodwin, if I loved you before I love you twice as much now. I can't believe how much you helped me."

She smiled. "It's what friends do."

The one side of his mouth capable of movement hitched up in a grin. "I've never had a friend do this for me before."

"I'm sure that's only because you've never had a friend capable of doing this before. Also, you probably never had a friend who loved you like I do. Outside of Dulcinea, of course." She made a face, rolling her eyes in a teasing manner.

He laughed, then grimaced. "Don't be cute; it hurts to laugh."

She stuck her tongue out, then pursed her lips. "I am what I am."

Sighing, his injured half smile returned and the twinkle in his eyes took on a wicked bent. "If I could kiss you without causing myself more pain, I would."

"I'll take you up on that in a few days." She rocked to her feet, the pain decreasing with every passing moment, but her hands hurting enough that she kept them from touching anything. "Stay where you are. I'm going to check with Dulcinea and see what's going on, then we're going home."

He folded forward, resting his forearms on his thighs and letting his head drop. "I'm not going anywhere."

"Good." She headed for the suite's living room. She found the goblin fae and the lieutenants surrounding the senator's thugs. Sutter had a bloody lip and Dulcinea's right hand was drawn back in a fist. "How are things going?"

Dulcinea dropped her hand and stepped away to speak to Harlow. "About as expected. They're all pretty tight-lipped. Doesn't matter. Cops are on their way up. They'll all be in lockup before the sun sets."

Harlow nodded. "Any idea where the senator is?"

"No." Dulcinea frowned. "And not for lack of trying to find out."

"I figured." Harlow hugged her arms to her body. Exhaustion was setting in, causing her vision to go a little unfocused and the lingering pain in her body to seep into her bones. "If it's all good with you, I'm going to take Augie home."

"Yeah, totally, go, we got this."

"Can you redirect the doctor to the house? Augustine's in bad shape. He still needs to be looked at."

Dulcinea pulled out her LMD. "I'm on it."

The suite door opened and Cy, in his own form, walked in with a small squad of uniformed police officers behind him.

"Go," Dulcinea said. "Get Augustine out of here before the cops decide they want a statement from him. I mean, they will, but they don't need to do it now."

Harlow gave her a little salute. "See you later."

With a nod, Dulcinea turned to deal with their new company.

Harlow jogged back to the bedroom. Augustine hadn't moved and for a moment, she thought he'd passed out again, but he lifted his head a few seconds after she entered, his lop-sided smile greeting her. "What's up?"

She pulled out her silver compact, flipped it open and flashed the mirror at him. "We're going home."

Chapter Twenty-eight

After an exceptional amount of fussing even for Lally, Augustine had been wrapped in blankets and relegated to the largest sofa in the library, which had also been wrapped in blankets to keep his bloody self from staining it. He lay there, waiting for Dr. Carlson to arrive, watching Harlow nod off in the chair closest to him. She was so beautiful, even with the tiredness of the past few days hanging over her like a shadow, that he was able to temporarily focus on something else besides how much his body hurt.

"Go to bed, Harley," he whispered.

Her head snapped up. "What? I'm awake."

He would have laughed if not for the pain it would have caused. He smiled instead, his face throbbing no matter what his expression. "You need sleep."

"I will. Right after the doc looks you over."

"I'm home now. I'm safe. You don't have to watch over me."

She tucked her knees into the side of the chair and curled up, eyes slightly more alert and twinkling with sass. "You're not the boss of me. I'll do whatever I want to do."

Hell's bells, he loved her. "Oh, I'm fully aware of that. But technically, since you're now one of my lieutenants, I *am* the boss of you."

"You keep telling yourself that."

He shook his head slowly, completely amused and bewitched by her. He wanted to thank her for saving his life, to let her know that he'd been fully prepared to die, beaten to a pulp by Sutter and his iron bar, and that if not for her, that's exactly what would have happened, but nothing he could think of seemed sufficient. "Thank you" didn't cover what he was feeling.

Her head slipped down to rest on the arm of the chair and a few moments later, the rhythm of her breathing changed. She was asleep.

And he hurt too bad to pick her up and carry her to bed. Anger at what Sutter had done to him welled up fresh and hot. He stared at the ceiling, knowing there was no outlet for his rage in the here and now, trying to store up what he was feeling for a time when he could act on it.

The sounds of movement and voices came from the back of the house and a moment later, Lally walked in, Fenton and Dr. Carlson behind her. Augustine put a finger to his lips, then pointed at Harlow.

Fenton frowned. "I think we should wake her. She's going to have to see this sooner or later." He pulled out his LMD and queued something up, shaking his head. "I wish you'd told me about this. I understand considering the stress you were under but this is going to be difficult to spin."

"Spin what? I have no idea what you're talking about."

He sighed. "Senator Pellimento held a press conference about thirty minutes ago."

"Yeah, I knew about that. She wanted me to confess to the murder of her son—she had the confession all written out and everything."

His brows rose behind the frames of his glasses. "So you're saying you didn't give her a taped confession?"

"Hell no." Augustine narrowed his gaze. "Are you saying she aired one?"

Harlow stretched. "What's going on?"

"Trouble," Lally answered.

Harlow straightened in her chair. "Like what?"

"Like this." Fenton set his LMD flat on the coffee table, then tapped the screen. The holoscreen flared to life with a video.

Senator Pellimento appeared behind a podium. "It is with the great sadness only a mother can know that I must announce my son, Robert Pellimento, was brutally murdered by the fae Guardian of this city."

"What the hell?" Augustine's bones heated with his anger.

Harlow was clearly awake now. "Didn't you tell her Giselle was responsible?"

"Yes, but she didn't care."

The senator continued. "The only good news in this situation is that the Guardian, Augustine Robelais, has confessed." The screen went black for a moment, then Augustine's face appeared. The camera was zoomed in and showed only from his shoulders up. No sign of the chair he'd been in, the restraints on his wrists or the tarp that had been spread beneath him to keep the hotel's carpet from absorbing too much blood.

His image began to speak. "I did kill your son."

The senator's voice could be heard off camera. "Why did you kill him?"

His image answered. "I hate humans. Not just the citizens of this city. All people."

Augustine untangled his arm from the blankets to point at the holoprojection. "I never said any of those things."

The color had drained from Harlow's face. She stared at his image.

The senator's voice asked another question. "Do you have anything else you wish to say?"

"The fae hate humans."

"Why is that?" the senator asked.

"We understand what it's like to have enemies."

"So you're saying that humans are your enemies? Why? What could humans want that the fae have?"

Augustine's lip sneered. "Power."

The screen went black again, then the senator reappeared at her podium. "With this shocking confession, I have no choice but to declare the entire state of Louisiana under martial law. New Orleans will be subject to a curfew starting immediately. No othernatural may be outside their home from sundown to sunup." She held up a piece of paper. "I will also be passing emergency legislation requiring all othernaturals to be regis-tered. I will not allow the human citizens of this great state to suffer the same tragic loss I have just because the othernaturals perceive us as a threat." She lowered the paper and took a breath. "Thank you for your attention. I will be unavailable for further comment and wish that my privacy be respected while I see to my son's final arrangements. Good night."

As she strode away from the podium, the holoprojection ended.

Augustine looked at Fenton and Harlow. "I swear, I never said any of those things. When she turned on the camera, I made a statement about how she ought to be impeached."

Harlow looked at him, pain in her eyes. "While you might not have said those exact things, you must have said those words. Did you have any idea she was filming you?"

"Not until I told her to turn the camera on."

Harlow shook her head. "She must have had the camera on the whole time. Then she asked you enough questions to get the words she wanted, and had someone splice this lie together. That manipulative—" She tossed off her blanket and stood up. "She's not getting away with this."

Fenton pushed his glasses back on the bridge of his nose. "I don't know, Harlow. She's a very powerful woman. This was a big step toward garnering the public's sympathy for the othernatural restrictions she's been secretly pushing." He sighed. "The days of those efforts being secret are now behind us, I fear."

Augustine tipped his head back and growled. "I wish Giselle had thrown the senator into that pond instead of her son."

Harlow began to pace. "We need a plan, we need a way to counteract this—"

Fenton's soft exhale interrupted her. "I appreciate your enthusiasm and while I agree with you, I don't see how we can go against this woman in a way that's going to make a difference. Do you have an idea?"

She stopped pacing to look at him. "We need to make a statement of our own. We need to make it public that she falsified Augustine's confession, that Giselle Vincent is the one responsible for her son's death, and we need to make people understand that they have nothing to fear from us or the varcolai or any of the othernaturals living in this city."

Augustine picked his head back up. "I'll give whatever statement you want me to but how are we going to get people to believe my word over hers? With the death of her son, she's got their sympathy. And how are we going to get anyone to even see it?" He looked at Fenton. "Where was that press conference broadcast to?"

"At this point, it's gone nationwide." Fenton looked at Harlow. "We have very little hope of getting that kind of coverage."

Harlow snorted. "You two really don't know what I'm capable of, do you?" She looked at Lally. "Will you put a pot of coffee on? I can't sleep yet. Too much to prep."

"You got it, sugar." Lally took off for the kitchen.

Harlow turned her attention to Dr. Carlson. "Get Augustine as patched up as you possibly can, but make sure all his visible injuries are documented with pictures. Include those photos in his file."

Dr. Carlson nodded as he stood up, bag in hand. "Absolutely."

She tipped her head at him. "And I don't want Augustine sedated. Give him something for the pain without knocking him out. I need him sharp."

"Yes, ma'am."

Augustine almost snorted. Dr. Carlson was a wise man not to contradict Harlow, not with the way she'd come to life and taken charge.

She focused on Fenton. "Do you have a way to contact the senator?"

"Yes, but why?"

"Because I need you to set up a meeting with her. Tell her if she wants an othernatural to crucify, Augustine will be happy to turn over the witch responsible for her son's death. Let Pellimento think he'll come alone. Make sure she does the same."

Augustine sat forward, even though it shot fresh pain through his body to do so. "Are you crazy? One, Giselle needs to be handed over to the NOPD. Two, there's no way I'm meeting with Pellimento again. And three, I appreciate the help but I don't think—"

"Trust me." She faced him, her earnest desire to help shining in her eyes. "Where's a place you'd feel safe meeting her?"

"Nowhere."

Harlow sighed. "Sutter and his men are behind bars. And she's probably riding pretty high right now, feeling like she's bested you. She might actually come alone." She pointed at Fenton. "Talk to your NOPD contact. Work it out so that she gets no police escort—or if she does, at least one that's on our side."

He nodded. "I'll get right on it. Would you like to share your plan?"

"I have recording equipment, too. And if things go the way I think they will, I won't need to splice a thing." She smiled. "We're going to turn the tables on her."

Fenton's mouth twitched. "I like that. How do you suppose we'll get eyes on this masterpiece of yours?"

She laughed, a sound that healed Augustine's soul. "Oh, Fenton. You know what I can do." She wiggled her fingers at him. "All you two need to do is play your parts. I'll take care of broadcasting it to the world."

⚜

Giselle huddled in the middle of the cell's barred wall, as far from the salt as she could get. The howling and wailing that had answered her first calls for help had died away, but now and then something lifted its voice in an attempt to be heard. Those constant, eerie cries combined with her inability to use her magic had her cringing at the slightest noise.

Her eyes had finally adjusted to the dim, phosphorescent light, which was both a blessing and a curse. The place was as dank and dreary as she'd imagined, but at least she could make out her surroundings. Even so, she refused to focus on whatever was being held in the cell across from her after glimpsing a shape that was in no way human.

She'd done some crying herself. Those tears were gone now, replaced by the realization that while she had no idea how long she was going to be here, there had to be a way to survive this ghastly place.

Unless they were going to let her starve to death. She swallowed, suddenly thirsty, and rocked her head back against the bars. Her stomach growled as if on cue.

Something scurried across her foot. She screamed, then lunged for it, grabbing the ratlike creature with both hands. If the fae thought she was just going to wither away and die in this place like a hapless victim, they were sorely mistaken. Giselle Vincent was not a quitter. She took a deep breath and snapped the creature's neck.

At least dinner was no longer in question.

Chapter Twenty-nine

Dr. Carlson had done what he could for Augustine, but Harlow knew by the way Augie was moving that he was still in a great deal of pain. Asking him about it wasn't going to help, so she kept him talking about anything and everything else. She glanced at the back door they stood beside. "What's the name of this place again?"

"*Le Belle et Le Bete*," he answered. "Beauty and the Beast. It's the oldest othernatural bar in the Quarter." He rapped on the brick wall beside the door. "And with the built-in protection this place has to hide it from humans, Pellimento will never know Sydra, Nekai and the goblin boys are inside for backup."

"You're sure? Because it sounds like there's a huge party going on inside there."

"There is." He smiled. "But to a human, this building not only looks abandoned; it sounds just as empty."

"I'll take your word on it." They were hidden behind a dumpster, awaiting Pellimento's arrival. She had seven minutes before she was late.

Augustine leaned against the wall. "You're sure all your stuff is where it needs to be and all in working order?"

"Positive." She pulled out her LMD, brought up the cam app and showed it to him. Six different screens showed six different views of the alley.

"I hope this works." He seemed on edge.

She couldn't blame him for that. His life was on the line here. "I promise you it will."

Two stray cats, a dusty gray and a bulky black tom, sauntered past the dumpster. Augustine smiled at them. "Nice of you two to make it."

The pair stopped and sat in front of them.

A second later, Harlow was looking at Dulcinea and Cy. She shook her head. "I'm never going to get over the fact that you two can do that. And Cy, I didn't even know you could do animal forms."

He shrugged. "Dulcinea gave me a few pointers."

Dulcinea grinned. "Where do you want us?"

Augustine nodded at the front of the alley. "At the entrance. You see anyone who looks like one of her hired thugs and you *discreetly* take them out. We can't risk an interruption until Harlow has what she needs."

"You got it, boss," Cy said. "Also, it's good to have you back."

"Thanks." Augustine smiled. "It's good to be back."

Dulcinea lifted her hand in a salute, then shimmered like a heat wave and became the gray cat again. Cy joined her in his guise as the black tom and together, they trotted back to the head of the alleyway. Cy jumped onto a discarded milk crate while Dulcinea curled up beside it.

"All right," Augustine said. "They're in place. Now you stay hidden. I don't like you in the alley at all. What if she wants to search it?"

"Then you distract her. Honestly, once you get her talking she's not going to think about anything but her own agenda."

"I hope you're right." He pulled out his LMD and checked the time.

"Robelais?"

The voice brought his head up. He walked out from behind the dumpster. "Senator. I was starting to think you were too scared to meet me."

Harlow crouched down, making herself as small as possible as Augustine walked toward the senator.

Pellimento laughed. "Too scared? Why? Because your band of misfit fae took down my mercenaries? Sorry, I'm not that easily deterred. Nor, as I'm sure you've come to realize, can my plans be so easily ruined. It's like you have no idea who you're dealing with."

Harlow watched the monitors on the cam app and smiled. The senator was the one who had no idea who she was dealing with.

But she would. In a big way.

⚜

Augustine realized his nerves were more about Harlow staying hidden than for his own safety. Pellimento would not take him prisoner again, not with Cy and Dulce close at hand and Sydra just a few feet away, listening in from the monitor Harlow had set up in *Belle's* back room.

He walked to the middle of the alley, giving Pellimento no reason to approach the dumpster. "I know very well who I'm dealing with. I am surprised you came alone."

"I wouldn't say I'm completely alone." She pulled a hand-gun from the small purse she carried. "This pistol holds fifteen rounds of specially made hollow points. Would you like to know what's special about them?"

"I'm sure you're going to tell me either way."

"They're not really hollow." She hefted the gun. "They're filled with a mixture of tiny iron pellets and iron shavings. After this bullet hits you, it will explode inside you and dissolve your guts into soup. Not a pretty way to go, but it works for me."

"And you know this because?"

She cocked her head to one side. "Really, Mr. Robelais? Do you think I wouldn't test my own weapon before I trusted my life to it? You're dumber than you look."

"And you're a liar and a manipulator out for your own agenda." Not to mention, pretty stupid if she thought she could get a shot off before he got to her.

She put a hand to her chest and looked aghast. "Mr. Robelais, you wound me. I'm only doing what's in the best interests of my constituents." Her hand fell away and her injured expression changed to one of superiority. "My *human* constituents."

A thrill zipped through him. This was exactly the territory they'd hoped she'd wander into.

"What have you got against the fae and the varcolai? And the vampires for that matter. They're not all bad."

She rolled her eyes. "If I've said it once, I've said it a thousand times. You're all abominations. *Unnaturals* is the word you'll soon be called." She sighed. "*Othernaturals* is so politically correct, isn't it? Like you all are just another extension of the human race." The glint in her eyes turned sour. "Well, you're not. I don't care if that witch did kill my son; you're the one who's going down for it. I'm going to make an example of you, Mr. Robelais. Just because you escaped me doesn't mean you're not still going to die a public death."

He put his hands on his hips. "So you do understand that I'm not responsible for Robert's death. But you still want to punish me."

She nodded slowly. "Now you've got it. Truth be told, that witch did me a favor. Robert has always been a difficult child. Willful. Feckless. More concerned with what my name could buy him than what his behavior might do to my name." She exhaled heavily, her chest rising and falling with the effort. "But that witch finally turned him into something useful. A martyr."

"You might be a worse mother than my own."

"I don't know, your mother sounded like a real gem to me."

"You would say that."

Pellimento raised the gun. "Where's the witch you promised me?"

Augustine laughed. "Did you really think I was going to turn over the one person who could clear my name? Just so, what, you could make her disappear?"

"Regardless of my plans for her, we had a deal." Her hand was steadier on the weapon than Augustine had imagined it would be.

"You want the witch? Drop the curfew. Rescind your lies about me. And leave all othernaturals alone."

Her gaze narrowed and her lip curled in plain disgust. "I will not rest until your kind are tagged and contained. Or exterminated. I'll take whichever comes first. Your kind are a plague and the sooner you're eliminated, the sooner humans will be safe again."

"My kind have existed beside humans since the beginning of time. Humans are in no more danger now than they were then. My kind are doctors and teachers, police officers and stay-at-home mothers. They work hard. They contribute to society. They love their children. They pay their taxes. They are not the enemy. You are." His blood went hot with anger, easing the pain still lingering in his bones from the beating he'd taken at her command. "This meeting is *over*."

"What's to stop me from shooting you right here? All I'd have to do is say that you attacked me and I shot in self-defense. People already think you're a murderer."

"And lose your chance to kill me in public?" He wagged his finger at her and started inching closer to the opposite wall. That also moved him slightly toward the senator, but his only thought was to get that gun aimed in a direction where it had less chance of hitting Harlow.

Pellimento paled as he came closer, her hand finally showing small tremors. She sidestepped away. "If you even try to touch me—"

"Touching you is the last thing on my mind." He nodded toward the exit. "You know my demands. You have an hour to make a statement and undo all the damage you've done."

She didn't budge. "Or?"

"Or…" He shrugged. "I guess you'll just have to wait and see."

"Are you threatening me?" She lifted the collar of her suit jacket toward her mouth and spoke into the lapel. "I'm being threatened. Do you hear that? The fae who murdered my son is now threatening me."

Cy and Dulce began to meow and hiss. Augustine gave them a little shake of his head as two police officers appeared at the mouth of the alley. She waved the gun in Augustine's direction. "Arrest him."

One officer started toward Augustine. He stopped at the senator's side. "Ma'am, we'd be happy to escort you out of here and back to whatever address you'd like to go."

Happy wasn't really how Augustine would describe the look on the officer's face. Minimal tolerance was more like it. Augustine raised his hand to his forehead in a small salute. "Officer."

Pellimento looked at the cop in horror. "What? Arrest him!"

The officer rested one hand on his gun belt. "Also, ma'am, I'm going to need to see your carry permit for that weapon." He held his other hand out. "Until then, I'll be taking possession of it."

She jerked the gun away from him. "I am a *senator* of the Southern Union."

"And I am an officer of the New Orleans Police Department. I'll give you one more chance to hand over the weapon and leave peacefully."

Sputtering like she might blow a vein, Pellimento gave the officer the gun and left with him. She kept glancing over her shoulder, sparks shooting from her gaze like bottle rockets going off.

Dulce swiped a claw at her as she walked past.

As soon as she was gone, Augustine released the breath he hadn't realized he'd been holding. The adrenaline in his system had blocked a lot of his pain. Now it came rushing back. He grabbed hold of the dumpster's edge as his vision started to tunnel in.

Harlow was instantly there, ducking under his arm to support him. "You don't look so hot."

"Don't feel it, either." He closed his eyes, trying to hang on to consciousness. "You get what you need?"

"Everything. You were perfect."

"Great." He almost managed a smile but every inch of him throbbed too much to figure out what his face was doing. Cy and Dulce reappeared in their fae forms. For a moment, he saw four of them. "I should... probably go back to the... the..."

Then everything went black.

Chapter Thirty

It's been an hour." Harlow walked from one side of Augie's attic room to the other. She'd set up a holovision in the room and since Dr. Carlson had left, they'd been monitoring the local news, watching for an indication that the senator might actually make some kind of apology and set things right.

Augie was propped up with a pile of extra pillows, a pain strip firmly attached to his ribs, which were now bound. He glanced at his LMD on the bed beside him. "Babe, it's been forty-five minutes."

Footsteps sounded on the landing. Fenton knocked on the door frame. "I hate to disturb you but Lally told me you were up here and—"

"You're not disturbing us." Augie waved one hand through the air like he was underwater, his smile still lopsided and his eyes glassy. She was okay with that. Meant the pain strip was doing its thing. "Come in, sit down. Show's about to start."

Fenton took a chair. "Thank you. How are you feeling, Augustine?"

"Great," he slurred. "Doc Carlson fixed me right up."

Harlow shook her head. "Dr. Carlson said he'll need at least a full day of bed rest, maybe two, before the damage from the iron is completely gone."

Fenton nodded. "Sounds reasonable. No word from the senator, I take it?"

"None." She went to the coffee table in front of Augie's couch and fired up her laptop sitting there, thrilled the pain in her hands was nothing more than a minor irritation now. "I'm ready to go, though."

His brows lifted. "You can do everything you need to do with that one machine?"

She smiled. "This one machine and my fae skills." She lifted one shoulder. "Also, I'm tapped into the computer lab at the Pelcrum. That is a serious amount of firepower you've got going on over there."

"Tapped in?" His brows furrowed. "That's a very secure system."

"No such thing as a very secure system. Not to me anyway." She bit her lip. "You don't mind, do you?"

"No, of course not." He splayed his hands on the chair's arms. "I guess I should stop being surprised by your abilities."

"My girl is amazing," Augustine volunteered.

"Yes, she is," Fenton agreed. He glanced at his watch. "I believe the senator's hour is up."

Harlow took off her gloves and cracked her knuckles. "Well, then, let's get this party started."

"Give her hell, Harley." Augustine lifted his hand, thumb up, and grinned.

"That's my plan." She attacked the keyboard, sending out the video segment she'd prepared while the doctor had been taking care of Augustine. She overrode satellite feeds and streaming webcasts, local, nationwide, international—wherever and what-ever she could access, becoming one with the machine. There was nothing off-limits to her.

The holovision flickered and the local newscast disappeared.

She typed one last command and sat back. "Here we go."

The senator's face appeared onscreen. The camera zoomed out to show more of her, revealing she held a gun. "This pistol holds fifteen rounds of specially made hollow points. Would you like to know what's special about them?"

The view switched to Augustine. Harlow leaned in. Her edit job had been fast and dirty. She prayed it came out the way she intended. He looked so pale, but she understood the pain he'd been enduring to make this meeting happen. He spoke. "I'm sure you're going to tell me either way."

"They're not really hollow." Pellimento lifted the gun higher. Her face practically gleamed with hatred. The night vision lens did not cast her in a pretty light. "They're filled with a mixture of tiny iron pellets and iron shavings. After this bullet hits you, it will explode inside you and dissolve your fae guts into soup. Not a pretty way to go, but it works for me."

Harlow glanced down at the dedicated website where she'd posted the video so that it would be available even after the telecast was over. She'd also linked to Dr. Carlson's report of Augustine's injuries, complete with the pictures she'd asked for. The hits were climbing rapidly.

The video continued, back to Augie now. "What have you got against the fae and the varcolai? And the vampires for that matter. They're not all bad."

Pellimento rolled her eyes. "If I've said it once, I've said it a thousand times. You're all abominations. *Unnaturals* is the word you'll soon be called."

"Hah," Augustine barked from bed. "This is going to finish her."

"We'll see," Fenton said. He twisted his hands together nervously and shifted his gaze back to the holovision.

Pellimento was glaring at Augustine. "I don't care if that witch did kill my son, you're the one who's going down for it. I'm going to make an example of you, Mr. Robelais. Just because you escaped me doesn't mean you're not still going to die a public death."

Augustine stared right back at her, hands on his hips. "So you do understand that I'm not responsible for Robert's death. But you still want to punish me."

Pellimento's slow grin came off as calculated and chilling. "Now you've got it. Truth be told, that witch did me a favor. Robert has always been a difficult child. Willful. Feckless. More concerned with what my name could buy him than what his behavior might do to my name." She sighed heavily. "But that witch finally turned him into something useful. A martyr."

Fenton shook his head. "She's digging her own grave."

"We hope," Harlow answered. She checked the site again. "Almost a million hits and three thousand shares. We're definitely getting eyes on this."

"Good." Augustine's voice was soft, his lids struggling to stay open.

"Rest, Augie. There's nothing more you can do right now anyway." Harlow dropped the volume on the holovision a few bars.

Pellimento's swan song was coming up. When the camera returned to her, her face was a mask of disgust. "I will not rest until your kind are tagged and contained. Or exterminated. I'll take whichever comes first. Your kind are a plague and the sooner you're eliminated, the sooner humans will be safe again."

The view switched to Augustine, who seemed filled with righteous indignation. He looked strong and beautiful, his bruised face giving him the appearance of a fighter unwilling to back down. "My kind have existed beside humans since the beginning of time. Humans are in no more danger now than they were then. My kind are doctors and teachers, police officers and stay-at-home mothers."

A tremor of emotion filled his voice, causing Harlow's breath to catch in her throat as he continued. There was no one who could deny Augustine believed the words he was speaking.

"They work hard. They contribute to society. They love their children. They pay their taxes. They are not the enemy. You are."

The video cut to Senator Pellimento being led out of the alley by the cop, then faded to black.

The screen flickered again and the local newscast reappeared. The anchorwoman seemed surprised, but not flustered. "As you just saw, our broadcast was interrupted by what appeared to be a video of Senator Irene Pellimento with a gun. We put a call in to the New Orleans Police Department and they confirmed that Senator Pellimento was charged an hour ago with unlawful possession of a firearm. Based on that report, we believe the date and time stamp on this video to be genuine. Our call to the senator's office has not yet been returned, but I can assure you we will be following this story very closely."

Fenton's LMD buzzed. He held a hand up. "I'd better take this." Harlow turned the holovision off as he answered. Augustine had finally fallen asleep, too. "Yes, Prime Quinn. I see. Very good. Yes, they both are. I'll tell her." He hung up, keeping his voice low and glancing at Augustine. "Let's go outside to talk."

She followed him into the hall, closing the door behind her so Augie could get the rest he so desperately needed. "What was that about?"

"The charges against Augustine have been dropped, but will be resumed unless we bring Giselle Vincent in." He hesitated as if searching for words. "What you did, with that video, was... amazing. You not only saved Augustine and his reputation, but depending on how this shakes out, the threat of Senator Pellimento may be one less thing for us to worry about. I can't pretend she won't still do whatever she can to make life for all othernaturals as uncomfortable as possible, but she's been exposed and that's a very good thing for us."

Harlow shrugged, a little embarrassed by the praise. "I was just doing what needed to be done."

"Prime Quinn would like to throw a dinner in your honor. When Augustine is up to it of course."

"That would be...wicked cool." She grinned, unable to help herself.

He smiled back. "Now, about Ms. Vincent."

Harlow nodded. "Yeah, about her. Where did you stash her?"

A curious light filled Fenton's gaze. "The Claustrum."

Her mouth came open. "Are you kidding me?"

His jaw popped to one side as he shook his head. "No."

"Are you going to get her and bring her back here?"

"I have to. I'll need to get Nekai to meet me at the Pelcrum when I bring her back. He's the only one who'll be able to bind her magic when she's once again on the mortal plane." He tipped his head to the side. "Of course, I could use some help fetching her from the Claustrum. Would you like to come?"

"That place terrifies me as much as it intrigues me."

"Is that a yes?"

She laughed softly. "That's a hell yes." She held up a finger. "Can you give me a second? I want to check on Augie."

"I'll wait right here."

She slipped back into the room. He was sleeping soundly. Despite his cuts and bruises, he'd never looked more handsome. "I'm a lovesick fool," she whispered to herself. Smiling, she bent and kissed him gently on the mouth. "I love you, Augustine Robelais. Now heal up. I have plans for you."

⚜

The clanking woke Giselle, who until that moment hadn't realized she'd been sleeping. Without the movement of shadows or a watch, time had lost meaning. Day, night, she had no idea. Around her, the noise level rose. Something was stirring the place into a frenzy.

Then she heard a familiar voice.

"This place is creepy."

"It does the job," a male voice answered. She recognized that one, too. The man who'd locked her in here.

She scrambled to her feet and backed away from the bars as he and Harlow approached. "What do you want?"

He studied her. "You. We've come to take you back to the mortal plane."

Surprise coursed through her. "You have?" Thank the goddess. She bit the inside of her cheek to keep herself from crying. She was finally going home. She couldn't wait to see Ian. "Let's go then."

The man twirled his finger through the air. "Turn around and back up to the bars."

She did as he asked. A moment later, he clamped handcuffs on her. Then he opened the cell and pointed toward the right. "Out."

She took a few steps forward then stopped. "I don't know where the hell I'm going. This place is a maze."

"Walk," Harlow said. "If you head in the wrong direction, we'll let you know."

Giselle started moving again. She kept her eyes focused on the dimly lit path, but as she passed other cells, it was impossible not to glance in. The things that glanced back at her quickly put that to an end. Things with too many teeth and limbs that were inhumanly long and eyes that glowed. Every now and then a whiff of something would pass her nose: flowers, bleach, dung.

Her skin crawled with the urge to be free. Once she was back in the human world and her magic was usable again, she was going to set both of the fools behind her on fire. They deserved it for what they'd done to her. Clinging to that thought, she kept moving until at last the dull light of the fae plane came into view.

Harlow fell into step beside her. "See? That wasn't so hard."

Giselle glared at her, but kept her mouth shut.

The man went ahead of them to unlock the massive gate surrounding the place. She shivered, not from being cold, but from utter disgust. "This place is miserable. Gray and windy and dirty and miserable. I'm so glad I'm not fae."

Harlow leaned in. "I'm glad you're not fae, too. Now shut up."

Giselle shook her head. "You have no idea the kind of power I wield."

"Lot of good it's doing you now." Harlow pointed her head toward the gate. "Go."

Giselle walked through. They'd see once she was back in the human world. Then they'd be sorry.

Harlow followed and the man locked the gate, then pulled out a mirror. He looked up. "Harlow." His gaze indicated something behind them.

Giselle turned at the same time Harlow did. Two shadowy figures floated toward them. Giselle backed up. "Keep Ava Mae away from me."

The man laughed. "Harlow, if you'd like a moment with your family, I'll take Giselle through and deal with handing her over to the police."

"The police?" Giselle whipped around. "What are you talking about?"

"That would be great, Fenton," Harlow said. "Thank you."

"What police?" Giselle repeated.

But Fenton just grabbed her arm and pulled her through the mirror without another word.

Chapter Thirty-one

Olivia materialized in time to pull Harlow into her arms for a hug. She hadn't expected to see her daughter again so soon. "How are you, *cher*? How's my boy?" She kissed Harlow's cheek. "I'm so happy to see you."

"We're both good. He took a little bit of roughing up recently, but he's on the mend. How are you?" Harlow's gaze slid sideways to land on Ava Mae. "How's life on the fae plane, Ava Mae?"

"We're just fine," Olivia said. She let go of Harlow and her solid form to wrap an arm around her other daughter's shoulder. "Ava Mae's settling in." She smiled at Harlow. "It's really good to have company."

Ava Mae nodded. "Good." She clung to Olivia's side.

Harlow's mouth turned up in a little half smile. "I'm happy to hear that. Do either of you need anything?"

"Just more visits from you and Augie." Olivia grinned. "More bourbon wouldn't hurt."

"Ick," Ava Mae said, her face scrunching up in disgust.

"I hear that," Harlow said.

Olivia gestured to the flat rock she often rested on. "Do you have time to sit and talk?"

Harlow nodded. "I have a few minutes."

Olivia led her daughters over and for a brief but glorious moment was overcome by the emotion of having them both with her. She wiped at her eyes. "Look at that, even ghosts can cry."

"What's wrong, Mom?" Harlow's gaze held the kind of concern Olivia wasn't sure she'd ever seen before in her daughter's eyes.

"I just love having you girls here with me. The last time I could reach out and touch both of you, you were babies. And you know that didn't last long." She perched on the rock. "This is just real nice."

Harlow sat on one side of her, Ava Mae on the other. Harlow linked her arm through Olivia's, who went solid just in time. "I'm going to find a way to get you back on the mortal plane with us, even if it's just for a visit."

"That would be wonderful." Olivia wondered if that would mean leaving Ava Mae behind. How did a mother make that kind of decision? "Tell me again, what happened to Augie?"

"Um..." Harlow rolled her lips in, making a tight line with them. "Short version is he had a disagreement with a woman that resulted in a run-in with some very bad individuals, but that situation is pretty much dealt with."

"A woman?" Olivia knew she must look judgey, but she wasn't about to have Augie breaking Harlow's heart.

Harlow smiled. "Not like that."

A new concern settled into Olivia's gut. "His mother?"

"No. A senator, actually." Harlow made a face. "You think his mother would cause him problems? I thought they weren't on speaking terms."

"They're not as far as I know. That woman..." Olivia shook her head. "She nearly ruined his life. I wouldn't put much past her."

Harlow seemed unconvinced. "He's Guardian of the city— and a good one. She's got to know that. Got to be proud of him now."

"I don't think so." Olivia sighed.

Ava Mae leaned against her, radiating worry and fear. "Mama."

"What's wrong?" Harlow asked. "Ava Mae looks upset."

"She's worried that I might be mad at her someday and not want to talk to her." Olivia glanced at Ava Mae. "Hush, now, child. That's never going to happen, so don't you fret." But as she turned back to her other daughter, distress darkened Harlow's eyes. It was clear she loved Augie and plain that any hurt against him was a hurt against her. Olivia patted Harlow's knee. "It's all right. Better his mother leaves him alone than interferes."

Harlow slid off the rock and onto her feet. "It's not all right." She kissed Olivia on the cheek. "I'll be back soon to visit some more, I promise. I just better get home and make sure there's nothing else I need to take care of with this business with the senator." She waved at Ava Mae. "Bye."

Ava Mae lifted her hand. "Bye."

Olivia watched Harlow pull out her mirror and disappear. Her mother's instinct told her home wasn't where her daughter was headed and the thing she had to take care of didn't involve the senator.

⚜

Harlow stared up at the enormous white building that loomed behind the stucco wall surrounding the property. This might be a bad idea, but she couldn't talk herself out of it, because bad idea or not, it seemed like the right thing. Like a thing that needed to be done. Potentially.

Or at least something she felt compelled to do.

She stood on Ursulines Avenue, studying the solid wooden gate in the wall in front of her and remembering the last time she'd been here with Ava Mae inside her and Father Ogun as her guide. She shuddered, happy that was far behind her and hoping that this visit would give her a better memory of this place.

That would require her to figure out a way to locate the woman she needed to see, however. A woman whose name she didn't even know. A woman whose face Harlow wouldn't have been able to pick out of a lineup if there was a gun to her head.

She sighed and glanced down the street. Maybe this was a dumb idea. Maybe she should just go home and be with Augie.

No. Running away from things had never served her well in the past and she wasn't that person anymore. She didn't want to be that person.

She peered through the narrow crack where the gate met the wall. A few nuns were walking in the garden. She focused on a spot in the far corner, one well shadowed by the trees, and used her mirror to travel there.

The grounds were beautiful, the place neat and quiet and peaceful. A half circle of statues surrounded the end of the walkway in the middle of the garden. In front of her was a small, slightly shabby building. She hugged the back wall of it, trying to get her bearings. Judging by the steam and smell of soap coming out of the high transom windows, it was a laundry.

Footsteps came toward her. Saying a little prayer that she wasn't about to get thrown out of a convent, she crouched down and peered around the corner. A woman walked toward the building pushing a large rolling laundry cart.

Harlow waited until she heard the door open and close, then stood up. The laundry woman had to know people, right? She was in charge of underwear. That had to put her on a first-name basis with anyone who lived here.

Harlow mustered a confidence she didn't feel and made her way to the door. Only a screen stood between her and the woman inside, who sang softly to herself as she sorted bedsheets.

Heart thumping, Harlow opened the door and stepped inside. "Excuse me? Could you help me?"

The woman turned. "What's that?"

Harlow knew those eyes. Those stormy sea eyes. "I, uh . . . I'm trying to find someone."

"You'll have to see the sisters up front." The woman's gaze narrowed. "But the convent's closed to visitors at this hour. You best come back tomorrow."

Harlow lifted her chin slightly and decided to test her theory. "Do you know Augustine Robelais?"

The flash of recognition in the woman's eyes lasted less than a second. "No."

Harlow nodded. So that's how she wanted to play it. "I'd heard his mother lived here and I had a message for her. Something important about her son."

The woman crossed her arms. "What's that?"

Harlow put her hand on the door handle. "Sorry, I can't tell anyone but her." If the woman couldn't at least admit to being his mother, she didn't deserve any more of Harlow's—or Augustine's—time.

The woman's mouth bent. "I'm his mother. What's he done now?"

With her admittance, Harlow's nerves disappeared. "Let's see, since becoming Guardian, he's saved the city on numerous occasions, saved countless lives, mine included, and stopped corruption in its tracks. And he's only been on the job a few weeks."

His mother snorted. "If you're trying to impress me—"

"No, I'm not. Truthfully, I'm not sure why I felt so compelled to talk to you, but I thought you should know that no matter what you think of your son, he is an amazing man. He's caring and thoughtful and fearless and the best person I know."

One side of his mother's mouth bunched up in a bitter smile. "And I suppose you're in love with him. You're fae, too, aren't you?"

"As a matter of fact, I am. On both counts." Defiance rose up in Harlow. "You know what else? I'm going to marry your son and we're going to have all kinds of fae babies." She closed her mouth quickly, unsure where that last bit had come from, but not entirely upset she'd said it.

"You really think he's all those things?"

"I do."

After a long pause, the woman picked up a piece of laundry. "If you think I'm coming to the wedding, I...don't know. Maybe. Maybe not."

Harlow's jaw unhinged. That felt like progress. Of a kind. "All right then." She was going to have to have a long talk with Augie when she got home.

His mother folded the dish towel in her hands and set it aside. "I saw the news. The statement the senator made. Then that video that came out after it—"

"I made that."

"That senator was going to kill him."

"Yes, she was."

His mother raised her head to look Harlow in the eyes. "I'm not saying I want to move in and have all my Sunday dinners with him, but maybe it wouldn't be the worst thing in the world to get to know the man he's become."

Harlow nodded. "I'll let him know. But that's all I'm doing. It's his decision what happens next."

"I understand." She turned and went back to her laundry.

Harlow stood there for a moment, trying to process everything that had just happened. Finally, she opened her mirror and slipped home.

⚜

"You smell like soap," Augustine whispered, opening his eyes to slits.

Harlow smiled down at him, teeth gleaming in the room's ambient light. "How are you feeling?"

"Actually...not awful. Better now that you're here. How are you feeling?"

She sat on the bed beside him. "Really good. Better now that I'm here with you." She took his hand and clasped it between her own. "Fenton turned Giselle over to the cops and she's confessed to the murders in the garden. Nekai zapped her with one of his weaver spells so that any magic she tries to use will backfire onto her. Apparently she found that out the hard way when she tried to immobilize Fenton."

Augustine grinned. "Nice."

She lifted one hand to gently touch his cheek. "There's talk that Senator Pellimento is going to be impeached. There's a whole subcommittee being formed to look into her secret dealings."

He frowned. "How long have I been out?"

"A little over a day."

"That explains why I'm feeling better."

She pretended to be injured. "I thought that was because of me."

"It is." He tugged her hands toward him and kissed her knuckles. "What else have I missed? Anything else major?"

"Sort of."

Her funny little smile intrigued him, but not as much as when she dropped his hand, stood up and started taking off her shirt. "What are you—oh."

Gleaming on her chest, right above the lacy cup of her deep red bra, sat a silver fleur-de-lis. The skin around the brand was still pink. "I hope you don't mind that I did this without you but I wanted to make it official. Are you mad?"

"No." He shook his head. "I can't believe you did it."

"Did you think I would chicken out?"

"No, I just…it's a *brand*." The Harlow who'd first walked into this house and his life was gone, replaced by a warrior woman who took his breath away.

"And it hurt like a mother." She started unbuttoning her pants.

His brows lifted. "Did you get another one I don't know about?"

"No." Her smiled was wicked. She dropped her pants to reveal matching underwear. Then she pulled back the covers and slid into bed beside him. "Although if you want to look for one, I'm not going to stop you."

He turned on his side to stare at her, ignoring the slight ache in his ribs. Harlow was in *bed* with him. "I don't even know who you are anymore."

"Some people might think I'm your fiancée."

"My what?"

"It's a long story." She leaned up and kissed him, hard. He reached to cup the back of her head and pull her in close. She broke away after only a few seconds. "We can talk about that later, Guardian Robelais."

"Oh, we will, Lieutenant Goodwin." He bent to kiss her again, his hands traveling over the glorious expanse of her skin. "Much later."

Acknowledgments

Here are a few of the people I need to thank for helping make this book happen: My whip-smart agent, Elaine. My editor, Susan, and the publishing team at Orbit. The fabulous Writer's Camp chicas—Leigh, Laura, Rocki. And the virtual camp members—Louisa, Amanda C., Amanda B., Julie and Kristen C. You are all such inspirations to me!

Then there's my House of Pain Street Team, one of the best groups of readers and cheerleaders an author could ask for. And last but not least, my readers! I love you guys!

A special nod to Damon Stentz for the Louisiana legal info.

I am also blessed with a wonderful family who give me their continuous support and an amazing husband who not only makes me laugh until I cry (often without meaning to) but is the best partner I could have ever hoped for to share this journey with.

extras

orbit

meet the author

Kevin Roberts, Intimate Images

KRISTEN PAINTER likes to balance her obsessions with shoes and cats by making the lives of her characters miserable and surprising her readers with interesting twists. She currently writes award-winning urban fantasy for Orbit Books and paranormal romance.

The former college English teacher can often be found on twitter @Kristen_Painter or on Facebook at www.facebook.com/KristenPainterAuthor where she loves to interact with readers. She's also the cofounder of RomanceDivas.com, an award-winning writers' forum. Sign up for her newsletter at KristenPainter.com to find out when her next release is coming out.

Kristen lives in Florida with her retired Air Force husband and a horde of feline dependents.

introducing

If you enjoyed
GARDEN OF DREAMS AND DESIRES
look out for

BLOOD RIGHTS

House of Comarré: Book 1

by Kristen Painter

Born into a life of secrets and service, Chrysabelle's body bears the telltale marks of a comarré—a special race of humans bred to feed vampire nobility. When her patron is murdered, she becomes the prime suspect, which sends her running into the mortal world... and into the arms of Malkolm, an outcast vampire cursed to kill every being from whom he drinks.

Now, Chrysabelle and Malkolm must work together to stop a plot to merge the mortal and supernatural worlds. If they fail, a chaos unlike anything anyone has ever seen will threaten to reign.

Prologue

Corvinestri, Romania, 2067

The servant trembled in front of the grand fireplace that had never been lit and never would be. "The girl...the girl is, well, it seems... that is, we cannot..." He bit at his lip.

The gilded mantel clock ticked toward sunrise. Tatiana yawned and rolled her hand through the air. "Go on."

His hands twisted, fingers knotting. "We cannot find the comarré, my lady."

Tatiana's veins iced and she stilled at the mention of the female blood whore. "What do you mean, you cannot find her?"

"We've searched Lord Algernon's manor, and she isn't there."

Tatiana and Lord Ivan had discovered Algernon's body just that evening, a rather unusual occurrence in a vampire death. Ashes yes, bodies no. "How long do you suppose he's been dead? Not more than a few hours, surely."

His hands fisted at his sides. "We believe two days, perhaps three. We think it happened just after the Century Ball, my lady. Perhaps that night or the next morning. We have no way of knowing exactly."

A spark of pain lit her palms. She glanced down at the tiny crescents of blood left by her nails, watched them vanish as she forced herself to relax against the velvet upholstered chair. Algernon's death meant the Elder position could be hers, but proving herself worthy of that title would require this chit to be brought to justice. The girl *would* be found. Even with a three-day lead, how far could she travel alone and unprotected? She was a simple comarré, bred for her blood and her social skills, nothing more than the vampire's equivalent of a geisha. The girl knew nothing of the kine world, just as humans knew nothing of this one. The girl would be simple to find among the kine. Like a sparkling gem in a mud puddle.

"Search again. Search the grounds as well."

"Yes, my lady."

"Now. Begone." Tatiana leaned her head into her hand. With Algernon's death, the council would have little choice but to appoint her Elder. Her reign would be a very different one from that old fool's. She would start with bringing that thin-witted girl before the council. By making an example of her to the other comarré. A dark joy lifted Tatiana's thoughts. When she was appointed Elder, Algernon's manor would be hers. Along with all his property in it. Not that she cared for any of his baubles and treasures but one, the one she and Lord Ivan had come to fetch when they'd found Algernon's body.

At last, the pieces were knitting together. All her work, her meticulous attention to detail, her endless studying of the prophecies, her personal sacrifices...finally, she would wear the mantle of power she'd been stitching these many years.

The taint of her past, the human years spent in poverty and squalor, those wounds could only be salved by the protection of great power. The ghosts of those who had used her, treated her like rubbish, those ghosts still haunted her, as spectral as the lost loves of her human life. Power could exorcise them, once and for all. She had to believe that. Or go madder still. Her fingers drifted to the locket around her neck.

The scent of kine had not dissipated. She looked up at the servant, dropping her hand from the locket. "Why are you still here?"

He shifted from one foot to the other. His head stayed bowed. "There is one other thing, my lady."

Tatiana sighed out the end of her patience. "What?"

"She appears to have taken a few of Lord Algernon's possessions."

Her nails drummed the chair's carved arm, wounding the old wood. "Such as?"

"As best we can tell, some jewels, gold coins—"

"Insignificant. Now go, search again." Finally, she could join Mikkel in bed, where he undoubtedly already chilled the sheets for her. Of all the paramours she'd had since her turning, he'd lasted the longest. Perhaps it was his youthful exuberance.

The minion stayed put. Fear wafted off him in delicious waves. Her stomach growled, causing him to jump.

"What else?" Bothersome mortal. Kine really were good for one thing and one thing only.

The servant shivered. "The ring you asked me to look for? It was not on Algernon's person or anywhere else in the house. I believe that the girl has taken it."

Bloody hell. The ring of sorrows, gone. Wood splintered beneath Tatiana's grip. That old dolt must have shown the girl the ring. Probably bragged about it. Algernon deserved to have his head removed from his neck. Unfortunately, the girl had beaten Tatiana to it. She forced the tip of her tongue against the razor point of one fang until blood coated her mouth. With pain came clarity. "How many searched with you?"

"Twelve."

She tested him. "And they also know the ring is missing?"

"No, my lady." Concern lined his forehead. "I told no one else, just as you instructed me."

She smiled. "You did well."

He relaxed and tentatively returned her smile. "Thank you, my lady."

In one lightning-quick move, she was beside him, her fingers threaded through his black curls. She snapped his head back, exposing his throat. His pulse fluttered like a wounded sparrow, his heart pounded wildly. Deliciously.

"My lady?" He paled beneath skin that showed an arrogant hint of tan. Did he think his ability to face daylight something to flaunt before her?

The tremor in his voice stroked pleasure over her skin. The clock chimed 6 a.m. Nearly sunrise, but she had work to do. Loose ends to tie up. A lifetime of planning to protect. The Nothos must be sent after the girl immediately. The unnatural creatures enjoyed a good hunt now and then, especially when put to the task by their vampire half-brethren. "You're positive no one else knows the ring is missing?"

"Yes, my lady, I swear it on my life." Indeed, he reeked of truth.

"You would mention that." She trailed a finger down the minion's neck. "Seeing as it's about to be required of you."

With a rabid growl, her human features disappeared as her facial bones shifted and her fangs descended fully. She sank them into her servant's throat, his cries filling her ears like chamber music, his blood disappearing down her gullet along with the secret of the missing ring.

She dropped his limp body to the hand-knotted Turkish carpet, licked a bead of blood from the corner of her mouth, and headed to her office. She'd make a note for Octavian, the head of her household staff, to remunerate the dead kine's family, but the cost was worth it. Killing soothed the painful memories of her past and what had been taken from her. It gave her the strength to face the enormous amount of work ahead.

She stopped at the door and glanced at the lifeless form fouling the perfection of her sitting room. She'd worked so hard to get where she was and sacrificed so much, she hated to see anything mar her home. She shook her head at the dead kine.

Had she been that vulnerable as a human? No. The streets had beaten the soft edges and innocence out of her before she'd lost her baby teeth. Humans were like that, turning on each other, picking the weakest among them apart, using one another for their own means. They deserved what they got at vampire hands.

Would the comarré be that vulnerable? Probably. The pampered creature had little chance of realizing what she possessed in that ring. Not even Algernon had fully understood it until Lord Ivan's explanation. How would a comarré know she held the key to a prophecy that might change the world? She was nothing but a blood whore. A piece of property, no different from the ring she'd stolen.

Tatiana smiled grimly. Well now, that wasn't true at all.

The ring had a future.

Chapter One

Paradise City, New Florida, 2067

The cheap lace and single-sewn seams pressed into Chrysabelle's flesh, weighed down by the uncomfortable tapestry jacket that finished her disguise. Her training kept her from fidgeting with the shirt's tag even as it bit into her skin. She studied those around her. How curious that the kine perceived her world this way. No, *this* was her world, not the one she'd left behind. And she had to stop thinking of humans as kine. She was one of them now. Free. Independent. Owned by no one.

She forced a weak smile as the club's heavy electronic beat ricocheted through her bones. Lights flickered and strobed, casting shadows and angles that paid no compliments to the faces around her. She cringed as a few bodies collided with her in the surrounding crush. Nothing in her years of training had prepared her for immersion in a crowd of mortals. She recognized the warm, earthy smell of them from the human servants her patron and the other nobles had kept, but acclimating to their noise and their boisterous behavior was going to take time. Perhaps humans lived so hard because they had so little of that very thing.

Something she was coming to understand.

The names on the slip of paper in her pocket were memorized, but she pulled it out and read them again. *Jonas Sweets,* and beneath it, *Nyssa,* both written in her aunt's flowery script. Just the sight of the handwriting calmed her a little. She folded the note and tucked it away. If Aunt Maris said Jonas could connect her with help, Chrysabelle would trust that he could, even though the idea of trusting a kine—no, a human— seemed untenable.

She pushed through to the bar, failing in her attempt to avoid more contact but happy at how little attention she attracted. The foundation Maris had applied to her hands, face and neck, the only skin left visible by her clothing, covered her signum perfectly. No longer did the multitude of gold markings she bore identify her as an object to be possessed. She was her own person now, passing easily as human.

The feat split her in two. While part of her thrilled to be free of the stifling propriety that governed her every move and rejoiced that she was no longer property, another part of her felt wholly unprepared for this existence. There was no denying life in Algernon's manor had been one of shelter and privilege.

Enough wallowing. She hadn't the time and there was no going back, even if she could. Which she wouldn't. And it wasn't as if Aunt Maris hadn't provided for her and wouldn't continue to do so, if Chrysabelle could just take care of this one small problem. Finding a space between two bodies, she squeezed in and waited for the bartender's attention.

He nodded at her. "What can I get you?"

She slid the first plastic fifty across the bar as Maris had instructed. "I need to find Jonas Sweets."

He took the bill, smiling enough to display canines capped into points. Ridiculous. "Haven't seen him in a few days, but he'll show up eventually."

Eventually was too late. She added a second bill. "What time does he usually come in?"

The bartender removed the empty glasses in front of her, snatched up the money, and leaned in. "Midnight. Sometimes sooner. Sometimes later."

It was nearly 1 a.m. now. "How about his assistant, Nyssa? The mute girl?"

"She won't show without him." He tapped the bar with damp fingers. "I can give Jonas a message for you, if he turns up. What's your name?"

She shook her head. No names. No clues. No trail. The bartender shrugged and hustled away. She slumped against the bar and rested her hand over her eyes. At least she could get out of here now. Or maybe she should stay. The Nothos wouldn't attempt anything in so public a place, would they?

A bitter laugh stalled in her throat. She knew better. The hellhounds could kill her in a single pass, without a noise or a struggle or her even knowing what had happened until the pain lit every nerve in her body or her heart shuddered to a stop. She'd never seen one of the horrible creatures, but she didn't need to in order to understand what one was capable of.

They could walk among this crowd without detection, hidden by the covenant that protected humans from the othernaturals, the vampires, varcolai, fae, and such that coexisted with them. She would be the only one to see them coming.

The certainty of her death echoed in her marrow. She shoved the thought away and lifted her head, scanning the crowd, inhaling the earthy human aroma in search of the signature reek of brimstone. Were they already here? Had they tracked her this far, this fast? She wouldn't go back to her aunt's if they had. Couldn't risk bringing that danger to her only family. Maris was not the strong young woman she'd once been.

Her gaze skipped from face to face. So many powdered cheeks and blood red lips. Mouths full of false fangs. Cultivated widow's peaks. All in an attempt to what? Replicate the very beings who would drain the lifeblood from their mortal bodies before they could utter a single word of sycophantic praise? Poor, misguided fools. She felt sorry for them, really. They worshipped their own deaths, lulled into thinking beauty and perfection were just a bite away. She would never think that. Never fall under the spell of those manufactured lies. No matter how long or how short her new life was.

She knew too much.

Malkolm hated Puncture with every undead fiber of his being. If it weren't for the bloodlust crazing his brain—which kicked the ever-present voices into a frenzy—he'd be home, sipping the single malt he could no longer afford, maybe listening to Fauré or Tchaikovsky while searching his books for a way to empty his head of all thoughts but his own.

Damn Jonas for disappearing without setting up another reliable source. Mal cracked his knuckles, thinking about the beating that idiot was in for when he showed up again. It wasn't like the local Quik-E-Mart carried pints of fresh, clean, human blood. Unfortunately.

The warm, delicious scent of the very thing he craved hit full force as he pushed through the heavy velvet drapes curtaining the VIP section. In here, his real face, the face of the monster he'd been turned into, made him the very best of their pretenders and got him access to any area of the night-club he wanted. Ironic, considering how showing his real face anywhere else would probably get him locked up as a mental patient. He shuddered and inhaled without thinking. His body tensed with the seductive aroma of thriving, vibrating life. The voices went mad, pounding against his skull. A multitude of heartbeats filled his ears, pulses around him calling out like siren songs. *Bite me, drink me, swallow me whole.*

Damn Sweets.

A petite redhead with a jeweled cross dangling between her breasts stopped dead in front of him. Like an actual vampire could ever tolerate the touch of that sacred symbol. Dumb git. But then how was she to know the origins of creatures she only hoped were real? She appraised him from head to toe, running her tongue over a set of resin fangs. "You're new here, huh? I love your look. Are those contacts? I haven't seen any metallic ones like that. Kinda different, but totally hot."

She reached out to touch the hard ridge of his cheekbone and he snapped back, baring his teeth and growling softly. *Eat her.* She scowled. "Chill, dude." Pouting, she skulked away, muttering "freak" under her breath.

Fine. Let her think what she wanted. A human's touch might push him over the edge. No, he reassured himself, it wouldn't. *Yes.* He wouldn't let it. *Do.* He wouldn't get that far gone. *Go.* But in truth, he balanced on the edge. *Fall.* He needed to feed. *To kill.* To shut the voices up.

With that thought he shoved his way to the bar, disgusted things had gotten this dire. He got the bartender's attention, then pushed some persuasion into his voice. "Hey." It was one of the few powers that hadn't blinked out on him yet. Good old family genes.

His head turned in Mal's direction, eyes slightly glazed. Mal eased off. Humans were so suggestible. "What'll it be?"

"Give me a Vlad." Inwardly, he died a little. Metaphorically speaking. The whole idea of doing this here, in full view of a human audience, made him sick. But not as sick as going without. How fortunate that humans wanted to mimic his kind to the full extent.

"A shot?"

"A pint."

The bartender's brows lifted. "Looking to get laid, huh? A pint should keep you busy all night. These chicks get seriously damp over that action. Not that anyone's managed to drink the pint and keep it down." He hesitated. "You gotta puke, you head for the john, you got me?"

"Not going to happen."

"Yeah, right." The bartender opened a small black fridge and took out a plastic bag fat with red liquid.

Mal swallowed the saliva coating his tongue, unable to focus his gaze elsewhere, despite the fact he preferred his sustenance body temperature and not chilled. A few of the voices wept softly. "That's human, right? And fresh?"

The bartender laughed. "Chickening out?"

"No. Just making sure."

"Yeah, it's fresh and it's human. That's why it's $250 a pop." He squirted the liquid into a pilsner. It oozed down the glass thick and viscous, sending a bittersweet aroma into the air. Even here in the VIP lounge, heads turned. Several women and at least one man radiated hard lust in his direction. The scent of human desire was like dying roses, and right now, Puncture's VIP lounge smelled like a funeral parlor. He hadn't anticipated such a rapt audience, but the ache in his gut stuck up a big middle finger to caring what the humans around him thought. At least there weren't any fringe vamps here tonight. Despite his status as an outcast anathema, the lesser-class vampires only saw him as nobility. He wasn't in the mood to be sucked up to. Ever.

The bartender slid the glass his way. "There you go. Will that be cash?"

"Start a tab."

"I don't think so, buddy."

Mal refocused his power. "I've already paid you."

344

The man's jaw loosened and the tension lines in his forehead disappeared. "You've already paid."

"That's a good little human," Mal muttered. He grabbed the pilsner and walked toward an empty stretch of railing for a little privacy. The air behind him heated up. He glanced over his shoulder. A set of twins with blue-black hair, jet lips, and matching leather corsets stood waiting.

"Hi," they said in unison.

Eat them. Drain them.

"No." He filled his voice with power, hoping that would be enough.

They stepped forward. Behind them, the bartender watched with obvious interest.

Damn Sweets.

The blood warmed in his grasp, its tang filling his nose, but feeding would have to wait a moment longer. Using charm this time, he spoke. "I am not the one you seek. Pleasure awaits you elsewhere. Leave me now."

They nodded sleepily and moved away.

The effort exhausted him. He was too weak to use so much power in such a short span of time. He gripped the railing, waiting for the dizziness in his head to abate. He stared into the crowd below. Scanned for Nyssa, but he knew better. She only left Sweets' side when she had a delivery. The moving bodies blurred until they were an undulating mass, each one undistinguishable from the next until a muted flash of gold stopped his gaze. His entire being froze. Not here. Couldn't be.

He blinked, then stared harder. The flickering glow remained. It reminded him of a dying firefly. Instinct kicked in. Sparks of need exploded in his gut. His gums ached, causing him to pop his jaw. The small hairs on the back of his neck lifted and the voices went oddly quiet, save an occasional whimper. His world converged down to the soft light emanating from the crowd near the downstairs bar.

He had to find the source, see if it really was what he thought. If it was, he had to get to it before anyone else did. The urge drove him inexplicably forward.

All traces of exhaustion disappeared. The glass in his hand fell to the floor, splattering blood that no longer called to him. He vaulted over the railing and dropped effortlessly to the dance floor below. The crush parted to let him through as he strode toward the gentle beacon.

She stood at the bar, her back to him. The generous fall of sunlight-blonde hair stopped him, but the fabled luminescence brought him back to reality. So beautiful this close. He rubbed at his aching jaw. *You'll scare her like this, you fool. You're all fang and hunger. Show some respect.*

He composed himself, then approached. "Looking for someone?"

She tensed, going statue still. Even with the heavy bass, he felt her heartbeat shoot up a notch. He moved closer and leaned forward to speak without human ears hearing. Bad move. Her scent plunged into him dagger sharp, its honeyed perfume nearly doubling him with hunger pains. The whimpering increased. Catching himself, he staggered for the bar behind her and reached out for support.

His hand closed over her wrist. Her pulse thrummed beneath his fingertips. Welcoming heat blazed up his arm. A chorus of fearful voices sang out in his head. *Get away, get away, get away...*

She spun, eyes fear-wide, heart thudding. "You're..." She hesitated then mouthed the words "not human."

Beneath his grip, she trembled. He pulled his hand away and stared. Had he been wrong? No marks adorned her face or hands. Maybe...but no. She had the blonde hair, the glow, the carmine lips. She hid the marks somehow. He wasn't wrong. He knew enough of the history, the lore, the traditions. Besides, he'd seen her kind before. Just the once, but it wasn't something you ever forgot no matter how long you lived. Only one thing caused that glow.

She bent her head. "Master," she whispered.

"Don't. Don't call me that. It's not necessary." She thought him nobility? Why not assume he was fringe? Or worse, anathema? But she'd addressed him with the respect due her better. A noble with all rights and privileges. Which he wasn't. And she'd surely guessed he was here to feed. Which he was.

She nodded. "As you wish, mast—" Visibly flustered, she cut herself off. "As you wish."

He gestured toward the exit. "Outside. You don't belong here." Anyone could get to her here. Like Preacher. It wasn't safe. How she'd ended up here, he couldn't fathom. Finding a live rabbit in a den of lions would have been less surprising.

"I'm sure my patron will be back in just a—"

"We both know I'm the only real vampire here." For now. "Let's go."

Her gaze wandered to the surrounding crowd, then past him. She sucked her lower lip between her teeth and twisted her hands together. Hesitantly, she brushed past, painting a line of hunger across his chest with the curve of her shoulder. *Get away, get away, get away...*

She was not for him. He knew that, and not just because of the voices, but getting his body to agree was a different matter. Her scent was so rich it numbed him like good whiskey. Made him feel needy. Reckless. Finding some shred of control, he shadowed her out of the club, away from the mob awaiting entrance, and herded her deep into the alley. He scanned in both directions. Nothing. They hadn't been followed. He could get her somewhere safe. Not that he knew where that might be.

"No one saw us leave."

She backed away, hugging herself beneath her coat. Her chest rose and fell as though she'd run a marathon. Fear soured her sweet perfume. She had to be in some kind of trouble. Why else would she be here without an escort? Without her patron?

"Trust me, we're completely alone." He reached awkwardly to put his arm around her, the first attempt at comfort he'd made in years.

Quicker than a human eye could track, her arm snapped from under the coat, something dark and slim clutched in her hand. The side of her fist slammed into his chest. Whatever she held pierced him, missing his heart by inches. The voices shrieked, deafening him. Corrosive pain erupted where she made contact.

He froze, immobilized by hellfire scorching his insides. He fell to his knees and collapsed against the damp pavement. Foul water soaked his clothing as he lay there, her fading footfalls drowned out by the howling in his head.

introducing

If you enjoyed
GARDEN OF DREAMS AND DESIRES
look out for

TRAILER PARK FAE

by Lilith Saintcrow

*Jeremy Gallow is just another construction worker, and that's
the way he likes it. He's left his past behind, but some things can't
be erased. Like the tattoos on his arms that can transform into a
weapon, or that he was once closer to the Queen of Summer than
any half-human should be. Now the half-sidhe all in Summer once
feared is dragged back into the world of enchantment, danger, and
fickle fae—by a woman who looks uncannily like his dead wife.
Her name is Robin, and her secrets are more than enough to get
them both killed. A plague has come, the fullborn fae are dying,
and the dark answer to Summer's Court is breaking loose.*

Be afraid, for Unwinter is riding…

Chapter One
A Different Beast

Summer, soft green hills and shaded dells, lay breathless under a pall of smoky apple-blossom dusk. The other Summer, her white hands rising from indigo velvet to gleam in the gloaming, waved the rest of her handmaidens away. They fled, giggling in bell-clear voices and trailing their sigh-draperies, a slim golden-haired mortal boy among them fleet as a deer— Actaeon among the leaping hounds, perhaps.

Though that young man, so long ago, hadn't been torn apart by gray-sided, long-eared hounds. A different beast had run him to ground. The mortals, always confused, whispered among themselves, and their invented gods grew in the telling.

Goodfellow, brown of hair and sharp of ear, often wondered if the sidhe did as well.

The Fatherless smiled as he watched Summer wander toward him through the dusk. She was at pains to appear unconcerned. His own wide sunny grin, showing teeth sharper than a mortal's, might have caused even the strongest of either Court unease.

Of course, the free sidhe—those who did not bend knee to Summer or her once-lord Unwinter—would make themselves scarce when the Goodfellow grinned. They had their own names for him, all respectful and none quite pleasing to him when he chose to take offense.

Summer halted. Her hair, ripples of gold, stirred slightly in the perfumed breeze. Above and between her gleaming eyes, the Jewel flashed, a single dart of emerald light piercing the gloom as the day took its last breath and sank fully under night's mantle.

Someday, he might see this sidhe queen sink as well. How she had glimmered and glistened, in her youth. He had once trifled with the idea of courting her himself, before her eye had settled on one altogether more grim.

The quarrel, Goodfellow might say, were he disposed to lecture, *always matches the affection both parties bore before, does it not?* The Sundering had taken much from both Courts, and that bothered him not a bit. When they elbowed each other, the space between them was wide enough to grant him further sway. Carefully, of course. So carefully, patiently—the Folk were often fickle, true, but they did not have to be.

He let her draw much closer before he lay aside his cloaking shadows, stepping fully into her realm between two straight, slender birches, and she barely started. Her mantle slipped a fraction from one white shoulder, but that could have been to expose just a sliver of pale skin, fresh-velvet as a new magnolia petal. Artfully innocent, that single peeping glow could infect a mortal's dreams, fill them with longing, drive all other thought from their busy little brains.

If she, the richest gem of Summer's long, dreamy months, so willed it.

"Ah, there she is, our fairest jewel." He swept her a bow, an imaginary cap doffed low enough to sweep the sweet grass exhaling its green scent of a day spent basking under a perfect sun. "Where is your Oberon, queenly one? Where is your lord?"

"Ill met by moonlight, indeed." She smiled, just a curve of those red, red lips poets dreamed of. There had been mortal maids, occasionally, whose salt-sweet fragility put even Summer to shame, and woe betide them if any of the Folk should

351

carry tales of their radiance to this corner of the sideways realms. "And as you are an honest Puck, I have come alone."

"Fairly." His smile broadened. "What would you have of me, Summer? And what will you give in return?"

"I have paid thee well for every service, sprite, and have yet to see results for one or two dearly bought." Summer drew her mantle closer. She did not deign to frown, but he thought it likely one or two of her ladies would take her expression as a caution, and make themselves scarce. They would be the wisest ones. The favorites, of course, could not afford to risk her noting such a scarcity, and so would stay.

"Oh, patience becomes thee indeed, Summer." He capered, enjoying the feel of crushed sweet grass under his leather-shod feet. A fingersnap, a turn, as if it were midsummer and the revels afoot. "As it happens, I bring word from a certain mortal."

"Mortal? What is a mortal to me?" Her hand dropped, and she did not turn away. Instead, her gaze sharpened, though she looked aside at the first swirling sparks of fireflies drawn by her presence. There was nothing the lamp-ended creatures loved more than her own faint glow by night. Except perhaps the Moon itself, Danu's silver eye.

"Then you do not wish to hear of success? O changeable one!"

"Puck." The fireflies scattered, for Summer's tone had changed. In her sable mantle, the golden hair paler now as her mood drained its tint, her ageless-dark eyes narrowing so very slightly, the loveliness of Summer took on a sharper edge. "I grow weary of this."

"Then I shall be brief. He has worked another miracle, this mortal of science. There is a cure."

She examined him for a long moment, and the Goodfellow suffered it. There was a certain joy to be had in allowing her to think he quaked at the thought of her displeasure. Far greater was the amusement to be had in knowing that the Queen of the Seelie Court, Summer herself, the fount of Faerie—for so the bards called her, though Goodfellow could have told them where a truer fountain welled—had very little choice but to dance to his tune.

She turned, a quarter profile of hurtful beauty, her black eyes flashing dangerous. The stars in their depths spun lazily, cold fires of the night before any tree was named. If an ensnared mortal could see her now, Goodfellow thought, he might well drop of the heartshock and leave the trap entire.

"And what is the price for this miracle, sprite?"

He affected astonishment, capering afresh, hopping to and fro. Under the grass was sere dry bramble, and it crunched as he landed. "What? I am no mortal tailor, to double-charge. All you must do is send your own sprite to collect it. The mortal longs for any breath of you, he entreats a word, a look, a sigh."

"Does he?" Summer tapped one perfect nail against her lips. There was a rosy tint a mortal might mistake for polish on its sweet curve, and it darkened to the crimson of her smile as her mood shifted again. *Changeable as Summer*, the free sidhe said. Unwinter was far less capricious, of course…but just as dangerous.

"Welladay." Summer's smile dawned again, and she turned away still further. "Does his miracle perform, he may receive a boon. I shall send him a sprite, dear Goodfellow, and our agreement stands."

"My lady." He cut another bow, but she did not see the sarcastic turn his leer had taken. "You do me much honor."

"Oh, aye." A girl's carefree giggle, and she moved away, the grass leaning toward her glow and the fireflies trailing. "I do, when the service is well wrought. Farewell, hob. I'll send him a familiar face, since mortals are timid." Her laugh, deeper and richer now, caroled between the shivering birches, a pocket of cold swallowing a struggling swimmer.

"Mind that you do," Goodfellow said, but softly, softly. He capered once more, to hear the dried brambles crunch underfoot, like mortal bones. He spun, quick brown fingers finding the pipes at his belt. He lifted them to his mouth, and his own eyes fired green in the darkness. Full night had fallen, and silver threads of music lifted in the distance—the Queen was well pleased, it seemed, and had called upon the minstrels to play.

He stepped *sideways*, pirouetting neatly on the ball of one foot, and emerged in a mortal alley. It was night here too, and as he danced along, the breathy, wooden notes from his pipes arrowed free in a rill. Concrete whirled underfoot, the mortal world flashing and trembling as he skipped across its pleats and hollows. They did not see, the dull cold sacks of frail flesh, and only some few of them heard.

Those who did shuddered, though they could not have said why. A cold finger laid itself on their napes, or in another sensitive spot, and the gooseflesh walked over them. None of them suited Goodfellow, so he ambled on.

A little while later, a mortal chanced across his path—a sturdy youth, strong and healthy, who thought the Fatherless a common, staggering drunkard. With the pipes whispering in his ear, luring him down another path, the mortal boy did not realize he was prey instead of hunter until his unvictim rounded on him with wide, lambent eyes and a sharp, sickeningly cheery smile.

Yes, Goodfellow decided as he crouched to crunch, hot salt against his tongue, bramble *did* sound like mortal bones, if it was dry enough.

Pleased by his own thoroughness, he ate his fill.

Chapter Two
Simulacrum

Jeremiah Gallow, once known as the Queensglass, stood twenty stories above the pavement, just like he did almost every day at lunchtime since they'd started building a brand-new headquarters for some megabank or another.

He was reasonably sure the drop wouldn't kill him. Cars creeping below were shiny beetles, the walking mortals dots of muted color, hurrying or ambling as the mood took them. From this height, they were ants. Scurrying, just like the ones he worked beside, sweating out their brief gray lives.

A chill breeze resonated through superstructure, iron girders harpstrings plucked by invisible fingers. He was wet with sweat, exhaust-laden breeze mouthing his ruthlessly cropped black hair. Poison in the air just like poison in the singing rods and rivets, but neither troubled a Half. He had nothing to fear from cold iron.

No mortal-Tainted did. A fullblood sidhe would be uncomfortable, nervous around the most inimical of mortal metals. *The more fae, the more to fear.*

Like every proverb, true in different interlocking ways.

Jeremiah leaned forward still further, looking past the scarred toes of his dun workboots. The jobsite was another scar on the seamed face of the city, the skeleton rising from a shell of orange and yellow caution tape and signage to keep mortals from bruising themselves. Couldn't have civilians wandering in and getting hit on the head, suing the management or anything like that.

A lone worker bee, though, could take three steps back, gather himself, and sail right past the flimsy lath barrier. The fall would be studded and scarred by clutching fingers of steel and cement, and the landing would be sharp.

If he was singularly unlucky he'd end up a Twisted, crippled monstrosity, or even just a half-Twisted unable to use glamour—or any other bit of sidhe chantment—without it warping him further. Shuffling out an existence cringing from both mortal and sidhe, and you couldn't keep a mortal job if you had feathers instead of hair, or half your face made of wood, or no glamour to hide the oddities sidhe blood could bring to the surface.

Daisy would have been clutching at his arm, her fear lending a smoky tang to her salt-sweet mortal scent. She hated heights.

The thought of his dead wife sent a sharp, familiar bolt of pain through his chest. Her hair would have caught fire today; it was cold but bright, thin almost-spring sunshine making every shadow a knife edge. He leaned forward a little more, his arms spreading slightly, the wind a hungry lover's hand. A cold edge of caress. *Just a little closer. Just a little further.*

It might hurt enough to make you forget.

"Gallow, what the hell?" Clyde bellowed.

Jeremiah stepped back, half turned on one rubber-padded heel. The boots were thick-soled, caked with the detritus of a hundred build sites. Probably dust on there from places both mortal and not-so-mortal, he'd worn them since before his marriage. Short black hair and pale green eyes, a face that could be any anonymous construction worker's. Not young, not old, not distinctive at all, what little skill he had with glamour pressed into service to make him look like just every other mortal guy with a physical job and a liking for beer every now and again.

His arms tingled; he knew the markings were moving on his skin, under the long sleeves. "Thought I saw something." *A way out.* But only if he was sure it would be an escape, not a fresh snare.

Being Half just made you too damn durable.

"Like what, a pigeon? Millions of those around." The bullet-headed foreman folded his beefy arms. He was already red and perspiring, though the temperature hadn't settled above forty degrees all week.

Last summer had been mild-chill, fall icy, winter hard, and spring was late this year. Maybe the Queen hadn't opened the Gates yet.

Summer. The shiver—half loathing, half something else—that went through Jeremiah must have shown. Clyde took a half-step sideways, reaching up to push his hard hat further back on his sweat-shaven pate. He had a magnificent broad white mustache, and the mouth under it turned into a thin line as he dropped his hands loosely to his sides.

Easy, there. Jeremiah might have laughed. Still, you could never tell who on a jobsite might have a temper. Best to be safe around heavy machinery, crowbars, nail guns, and the like.

"A seagull." Gallow deliberately hunched his shoulders, pulled the rage and pain back inside his skin. "Maybe a hawk. Or something. You want my apple pie?" If Clyde had a weakness, it was sugar-drenched, overprocessed pastry. Just like a brughnie, actually.

Another shiver roiled through him, but he kept it inside. *Don't think on the sidhe. You know it puts you in a mood.*

Clyde perked up a little. "If you don't want it. How come you bring 'em if you don't want 'em?"

Insurance. Always bring something to barter with. Jeremiah dug in his lunchbag. He'd almost forgotten he'd crumpled most of the brown paper in his fist. Daisy always sent him to work with a carefully packed lunch, but the collection of retro metal boxes she'd found at Goodwill and Salvation Army were all gone now. If he hadn't thrown them away he had stamped on them, crushing each piece with the same boots he was wearing now. "Habit. Put 'em in the bag each time."

She'd done sandwiches too, varying to keep them interesting. Turkey. Chicken. Good old PBJ, two of them to keep him fueled. Hard-boiled eggs with a twist of salt in waxed paper, carefully quartered apples bathed in lemon juice to keep them from browning, home-baked goodies. Banana bread, muffins, she'd even gone through a sushi phase once until he'd let it slip that he didn't prefer raw fish.

I just thought, you're so smart and all. Ain't sushi what smart people eat? And her laugh at his baffled look. She often made little comments like that, as if... well, she never knew of the sidhe, but she considered him a creature from a different planet just the same.

"Oh." Clyde took the Hostess apple pie, his entire face brightening. "Just don't stand too near that edge, Gallow. You fall off and I'll have L&I all over me."

"Not gonna." It was hard taking the next few steps away from the edge. His heels landed solidly, and the wind stopped keening across rebar and concrete. Or at least, the sound retreated. "Haven't yet."

"Always a first time. Hey, me and Panko are going out for beers after. You wanna?" The waxed wrapper tore open, and Clyde took a huge mouthful of sugar that only faintly resembled the original apple.

"Sure." It was Friday, the start of a long weekend. If he went home he was only going to eat another TV dinner, or nothing at all, and sit staring at the fist-sized hole in the television screen, in his messy living room.

Ridiculous. Why did they call it that? Nobody did any *living* in there.

"Okay." Clyde gave him another odd look, and Jeremiah had a sudden vision of smashing his fist into the old man's face. The crunch of bone, the gush of blood, the satisfaction of a short sharp action. The foreman wasn't even a sidhe, to require an exchange of names beforehand.

I'm mortal now. Best to remember it. Besides, the foreman wasn't to blame for anything. Guiltless as only a mortal could be.

"Better get back to work," Jeremiah said instead, and tossed his crumpled lunchbag into the cut-down trash barrel hulking near the lift. "Gotta earn those beers."

Clyde had his mouth full, and Jeremiah was glad. If the man said another word, he wasn't sure he could restrain himself. There was no good reason for the rage, except the fact that he'd been brought back from the brink, and reminded he was only a simulacrum of a mortal man.

Again.